PASSION'S PROMISE

Feigning a defiance she did not feel, Delilah steeled herself and looked him straight in the eye. "I would do anything to stay at Shadows-in-the-Mist," she said. "Even allow myself to become employed by a Yankee-Doodle gambler."

Grant laughed aloud and took both her hands in his. "Miss Delilah Wickley," he said, "you can stick a feather in my hat any old day and you can call it anything you please."

"In the meantime," she said quietly, "I would like to reside aboard the riverboat."

"But you will take your meals with me," Grant insisted. "At the main house." He was standing so close to her that she could feel the heat of his breath on her cheeks. "I insist," he said, stepping even closer; his slim fingers gently massaged her wrist.

Without warning, his hand dropped hers and slid to the small of her back. The breath of space between them became nonexistent as he claimed her trembling mouth in a deep, wild kiss. In spite of herself, Delilah pressed herself against him, unable to prevent her body's betrayal of the hatred she had sworn for this loathsome, despicable man . . .

DISCOVER DEANA JAMES!

CAPTIVE ANGEL   (2524, $4.50/$5.50)
Abandoned, penniless, and suddenly responsible for the biggest
tobacco plantation in Colleton County, distraught Caroline Gil-
lard had no time to dissolve into tears. By day the willowy red-
head labored to exhaustion beside her slaves . . . but each night
left her restless with longing for her wayward husband. She'd
make the sea captain regret his betrayal until he begged her to
take him back!

MASQUE OF SAPPHIRE   (2885, $4.50/$5.50)
Judith Talbot-Harrow left England with a heavy heart. She was
going to America to join a father she despised and a sister she
distrusted. She was certainly in no mood to put up with the insulting actions of the arrogant Yankee privateer who boarded her
ship, ransacked her things, then "apologized" with an indecent,
brazen kiss! She vowed that someday he'd pay dearly for the lib-
erties he had taken and the desires he had awakened.

SPEAK ONLY LOVE   (3439, $4.95/$5.95)
Long ago, the shock of her mother's death had robbed Vivian
Marleigh of the power of speech. Now she was being forced to
marry a bitter man with brandy on his breath. But she could not
say what was in her heart. It was up to the viscount to spark the
fires that would melt her icy reserve.

WILD TEXAS HEART   (3205, $4.95/$5.95)
Fan Breckenridge was terrified when the stranger found her near-
naked and shivering beneath the Texas stars. Unable to remember
who she was or what had happened, all she had in the world was
the deed to a patch of land that might yield oil . . . and the fierce
loving of this wildcatter who called himself Irons.

*Available wherever paperbacks are sold, or order direct from the
Publisher. Send cover price plus 50¢ per copy for mailing and
handling to Zebra Books, Dept. 3765, 475 Park Avenue South,
New York, N.Y. 10016. Residents of New York and Tennessee
must include sales tax. DO NOT SEND CASH. For a free Zebra/
Pinnacle catalog please write to the above address.*

CAROLINE BOURNE

RIVERBOAT SEDUCTION

ZEBRA BOOKS
KENSINGTON PUBLISHING CORP.

In loving memory of Bubba,
and seventeen years of friendship

Thanks, Mom, for the use of
your poem, "The Rose"

ZEBRA BOOKS

are published by

Kensington Publishing Corp.
475 Park Avenue South
New York, NY 10016

First printing: June, 1992

Printed in the United States of America

Part One

One

The morning was warmer than usual for the first week of February. Delilah kept to the trail winding through great stands of hardwoods and pines, occasionally pausing to watch a shy slider turtle tuck itself into its shell or a coachwhip snake curl into a braided coil. Only a hundred yards farther on Bayou Boeuf, the sunlight glinted suddenly on the shiny green armor of a tiger beetle hurtling past her with flying leaps that frightened her mare. Calming the spirited horse, she moved onto the narrow path skirting the bog and crossed into the meadow toward Ellie McPherson's home on Lamourie Bayou.

Dismounting at the carriage house, Delilah handed the reins over to Lancie, the freed black man employed by Ellie. Under normal circumstances, Lancie would have teased her about her suitors, but today he took the reins with little more than an abstracted grunt. Delilah smarted from his lack of attention. Had she been one of the high-and-mighty belles on the bayou, she might have reprimanded him for his rudeness. Instead she drew her hands to her hips, more to portray her indignation than to smooth down the wrinkles her four-mile ride had impressed into her skirts. "Well, what is wrong with you today, Pickle-Puss?" she asked. "Not so much as a 'good morning'? You don't want to know about my beaux?"

Lancie halted, his tall ebony frame half turning back. As his hand moved to rub the muzzle of Delilah's mare, he replied, "Sorry, Missy—" He drew a deep, dramatic sigh. "Miz' El, she done invited that Yankee-Doodle gambler from de river to visit. I don't like it. Naw'm, don't like it a bit!"

Dropping her hands, Delilah released a small laugh, her golden-brown eyes twinkling with mirth. "So that is it, you old rooster! Protecting the mistress from male prowlers! Especially Yankee-Doodle ones!"

Only now did a smile grace Lancie's face. Indeed, he was very loyal to Miss Ellie. She had kept him and his mother on at the cottage as employees when they'd unexpectedly found themselves freed by her father on his deathbed. "I believe Miz El can take care of herself, Missy."

Ellie's eighteen-year-old son Maden chose that moment to exit the carriage house, leading a lame harness horse. Looking in her direction, he smiled his pleasure. "Missy, didn't know you'd ridden up. Ma's at the house."

"What's wrong with the gelding?" Delilah asked.

"Picked up a stone. He'll be all right. Did ya hear, Missy, the folks of Smith's Landing are thinkin' about renaming the place for that racehorse belonging to Mr. Wells."

Delilah flinched at mention of the famous horse, Lecomte, which Mr. Thomas Jefferson Wells had raced to prominence all over the country. "Bella could outrun Lecomte if she put her mind to it! Why, just the other day—" She caught herself just in time. She had ridden with one of Mr. Wells's employees, who had taken a horse from its stall without permission, and she had promised him faithfully she would say nothing about his little mischief.

Delilah's only response from either man in her immediate presence was a boisterous round of laughter, as neither seemed aware she had caught herself in midsentence from divulging a confidence. As far as they were concerned there wasn't any horse on the bayou—or in the state of Louisiana—ever going to get a nose on Lecomte.

Halting his laughter, Maden fixed his eyes on Delilah's face, then immediately felt the color rushing into his cheeks. When she smiled, he quickly glanced away, though not without first assessing her careful appearance.

She was especially lovely today, her long sable-colored hair held back in a velvet ribbon, her brown riding habit a little snug, and her skirt scarcely midway to her calf, betraying her dusty riding boots. Her heart-shaped face beamed, her cheeks as pink as if she'd rubbed them briskly with a mullien leaf. But they were not too pink to hide the scratch upon her right cheek.

Spying the small wound at the same time as Maden, Lancie dropped the reins of the horse, approached Delilah and pinned her chin firmly against his fingers. Had she been any other white woman, he would not have been so bold as to touch her. "Where'd you git dat scratch, Missy? Somebody been abotherin' you? Not that pawin'-all-over boy from the Wells place, huh?"

Easing her chin away, Delilah briefly touched her fingers to his thick wrist. "Lancie, stop worrying about me! It's merely the sting of a twig that caught me unawares on the trail. Besides, Bella is the fastest horse at The Shadows and she wouldn't let anyone get close enough to do me harm." Delilah smiled her sweetest smile. "Now," she said in parting, "you quit worrying about the women on Bayou Boeuf and win your Daisy's heart before my father runs you off. It's darn near about time, Lancie, that you tied yourself down to skirts! And you help him tie Daisy down, Maden, do you hear me?"

While Maden joined Delilah in the gentle kidding, Lancie found himself thinking about the pretty Daisy at Shadows-in-the-Mist. He knew he had already won her heart. What he did not have was Angus Wickley's permission to marry her. She was a slave . . . he was a free

9

man . . . and it just simply wouldn't work. That truth made Lancie hate Delilah's father, because he was master of the woman he wanted for a wife.

Shaking off his gloomy thoughts, Lancie returned to the subject at hand. "Don't you be acussin', Missy. Go on up to the house. Stable ain't no place fo' a lady."

"Oh, Lancie!" Delilah clicked her tongue. "I'd go wading in a bog if I took a mind to it. Maybe I don't want to be a lady!" Pivoting on the heel of her boot, she marched off, her head held high and proud. Soon, though, she halted, turned back, and smiled. "Give Bella a little grain, Maden?"

"Sure, Missy. I'll put some spirits in it . . . Maybe she'll be able to hold her own against old Lecomte."

When Delilah turned to put distance between them, Maden spoke to the man who outweighed him by a hundred pounds. "Sure is a fine-lookin' lady. Wish I was a few years older."

"You keep dem eyes off Missy!" Lancie ordered sternly. "She gonna git better'n a worthless pup!"

Grinning, Lancie watched her move toward the wide, washed-cypress house Ellie McPherson called home. He said a private little prayer that when Delilah decided to marry—and the time was certainly approaching, if not passing her by—that she'd get a man who deserved her. He knew of no other twenty-two-year-old woman on the bayou—black or white—who had not already taken a husband. As for him . . . if he couldn't have Daisy, he didn't want anyone.

As Delilah sauntered across the lawn, her gaze moved fluidly over the large cottage, festooned with elaborately carved trim, its planked porch and first floor built upon brick columns eight feet high to allow for the spring flooding. It had been her home once, the house her father had built when he and her mother Irene had first moved into central Louisiana from New Orleans. Delilah had been born in this house.

Rather than lay it to waste when Angus's own plantation had profited and he'd built the bigger house to the east, her father had sold the cottage and seventy acres to Charles and Ellie McPherson. Delilah remembered her childhood, scampering about on that wide porch—and the many happy hours spent sharing confidences with Daisy, the love of Lancie's life, a slave girl born on the same night as she. The two girls had grown up together in the protected environment of Shadows-in-the-Mist. They had shared many adventures, and to this day they were the closest of friends.

The cool February wind stung Delilah's cheeks. Only then was she aware of the moisture sheening her amber eyes as memories of her mother came back to her. As Ellie McPherson quickly traversed the wide porch steps, holding up the hem of her simple cotton gown, Delilah flicked away the offending evidence of her reminiscences. She dearly missed her mother; it seemed like only yesterday that she'd sat beside her, asking a world of questions and receiving short, brittle replies. As a child, Delilah had felt that she annoyed her mother terribly and that the woman would rather not have had her around.

"Delilah!" Ellie took her hands and squeezed them gently. "I didn't expect you until the end of the week! Did you hear that Smith's Landing might be renamed Lecomte?"

"Horse feathers!" Delilah retorted. "I heard all about it from Lancie and your son. Mr. Wells's silly old horse, and those simpletons at Smith's Landing who would consider such a change, are of no interest to me!" Ellie's look coaxed a smile from Delilah. "Now enough of this nonsense! Tell me about your Yankee-Doodle gambler."

Ellie frowned her disapproval. "Lancie has been talking. He is a meddling old warrior—"

"Oh, do tell me about your Yankee, Ellie," she urged, linking her arm through that of her older friend for the return journey to the house. Within moments they entered the long hallway, then the beautifully furnished

11

parlor to the left with its graceful mahogany furnishings glistening against the hearth where a fire blazed. "I sense your hesitation," Delilah continued, tossing her riding quirt to a claw-footed table. "Am I to assume you have a gentleman admirer in this gambler who has ruffled Lancie's feathers?"

In the moments that it took Ellie to answer, Delilah studied the large, comfortable parlor, its red-flocked wallpaper and marble fireplace, its sideboards and cabinets exhibiting rich English china and sterling silver serving pieces.

"He's just a man I met on a journey downriver some years ago," Ellie replied. "He's really quite charming."

A memory registered in Delilah's mind. "Is he the man who was responsible for Charles's death?"

Ellie McPherson shuddered at the memory. She had never told Delilah—or anyone else along the bayou—the truth about that night, though she had wanted to. She was sick and tired of everyone believing Charles was a faultless man. "He was there that night," she replied after a moment. "But I can hardly call him responsible."

"Why don't you hate him, Ellie?"

"What happened that night was more Charles's fault than Grant's. I will not hate him." Placing her hand lightly on Delilah's arm, Ellie continued. "You know I prefer not to talk about what happened. Now . . . would you care for tea?"

It infuriated Delilah that Ellie would give her no details. Weren't they the best of friends? "That would be nice," she responded, miffed by Ellie's secrecy.

"Miss Mandy?" Ellie called to Lancie's mother. Presently, a short, plump woman, her oversize white apron and gathered cap blindingly white against her dark face, entered the parlor and smiled her greeting to the younger woman. "Would you be so kind as to bring a tray of tea?" Ellie requested.

"Yas'sum. You sho' is looking spritely and purty today, Missy," Miss Mandy said before departing.

"Thank you," she said softly. When Miss Mandy left the room, Delilah leaned across the settee. "How has she taken Dr. Miller's news?" she asked Ellie.

A deeply pained frown invaded Ellie's brow. "Grimly, as anyone would expect. She refuses to accept that she has so little time left and insists on going about her chores. Tylas—Dr. Miller—says to let her carry on as usual. When she goes, it will be very sudden."

"Oh, I see . . . Well, perhaps that is best." Lifting her gaze, Delilah caught the momentary sheen in Ellie's blue-green eyes. This seemed to be her morning for bringing up subjects no one wished to discuss. She should have stayed on the trail and not sought human companionship.

"Now, tell me, my young friend, what has brought you to the cottage today?"

Delilah delayed her answer while Miss Mandy entered with a small tray containing a steaming pot of tea and delicate china cups. "It's Father," she replied, her eyes following the movements of the retreating servant. "His financial straits are making him a vicious old bull to live with. He sold Swainie's family to Mr. Thomas Jefferson Wells so that he could make a payment to the New England Mortgage Company, but he didn't get nearly enough to stop the threats of foreclosure."

"I wish there was something I could do to help," Ellie replied, putting her hand upon Delilah's. Withdrawing her touch, Ellie poured the tea, sweetened it to Delilah's taste, and handed her a cup. "If only Angus would remember where he buried that gold."

If only . . . Delilah mentally echoed Ellie's words. "I'll never understand why he buried it to begin with, rather than depositing it in the bank. Dear Lord, Ellie, do you realize he buried enough gold to pay off the mortgage on The Shadows—with money to spare? His memory is getting worse every day. Just this morning he left the house without his boots. I just wish I could run away and hide somewhere." Delilah didn't like thinking about that

13

night her father had run the rig into Bayou Boeuf, resulting in the death of the slave Lathrop, any more than Ellie wanted to talk about Charles's death. She and Daisy were never able to decide whether Delilah had pulled Daisy from the swift currents of the bayou, or the other way around. However it had happened, the two little girls had then dragged Angus Wickley onto the bank before the bayou could claim him, as it had Lathrop.

But that was all in the past; the present was proving to be the dilemma. Since her mother's death, Delilah had done the best she could to help her father run Shadows-in-the-Mist. She kept all the books for the plantation and met with other planters on the bayou. She had also made the selling and purchasing arrangements (though she would never have agreed to sell Swainie's family) and she had talked to the bank in Alexandria about taking acreage in payment of debts owed there. She had brought up the subject to her father of selling the riverboat, but he had immediately sprung into a black fury. She was hitting more brick walls than a trapped and frantic sparrow.

Delilah looked up from her tea when Ellie spoke. "I have an idea, Delilah. My friend, Grant Emerson—"

"The Yankee?"

Ellie slightly nodded. "Yes, the Yankee. I sent an invitation to him to visit. I've recently learned that the Parlington plantation near Lafayette will go up for sale this spring and he had expressed an interest in purchasing such a place. He's wealthy, very generous, and interested in land investments. About your father's situation, Delilah, I may be able to implore him to buy a share in The Shadows—"

"No!" Delilah jumped to her feet, upsetting her tea. "I will not have The Shadows bailed out of debt by a Yankee-Doodle gambler who would probably want to rule the place with a bullwhip!"

Surprised by her outburst, Ellie calmly set down her

14

teacup and rose. "Is it because he's from the East, or because he's a gambler?"

Delilah instantly regretted her outburst. Ellie was merely trying to help her find a solution to a very serious problem. She should not have reacted so fiercely. Turning, she took Ellie's hands, her eyes moving over a face that did not betray her thirty-six years of age. "Forgive me, El. I guess the antics of Father have my nerves a bit frayed. I did not intend to demean your friend. But I could never accept such an overture from a stranger."

"And a Yankee-Doodle one at that!" Ellie laughed, attempting to quell the tension. "Just don't you worry, my young friend. Everything will work out."

Suddenly, the sound of a galloping horse broke the stillness of the morning. Both women rushed to the door just as Philo, a stable hand from The Shadows, dismounted. "Miz Delilah, ya best git back home right now. Somethin' bad's ahappenin'."

A chill of apprehension traveled the length of Delilah's spine. "What has happened, Philo?"

"Yo' pappy, he done hol't hisself up in de Big House wid a gun!"

A strangled cry ripped at Delilah; she made several unsuccessful attempts to speak. Ellie McPherson spoke sharply. "What has brought this about, Philo?"

The elderly man had removed his hat in respect to the women. He held it firmly to his chest. "Mr. Penrod from de bank, he done brought a—a 'viction notice, an' Massah Wickley, he s'posed to be off'n de Shadows in five days. He hol't up in de house sayin' he shoot his brains out 'fo' he leave de Shadows. Lawd, Missy, we real scared. We sent fo' de sheriff in Alex. We thinkin' maybe you can talk some sense into yo' pappy."

The rush of panic and fear was almost more than Delilah could bear. She took several deep breaths, her fingers clawing at the slim column of her throat. "Dear God, Ellie . . ." She finally found her voice. "I can't lose my father—"

15

"Angus is as strong as a bull," Ellie assured her. "He's just scared. Hurry home with Philo and talk to him. He'll listen to you, Delilah . . . he loves you so. And if there's anything I can do—"

Briefly touching her hand to Ellie's, Delilah whispered, "A little prayer might help."

By the time Delilah and Philo crossed the Old Texas Road just south of Smith's Landing, carriages and horses scurried toward Shadows-in-the-Mist, morbidly drawn to the impending tragedy that had been spread along the bayou by gossiping tongues. Delilah almost became physically ill when she dismounted at the porch of The Shadows and saw those curious interlopers being held at bay by the plantation slaves and the constable from the landing. The distraught cook, Mozelle, normally as stalwart as the fiercest bear, met Delilah at the door. Behind her stood Trusdale, their French-speaking butler, who rolled his eyes upward and shook his head.

"The massah, he be's in the study," Mozelle wailed. "He says only way he leave dis land be's in a long pine box."

"Hush, Mozelle! Hush that nonsense!" Delilah spoke sternly. "You're not making matters any easier. You go tell Philo that I want all these people off the plantation immediately!"

"Mademoiselle," Trusdale spoke up, "he will not shoot himself. He is just trying to gain sympathy."

Delilah clicked her tongue, her eyes narrowing as she met the big man's gaze. She didn't like Trusdale and could not understand why her father had purchased him on his last trip to New Orleans. Trusdale, because he was educated and spoke like a true Frenchman, had always tended to look down on the other slaves.

Shaking off the anger she felt, she spoke to Philo. "Please, try to make these people leave!" Though she knew his efforts would prove futile, she simply had to be alone with her father, without an audience. As she moved through the house, sending the other servants outside, she could hear her father humming a tune Philo often hummed at the stable. He must have heard the resonant voice of The Shadows' oldest slave that morning and allowed the tune to settle peacefully into his soul.

When the house had been emptied, Delilah moved slowly down the corridor toward the study, her father's favorite room. Her breathing all but ceased as she stood outside the door, then opened it just enough to see him sitting at the game table, the chess pieces unmoved since the last visit of Mr. Thomas Jefferson Wells. Wells and her father played chess in the large, comfortable room every Thursday from two to four in the afternoon. A game not completed by four o'clock was resumed the following week. Though hooded, moisture-sheened eyes scanned the chess pieces, the deeper concentration of the big barrel-chested man was on his favorite hunting rifle. His hands caressed it almost lovingly.

When Angus Wickley caught the delicate scent of his daughter, he looked up, immediately ceasing his absent-minded humming. "Delilah, girl—"

"Papa, what are you doing inside the house? You should enjoy the outdoors before the rain comes." All at once, she noticed that he appeared much older than his actual age of fifty-four. But perhaps the agony of defeat had simply masked his mature good looks. Even his thick silver-gray hair and sweeping sidewhiskers seemed to have thinned in the hour or two since she had last seen him. Delilah stepped into the room, her hand outstretched. "Here," she entreated further. "Let me take your hunting rifle out to one of the men for a good cleaning."

"Stop, Daughter!" Without arising, the hand of Angus Wickley came up in an almost threatening gesture. "The gun doesn't need to be cleaned. Now . . . sit. We need to talk."

First and foremost in Delilah's mind was relieving her father of the rifle because she did not know if he felt desperate enough to use it. If only she had been present when Hugh Penrod had arrived with the foreclosure and eviction notice, she could have intercepted it and broken the news delicately. As she took a chair across from Angus, she spied a crumpled bit of paper on the normally immaculate floor. "What is that, father?"

Angus Wickley dropped his glance, then retrieved the offending notice. "It is the end of our lives, Delilah girl, as we know them. Thank God you're strong . . . like your mother."

Her mother had been anything but strong, but it was not the moment to pick an argument. Delilah had to buy time, to gentle her father's mood and shine a light of hope into the dark desperation reflected in his eyes. She might have accomplished that task within the span of a minute or so if the tall case clock against the wall had not suddenly chimed the hour of ten. Startled, she lurched from her chair and was immediately faced by a puzzled look. She shrugged lightly. "Sorry, Papa, I guess my nerves are a bit frayed."

When he did not reply, Delilah took a moment to study him. His one hand absently stroked the rifle while the other gently touched each of the chess pieces without moving them. Before that cold December night on the bayou, he had been the towering oak to which she had run for protection; now he was like a willow, his eyes downcast, the tenuous branches of his soul dragging the ground. She wanted so much to provide the strength he had so often provided her, yet he seemed as far away as the sun. She felt that if she reached out to touch him, she would find only empty space. She felt that if she spoke her heart, he would close his own and her words would be wasted. Yet she could not sit by and watch him destroy himself.

She prepared to speak those words gathering in her heart, but he interrupted her thoughts. "I put a jewel case on the bureau in your sleeping chamber, Delilah," he said gruffly. "It holds the treasures that were your mother's and should fetch a pleasing penny if the need arises. Should anything happen to me—"

Delilah shot to her feet. "Nothing is going to happen to you, Papa. It doesn't matter about The Shadows . . ." Oh, but it did. It mattered so much to both of them. Gathering her thoughts once again, she continued. "What matters is that you and I have each other, and together we can weather any storm. That is more precious than land and a house and all that it holds. Oh, please, Papa, everything will work out. Perhaps the mortgage company will let us keep the riverboat. We could live there until we decide what to do." Her gaze met his hooded one. "Papa, couldn't you try to remember where you buried the gold? It could mean the difference between keeping The Shadows and losing it."

His eyebrows gathered in a perplexed frown as though a thousand muddled thoughts were pulling together within his brain. "The gold . . . the gold, Delilah girl? I told you, Lathrup was with me when I buried it. Ask him."

Pain creased Delilah's brow. Would it do any good to remind her father, for the hundredth—no, the thousandth—time, that Lathrup had died that night in the bayou? She thought not.

Angus Wickley looked up at his tall, slender daughter, his heart suddenly arush at her beauty and grace. How much like her mother she was—prideful, but every bit the lady; strong, but smart enough to display a moment of vulnerability when it would be to her advantage. She was his companion and his life. Since Irene's death, she had taken the weight of the world on her shoulders, managing the plantation as skillfully as any man, making decisions and earning the respect of other planters on the bayou. She had proved more adept at plantation life than the son he had wanted could ever have been. She had sacrificed the pleasures a woman deserved to be a dutiful daughter. She had held her would-be beaux at arm's length because The Shadows — and her father, the only person in the world who held the key to saving The Shadows — came first.

But now it was time for one way of life to end and another to begin. Delilah was right. Things would work out.

"Delilah girl . . ." Gently, Angus Wickley placed the rifle against the leg of the game table. "Be an angel and fetch your papa a shot of his favorite brandy from the parlor. Then we shall talk, just you and me."

Though she couldn't remember the last time her father had taken a drink, Delilah breathed a sigh of relief. The anguish in his voice was replaced by hope. She heard the strength there, the optimism . . . the invincible love of a father for his daughter. "I'll be right back, Papa. Just remember that no matter what happens, we have each other."

He did not reply, except to favor her with a sad smile.

Delilah resisted the urge to run to the parlor and accomplish the diversion quickly, choosing instead to remain calm and undaunted. She could hear the murmurings of the interlopers on the lawns. A wide-eyed Philo peered in at the front door just as she reached the parlor entrance.

"Massah Wickley, he be's calmin' down, Missy?"

Delilah smiled sadly, looking past him to give comfort to the tearful Mozelle. "He's better . . . asking for a glass of his favorite brandy." With gentle admonishment, she continued. "You didn't get rid of our *dear* neighbors, Philo?"

"Dem whites, Missy, dey ain't gonna listen to us black folk."

"Well, perhaps the rain will chase them off," she said, watching the first droplets puddle against the planked porch.

With Philo's parting, Delilah rushed to the liquor cabinet and found a half-empty bottle of peach brandy. Taking up a clean goblet, she turned toward the corridor.

Thunder suddenly rent the sky, but even its moment of intensity did not diminish the sharp, single burst of rifle fire from inside the house. Delilah's cry was simultaneous to the decanter crashing to the highly-polished floor, sending glass and amber rivers of brandy swirling around her trembling form. As her fingers rose to dig at her temples, it seemed that a hundred pairs of masculine boots thundered past her. Managing to regain her senses, she rushed toward the study, only to be caught in the powerful arms of Thomas Jefferson Wells, who had just arrived at The Shadows hoping to talk some sense into his good friend.

"Don't go in there, Delilah," he ordered brusquely, his strong voice touched by emotion, fearing the worst. "Let the men see what has happened."

But Delilah would not be held back. She jerked herself free and rushed past him. There, in the panelled study, sat her father, surrounded by half a dozen men. When Delilah's anguished gaze met his own, he explained sheepishly. "The blasted thing went off, Delilah girl. Better get one of the men to mend that hole up there—"

Laughing and crying in the same moment, Delilah rushed into his arms and held him tightly. The other men, sensing that she had the situation well under control, quietly left the room.

Later, when the excitement had died down, Delilah retired to her room for a few hours of solitude. She didn't know what her father expected them to do after they left The Shadows, but for now, he acted as if he hadn't a care in the world. She had left him in the study with Mr. Wells, the two of them mulling over the game of chess they had begun the week before.

His good mood carried over into the evening. At dinner, he chatted pleasantly about little things, reminisced on the past, and brusquely evaded speculations on their future away from Shadows-in-the-Mist. He remarked that repairs needed to be done on the riverboat, and that perhaps they could invite a few good friends on an overnight bayou excursion. It was almost as though he had forgotten about the eviction notice.

That night, Delilah could not sleep. She paced her room until well past midnight, then sat in the wicker chair, holding the embroidered pillows to her and watching a gentle rain streak the windowpanes. When dawn filtered through the trees, sleep had still not come to her, and yet she was not tired. She knew only that there was much to be done in the few days before The Shadows would be only a memory.

A knock sounded at the door; then the pretty brown-skinned Daisy opened the door and peered in, her dark eyes scanning the dim interior for Delilah. When she saw her sitting peacefully in the wicker chair, she approached, dropped to her knees, and gently wrapped her arms around Delilah, she was weeping.

Delilah returned the embrace. "Why this emotion, my friend?" she asked.

"It's yo' papa, Missy. When he wasn't up 'bout five, like usual, Trusdale went in to wake him. Missy, yo' papa died peacefully in his sleep last night."

Delilah did not cry. As if her body had suddenly drained of strength, she held Daisy for a long, long while, until the sun filtered in and settled upon her pale features. Her dear father — close to losing the home that had meant so much to him — had quietly willed himself to die. She had no doubt of it.

She remembered very little after that. Existing in a vortex of numb silence, she was only vaguely aware of strangers wandering aimlessly through The Shadows, of words of comfort and consolation, of weeping servants and sharply barked orders muffled by a driving rain. When the funeral coach arrived at midmorning to take her father away, she sat quietly on the divan watching a silent, emotional Ellie McPherson move about the parlor. She had covered the mirrors in traditional black

22

drapes to ward off the evil spirits that might be attracted to the shiny surface. Candles had been lit all about the room, the hands of the grandfather clock silenced, and the bier was set up to accept her father's casket when he had been properly laid out.

What had happened to her wonderful life . . . and the father she had loved so dearly?

After the funeral, Delilah stood alone for a few moments to say goodbye to her father in her own special way. Suddenly, dozens of cardinals, the ruby-red bodies of the males like animated Christmas ornaments, perched in a small, bare oak just beyond the cemetery. Delilah remembered something her father had said a long, long time ago, when she had been frightened by the sudden passing of one of their slaves. "Never be afraid of death, Delilah girl. When someone dies, their soul becomes a cardinal and soars gracefully to heaven on scarlet wings. Nothing can touch it, not arrow nor bullet nor falcon, for the Lord's hands shield that precious soul from all harm until it is safe in his Sacred Kingdom. No, Delilah girl, death is not to be feared. You will never be safer than then."

As the birds suddenly took to wing, Delilah wondered which of those lovely jewels had appeared to take her father's soul on its final journey, soaring with the majestic winds of Bayou Boeuf . . . and onward into the clouds.

Turning, she stood for a few more minutes in the shade of a pine, her fingers loosely linked against the gathers of her somber gray gown. The house her father had built and named Shadows-in-the-Mist stood majestically upon the barren lawn, catching the full attention of the young melancholy woman who had just buried the last of her immediate family. In just a few short weeks a blanket of green would gently cloak the hills and the azaleas would spring into profuse bloom. The magnolias would bear large, bold white flowers and the breeze would carry their sweetest fragrances on a peaceful journey along the bayou. But she would not be here to enjoy it as in seasons past. The Shadows was lost to her forever. Soon—oh, so painfully soon—uncaring hands would manipulate for profit the lands that she had cherished simply for their beauty.

The exquisitely proportioned plantation house of pink brick stood against the somber horizon, its neoclassic columns painted a cool white. The shells covering the circular drive glistened in the fading light as the first rain of the day threatened above the timberline.

Delilah had many duties to attend to in the two days remaining before the eviction. Gathering her wits, and sending her somber thoughts to some far-distant place, she breathed deeply, turned, and whispered, "Farewell, Father," then began the short trek down the hill toward the carriage house. She soon located Philo, who was taking a moment after the funeral to partake of his first meal of the day.

"Philo?"

Swallowing his last morsel of food, Philo came to his feet. "Missy be wantin' Bella saddled up?"

Delilah kicked at an imaginary stone, only now noticing the thin coat of dust clinging to the hem of her dreary gray crepe skirts. "Yes, Philo . . ." She gently shrugged. "I don't want you to think ill of me or to fancy that I'm doing something dreadful, but . . ." She had trouble searching for the right words, "As you know, Bella is my favorite horse. There are many others at The Shadows and she will not be missed. I want you to take her over to Miss Ellie's place and request that Lancie keep her there in the stable." Misunderstanding Philo's look, she continued with haste. "You can't really call it theft, Philo. Bella is mine. Father gave her to me for my last birthday and she shouldn't be considered property subject to seizure. Do you understand?"

24

Bewilderment masked the old gentleman's deeply-lined features. "Sho', Missy. Philo, he wuz jes' gonna ask which o' dem saddles Missy be wantin'—the li'l odd one o' dat one made fo' de ladies."

"I don't want the sidesaddle, Philo. I want the English saddle and the proper tack. Now, you'll do this for me this morning, without delay?"

"Sho', Missy. I be's ridin' out 'most fo' Missy reach de Big House."

Dropping her eyes, Delilah pressed her mouth into a thin line. When her gaze again met Philo's, she attempted to still the quiver in her voice as she spoke. "I do hope that . . . whoever ends up owning The Shadows will be good to your people."

The old man's eyes misted. "Ain' nobody be's a'good to us as Missy an' Massah Wickley . . . when he was in a good mood," he softly amended, remembering the times Angus Wickley had dealt punishment—though never severely—to the slaves. "Don' worry, Missy, we be jes' fine." Then, drawing up his shoulders as he turned, he began to hum his favorite hymn. The tears were there, clinging to his haunting voice.

Delilah drew her shoulders up straight and turned toward the house. But she paused again, her own emotions threatening her equilibrium, her remembrances of her childhood at The Shadows so painfully clear that she maintained her dignity only with great effort. Her girlish dreams, of mirrored ballrooms, well-groomed cavaliers, and giggling beaux were like moving pictures inside her head—the dreams of a young girl that had never materialized. But could she have survived plantation life without them?

She thought not. Over the years, while she had performed her dreary duties, she had kept the dreams at the back of her thoughts. They had been almost as important to her as the plantation . . . and her dear father and mother.

Linking her fingers at her back, she resumed the short

25

journey to the house her father had built on Bayou Boeuf.

Leaving Shadows-in-the-Mist was like abandoning an old and dear friend.

Two

Grant Emerson stepped from the gangplank of the steamboat *Rodolph* onto a crowded dock. The *Rodolph* made regular trips up the Mississippi River, through Old River, and up the Red to the town of Alexandria in central Louisiana. He would not have made the trip until the spring, but a missive from the pretty young widow, Ellie McPherson, had brought him through the haunting river channels three months earlier than usual.

Bearing down on his silver-studded cane, Grant moved with an unsteady gait toward the depot of the Red River Railroad to check the schedule of runs to Lamourie Bayou. Then he turned northward, toward the branch office of the New Orleans Canal and Banking Company. After many days in his cramped quarters aboard the *Rodolph*, he found the half-mile walk invigorating, despite a recent rain that had turned the roadways to mud and slush. His highly-polished black boots sank into the deep ruts as he moved precariously northward; by trip's end, each was weighted down by clumps of clinging red clay. He paused at a community watering trough to dab at the clots with his handkerchief, accomplishing little more than shifting the mess from one place to another. By the time he arrived at the bank, mud spattered his black trousers and the cool March wind had left his flaxen hair a mass of disarray framing his angular face. The deepening color of his blue eyes closely matched the threat of rain washing across the eastern horizon.

Entering the small, dimly-lit branch office with its prisonlike teller windows and expressionless male employees, Grant removed his hat and scanned the faces behind the littered desks for his banker. Momentarily, he spied the tall, thin man exiting the office of the manager. Their gazes instantly met and surprise marked the older man's face.

"Grant Emerson!" Hugh Penrod moved through a waist-high swinging door and offered his hand. "I didn't expect to see you until June. What brings you to Alexandria in March?"

Grant did not admit that he'd been invited by Ellie McPherson. "Making a deposit," he replied, grasping Penrod's gnarled hand. "And checking on my funds."

Penrod motioned him to a small, clean office to the right. "Take a chair, Grant," he offered. "I'll pull your record."

Grant had just made himself comfortable in an overstuffed leather side chair and picked up a copy of *The Alexandria Gazette* when Hugh Penrod returned, closing the door behind him.

"Have you seen Mrs. McPherson lately?" Grant inquired.

Penrod smiled. "She was in depositing her household funds yesterday morning." Thoughtful silence marked the older man's brow for a moment. "In fact," he continued on a sigh, "now that I think about our conversation, I should have expected you'd make an early trip."

"What do you mean?" For the present, the banking records being pushed across the desk toward him were the least of Grant's concern. "Tell me, Hugh, why Ellie was so anxious that I make this trip?"

"She was hoping you'd take a look at the Parlington place near Lafayette. But now the Wickley plantation is available . . ." Hugh cringed at his recollection of Angus Wickley's death. Despite the deterioration of Angus's health over the last few years of his life, Hugh felt personally responsible, since he was the one who had delivered the seizure and eviction notice. "The place was seized by the New England Mortgage Company for which we are bonded agents. Since we hold a second mortgage, I have recently filed a lien against the property. It goes up for sheriff's sale on the third Wednesday of this month and, I understand from Ellie, you have been interested in a good land investment."

Grant leaned back, cupping his hands behind his head. He smiled pleasantly. "And I suppose you've determined that I have funds enough in my account here to pay off your lien and the lien of the first holder?" When Hugh Penrod's humorous expression answered his question, Grant continued. "So why don't you tell me about the place, Hugh, in the event that I am, indeed, interested?"

With an excitement that seemed almost childlike, Hugh Penrod stretched out his hands. "Seven hundred acres of prime pasture and planting, seventy healthy slaves, thirty men, twenty-four women and sixteen young'uns under the age of fourteen, a fine house completely furnished, two silos for grain, a stable and carriage house, a smoke house and, would you believe it . . . a riverboat permanently installed on the bayou, down the lawn from the main house. Angus Wickley purchased it on a whim at the auction of a bankrupt shipping company and transported it to The Boeuf. Blast! You should have seen the trouble he went to to get it there. As you know, The Boeuf is too narrow and too shallow to allow for the boat, but Angus was determined to get it there.

Calling for volunteers from the surrounding plantations, he carefully removed her paddle, sending it on ahead of the boat, then put two hundred darkies to work for the better part of three weeks rolling the blasted thing on logs from the Red to The Boeuf, tying up traffic and the sheriff threatening to fine him for being a nuisance. But he'd paid twenty thousand dollars for her and he said he'd lay down and die rather than give up the struggle. Finally, when the paddle was reattached and the boat was being rolled into The Boeuf, it promptly got that blasted paddle wheel stuck four feet into the mud, and the back half of her hull was just sucked under. She's moored, but there's no need for it. The mud holds her down in the back like glue and in a good throe of wind the front half of her bobs around like a broken neck. She'll be sitting there forever, connected to the shore by a single gangplank. Kind of good-looking, though, and folks here and about like to see her there. But she's fallen to neglect. If you buy the place, you might want to invest a little money in her."

"What makes you think I wouldn't sell it and get it off the bayou. If it doesn't serve a purpose, why keep it?"

Hugh sat back in his chair and laughed. "I know you've got an ache for the riverboats, Grant. And I suspect you'll grow to love *Bayou Belle* as much as the people here and abouts. No . . . you wouldn't sell it."

Grant smiled again; perhaps Hugh was right. "Does the place have good accommodations for the slaves?"

"Cabins less than ten years old, with good drainage and a clean water supply. The big house is set in a deep, shaded grove of live oaks just a hundred yards up from the bayou. You need to get off that blasted river, Grant, and settle down. Besides, rumor has it that Angus Wickley buried half a million dollars in

30

gold somewhere on the place and forgot its whereabouts after a grievous injury. Treasure-seekers have been run off the place for the past ten years or so."

"And do you believe it exists?"

"Hell . . ." Hugh linked his fingers behind his head. "There's no doubt about it. I received several reports from men who saw the gold, including Mr. Thomas Jefferson Wells of Dentley Plantation. He was out on the road that night when Angus was returning from New Orleans. Angus was damned lucky he wasn't robbed while transporting it to The Boeuf. But his luck ran out, and for some insane reason he stopped somewhere along the bayou, buried the gold, and plunged the rig into the bayou. His slave was killed, but Angus and the two children, his daughter and the slave girl her same age, survived. I don't think the gold will ever be found."

"Why the hell did he bury it so close to home?"

"No one knows. We don't even know where he got it."

"And the old man didn't say?"

"Something happened to him after that night. He never was the same, couldn't remember himself where he'd gotten it." Changing the subject, he continued. "Now . . . what do you think? You going to look at the place? We'd sure be pleased if you settled down here and found a good woman who'd keep you here."

Grant had made many friends in the Red River port town, in the three years since he'd first escorted Ellie McPherson to her home on Lamourie Bayou after the incident just out of St. Louis that had left him lame. Acquaintances expected that he'd be Ellie's second husband, but the truth was that they were, simply, very good friends. "I'll settle down," Grant said, "when I find a woman strong enough to hog-tie me. Now . . ." Once again cupping his hands behind his head, he continued. "About this place, Hugh. Who's running it?"

"Now that the family's gone . . ." Hugh deliberately did not mention the death of Angus Wickley, "the place is being held down by some of the more reliable slaves, an old fellow by the name of Philo, his son, Philbus, and a French-speaking niggah named Trusdale. Miss Ellie's been over there a few times to make sure the house is being kept clean and to gather some of the personal effects of the previous owner's daughter. You interested, Grant?"

Grant exercised perfect control. He certainly did not want to appear too eager and have the price suddenly shoot up. "Might be, Hugh. You slide the figures across the desk to me and I'll decide whether I take a look at the place." Taking up a pen and dipping it into the inkwell, Hugh hastily scrawled some figures on a sheet of bank stationery. Grant looked down only when the sheet of linen paper stopped just short of his waistcoat. Thoughtful silence darkened his brow, then he glanced up, his gaze catching Hugh Penrod's waiting one. "Yep, I'll be taking a look."

The banker smiled his pleasure. "I'll have one of the boys draw up a letter of access. You take all the time you need at the place. The darkies out there will cooperate . . . I'll see to it."

"The plantation's near here?" Grant asked.

"Near a place called Smith's Landing on Bayou Boeuf about sixteen miles south . . . hardly more than a couple of taverns and a general store. But there is a railroad depot connecting to Lamourie Bayou and to Alexandria. And . . ." Hugh smiled broadly, "separated from Ellie McPherson's place by little less than an hour's ride by horseback. Why don't you take Ellie when you look at the place. She's familiar with the land and knows most of the slaves."

Grant rose to his feet. "I just might do that,

Hugh," he replied. "Now, I need to make a deposit before I leave."

Grant Emerson saw hope at the end of what had been a wasted five years of his life. At the age of thirty-two he was ready to settle down and try to put his past mistakes behind him . . . especially those that had compelled him to leave behind his life in Massachusetts.

Bayou Boeuf moved with silent majesty through the fertile fields of central Louisiana. That early Sunday morning, as the carriage clipped along a well-traveled road, Grant saw more than the beauty; he saw the haunting sanctuary he had secretly been seeking for five years. As the house suddenly came into view, an excited Ellie McPherson tucked her hand into the crook of Grant's arm. "There it is, Grant," she whispered. "Shadows-in-the-Mist."

Grant was impressed, but he couldn't imagine himself needing so much room. It appeared to be a house that a woman's loving hands should nurture, a house whose many rooms should be invaded by the scampering feet of mischievous children. He almost felt guilty considering the purchase. The house deserved a family.

Grant noticed at once the pathetic contrast between the large brick house and the humble, though sturdy and freshly whitewashed, planked slave quarters circling a bend in the bayou. Many slaves, enjoying the one day that no work was expected of them, moved among the cottages that appeared much too small to accommodate their large families.

The wide, greening lawns surrounding the house were studded with handsome oaks and spreading pecan trees. Off to the right a trellised gazebo graced a slight rise, the new blooms of a wisteria hanging in long, lavender fingers over its domed roof. Everywhere Grant looked, an early spring heralded a new and exciting season. And there, a permanent fixture on the current of Bayou Boeuf, was Angus Wickley's notoriously frivolous purchase — the large white riverboat with peacock-blue trim and the name, *Bayou Belle,* in large blue, gold-trimmed letters across the wall of the lower compartments.

She was a good size, about a hundred and forty feet long by twenty-eight side. What the commercial shippers called "the women's quarters" appeared to be about thirty feet long belowdecks, and she was topped by an elegant roundhouse. An exquisitely decorated deck surrounded by iron railings and nettings half hid a line of fancy wooden deck chairs that needed a good coat of varnish.

The sight of the *Bayou Belle* brought five years of memories rushing upon Grant. The riverboats that plied the Mississippi were a little larger than the one sitting serenely — and crippled — before him, and he recalled the many nights he'd sat among men adept at such games as poker, whist, brag, and three-card monte. He'd made a fortune being "a lucky gambler" and had never once cheated. He prided himself on that, although the ordinary man might consider that occupation nefarious, underhanded, and indicative of a criminal mind.

"What are you thinking, Grant?"

He started at Ellie's softly voiced question. "Just remembering," he replied after a moment, turning his gaze from what he considered the "jewel" of the plantation he was thinking about purchasing.

Alighting the carriage, Grant retrieved his cane and offered his hand to Ellie. At that moment, Philo came out of the carriage house. "Miz El, you be visitin' a'gin so soon? Lawd, what the Missy done fo-'got dis time?"

"Philo, this is Mr. Emerson, the gentleman Mr. Penrod advised would be wanting to see The Shadows. Will you kindly take charge of the morning after he has seen the house and show him the rest of the plantation?"

Philo's coal-black eyes darkened even more, an unfathomable depth of contempt and silent loathing. So this was the Yankee-Doodle gambler interested in The Shadows? His mood changing noticeably, Philo replied, "Yas'sum, Miz El, Philo'll saddle a couple o' hosses. Don' know what a stranger be wantin' wid dis rundown ol' plantation."

She and Grant turned toward the house. "Is it just me?" Grant asked. "Or do they dislike anyone interested in this place?"

"They loved the Wickleys, that's all, as much as the Wickleys loved them. Change is hard for them."

"And these Wickleys . . . they loved this place as well?"

"With all their hearts and souls," Ellie replied quietly.

"Then why did they leave?"

"Well . . ." Ellie chose her words very carefully. "Angus Wickley died and his daughter could not run the place alone." Though she knew Delilah was more than capable of running the plantation, she did not amend her small lie, even in deference to her dear friend.

Grant imagined there was much more to it than that. If he could separate himself from Ellie for a few minutes, he knew one of the slaves might be more than willing to fill in the details. Thus, when they reached the gallery and were met by Mozelle, whose look was every bit as hostile as was Philo's, Grant turned to Ellie. "Why don't I take a look at the house by myself, Ellie?" he asked. When her look darkened with surprise that she should be excluded from the

35

tour, he continued so that only she could hear. "I've got a distinct feeling that sabotage might be in the making here. I'd like to hear what these people have to say if you're not around. After all, they respect you and would say nothing to displease you."

Ellie's look hinted at some degree of understanding. "Where is Trusdale?" she asked Mozelle, believing he would be the least offensive of the house servants.

"Trusdale, he be over at Mistah Montfort's at Wellswood. Mistah Penrod, he say it be all right, since his man, Ol' Peck, be laid up."

"Oh, I see. Then you will be showing Mr. Emerson the house?"

Her eyes narrowed spitefully. "Yas'sum, Miz El."

"Have you a pot of boiling water in the kitchen? I might enjoy a cup of tea while you look around."

"Yas'sum, Miz El."

Ellie watched as Grant joined the servant for the tour of the house, then made her way toward the kitchen where she had so often sat with Delilah, sharing in the gossip that flowed along the bayou as quickly as the current. The house rang with silence where Delilah's happy laughter had once been heard, and the absence saddened her.

Out of hearing range of Ellie McPherson, Mozelle gathered her apron into a ball between her nervous fingers. "What a stranger be wantin' wid dis big ol' rundown house?" She asked Grant.

Grant could see at first glance that the house was sturdy, immaculate, and richly furnished. Were Mozelle and Philo seeing something that he could not? "What is wrong with the house?" he asked, following her on the stairs.

Halting at the landing, Mozelle narrowed her eyes. "Dis big ole house eat up wid de termites, sur'nuff. An' it be's sittin' on a Injun graveyard. If ya smart,

Mister Yankee-Doodle, a' ya be hoppin' back in dat carriage and skee-daddlin' faster'n a rabbit."

Grant maintained his composure. He imagined that owning a place like Shadows-in-the-Mist would prove to be quite a challenge . . . and one that he was more than willing to face. "I'd like to see the upstairs if we could continue," he said as politely as he could.

In the next few minutes, Mozelle threw open door after door, pointing out the defects and deficiencies in each room, which on each occasion Grant failed to notice. But when she came to the last door, she turned toward Grant, narrowed her eyes, and drew her hands to her wide hips. "Dat be's Missy's room. Ain't no business o' yer'n goin' in."

"Is Missy still in there?" Grant asked.

A bit of color invaded Mozelle's dark face. "Ain't nobody in dere, Mr. Yankee-Doodle."

"I have a name, Mozelle, and it's not Yankee-Doodle."

"Ya' from de Nawth, ain't ya? Then ya be Mr. Yankee-Doodle."

She was a most infuriating woman, and as bold as a cavalier's cockade. Grant felt his patience waning. "I'd appreciate it if you called me Mr. Emerson."

"Sho', Massah Emerson, if'n that be what ya want."

If anything could rile Grant's feathers, it was being called Massah! She had succeeded in incensing him. "You're either going to cease that vicious tone with me," he said, "or when I buy this place I'll sell you to the lowest human vermin I can dredge up from a city sewer. Do you hear me?" He wouldn't, of course. Grant abhorred slavery; it made his skin crawl.

Mozelle's black eyebrows had shot up in surprise. "Yas'sir, I hear ya loud an' clear."

Fighting back his moment of ire, Grant pushed open the door to the room Mozelle had attempted to

37

bar him from. The anger left his eyes as he scanned the large, feminine bedchamber with its spotless pink-and-white flocked wallpaper, rich furnishings, and canopied bed covered in antique lace. At the south window sat a white wicker rocker plumped with hand-embroidered pillows, over which hung a delicate fringed shawl. He could almost imagine the woman who had occupied and enjoyed this room and felt that he had, indeed, invaded a private sanctuary. Dropping his gaze, he pulled the door closed.

"I'll see the rest of the house now, Mozelle."

"Yas'suh, ya be wantin' to see the room where Massah Wickley jes' pert near blowed his brains out wid a gun?"

Grant had had just about enough. Firmly gripping the servant's upper arm, he pulled her around to face him, infuriated by her narrow, rebellious look. "Before we reach the bottom of the stairs, I want to hear one good thing about this house come out of your mouth. And I'll tell you one more thing: If I wasn't interested before I got here, after this nice, informative little chat I've had with you, I'd pull my last penny from the bank to buy this place." Releasing her, and pulling down the waistcoat that had suddenly tightened across his chest, Grant turned toward the stairs.

By the time he had finished seeing the house — alone — and sought out Ellie McPherson in the kitchen, Grant had managed to regain a bit of his lost composure. But his normally crystal-blue eyes were still fiercely dark and that was the first thing Ellie noticed. "What's bothering you, Grant?"

"Not a thing, Ellie," he replied, averting his gaze when Mozelle, her arms crossed, sauntered into the kitchen behind him, "but when I buy this place," he continued, gesturing toward Mozelle with his right hand, "I'm going to sell that woman to the devil.

Right now, I'll take that ride over the lands and will be back within the hour."

When Grant had left the house, Ellie looked quizzically toward Mozelle. "What on earth did you do to him, Mozelle?"

Shrugging, a light of innocence beaming in her dark eyes, she softly replied, "Don' know, Miz El. Must be dat hotter'n a pot Yankee-Doodle blood runnin' through dem veins o' his . . ."

Grant sauntered across the lawns, allowing the cool March morning to quell his ill temper. Philo appeared from the carriage house with two saddled horses. In his dark eyes beamed the same rebellion Grant had seen in the eyes of the feisty house servant.

Resting his cane against a narrow bench, Grant mounted the gelding. Before reining about, he pointed a finger at Philo. "If I hear one thing about boll weevils or poor soil, cursed grounds, or dying crops," he bellowed, "I swear to the Almighty . . ." He left the threat hanging, feeling that he'd successfully gotten the message across.

Delilah had awakened early that Sunday morning, eaten a light breakfast in the dining room of the Exchange Hotel, then returned to her small room at the west end of the second-floor corridor. Drawing a chair to the window, she stared across the railroad tracks running parallel to the levee and watched the riverboats on Red River. She dropped her elbows to the windowsill, her chin resting heavily upon her linked fingers.

In the past four weeks her world had turned topsy-turvy. She recalled the many afternoons she had spent confined to the rooms of The Shadows, kept indoors by foul weather, domestic duties, or a momentary bout of illness that never really amounted to anything. Her weary sighs had been childlike then, a bored, repressed, spoiled belle wanting only to pursue her personal pleasures; now they were the sighs of a worried woman who had suddenly found herself alone and homeless, and who did not know what tomorrow would bring.

She thought of her dear father and a smile lit her face. He was where he had been happiest — at his beloved Shadows-in-the-Mist — in peaceful repose beside his wife Irene, both their graves shaded by the ancient boughs of a live oak. "I miss you, Papa," she whispered, touching her fingertips to the cool pane of glass.

Again she sighed, averting her gaze from the window. She needed to place her priorities, among which were retrieving her horse from Ellie's stable. Mr. Pinchon at the livery had agreed to stable Bella for a dollar a week.

But should the horse be a priority? She could not live at the Exchange Hotel for the rest of her life and her future was uncertain. She would have to find work somewhere, perhaps at one of the small shops on Main Street. Things had to work out, she thought. Hadn't her papa said that they would?

Masculine bootsteps clipped in the corridor outside. Momentarily, a light rap sounded at the heavy wood door. Smoothing down her skirts, she approached and soon met the gaze of the Exchange manager, Mr. Pitman. His brows were pinched and worried.

"Miss Wickley, please understand that I am sympathetic to your recent loss, but you have not paid your hotel bill for the past week — "

She certainly had not meant to be so irresponsible;

40

shame forced her to drop her eyes. When she again lifted them, she said quietly, "May I have until tomorrow morning, Mr. Pitman? I promise that I will have the money then."

The portly gentleman pulled at his stiff collar. "Very well . . . but I must also ask for a week in advance, Miss Wickley. The owner checks the books once a week and he has expressed concern—"

"I will have the money tomorrow." Annoyance hardened her voice. "Good day."

He bowed perfunctorily as he stepped back from the door. When Delilah again found herself alone, she opened the bureau drawer and removed the smooth mahogany box her father had placed in her room the morning of his death, the jewels that had been her mother's nestled among the plush velvet interior. She had already sold a rare cameo brooch to Mr. Garrett at the general store to pay her expenses for the past month. As her fingers moved gently among the items, she wondered which she could bear to part with now.

Inside the box were several valuable items of jewelry mingled with antique costume pieces of little more than collector's value, among which were a gold locket with a dozen perfect emeralds nestled among the engraved vines—a favorite piece of her mother— several strands of pearls, a pansy brooch-pendant of gold and diamonds and one of rose-cut diamonds set in silver, a lapel watch that probably had not worked in years, a rare cabochon-gem necklace. How lovely her mother had looked in her jewels. After a moment Delilah removed an oval locket of paste, enamel, and gold, a piece she could not recall her mother ever wearing. Perhaps Irene Wickley hadn't liked the gaudy locket with its bow and tangled cipher. Firmly implanting that possibility in her mind to justify her action, Delilah separated the locket from the rest of the box's contents and closed her fingers over it. "We'll see if Mr. Garrett will pay a fair price for this tomorrow," Delilah said quietly, clutching the locket to her chest.

That chance was as remote as the moon. He'd paid only twenty dollars for the cameo brooch; it was probably worth ten times more.

Delilah returned to her window seat and watched a riverboat pull from its moorings. Her thoughts were of Shadows-in-the-Mist, a dear man she had lovingly called Papa, and the ruby-red cardinals gracing the boughs of a single strapling oak.

Three

That Monday morning, Grant exited the bank and stood for a moment on the boardwalk, his crystal-blue eyes scanning the roadway and the stirring of humanity. He needed a cup of coffee, a new pair of boots, and a shave. Therefore, he turned north toward Main Street and the neat row of businesses overlooking the river.

Hugh Penrod had been in a devil of a mood that morning, although he did manage to show his pleasure at Grant's decision to bid on The Shadows. Perhaps the man had gotten out of bed on the wrong side or had suffered through a spat with a bickering wife. Whatever, Grant hoped Penrod's mood would have improved by the time of their afternoon appointment.

As Grant moved northward, feeling the nail dig into the sole of his left foot, he set his first priority of the morning. A few minutes later he stepped onto the Main Street boardwalk and entered Garrett's General Store. Looking around the dimly lit room at the mélange of merchandise—dry goods arrayed along the left wall, groceries and kitchenware on the opposite side—he spied the boxes of men's shoes and boots at the rear. Nearly upsetting a barrel of crackers, his movements drew the attention of the proprietor, who had been setting up bolts of calico in a small alcove which advertised the fabric for five cents a yard.

Grant's eyes had just started to adjust to the dimness when his gaze caught the outline of a potbellied stove, which he at first mistook for the proprietor. When the somber-faced gentleman stepped forward, Grant smiled to himself as he assessed the similarity. "I'm in need of a new pair of boots."

Pointing to the back of the store, Mr. Garrett told him he should find what he wanted against the wall.

Behind a shelf of kerosene lamps, preserves, and canning jars, Grant searched among the boxes of boots and shoes for footwear similar to his own. He finally located a pair of straight boots that appeared to be his size and sat on a sturdy barrel to try them on.

His own well-worn boots slid off easily, but pulling on the new ones proved to be quite a chore. Concentrating on a particularly stiff heel, he did not hear the door of the general store open.

Delilah Wickley had awakened just as the first rays of sunlight touched the horizon. Taking the early train to Lamourie Bayou, she had enjoyed Ellie's company for an hour, then rode Bella the sixteen miles back to Alexandria. Stabling her with Mr. Pinchon, she then bathed and donned a clean dress before stepping from the Exchange Hotel onto the boardwalk. The long ride had refreshed her; she didn't feel nearly so glum about having to sell another piece of her mother's jewelry.

44

Mr. Garrett smiled dutifully when she stepped up to the counter. "Miss Wickley, how may I serve you today?"

Looking into the glass case, she saw that he still had not sold the cameo brooch. "I was hoping you might buy another piece of my jewelry, Mr. Garrett," she replied. She looked askance, as if she did not trust the gentleman to be tolerant.

"Miss Wickley . . ." John Garrett frowned, his thick brows settling heavily over bloodshot eyes, "I purchased the last piece because your father was an old customer and because you were in need. As you can see, I have not sold the brooch—"

"Perhaps if you hadn't put such a high price on it . . ." She couched her moment of anger because she really needed to make the sale and she didn't imagine that John Garrett would tolerate her impertinence. She continued on a softer note. "People here about cannot afford to pay fifty dollars for a brooch . . . And you only gave me twenty for it," she mumbled, then, hastily pulling the paste-and-enamel locket from her reticule, she pushed it across the counter toward him. "Please, won't you consider purchasing the locket? It isn't as expensive a piece as the brooch and I would consider a lesser price."

Mr. Garrett drew a deep breath. He would have to learn to say no to a pretty face, but today didn't seem to be the day. "Let me see, Miss Wickley, I could offer you five dollars . . ."

Grant looked up from his struggle when the velvet-soft entreaty of the feminine voice reached his ear. At first, he caught only the crisp, ironed cotton of her billowing lavender-and-gray plaid skirts, then the rich tresses the color of mahogany cascading to a slim, tightly-clothed waistline met his eye. When she stepped back from the counter to emphasize her dismay over John Garrett's offer, a lovely feminine profile rewarded his efforts to gain a fuller view.

He noticed at once that the lady carried herself with unpretentious confidence. She might desperately need the money the locket would bring her, but the need did not reflect in her proud stance. When she nervously tidied her hair with a single toss of her head, he caught the twinkle of golden eyes suddenly darkening with determination and a full, sensual mouth pinched to portray her unspoken indignation. Her high cheekbones were rosy, possibly with embarrassment at having to sell her jewelry. In all his worldly travels, Grant had never seen such loveliness epitomized in one human form. He imagined that if his fingers grazed her cheek, it might be like caressing the petals of a dew-kissed morning rose.

Before fully assessing the situation, Grant raised one finger, capturing Garrett's attention. "Excuse me a moment while I tend another customer," the storekeeper said to Delilah and momentarily stepped into the dim aisle where Grant sat, holding one of the straight boots against his stocking foot. "May I help you, sir?" he asked.

Pulling twenty-five dollars from his change purse, he pressed it into the man's hand. "Discreetly offer the young lady this money for the locket . . . as if you have reconsidered."

"Sir?" John Garrett kept his voice low so that only Grant would hear. "You wish to purchase the locket without Miss Wickley being aware of it? It really isn't worth this price."

Grant arched a pale eyebrow. "Wickley? Of the

plantation Wickleys?"

"Used to be. Her father died and the place is up for sale. Now . . . about the locket. It really isn't worth —"

Grant cut him off. "If it isn't, then I will have made a mistake," he said. "It won't have been my first."

Shrugging his shoulders, John Garrett hid the bills inside his fist and returned to the front of the store.

Delilah had waited patiently, though her foot tap-tap-tapped upon the planked floor. When John Garrett slipped behind the counter, she again held the locket out to him. "Though I am disappointed in your price, I really have no choice, Mr. Garrett, but to take —"

"Miss Wickley!" His sudden inflection startled Delilah and before she could withdraw her hand in surprise, he had taken the locket from her palm. "I failed to notice that it is a French piece of the last century. Yes . . . yes, I do believe it might fetch more. I could offer you, say, twenty-five dollars?"

"Twenty-five dollars!" Delilah's amber eyes filled with happy surprise.

The gentleman made the pretense of removing the bills from a box beneath the counter when in truth they lay curled in his fist. "Is the amount to your liking?"

Delilah nodded her agreement, the pink once again suffusing her cheeks. "Thank you . . . thank you so much."

When Delilah tucked the bills into her reticule and left the store, Grant, still wearing his old boots and carrying the box with the new, moved into the light. "So, that is Miss Wickley," he reflected, watching the bounce of her skirts disappear along the boardwalk.

"Here is the locket, sir. A waste of good money, if you ask me."

I didn't ask you, Grant wanted to say, but instead replied that he would take the boots. "And a pair of bootjacks, if you have any." He dropped the locket into an inner pocket of his jacket. "Have you any other pieces the lady has sold you?" he then inquired of Mr. Garrett.

John Garrett had just retrieved a pair of bootjacks, shaped like a reclining and very buxom woman, from a high shelf. He tucked them into the box with the boots and then removed Delilah's cameo brooch from the display case.

Taking the brooch, Grant immediately recognized the exquisite Italian workmanship of the turquoise-blue glass cameo with its tumbling hair of tooled gold. He had once processed similar pieces through his warehouse in New York. Where would a Southern lady have found such rare pieces of jewelry? "How much do you want for it?" he inquired.

"Fifty dollars."

Grant visited his most discerning look upon the proprietor. "After you gave Miss Wickley only twenty for it?"

Garrett puffed up like a banty rooster, surprised that a new customer should be so bold as to question his business practices. "Do you want the brooch or not?" he curtly asked.

"I'll take it," he replied, "and the boots and the jacks, too. I'll be staying in Alexandria for a while and would be interested in opening an account at your store."

"I'm sorry, sir, I don't know you well enough to—"

Grant pulled a few bills from his change purse. "I don't know you either, sir, but since you are an established businessman, I wish to deposit my funds with you at this time to cover future purchases and to assure you of my good intentions." Meeting the storekeeper's surprised gaze, he continued. "If Miss Wickley brings any other items to you, please pay for them from funds in my account . . . at the price she wants, not *your* price."

The proprietor ignored the biting remark. "You are, sir, a connoisseur of jewelry? I could acquire far more valuable pieces for you from here and abouts—"

"I will purchase items only from Miss Wickley, and I trust you to be discreet." When John Garrett gave him a furtive look, he continued with haste. "It is my intention to be the high bidder Wednesday on the Wickley plantation. I am interested in returning any valuable pieces to the place. I am not only interested in jewelry, but in anything that comes from The Shadows, be it jewelry, an item of furniture, or a canning jar. I trust you to use good judgment in making purchases from Miss Wickley."

"Very well, sir. And to whom—and where—shall I send word of any such purchases?"

"My name is Grant Emerson and I am staying at the Exchange Hotel, room 22."

Delilah returned to the livery to pay Bella's board for two weeks, then to the hotel to pay her bill. Moments later, she unlocked the door to number 20 and fell heavily to her bed. Smiling as her gaze followed the flickering lights on the ceiling, she thanked Providence for triggering a little compassion in the usually staid Mr. Garrett. She never dreamed that he'd give her so much for the gaudy locket. Though her mother probably had never worn it, she had not really wanted to sell it. The good price she received made the necessity a little easier to live with.

If only she knew where her father had hidden all the gold so that she could buy back The Shadows. . . . But she and the slaves had been searching for years and had failed to find even the smallest clue. The sale would be held on Wednesday. Perhaps Mr. Thomas Jefferson Wells would purchase the place, then let her live there and take care of the house.

Her smile faded. Though Wells and her father had been good friends, she knew he would not want the land. He had enough to take care of as it was at Dentley and had been devoting most of his time to his racehorse. Perhaps no one would be interested in buying it and the plantation would fall to neglect until the mortgage holders could unload it.

Delilah knew there was absolutely nothing she could do to save The Shadows from sinking into the clutches of uncaring hands. She feared for the well-being of Philo, Mozelle, her dear friend Daisy, and all the other slaves. What would become of them? Would they be scattered among other plantation families along the bayou, never to see one another again? Oh, why had her father managed the plantation so carelessly? She wondered if there was anything she could have done while he was alive to safeguard the future of Shadows-in-the-Mist.

She had asked those same questions of Ellie that morning when she'd visited and, of course, Ellie had assured her that she had done everything possible to help her father. Dear Ellie! What would she have done without such a friend to lean on in her time of need? Perhaps she should have taken Ellie up on her offer to live at the cottage. But her foolish pride prevented her from accepting help from anyone, even her closest friend. Her father had failed in life; she wanted only to prove that a Wickley did have the spirit and motivation to succeed, even when every day was nothing more than a dismal repetition of the previous one.

It would accomplish nothing to worry about it. What would be would be . . . Delilah moved from the bed toward her favorite chair by the window, taking a book of poems from the bureau with her. She would read the bittersweet sonnets until her stomach grumbled its protests at being hungry and she would eat another silent meal alone in the dining room below.

Bootsteps, mixed with the tap of a cane, clipped on the corridor floor, followed by a clink of keys and the door to number 22 across from her own room being shut. She had not met the room's occupant, but she had heard him coming and going for the past few days.

He was probably old and decrepit and needing the cane for support, a mean, bitter man who had abandoned a pitifully weak wife to run their humble farm alone. Or perhaps he was a veteran of the Mexican War and had barely escaped the Mexican cutthroats, dragging himself across the wilderness of Texas with a bullet in his leg. Perhaps he was a French aristocrat who had taken the thrust of a rapier . . .

Delilah smiled to herself. At least her imagination was still intact.

A miasma hung in the atmosphere that Wednesday morning, a stench of foreboding that stung Delilah's delicate senses. She paced back and forth in her

51

small hotel room, her fingers damp with perspiration as they linked nervously together. She wanted to be on the courthouse steps at that very moment, hearing the announcement of the sale of The Shadows and getting a glimpse of the purchaser; yet her heart forbade her to leave the room that had become a self-imposed prison. For the first time since leaving The Shadows, tears stung her eyes, tears which she stubbornly sniffed back and refused to acknowledge as anything other than a late winter cold trying to surface. Her shoulders ached from tension and her stomach felt all aflutter, reminding her that she had not eaten since noon of the previous day. But how could she possibly eat when her life's blood was falling into calloused hands? Some usurper might, even now, own the very land that cradled the bodies of her mother and father.

Delilah moved from the rug that muted her pacing footfalls and onto the hardwood floor to seek the solace of her favorite chair by the window. She dropped to the plush fabric, rested her cheek against the back of her hand, and watched the activity on Red River. Whether only a few minutes passed or an hour or two, she really wasn't sure, so many thoughts flooded her mind. But when the light knock sounded at her door, she could not sort out a single one for remembrance.

Though it was not her intention, she took more time than necessary to answer the knock. In the dim light of the corridor stood Ellie, her crisp black-and-white traveling gown accented by a broad-brimmed winter hat upon which perched a stuffed dove whose wings spanned the top of Ellie's head. It was all Delilah could do to cut her gaze from the creation and smile in greeting for her friend. Only then did she notice the worry creasing Ellie's brow.

Taking her friend's gloved hand, she coaxed her into the room. "Dear Ellie, I wasn't expecting you in town until Friday. Something has happened? Maden is all right? Lancie—"

"Everyone is well, Delilah." Ellie sat upon a small settee and, keeping Delilah's hand in her own, she motioned to her younger friend to sit beside her. Her dark eyes met Delilah's amber ones. "I wanted to tell you before someone else did that . . . It is just that . . ." Ellie fought for the words, "at the sheriff's sale this morning, a proper bid was received on The Shadows. It has a new owner."

Delilah could not prevent tears from moistening her eyes. "Do tell me, Ellie, that someone decent and caring has my father's land—my land."

"The purchaser *is* very decent and very caring, my friend." Ellie rose from the settee so suddenly that the movement startled Delilah. "Do you remember last month when I told you about an acquaintance . . ." Giving a small, nervous laugh, Ellie continued. "The one Lancie was so upset about—"

"The Yankee-Doodle gambler? Yes, I remember, Ellie. What does he have to—" What Ellie was trying to say suddenly hurtled into her brain. "No, Ellie, please don't tell me—" Rising, she took Ellie's hands to squeeze them. Pain darkened her golden eyes. "He did not buy my father's land? That despicable man is not the new owner of Shadows-in-the-Mist!"

Tears stung Ellie's eyes. She wanted to comfort her friend, but also to defend the man she so easily insulted. "He's a good, kind man, Delilah. No one could treat the land—and the slaves— better than he will—"

"No! No!" Delilah clutched at her temples. This

53

could not be happening. A gambling swine from the Mississippi could not possibly have moved into the peaceful community and set down his venomous roots . . . not on the land her father had loved . . . not on the land where her dear parents lay buried. It could not happen. "But you said . . . Ellie, he was supposed to." Delilah stumbled over the words, "The Parlington Place near Lafayette—he was going to look at that land. Not The Shadows—not my father's—" Delilah dropped into the chair by the window. Ellie stood silently by while the most vicious accusations formed in Delilah's mind. When at last she cut her gaze back to Ellie, the tears were gone and her eyes were narrowed with something, almost akin to hatred. "You knew all along, didn't you, Ellie, that the bank was going to take my father's land away from him? You knew when you invited that despicable man to visit you at the cottage. You never had any intentions of showing him the Parlington plantation. It was my father's land all along. What a fool you played me for—"

"No, Delilah . . . no—" Delilah's accusations caught in Ellie's throat as she moved cautiously toward her. "That is not true. I had no idea—"

"Please, leave me, Ellie—"

Falling to one knee beside Delilah, Ellie tried to take her friend's hand. Delilah, however, curled it into an unrelenting fist. "We've been friends too long, to tell each other lies, Delilah. I swear I did not know the bank was taking The Shadows. I swear!"

"Yes, you did," Delilah accused, her voice a soft monotone. "I do not see how we can possibly remain friends. You have betrayed me and I can never forgive you." If she noticed Ellie's tears, she gave no evidence of it.

Ellie knew there was no arguing with Delilah in this state. She had known Delilah long enough to know that in a few days she would allow herself to think more clearly and would understand the error of her cruel judgment. With that in mind, Ellie gracefully rose from her knee, touched her fingers to Delilah's wrist, and left her friend to her grim solitude. She knew pain churned deep inside Delilah and that it had formed the foundation of her thoughtless accusations.

In a few days, Delilah's heart would tell her that no deception had taken place. But until then, Ellie could not allow Grant to see the pain in her eyes.

By the time she reached the carriage where Grant awaited her, she had managed to subdue her tears. But still the pain in her eyes was like a mirror. As Grant alit the carriage to assist her, his narrowed eyes held her moisture-sheened ones. Surrendering his politely proffered hand, she sat very still as he seated himself beside her.

"She didn't take it well, did she?" he asked quietly.

Ellie managed the smallest of smiles, drawing her hand to her hairline to brush back a recalcitrant lock of auburn hair. "Not well at all."

"What did she say that has upset you so?"

"I would really rather not discuss it, Grant."

Her tone left no room for argument. Suppressing his curiosity for details, he flicked the reins at the harness mares, stirring them into movement.

Grant had packed his one canvas traveling bag, which bulged with his few personal items on the seat behind them. He would drive the sixteen miles to Lamourie Bayou, leave Ellie at her cottage, then would take up immediate residence at Shadows-in-the-Mist.

Thinking about Mozelle, he smiled to himself. Winning her over would be like pulling a tooth with tweezers.

Four

Mozelle moved absently around the large kitchen, flicking her wash rag at pots and pans, cursing the inanimate objects that got in the way of her toes, and generally trying to make life miserable for her young kitchen assistant. Daisy shrugged her shoulders, trying as patiently as possible to allow Mozelle's insulting remarks to pass without comment.

Mozelle's husband, Philbus, had ridden hard from Alexandria that morning to spread the news among the slaves that the Yankee-Doodle gambler had purchased The Shadows at sheriff's sale. As far as Mozelle was concerned, that news was as devastating as an infestation of rats no poison could kill.

"Ain't gonna fix dat white dog no decent victuals," she mumbled, continuing her haphazard journey across the ceramic floors with her rag. "Lawd done condemned us all to hell! Dat devil fo' sho' gonna be tearin' up some backs wid de whip, jes' like all dem nawthun troublemakers a comin' into de South. Lawd, what we's folks done already did do to make ya so mad! We be good. Massah Wickley say we de goodest slaves on de bayou . . . in de state . . . in de *country!*" Kicking out at the cat that inhabited the kitchen with no true intent to assault it, Mozelle continued. "Fo'give me, Lawd, but I's gonna poison dat Yankee-Doodle dog . . . gonna poison de first meal he demand from me."

Daisy, drawing her hands to her slim hips, felt her patience beginning to wane. "Mozelle, you carryin' on like dis jes' 'cuz Trusdale be over at Wellswood an' cain't knock ya down a peg or two—an' don't nobody knows what de new massah ain't a goin' ta be a real fine massah. You jes' plum scared the new massah be sellin' you off to dat white gutter trash like'n he said."

Mozelle's eyes narrowed. "You Miz Uppity High Yella, with yo' light skin, an' widout Missy to be a lookin' out fo' ya like'n she always done, de new massah might be acallin' ya to his bed at night. Ya's be aspreadin' dem skinny ol' legs 'neath the massah and he'll be atakin' his pleasures wid ya. An' what'll ol' Lancie be thinkin' 'bout sharin' ya wid yo' massah, huh?"

Daisy frowned wryly. "Don' be asoundin' so bad to me, Mozelle. I seen de new massah when he here a lookin' at de place, and he mighty fine lookin', if'n ya ask me—"

"I ain't askin' ya, Miz Uppity Britches. Ya bes' be watchin' dat smart mouth o' yor'n, or dis here rag be apoppin' blisters on yo' lips. Mozelle ain't gonna take no sass off no wench likes you!"

The back door slammed and Mozelle's father-in-law, Philo, rushed into the kitchen. "Lawd, Missy jes' scoot down from her hoss at the stable. An' Philbus, he say when he pass by Miz El's place on de way from Alex dat Mr. Yankee-Doodle be dere, mos' likely on his way to de Shadows. Lawd, ya two women, bes' be gittin' Missy a skee-daddlin' befo' dat devil from de Nawth ketch 'er on 'is land an' swat her backside somethin' fierce."

"No one will swat my backside and live to tell about it," Delilah Wickley remarked casually, strolling into the kitchen as though she had never been away from The Shadows.

Rushing to hug her former mistress, Mozelle spoke quickly. "What ya be doin' here, Missy? Dat dog from de Nawth be arrivin' most any minute. Lawd, Missy, ya done los' yo' mind!"

Delilah hugged Mozelle, then touched her mouth in a gentle kiss against her smooth cheek. "Will you bring my horse up to the kitchen entrance so that I can make a quick getaway if he shows up?" she asked Philo over her shoulder.

"Sho', Missy . . ." Philo turned, scratching his graying head as he prepared to leave. "Lawd, what be dat gal up to now?"

Delilah drew Daisy, who had quietly approached, into a warm hug. "I sure could use some of that coffee on the stove," she said. "Is it all right if I pour myself a cup?"

"Ya's sits down, Missy," a sniffling Daisy replied. "I bring it to ya."

When Daisy moved toward the stove, Mozelle studied Delilah. "Missy, ya sho' is lookin' good. Lawd, but we done miss ya somethin' fierce. Big ole' house jes' ain't been de same widout ya sweet presence. Yo' room jes' the way ya's left it, Missy, an' if Mozelle have any say-so a'tall, it'll be dat way till the Lawd calls me home!"

Delilah smiled her sweetest smile. "I'm sure the new master of Shadows-in-the-Mist will be making some changes. I won't be surprised if my room is the first to go." When Mozelle started to protest,

Delilah continued with haste. "But that's the least of my worries, Mozelle. Come, let's sit at the table and talk."

Mozelle's eyes narrowed suspiciously. "What ya is up to, Missy? Ya got dat look in yo' eyes, dat look dat made yo' papa threaten to take the willow switch to ya . . ."

Delilah smiled devilishly, even as sadness dimmed the liquid gold of her eyes. "Let's talk, Mozelle, and if you're not willing to help me, well . . . I'll understand."

Half an hour later, a very pleased Delilah eased her mare slowly along the muddy fringe of Bayou Boeuf, pausing occasionally to breathe deeply of a warm breeze or the delicate scent of hyacinth blanketing the water. She loved the bayou—its deceptive calm where time seemed to have stood still, an Eden where wildflowers grew like badges of boldness.

Overhead, the clouds writhed, driven by the gentlest of winds. At the edge of the woods, a young buck darted into the shadows of a moss-enshrouded oak, his white rump patch flashing in alarm. "That's it . . ." Delilah said, easing her mare ahead on the trail. "Run away, you skittery coward." She wasn't really speaking to the deer; rather, she imagined it the personification of the despicable northerner who had usurped Wickley land, fleeing the smallest of the bayou's dangers.

A pirogue moved smoothly over the bayou current, quelling her moment of anger. Hearing the deep, resonant serenade of its occupant, she halted the horse to listen.

"Ain't nothin' gonna git me if I stay on cou'se,
"Ain't nothin' gonna git me, not a shied-back
      hoss,
"Ain't nothin' gonna git me if I don't wanna
      be,
"Ain't nothin' gonna git me if I shimmy up a
      tree,
"Ain't nothin' gonna git me in dis worldly
      place,
"But the Lawd's gonna git me when I meets
      His grace.
"When dat day comes, massah, knows what
      I'll be,
"Free, free, free, massah, free, free, free."

Recognizing now the haunting voice of one of the young slaves from The Shadows, she waved her hand. Her gesture was returned with so much enthusiasm that the shallow-bottomed boat nearly toppled him and his well-stocked line of bream and *sac-a-lait* into the water.

Suddenly, with only an increase in wind speed as warning, the sky became gray and bloated. Delilah coaxed her mare into a lope, scarcely reaching the protection of a thick stand of cypress before huge drops of rain scarred the bayou surface.

In the next few minutes, the sky darkened miserably. Sheet lightning, followed by the distant rumble of thunder, tumbled into the silence of the bayou. A line of water-ash trees on the other side suddenly appeared as friendly ghosts on the bank. The rising force of the storm bent palmettos forward, their flat-fingered leaves raking the murky waters.

In the long, lonely hour the storm imprisoned her among the cypress, Delilah mulled over her conversation with Mozelle. Though the servant had said nothing to confirm it, Delilah was almost certain she had been apprehensive of her plan and had entered into her mistress's scheme simply out of love and loyalty. Delilah felt a trifle guilty about that.

Presently, the rain let up, enabling her to coax the mare back onto the muddy trail. If she rode at a leisurely pace, she would be back in Alexandria before the setting of the sun. In the confines of her hotel room, she would lay the groundwork for her future security.

Pleased with her thoroughness of thought, she didn't even care that she was soaking wet.

Grant Emerson sat quietly in the study, his pale-blue eyes scanning the pages of the business ledger lying open upon the desk. Putting aside his admiration of the flowing feminine hand that had recorded the entries, he could see why the plantation had not thrived under the direction of the former owner: exorbitant prices had been paid for seed and supplies and low prices paid for the harvested produce. Angus Wickley had not sold cattle during the more profitable season of the year and had waited too long into the rainy season to pick the cotton. And what was this expense — fifteen hundred dollars for a white-stockinged Thoroughbred mare? In the week since he'd been at The Shadows he had not seen a single horse worthy of such a price. Had plantation property been unlawfully removed before he'd taken possession?

Settling back for a moment and rubbing his eyes, Grant sighed. His stomach grumbled its protest at being denied decent food since he'd taken up occupancy of The Shadows. He couldn't bear the thought of one more oversalted, undercooked egg, glass of spoiled milk, or strip of beef so tough it might have been left out in the sun to dry. He'd tried to be tolerant of the cook—that blasted Mozelle—but even his kindness had failed to affect her. She'd looked at him as she might have a mangy dog and her sarcastic *Yas, suh, massah, suh*'s had thoroughly prickled his nerves. Though he had initially resolved to leave things as they were, he knew now he would have to make some changes.

Thinking of Mozelle forced him to remember separate conversations he'd had with Hugh Penrod and Ellie McPherson in the last week. Both had advised him not to insist right away that the slaves call him Mister rather than Master. It would accomplish nothing but tension and embarrassment if a mistake was made in addressing him, and it was best to gain some degree of popularity with these very sensitive people before requesting a change in the age-old tradition. The advice of his friends had made sense; he would not force the issue.

Deciding that two weeks was long enough to be patient with The Shadows' feisty cook, Grant moved into the corridor and toward the back of the house.

Mozelle was surprised to see him enter the kitchen. Her questioning eyes followed his movements.

"Where is the girl who works with you?" Grant asked.

"Daisy, massah, suh?" Mozelle questioned, wiping

63

her hands on an oversize white apron.

He bit his tongue to keep from responding to her sarcastic tone. "Daisy . . . where is she?"

Mozelle couldn't control her wry grin. So, the young master was lookin' to Daisy as a bed wench after all. "She jes' took some slop out to de hogs, massah, suh. Be right back." Lifting her chin with impertinence, she asked, "Massah needs Mozelle to do somethin'?"

Grant crossed his arms. "I think you've done quite enough these past few days," he replied. "I'll wait for the girl to return." Just at that moment, the back door opened and Daisy entered. Her surprise at seeing her new master in the kitchen caused her to drop the slop pan with a loud clatter. When Grant said politely, "Daisy, I want you to prepare me a breakfast fit for a king," her eyes widened.

Daisy curtsied impishly. "Massah, suh, Mozelle, she say she 'sponsible fo' massah's meals," she replied. "I's jes' her helper."

"Not any longer," Grant said, feeling the penetrating gaze of the older servant upon him. "Starting today—in fact, this very minute—*you* are the cook and *she* is your helper." Mozelle drew a surprised breath. "From now on," he continued, "if my meals aren't perfect, not to mention *edible*, I'll consider you personally responsible and the proper punishment will be dealt." Though he had no intentions of punishing the pretty young slave girl for any lack of culinary talent, he embellished his threat. "Do you understand?" he asked sharply.

"Yas suh, massah," she replied, scarcely able to restrain the glee from flashing across her face. "I be de cook, and Mozelle, she be de helper. Massah be wantin' a meal now?"

"I certainly do. When my place has been set in the dining room, you send your helper out to the stable to fetch me if I am not already back."

Had Grant looked in Mozelle's direction, he'd have seen not anger, but tears clouding her ebony eyes, tears which were caused by her realization that she'd gone too far in her rebellion.

Within moments, he was moving on a deliberate course toward the stable. But his progress was halted by the strange sight of a slave girl with two dozen brightly adorned braids, a loose bottom lip, and graceful hands carefully placing frog ornaments in a half circle on the ground between her parted legs. She looked up and smiled eerily, her eyes blank of emotion. He contemplated the strangeness of the sight for a moment, then continued his journey toward the stable.

Philo, sitting on a small stool and pulling nails from a horseshoe, respectfully rose as he approached. "That be Peculiar, massah. She ain't right in the haid, an' Massah Wickley, he ne'er s'pected no work out o' her."

"I can see why" came Grant's soft reply.

"Massah be's wantin' a hoss saddled up?" Philo asked politely. In the past few days he had seen only gentleness in the northerner they had all been prepared to despise.

"In about thirty minutes I'll be wanting to ride over to Mrs. McPherson's to look at a mare and colt. Ask Philbus if he would mind riding with me."

"Yas, suh, massah."

Grant turned to retrace his steps to the house, then again faced the old black gentleman. "By the

65

way, Philo, have any horses been sold off the plantation in the past few weeks?"

"Naw, suh, not since Massah Wickley sold off'n a dapple geldin' to Mistah Wells befo' Chris'mas."

"What about a Thoroughbred mare with white stockings?"

Silence. Philo made a pretense of lifting his fingers to scratch at his head, as though he wasn't sure what his new master was talking about. He knew very well that he was inquiring about the mare Delilah had taken from the plantation the week her father had died, but loyalty to the daughter of his former owner compelled him to withhold that truth. After all, the new master had many other horses on the plantation; he would soon forget about that one. "I jes' don' know, massah, suh. Right off hand, I couldn't say. Maybe they was such a hoss, an' maybe they wasn't. I jes' don' rightly recall."

Grant had read the old man's face as easily as he might have a child's nursery rhyme. He imagined that the daughter of the former owner was somehow tied to the disappearance of the horse and that she still had the loyalty of these people. "Well," Grant easily conceded, "if you remember anything, you let me know right away." He forced a stern look upon his face, even as humor rested behind his gaze. "Rest assured," he warned Philo, "I *will not* forget about a missing fifteen-hundred-dollar horse until this little mystery is solved."

As he resumed his way to the mansion, Grant found himself once again thinking about Delilah Wickley. Since he had seen her that one time in Garrett's Mercantile, scarcely five minutes had passed that the vision of her hadn't entered his mind. He didn't imagine he'd ever seen a profile more gently and perfectly sculpted than the one she had revealed to him in the mercantile. She came to him during his most mundane of thoughts, and in his dreams at night. He wanted so badly to feel the softness of her skin, to ease his fingers through her rich mahogany tresses. He wanted to feel the whisper softness of her breath upon his cheek, her mouth pressed gently to his own. He imagined her in the arms of another man and jealousy raged within him.

So deeply lost in his thoughts was he that he scarcely realized he'd entered the house until a brightly smiling Daisy was curtsying briskly before him. "Massah, suh, yo' breakfast plate is on de table."

"Am I going to enjoy my meal?" he inquired, arching an eyebrow.

"Massah, if it ain't to yo' likin', ya's can tie me in de barn and whop me good!"

Grant managed a small smile. "I hardly think that will be necessary." A thought came to Grant. "Tell me, girl, aren't you seeing the man who works for Miss Ellie?"

Beneath her pale golden skin, Grant was sure he'd seen the rush of color suddenly drain from her features. "Y-yas, suh, massah . . . it be me. Ya ain't a goin' ta make me stop seein' him, is ya, massah?"

"Not if you enjoy his company," Grant replied.

Daisy smiled. "Thank ya, massah, suh." As she walked off, Grant reflected how he abhorred slavery and the idea that a man would consider other human beings as chattel. But in the South, slavery was an institution. Until he had established himself as a planter on the bayou and learned how freed persons of color could sustain themselves, he could not entertain the notion of freeing the men and women who served Shadows-in-the-Mist.

Moments later, Grant found himself thoroughly enjoying a breakfast of ham, scrambled eggs, biscuits with muscadine preserves, and fresh, sweet milk. When he had gotten his fill, he sat back and closed his eyes. He envisioned a rose-frocked young woman with amber eyes and flowing chocolate-colored tresses sitting at the opposite end of the elongated dining table, looking up from her meal just long enough to ask him if he was enjoying his own. The face was that of Delilah Wickley. Enjoying his daydream, he could almost detect the sweet aroma of her essence, and hear her delicate breathing within the room . . .

Enough! he chastised himself, pushing himself up with something of a grunt. Retrieving his cane, he moved from the dining room and once again left the house.

Philbus waited at the stable with two saddled horses. Approaching and taking the reins of the gelding, Grant drew himself into the saddle, then tossed his silver-headed cane to a mound of hay against the stable wall.

Delilah Wickley was not sure how much longer she could bear these long daily rides to the bayou and accomplish nothing by sunset. This morning, she had taken up her usual position at a small clearing at the edge of the woods, where she could see the trail leading to Shadows-in-the-Mist for a good quarter-mile before it once again plunged into the deep shadows of the trees.

How much longer was that blasted Yankee going to hole himself up at The Shadows? Delilah wondered, crouching wearily against the trunk of a massive oak. Picking up a fallen leaf, she began cutting a face into its odd shape with one of her long fingernails.

The sounds of the bayou soothed her nerves — the gentle movements of an alligator, only its eyes breaking the water's surface, the faraway sounds of a flicker drumming its energetic beat in its search for bark beetles, the plod of horses hooves . . .

Horses! Delilah rose slightly on her knees to gain a better view. Cupping her hands across her finely-arched brows to block out the eastern sun, she soon saw two riders, one white and one black, emerging from the forest trail. She recognized Philbus only by the floppy hat he always wore; the other man, a stranger to her, had to be none other than the new master of Shadows-in-the-Mist. Because she had expected a stout man, she was a little surprised by his tall, slim build and the grace with which he sat his horse. Gritting her teeth as she reminded herself how much she loathed him, she crept into the edge of the woodline where she'd tied Bella.

She had rehearsed her plan in her mind many times over during the long, lonely rides from Alexandria; now, as she prepared to put it into action, she wasn't so sure of it. Suppose something should go wrong?

No! She couldn't think like that. She had to be optimistic. She had made a promise to her father, and if it was the last thing she did in life . . .

Taking a long, deep breath as she drew herself

gracefully into the saddle and absently rubbed her fingers through the coarse hairs of Bella's flowing mane, Delilah plotted her course. Then, with a gentle nudge to the flanks of the spirited mare, she bounded onto the bayou trail.

Keeping her eyes on the approaching men and discreetly spurring Bella ahead, Delilah suddenly screamed out. "Help! Help! Please, someone help me!"

The sight of the tall, slim Delilah Wickley surging down the trail toward him on what appeared to be a runaway horse took Grant Emerson by surprise. He cast a look at Philbus, puzzled by the grin on the slave's face.

"Philbus!" Grant fought to restrain his own horse from responding to the rapid approach of the runaway. "Stop that woman's horse!"

Philbus, along with the other slaves at The Shadows, had been warned that their former mistress had a plan to take back her father's plantation and that they were not to interfere. Snatching the first thought that came to his mind, he responded, "Dat white trash, massah? She be able to take care of 'erself."

Suddenly, Delilah's horse sped off onto a trail to the left, straight into a forested glen just a hundred yards from the approaching men. Groaning his outrage at Philbus's words, Grant spurred his horse ahead on the trail, then turned in the direction she had gone.

Delilah Wickley! What the hell was she up to? he wondered, catching sight of her fast-moving horse on the trail ahead of him. And why had

Philbus referred to her in such a derogatory way when he had to have known who she was? Ducking branches and twigs, some of which managed to snag and tear at his jacket, Grant had almost caught up to her when her horse suddenly halted. Just then, Delilah tumbled across Bella's neck, landing full upon hard ground among a stand of cypress stumps.

Pulling up the gelding, Grant jumped down from the saddle, instantly cursing the absence of his cane. He saw her lying there, her body twisted, her face toward the ground, and the thick, rich masses of her hair in disarray all about her. Dropping unsteadily to the ground, he turned her over and drew her up against him.

What if she was dead? he thought, his fingers brushing at a patch of mud clinging to her face. Her skin was as soft and silky as he'd imagined a hundred times in his dreams, her full, sensual lips slightly parted, betraying not the least sign of life. He wanted to kiss her, but he resisted the urge as he gently shook her, hoping to stir some reaction.

Momentarily, her eyelashes flickered. Breathing a sigh of relief, Grant watched her exquisite face for further signs of life.

Delilah had not meant to allow Bella to toss her into the stand of cypress stumps; if she'd hit one of them, she could have been seriously hurt. What she had intended was to drag the mare to a halt a little farther on the trail, then carefully pitch herself into the soft woodline. But Bella had been spooked by a rabbit and had unintentionally changed her rider's plans.

71

Delilah felt a hard-muscled chest against her soft shoulder. His masculine smell assaulted her senses and she hesitated to open her eyes. *Oh, please, let him be a gaunt, ugly man!* Let him be what she expected a Yankee to be, an arrogant, gravel-voiced creature she would take great pleasure in deceiving! With that in mind, she gently opened her eyes, expecting to be rewarded with the countenance of just such a rogue.

Delilah was unprepared for the remarkably handsome face so close to her own that it startled her. The morning sun was behind him, casting an almost blinding glow around the fringes of his pale golden hair. She had never seen eyes so exquisitely blue and sincerely marked with concern for her, or features so perfectly chiseled. Hypnotized by the nearness of his muscular frame as he cradled her against him, she cut her gaze from his only when Philbus, astride the big gelding he had claimed as his own, hovered over the two of them.

Delilah's eyes narrowed in warning as Philbus frowned disapprovingly. Thinking that he might give her away, she spoke hastily to Grant. "Thank you for your kindness, sir. I don't know what I would have done if you hadn't come along. I am not a very good rider and my horse got spooked—"

Her soft, sultry voice pleased him, even as her words gave her deception away. Just the day before, old Philo had mentioned what an extremely good horsewoman his former mistress was. So! Miss Delilah Wickley had every intention of hiding her identity from him. He could not help but be curious as to her motives. Besides, he had a pretty good idea that the fifteen-hundred-dollar horse missing from The Shadows might very well be the one standing at the edge of the woodline. On the spur of the moment, Grant decided to play along with Delilah's little game.

"I do hope you have not been hurt badly, Miss—?"

"Freeman . . . Missy Freeman," she easily lied, employing her mother's maiden name with ease. "Please accept my humblest apologies for taking up your time." She made an attempt to rise, but, drawing the back of her hand dramatically to her cheek, feigned weakness and slipped back into the cradle of his arms, from which position she gave him an apologetic smile.

Grant's uncertainties over the past few days that perhaps he had not sown his wild oats sufficiently before settling down to plantation life quickly diminished. With a woman around as beautiful and feisty as Delilah Wickley, how could life be boring? Meeting the golden depths of her eyes, he favored her with a brief smile.

"Well, Miss . . . Freeman. I must insist that my man here take you back to the plantation where you might comfortably regain yourself."

"How very kind of you, Mr—?"

"Emerson . . . Grant Emerson."

Delilah forced a pained look. "Is your home far, Mr. Emerson?" She asked in her sultriest voice, ignoring Philbus who dramatically rolled his eyes heavenward.

Grant started to reply, but Philbus, who had dismounted his horse, helped him. "Wants me to take de lady to de Shadows, massah?" he asked.

Only then, as Grant regained his footing with some trouble, did Delilah notice that he was lame. But that did not detract from his statuesque height in her eyes; rather, it gave him an aura of quiet dignity.

When Grant caught her gaze upon his lame leg, he was embarrassed. He moved a few feet away before he answered Philbus. "Yes, take her to The Shadows, Philbus." His gaze seemed to hold the forest across her shoulder as he addressed her. "Please enjoy the amenities of my home for as long as you require, Miss Freeman."

Grant did not take another step until Philbus had gently picked her up in his arms, positioned her on his saddle, took the reins of her horse, and mounted behind her. He did not want her attentions drawn to his awkward gait.

Grant watched Philbus ride away, Delilah held firmly to the saddle in front of him. He was curious not only as to Delilah's motives but as to those of the slaves of Shadows-in-the-Mist. What could they possibly gain by her charade?

But was he being too rash in assuming conspiracy? Perhaps Philbus was acting alone.

He couldn't help but be pleased at the prospect of Delilah's company at The Shadows. But damn . . . why did he have to be lame, and embarrassed by it to boot?

He had no doubts she would still be at The Shadows when he returned from Ellie's. He wished now he hadn't promised that he'd come see the horses, for he wanted only to return to the plantation and see for himself how perfectly Delilah Wickley fit into his new home on Bayou Boeuf.

Five

Delilah wondered why Philbus had said nothing since they entered the trail dipping into the woodline. She sensed his penetrating gaze and the words of admonishment and disapproval he had not spoken. When she was sure Grant Emerson was shielded from them by the depth of the woods, she spoke quietly to the slave. "You may stop now, Philbus, and let me mount my own horse."

Though Philbus halted, he hesitated to help her down. And only when she tossed her head, fixing her narrow gaze to his own disapproving one, did he ask what was on his mind. "What ya be's up to, Missy? Massah Emerson, he bound to find out who ya is, an' he ain't a gonna be none too pleased that we's keepin' secrets. He's prideful, too. Din't ya see de way he stood der widout mountin' his hoss, 'cause he din't want ya to be a lookin' at his bum leg?"

With a disgruntled "harumph!", Delilah slipped to the ground from between Philbus's arms. Taking Bella's reins from him, she drew her slender hands to her hips. "So he's lame, Philbus! Why should he be concerned about that? *I'm* certainly not! Besides, it doesn't make him any less of a man. Being a Yankee makes him less of a man!" As Delilah mounted her horse, she couldn't help but remember fathomless blue eyes beneath sun-colored eyebrows and the gentleness with which Grant Emerson had held her against his chest. "Come, Philbus . . ." She continued, her voice softening, "you must take this poor injured young woman to The Shadows where she can rest."

When Delilah started to nudge the horse past Philbus, he took the reins and halted her progress. "I ask, Missy, what ya be's up to?"

Anger glistened in her eyes. "I'm going to find that gold and buy back my father's land, Philbus. You should be happy that I'm so determined. Do you want to be the property of that Yankee-Doodle gambler?"

Philbus shrugged his shoulders. "Don't want to be de property o' nobody, Missy," he replied. "Not even you. Jes' want to be my own man. Maybe go to Texas and be a cowboy. 'Sides, what makes ya think ya kin find that gold when ever'body been lookin' fer nigh on to ten years an' ain't found it yet?"

Delilah sighed deeply. For many years, Philbus had been very vocal about his desire for freedom. Few people would have tolerated such an attitude from a slave; her gentle father had been one. "Won't you help me, Philbus?" she implored with quiet dignity. "Do you know what manumission papers are?"

Philbus shrugged. "Sho', Missy. Dey be freedom papers."

Delilah leaned across her saddle, her narrowed gaze fixed to that of the slave. "If father hadn't lost the plantation," she said, "he would have ultimately freed all your people. That was his goal. And I promise you, Philbus, in honor of my father, that the day I can once again call The Shadows my home, you'll have your freedom papers, as will Mozelle and your father and anyone else who wants them."

"An' who do ya thinks gonna do de work at de Shadows?"

"Freed slaves still have to work for a living, Philbus," she reminded him, exasperation easing into her voice. "As far as I know, everyone is happy at The Shadows—or they were when my father was alive. Surely, they would stay on for wages."

Philbus's slitted gaze caught her own pleading one. "Then what'll ya be wantin' me to do, Missy?"

Delilah straightened in the saddle, "If you do nothing but keep quiet about who I am, that will be help enough for me," she replied. "Thank heavens Trusdale is at Wellswood! He wouldn't keep my secret for even a minute, that old rascal." Her tone calmed. "I'm hoping you will help me find the gold, Philbus. But even if I don't, I *will* get The Shadows back."

"Dat gold. Dat gold, Missy! I's sick 'n tired o' hearin' it! Don't ya know dat gold be found an' they's be some questions asked, likes 'where yo pappy got dat gold'? Lawd, if'n Mista Wells hadn'a met yo pappy on de road an' yo pappy showed him dat gold right then an' dere, ain't nobody here 'n abouts believe it even exists."

"Are you enjoying getting snippity, Philbus?" Delilah asked. "You're talking to me like I'm still a child."

Philbus smiled slightly before his tone once again grew serious as he changed the subject. "An' what makes ya think they's anything ya can do to git back de Shadows, Missy?"

"Oh, Philbus!" Exasperation laced her voice. "I can buy back the plantation when I find the gold. And if Grant Emerson won't sell it, I'll make his life miserable. If I can somehow manage to convince him to let me stay on at The Shadows, there are any number of things I can do to ruin him. I know that plantation like the back of my hand. And, believe me, there isn't anything I wouldn't do to get it back!"

Philbus crossed his wrists upon the pommel of his saddle. "Sho', Missy, ya's can do jes' about anything to ruin him. But, say, if'n ya don't find dat gold an' ya do ruin him, Massah Emerson, he jes' sell de Shadows to somebody else. Jes' 'cause ya might ruin him don't mean ya'd be gittin' de Shadows back. Face it, Missy, if'n ya ain't got money, yo ain't never gonna git back de Shadows."

Delilah studied Philbus's strong features. Why did this kind, decent man have to speak the truth when she preferred to exist in her dream world? If Grant Emerson could not make a go of Shadows-in-the-Mist, he would simply sell to someone who could. He would probably care about nothing more than recouping his initial investment. "Then I guess there is only one thing I can do, Philbus."

"An' what dat be, Missy?"

Delilah lifted her chin in a prideful gesture. "If I don't find my father's gold, I guess I'll have to marry the Yankee-Doodle gambler. As his wife, The Shadows will be just as much mine as his. Then . . ." She grinned almost wickedly, "I'll make his life miserable and run him off!"

Reining her horse about on the trail, she put distance between herself and Philbus.

78

"Lawd, dat gal's gonna git herself in a heap o' trouble," he mumbled, coaxing his horse into the stirrings of Bella's dust. He liked the idea of Delilah Wickley being at Shadows-in-the-Mist. It would be like old times, keeping the mischievous young missy out of the arms of trouble. Then again, her plan might backfire . . . she might actually grow fond of the man she had sworn to hate.

Grant rode at a leisurely pace, even as he wanted to nudge the horse along, accomplish his visit to Ellie's, and return posthaste to The Shadows. When he pulled into the carriage yard beside Ellie's cottage, he at once saw the mare and colt in a small pen off to the right. Ellie was leaning against the fence, watching Maden groom the mare. She turned, shielding her eyes from the sun as Grant rode up. "What did I tell you?" Her voice reflected her excitement. "Aren't they a fine pair?"

When Grant dismounted, she tucked her arm into his, coaxing him toward the pen.

Grant was glad of her support, since he did not have his cane. "You are certainly in a good humor this morning." He smiled at the pretty, dark-haired Ellie. "And, yes . . . they are indeed a fine pair."

Since Charles's death three years before, Ellie had maintained her cottage and grounds with the money she made selling horses at a profit. Usually, she had run-of-the-mill stock, but the mare and colt were top of the line.

"So, Grant, what will you give me for the pair?"

Grant stood at the fence, his right arm resting across the wood rail. "Let me take a closer look, Ellie," he said, then remembered the absence of his cane. He did not want to risk his bad leg giving out from under him on the short walk into the pen. "No, I can see them well enough from here."

Lancie, who had been tending to tack in the carriage house, approached from behind. Grant turned as his shadow suddenly loomed. Lancie carried a walking cane he'd made from a sturdy piece of cypress. He offered it to Grant. "Made this here walkin' stick, Mista Emerson, when I broke my foot las' year. You welcome to it."

It was the first kind gesture Lancie had made to him. In the past few weeks it had been very evident to the hired hand that Miz El was merely the Yankee's friend and that he had no interest in her as a future wife. Keeping his employer from being hurt was much more important to Lancie than her friendship with a man from the North.

Grant took the cane from him appreciatively. "Thank you. I'll return it before I leave."

"No need, Mistah Emerson. You's can leave it in Miz El's place so's it'll be handy when you's come ag'in." He began his retreat, but quickly turned back. "Mistah Emerson, will you be mindin' if I be visitin' Miss Daisy at de Shadows? Massah Wickley didn't mind when he wuz livin'."

"And neither do I. But you make sure to treat Miss Daisy proper."

"Sho', Mistah Emerson. Thank you now."

When Lancie moved back into the shadows of the carriage house, Grant turned to Ellie. "Well, what do you think about that?" he asked.

"I think . . ." Ellie replied, taking a place beside him as they entered the pen, "that Lancie's beginning to see that you're not as bad as all that."

"I'm afraid to ask how bad 'all that' is." Grant

80

laughed, dropping his arm across Ellie's slim shoulders. "Come on, let's look at these horses that you think are worth a pretty penny."

"They are a great pair," Maden interjected, handing the mare's lead to Grant. "I tried to talk Ma into keepin' 'em, but she says she'd rather you had 'em."

"How about it, Maden?" Grant asked. "You want me to turn down a sale on these two?"

Maden grinned. "Sure, Mister Emerson, an' my ma'll be taking a stick to me for the first time in quite a few years."

"I'd do no such thing, Son." Ellie joined in the gentle chiding. "Now get on in the carriage house. Lancie probably needs your help."

Moments later, as they left the horses once again in Maden's care and moved toward the cottage, Grant made his offer. "I'll give you eight hundred dollars for the pair, Ellie."

Ellie was elated; she had expected half that amount. "For that price, I should throw in a couple of good horses from the pasture."

Grant laughed. "Tell you what, rather than the extra horses, how about some of that good female advice you always seem to have on hand."

Scarcely had they seated themselves in the parlor of Ellie's cottage before Miss Mandy entered, carrying a tray of hot tea and muffins.

"Sho' nice to see ya ag'in, Mista Emerson," the pleasant lady greeted him. "Baked some fine blueberry muffins 'cause I know's they yo' fav'rit."

"Ellie, I'm going to have to steal this fine lady away from you," Grant remarked. "I'd never have to go to bed hungry."

The stout servant drew her hands to her wide

81

hips. "What you say, Mista Emerson, ain't dat Mozelle a feedin' you good?"

Grant smiled, taking the cup Ellie offered him. "For the past week Mozelle has tried to poison me," he answered Miss Mandy's inquiry. "Daisy is the cook now."

"Lawd!" Shaking her head, Miss Mandy turned, retracing her footsteps to the kitchen.

"Did you relieve Mozelle of her kitchen duties?" an astounded Ellie asked. She could not remember a time that Mozelle had not been the cook at Shadows-in-the-Mist.

"I demoted her to cook's helper," Grant replied, "until she stops sabotaging my meals. When *she* comes around, *I'll* come around."

"The doctor came by today to see about Miss Mandy," a very solemn Ellie informed Grant, changing the subject. "He doesn't expect that she'll last out the year."

"I'm sorry," Grant said. "She's a dear woman and I know how much you care for her."

"Yes. And my father was very fond of her, and, of course, of Lancie, too." Ellie sipped her sweetened tea, studying Grant in the moment of silence. His golden hair was windblown from his ride along the bayou, his angular face slightly flushed. That he had something on his mind besides Mozelle was clear. She placed her cup gently on her saucer. "What has happened this morning, Grant, to put you in this thoughtful mood?" she asked him. "You look as though you are a thousand miles away."

Grant smiled. "Actually my thoughts are only as far away as The Shadows." Setting down his cup and leaning toward Ellie, he continued. "This morning when Philbus and I were riding over here, we came upon a young woman on a runaway horse. By the time I reached her, she'd been pitched to the ground—"

"Oh, dear . . . was she hurt?"

"She claimed to have been hurt. I had Philbus take her back to The Shadows where she could rest." Ellie's questioning eyes sought more information. "The lady was Delilah Wickley," he stated. "But she said her name was Missy Freeman."

Ellie was surprised. "The blacks among the bayou have always called her Missy. Freeman was her mother's maiden name. What is our Delilah up to?"

"I was hoping you might know, Ellie."

She shrugged her slim shoulders. "I'm afraid I don't, Grant, unless she wants to search for her father's missing gold."

"Bah! I don't believe it exists."

"Oh, it exists. Mr. Wells saw it for a fact. The only thing is, nobody knows where Angus got it." Ellie allowed herself the indulgence of a smile. "Delilah hasn't come around as I thought she would." Ellie had never gone into the details of her conversation with Delilah. It was still a little painful to think of, let alone talk about. "I wish there was something I could tell you," she said linking her fingers. "What do you plan to do?"

"I plan to go along with her little game until I know what she's up to. Even Philbus pretended that he didn't know who she was. I'm curious as to how the other slaves at The Shadows will react. To be perfectly honest, Ellie, I sense a conspiracy between our Miss Delilah Wickley and the people at The Shadows. I guess what I need to know is if I have anything to fear from Miss

Wickley being at my home."

"If you mean, will she attempt to sabotage your life or burn your house down, I really don't think so. Delilah has a bit of a temper, but she is good and kind, and well loved by everyone on the bayou. I believe the only harm Delilah might do you is of—" She'd been about to say, "the heart," but on the spur of the moment decided against it. When it came to matters of the heart, she was sure Grant could take care of himself. After all, hadn't he treated her with sisterly affection rather than showering her with the amorous attention she had hoped for after Charles's death? She was almost envious of Delilah for being able to ignite the flames she now saw in Grant's eyes just at the mention of her name. Color rushed into Ellie's cheeks as she suddenly realized that Grant was scrutinizing her. "How embarrassing," she apologized. "I forgot what I was going to say."

That he had not guessed the direction of her thoughts was evident as he asked, "So, Ellie, what should I do about our Miss Wickley?"

Ellie's fingers wrapped gently over his wrist. "Do be kind to Delilah, Grant. Try to remember that she has lost not only The Shadows but her father as well and that she has not been thinking clearly of late. And please . . ." she added, "I beg of you not to do anything to embarrass her."

"Then I should not allow her to stay at The Shadows for any length of time?"

"I imagine it might cause a stir of gossip along the bayou. But . . . if she is truly hurt, I don't see where a short stay would do any harm. You must remember that she has no home now other than the hotel in Alexandria."

"The last thing I want to do . . ." Grant gave her a boyish smile, "is tarnish our Miss Wickley's reputation."

Grant found himself preoccupied with thoughts of his unexpected houseguest. When at last Maden announced that the horses were ready to begin the journey to The Shadows and he had left Ellie with the appropriate parting amenities, his preoccupation stirred him into a faster pace along Bayou Lamourie. When he entered the trail abutting Bayou Boeuf with The Shadows only a half mile away, he felt his heart beating against the fabric of his shirt.

He could not face the possibility that perhaps she'd had second thoughts and had terminated her trickery.

She had to be at The Shadows.

He longed for the excitement of her.

"I's jes' never thought ya'd do it, Missy," Mozelle fussed at the seated Delilah. "An' when I tol' ever'body else what ya's plannin', dey's think ya chicken out, too. Lawd, Missy, ya's a'bad as when ya's a li'l thing, chasin' about an' gittin' in one scrape after de other. What we's gonna do wid ya?" Mozelle placed a steaming cup on the table in front of her. "Now, drink dis here tea a'fo' I fo'gits I's a lady!" she said.

Delilah sighed patiently. "I've sure missed your fussing, Mozelle. I do declare, you're getting better at it every time I see you." Patting the table, she continued. "Why don't you pour yourself a cup of tea and sit down with me."

"Harumph!" Mozelle sniffed, her eyes cutting to the flitting Daisy. "Li'l Miz Uppity Britches over dere, why she jes' might tell de massah *her* kitchen helper is asittin' on her hiney bein' wo'thless. Huh, Miz Uppity Britches!"

"Why's don' ya jes' hush, Mozelle," Daisy snipped. "I ain't a gonna do no such thing!"

Delilah laughed. "Will the two of you hush up? Why, I've never heard such carrying on!"

"She jes' mad 'cause I's de kitchen boss now!" Daisy accused.

"That's enough," Delilah admonished lightly, "or we'll have to put you two bickering females in a pen and let the feathers fly." Rising, she continued. "My tea is a little too hot. I think I'll look around upstairs until it cools off."

Mozelle drew her hands to her ample hips. "This ain't yo' house anymore, Missy. I be patient when ya first come in dis mo'nin' and go snoopin' all through de first floor. Don't ya be touchin' nothin' up dere what ain't none of yo' business. The new massah, he likes things jes' so . . ."

"Do you really care what the new massah likes, Mozelle?" Delilah asked.

She shrugged absently. "Naw'm. I jes' don't want him to be ayellin' at ya or nothin'."

"Don't worry about me. You just warn me if he rides up to the stable. I wouldn't want the Yankee-Doodle gambler to catch me walking around. After all . . ." She smiled mischievously, "I've been grievously injured."

Delilah sauntered through the door as though time was of no concern. "Dat gal, she be wantin' to see if de new massah done fool't wid her bedroom," Mozelle remarked to Daisy.

That was exactly what Delilah wanted to see. She knew she'd left personal belongings in her bedroom—a seldom-used shawl, day gowns she'd intended to distribute among the women of The Shadows but had somehow never gotten around to, a box of combs and brushes she'd stored in a cabinet. She wanted to see all her things carelessly tossed about for disposal at the direction of the new owner. She wanted to see that small evidence of his callousness. She wanted to see the door standing open to allow the essence of her to disperse into the atmosphere, leaving him no reminders that others had occupied the house before him. She wanted to see how very much he loathed the former owners so that she could justifiably loathe him in return . . .

But as she ascended the stairs and entered the wide corridor, she saw that the door to her room was closed. Stealing her way up to it as if she expected someone to jump out and snatch her, she allowed her hand to fall gently to the handle. *Yes, let me see my room turned inside out, my bedcovers ripped asunder, my airy lace curtains replaced with heavy masculine draperies that would allow no sunlight, my delicate furniture replaced with gaudy, gargantuan pieces that only a Yankee could like!*

Feeling the anger swell within her like a tidal wave, Delilah pushed the door open with a brittle expletive, expecting to find an ugly transformation.

She was immediately surprised . . . and wary. The Yankee had been at The Shadows for the better part of two weeks and not a thing within her room had been touched. Moving across the plush Oriental carpet in its subtle shades of pink and blue and cream, she touched the fragile gossamer floating from the high canopy of her bed, its lace coverlet still a little crumpled where she had last lain upon it. Tears came to Delilah's amber eyes, tears which she flicked away before they reached the smooth curves of her cheeks. There on the bedside table was the book she had been reading the morning she'd left The Shadows. There on the wicker chair by the window were the pillows she and her mother had embroidered together. She threw herself among the feather-filled memories and hugged them to her slender frame. "Oh, Delilah, could you have misjudged him?" she asked herself in a soft whisper. "Have you seen anything changed within the house, even as hard as you've looked?"

Masculine voices in the direction of the stable drew her attention to the wide, spotless window. Grant Emerson was returning, leading a dapple mare, an untethered colt frisking at her side. She watched as Philbus took the reins of Grant's horse while he dismounted, simultaneously holding his cane up to him. All thoughts of rushing downstairs to throw herself upon the divan as was appropriate to a "grievously injured" woman flew to the wind as she watched him, the noonday sun catching the brilliant gleam of his pale hair, his tall, muscular frame casting a shadow almost as long as Philbus's own. "Could I have misjudged him?" she again asked herself, her fingers holding tightly to the windowsill.

But as she watched him cross to the house, he suddenly halted, his deep voice cutting into the morning with words that could gain no clarity from her distance. One of the young women, carrying a basket of clothing to the scrub boards, immediately answered his summons.

While Grant's right hand held fast to the cane, his left flailed the air at the slave, who had set her basket on the ground. Her head fell dejectedly, and Delilah imagined that the new master of Shadows-in-the-Mist had reduced the poor thing to tears.

"You devil and you varmint!" she spat, her fingers clutching the sill so tightly that pain shot into her wrists. "Of course I have not misjudged you . . . treating a pregnant woman like the lowliest of dogs!"

Grant was furious. By the time he had dropped his hand to Kimmie's shoulder to give assurance his anger was not with her, he heard her soft sobbing. "I am not angry with you, girl," he comforted her. "I want to know who sent you out with that basket of clothes. You must be close to your time and you don't need to be carrying a load like that. Now, hush, stop that crying."

Philbus approached. "What de matter, massah, suh. Dat girl bein' bad?"

Grant's fingers gently massaged Kimmie's shoulder in an attempt to control her weeping. "She's near her time and I simply didn't want her to be carrying a load like that. I don't expect work out of a woman who is about to give birth."

Would the Yankee never cease to surprise him? "It ain't been like dat befo', massah. Ain't never no mind made to one of de wenches what's gonna drop a babe. Dey work right up to de minute de pain starts, an' den dey's back in de field or whatever be dey job when de young'un pops out."

Grant's piercing blue eyes cut to Philbus. "Well, I won't have it. I'm master here now, and as much as I was trying to avoid it, changes will have to be made. You spread the word that I want to talk to everyone tomorrow morning at eight." He again faced the slave girl. "Young woman . . ." Grant's voice softened, "what is your name?"

"Kimmie, massah, suh," she sniffed, her gaze cutting shyly to his.

"You go on back to your cabin and you let someone else do the heavy work. Do you understand why this is necessary?"

Her fingers twisted through the folds of her calico gown. "No, suh, I's don't."

"A woman in your condition should take good care of herself and not do anything to endanger her health. When is your baby due?"

"Mos' any day, massah, suh."

"Don't do any work until I tell you it's all right." he ordered lightly. "Do you understand?"

"Yas, suh, massah, suh," Kimmie answered, bending to pick up the basket.

Grant's cane landed in the middle of the clothing. "I'll get one of the boys to take these out to the scrub boards and instruct another woman to wash them."

Philbus stood a few feet away, his glance one of admiration. The kind actions of the new master made him ashamed that he'd lied to him about Delilah Wickley. But he couldn't help but wonder if Grant Emerson was truly concerned about the health of the young woman or was simply protecting the welfare of a new asset—the slave baby who would soon be born?

To justify the quiet rebellion of all the slaves at Shadows-in-the-Mist, Philbus wanted to believe the latter. But that was a pretty hard order to fill. For only the second time in their lives, a white man was treating them all like human beings; in fact,

Grant Emerson treated them even more humanely than Angus Wickley had in the last ten years of his life. After his accident, he had developed a vicious streak, though he displayed it only often enough for them to remember it.

The Yankee-Doodle gambler, with his kind and gentle ways, almost made Philbus forget Angus Wickley.

Almost.

Six

When Grant entered the house, Delilah was lying on the divan in the parlor, a cool cloth across her forehead. From beneath the fringes of her thick lashes, she watched his slow, deliberate movements. How could he appear to be the epitome of gentleness and yet have been so cruel to Kimmie? Delilah's mouth pinched into a thin line as she mentally reinforced her loathing for him. She could still feel her heart beating fast after her quick flight from her former bedroom, a pace she was now sure quickened because of his despicable nearness.

Grant entered the parlor, halted, began a quiet retreat, then again turned toward the divan where Delilah rested.

"Miss Freeman?"

She managed to act a little startled. Pushing the cloth away from her eyes, she met his gaze. "Mister Emerson . . . I didn't hear you approach." Attempting to rise, she feigned weakness, her thick, dark tresses again touching the pillow. "Oh, dear, I thought I'd recovered sufficiently to make my way home."

"There is no need to hurry." Grant's right hand absently caressed his cane. "I'll be happy to send one of my people to your home to assure your family of your well-being."

Her eyes widened in surprise. "There is no need. They don't usually worry about me until darkness has fallen, and surely by then—"

Grant wondered just how far she would go with her deception. She had no family and no home, just a room at a hotel where no one monitored her actions. He felt a moment of anger quicken the pace of his heart, though his features did not mirror the emotion. "I must insist, Miss Freeman," he said on a note of finality. "I will bring pen and paper so that you might compose a note."

"Well . . ." Delilah's thoughts revolved at an incredible speed. "Perhaps if you sent your slave Philbus. My family trusts him—"

Grant was well aware that an eavesdropping Mozelle stood in the shadows just beyond the doorway. When he called her name, she started for a moment, then entered the parlor, her arms crossed behind her back. "Philbus will be needed to carry a message. Take word to him." He returned his look to Delilah, "Simply tell Mozelle where you live and she will pass the information on to Philbus," he instructed her.

Delilah shrugged lightly, her gaze cutting between Grant Emerson and the silent Mozelle. "There is no need. Philbus knows where I live."

Grant frowned inwardly. He hated lies. He hated conspiracies. Were Delilah Wickley not so lovely and were he not trying to win the trust and respect of the slaves, he was sure some of his civility might be lost. But he forced a small smile. "Then it shall be done," he said. "Please inform your family that you are most welcome at The Shadows for as long as you wish—need—to stay." Bowing lightly, he turned, the thick braided rug muffling his footfalls until he was well out of sight. Only then did Delilah's gaze again meet Mozelle's.

"Ya should be ashamed of yo'self, Missy," the slave softly admonished. "Now ya is here, how ya gonna stay widout him bein' 'spicious. Lawd, Missy, ya's gonna git de lot of us strung up and whipped real good. An' de massah's bein' so nice to ya."

Delilah swung her booted feet to the floor. "Why are you defending him?" she asked irately. "He just gave a good tongue thrashing to poor Kimmie, her being big with child and all."

Mozelle's toe tapped in outrage. "De massah ain't done no such a thing, Missy."

"I saw him." Delilah flung her arm for emphasis. "I saw him cutting that poor girl down to size, refusing to allow her to pick up her basket of clothes! I was watching from the window of my room."

Mozelle kept her voice deliberately soft. "Dat ain't yo' room, an' like I says, he ain't done no such thing to Kimmie. Ya's need to be amindin' yo' own business when ya don't know what's ahappenin'."

"My Lord, Mozelle." Delilah shook her head. "What has happened to you? You were as fired up as a lightning-struck rooster the last time I was here. Now you defend him."

Mozelle shrugged her shoulders, her face drawn into a frown. "I sho' don't like dat Yankee-Doodle feller, Missy, but he be de massah of de Shadows, and I's jes' de slave."

"That never stopped you from speaking your mind before, Mozelle."

Mozelle turned, preparing to leave. "Things is

diff'rent now. I best be huntin' down Philbus to take dat message ya is gonna write, Missy."

When Mozelle encountered Grant in the foyer, she attempted to cut her gaze from his critical one. But when he spoke her name, she halted and turned back.

"Do you know anything about this young lady?" Grant asked in a quiet voice.

Her eyebrows shot up in surprise. "Ever'body on de bayou here 'n abouts calls her Missy."

"Is that all you know?"

Mozelle suspected that her new master was baiting her. She felt a rekindling of the annoyance she had felt just that morning when he'd given her job to Daisy. A pang of guilt seized her. It had taken only seconds for the news to reach the house of his concern for Kimmie, and in the two weeks that he'd been at The Shadows, he had been kind and sensitive to the needs of the people and had done nothing that would give them reason to dislike him. When she continued, her eyes downcast, she held back all her knowledge of her former mistress, though she could not outright lie to him.

"Sho', massah," she replied, "I knows dat girl's a fine rider an' I knows lots o' folks along de bayou know her and I knows, fo' sho', dat nobody ain't got nothin' but kind words fo' her. I knows, massah . . ." Sheepishly, her eyes met his briefly, "dat girl come from a real fine family an' ain't nobody finer'n Missy."

"Strange," Grant mused. "When Philbus and I met her on the trail, he called her 'white trash.' Can you imagine why he might have said that about so fine a lady?"

Mozelle slowly shook her head. "Philbus, he jes'

not be wantin' ya to waste yo' time on 'er when ya's goin' over to Miz El's place to see de horses." She paused a moment. "I's dismissed now, massah?"

Where there had been hostility just that morning, Grant now saw shame in her lowered features. "You're dismissed," he replied quietly. "Why don't you and Daisy prepare a simple lunch that I can enjoy with Miss . . . Freeman."

"Yas, suh."

When Mozelle was out of sight, Grant turned toward the parlor, a box containing pen and paper tucked beneath his left arm. While Delilah kept her eyes closed, he set the items down on a small, bare table and drew it across the carpet to the divan. Instantly aware of him, Delilah opened her eyes, briefly met his gaze, then shifted her attentions to the table and its contents.

"I have brought writing implements, Miss Freeman. After you have written your message, would you care to have lunch with me?" Her eyes dropped and a shame identical to that Grant had seen in Mozelle's face now marred her lovely features. But just as fleetingly as that look had come upon her, he now saw pools of hostility darken the rich gold of her eyes. He imagined that she must hate him very much, though he knew not the reason why.

Crimson rushed into Delilah's cheeks as his eyes held her gaze, transfixed. She wondered if he had guessed at her inner rebellion as the woman within her responded to the masculine nearness of him. "Thank you, sir," she responded, dropping her gaze. "You are most kind."

Grant's smile came easily in spite of the circumstances. He liked being near the beauty reclining

96

upon the divan, even if her motives were questionable. He remembered that day in the mercantile when she had sold the brooch. Watching her proud loveliness against the dim interior of the store that morning had quickened the pace of his heart; the nearness of her now quickened it, too, and he worried that she might see the movement against the thin material of his shirt.

Delilah, however, could not cut her gaze from his eyes. She imagined that if they were crystals they would look lovely set in a pendant; she imagined that the strands of his shoulder-length hair, like molten gold, would be lavish and lush spun into a scarf to wear about her shoulders. She imagined that his tall, slim yet muscular form would mold perfectly against her own soft body . . .

Delilah drew in a quick gasp of air. The narrowing of Grant's eyes as she did so was a clear indication to her that he had read her thoughts. The color deepened in her cheeks, but she somehow managed to bury her face into the soft folds of the pillow without looking every bit the fool.

Grant smiled. "Write your note, Miss Wic—Ummm, *Freeman,* and share lunch with me."

He hadn't been the least effective in halting his verbal folly. As Delilah realized that he was very aware of her true identity, she was almost certain the folds of the pillow had become bricks. How could she save face now? He must think her every bit the fool. Miss Wickley! He'd been about to say Miss Wickley!

Grant was not ready to play all his cards. The lovely Delilah Wickley was playing a game with him and he did not want to lay down his hand. After he managed to place his thoughts in some

97

semblance of order, he smiled at her. "Please forgive me for forgetting your name for the moment," he said. "The former owner of this house was named Wickley and I have heard them mentioned so often that I almost addressed you as a Wickley." His smile widened mischievously. "And I really do owe you an apology," he continued on a teasing note. "I hear the old gentleman had a terribly hard-headed daughter. Did you know her?"

Delilah's eyes widened. She felt her knuckles tighten against the folds of her riding gown enough to cause pain. She forced a smile as her gaze met his own. "Yes, I did know her," she replied. "She was—is—about my age. But . . . we never got along. Different social classes, you understand. You can't mix oil and water with any degree of success."

Grant's smile was so brief as to be nonexistent. "Are you saying then that this Delilah Wickley is a bit of a snip?"

"A snip and a snooty witch," Delilah replied without pause. "You wouldn't like her in the least. Believe me—"

Without quite realizing he'd made the move, Grant's palm briefly covered Delilah's warm hand. "You don't look like the kind of lady who could be dishonest. Of course I believe you. I do hope I don't have occasion to run into the dreadful woman. Thank you for the warning." Smiling warmly, he continued. "You write that missive and I'll have Philbus deliver it to your family. I'll see how the ladies are coming with lunch."

When he was well out of sight, a tight-lipped Delilah mumbled, "Dreadful woman, indeed! The worst is yet to come, *Mister* Emerson!"

* * *

Grant had worried that plantation life might seem a little dull after his years of excitement on the great river geographically dividing the nation. But the presence of Delilah Wickley in the house was every bit as exciting as playing a winning hand of cards at a game of high stakes. He wished there had been no other women before her in his life . . . especially one. He cringed as the mental image of Madeleine Vail crawled through his memories, like the clinging fronds of a poisonous vine. Would he ever escape that mistake in his life? Would the obsessed vixen let him?

Shaking off the unpleasant thoughts, Grant moved toward the stairway and his chamber on the second floor. There, he changed his shirt and jacket, brushed back his golden hair, and drew a tie beneath his collar. He looked forward to the game of cat-and-mouse with Miss Delilah Wickley, whom, he was sure, considered herself the predator. Smiling to himself as he considered all possible moves in the challenging game before him, he turned toward the corridor.

Entering the parlor brought him face to face with Delilah. He smiled, even as her eyes widened in surprise at the near encounter. "Are you feeling better?" Grant asked.

"A little. Your maid, Mozelle, announced that lunch was ready and I thought it rude to ignore her summons. I was coming to meet you."

Politely, Grant extended his arm, waiting for her own to link through it. When it did, he was almost sure he felt her shudder. Was he that repulsive to her? He frowned inwardly, even as his smile remained. "Tell me, Miss Freeman . . ." he began on the short walk to the dining room where he helped to seat her, "have you heard the story of gold being buried somewhere on this plantation?"

Delilah gulped. Is that why he'd bought The Shadows? The lure of gold? "Why . . . yes, Mister Emerson. I'm sure everyone along the bayou — indeed, in all the parish — has heard the story. I doubt that it's true, though. The Wickleys were notorious storytellers."

Placing his cane against his chair as he sat, Grant's eyes, laced with humor, continued to hold Delilah's golden ones. She was a most stunning beauty, even with the very noticeable patch of dirt staining her sleeve. And she must be very agile to have been able to pitch herself from her horse without doing harm to herself. He had no doubt that her mind was as agile, for she'd already impressed him with her dexterity of thought. "It would do me great honor if you'd call me Grant."

Delilah arched a sable eyebrow. "Very well . . . Grant." She lowered her eyes to nervously pick over the plate of food, consisting of thinly-cut beef and lettuce between slices of Mozelle's freshly-baked bread, potatoes cut in wedges and steamed, with garnishes of parsley and small blocks of cheese, a tall glass of iced tea with a slice of lemon . . . Oh, didn't Mozelle remember that she hated iced tea?

"And am I still required to call you Miss Freeman?"

Her concentration broken by Grant's quietly spoken question, Delilah looked up quickly. "Oh, please, forgive my rudeness. Of course not. Please call me Missy." She pointed her finger timidly at the plate. "May I eat this now?" she asked. "I'm famished."

Her childlike qualities and womanly charms warmed him. "Please, enjoy your meal," he replied.

Philbus had ridden along the bayou just far enough to see little more than the rooftop of The Shadows upon the timberline. Dismounting his gelding, he dropped against a live oak and picked up a twig. Behind a fencerow, the few well-fed cattle owned by The Shadows grazed contentedly in green pastures. At the bayou, he raised his hand in greeting to Old Granny, the eldest of the female plantation slaves, who sat on a wooden bucket, the fishing line of her cane pole disappearing beneath the surface of the water just a few ripples from the hull of *Bayou Belle*. A big yellow dog, her constant companion, slept peacefully at her side, perking an ear occasionally when a sound erupted from the bayou.

After a few moments, Philbus rose, remounted the gelding, and rode at a leisurely pace, dismounting at scarcely fifteen minutes after his departure.

In the kitchen, Mozelle informed him that the master and Missy were lunching in the dining room. Philbus had removed his hat upon entering the house, and as he moved slowly toward the dining room, he held it almost possessively to his massive chest.

Delilah's eyes widened in surprise upon seeing him. He certainly had not taken enough time to carry a message anywhere, let alone a phantom home westward on the bayou. Standing just inside the door, Philbus waited to be noticed by his new master. Grant finally looked up.

"Yes, what is it, Philbus?"

The brawny slave cut his eyes from Delilah's and spoke humbly. "Massah, on de trail, I met up wid Missy's pa alookin' for her. He'd be right obliged, he said, if Massah'd be neighborly enough to let Missy stay on at de Shadows whilst he goes to N'Awleans fo' a week or so."

Delilah promptly choked on a morsel of meat. Alarmed by the reddening of her features and the moisture sheening her golden eyes, Grant was immediately beside her, slapping her full upon the back. "Are you all right, Miss Freeman?"

"I—I just need . . . to get my wind." She coughed out the words, averting her narrowed gaze toward Philbus. His announcement had not been part of the plan and Delilah was surprised that he'd so boldly come up with it on his own. Or had he? As she calmly pushed away her half-empty plate, she continued in a soft, controlled tone. "Since my . . . pa has made arrangements for me, perhaps your slave would be so kind as to fetch a few of my things from my . . . home."

"Sho', Missy," Philbus replied without a moment's delay, immediately flashing an apologetic look to Grant Emerson. "That's if, massah, it be's all right."

As Philbus left the room, Grant returned to his chair. Linking his fingers beneath his strong chin, he curbed a moment of annoyance as he remarked to his guest that he would understand if she was troubled by her father's request. "A woman your age would be expected to make her own decisions and take care of herself," he said. "Of course, if you do not wish to stay—"

"If it is what my father wishes, then I will obey him. He is merely concerned for me. We have,

102

after all, had trouble with poachers on our place the past few weeks."

What an outstanding liar she was! He wanted so much to be angry with the deceptive little creature, but the truth was that he found her very entertaining. She had perfected lying to an art; he wondered how adept she was in other fields . . . such as lovemaking.

As visions of the porcelain-skinned beauty lying naked in his arms filled the darkness behind his closed eyelids, Grant's body tightened into an iron-hard betrayer of his vulnerability. If he didn't relax, he was sure she would notice the physical change in him. An ache crawled down his body, entering his groin so quickly that he felt compelled to slip lower into his chair. Crimson flashed across his high cheekbones; he brought his fingers up to brush at a fallen lock of hair. The way she looked at him indicated that she might be more perceptive than he wanted to believe.

Surging forward, Grant's voice took on an almost graveled tone as he continued. "Well, my young houseguest, will you think me rude if I leave the table to tend business?"

"Of course not. I certainly don't want to get in the way. Couldn't you try to pretend I'm not here?"

That request was like asking Atilla the Hun to plant begonias for his mother. But, miraculously, the formation of words had managed to quell the desire that had rocked his body just moments before. Grant stood and took up his cane. "There is a lovely chamber on the second floor which will accommodate your needs during your stay," he said casually. "Please, make yourself at home."

The sincerity of his words again heightened her

guilt. Daring to meet the steady gaze of his crystalline eyes, she managed the smallest of smiles, then allowed a moment to pass before replying to him. "That is very kind of you. I wouldn't have expected such a gracious host of a . . ." Yankee-Doodle gambler! Crimson flooded her cheeks as she caught herself in midsentence. She certainly could not allow the insult she had almost spoken to fall from her tongue. Catching her lost breath, she continued somewhat precariously, "of a . . . a gentleman who has yet to have time to settle into a new home."

Her full, trembling lips, ever so slightly parted, warmed Grant. For the briefest of moments, the lies and the deceptions did not matter, only that she was here, vibrant and womanly . . . passionate. The slight throb in the slim column of her throat drew his attentions, the long, tapered fingers of her hand slowly rising to cover it, then her thickly-fringed golden eyes, almond-shaped, catlike, and seductive, silently observing the direction of his gaze . . .

He turned and fled before his traitorous body gave away all his secret cravings.

Scarcely had Grant disappeared into the corridor before Daisy appeared to draw out a chair and sit beside Delilah. They had been childhood friends for as long as either of them could remember. They had been together that stormy night the wagon in which they'd been hiding had plunged into the frigid currents of Bayou Bouef . . .

Delilah shuddered as she tossed the horrid memory from her mind. "Do you think he knows who I really am, Daisy?"

"Don't know, Missy. Trouble right now is Mozelle. She's fierce mad—"

"About your taking her job?"

"Naw, ain't nothin' to do wid dat. Mozelle, she's a thinkin' that when de massah finds out, that he'll be sellin' us all off. Mozelle's thinkin' maybe you ought'n to tell him yo'self."

Delilah's gaze softly swept over her friend's pretty face. "And what do you think, Daisy?"

"I's thinkin', Missy, that ya ought to follow yo' heart." With a big grin, she added, "And be glad Trusdale's gone, 'cause he'd be blabbin' fo' sho'!"

"Well, if you think I should follow my heart, then I shall have no consideration whatsoever for our Mr. Grant Emerson," Delilah replied in a suddenly vehement tone. "It is his fault my father died . . . his and Ellie's. Ellie knew the bank was going to take the plantation. She invited that . . . that Yankee-Doodle gambler to come here to take my father's land."

Daisy calmly shook her head. "That's a mighty big hate fillin' yo' heart, Missy."

Pushing herself to her feet, Delilah gave Daisy a scathing look. Flinging back the rich, tangled locks of her hair, she moved toward the stairway and her old bedchamber on the second floor.

She wanted to slam the door to vent her fury, but she dared not. It might require explanations to the new master of the house. She hated him. Hated him! He and Ellie, the conspirators. How could she have been so blind, all these years, thinking that Ellie was her friend?

Throwing herself upon the bed, she made a feeble attempt to pummel her fist against the coverings, managing only to catch one of her long fingernails in the delicate cream crochet.

But she gave little thought to the torn nail as she

turned onto her back and tucked her hands behind her head. As the sun caught one of the crystals of the chandelier and cast its ray full upon her features, she mumbled beneath her breath, "Grant Emerson, you just wait. I am going to be your worst nightmare . . ."

Seven

Actually, Grant's worst nightmare was a thousand miles away, and at that precise moment turning toward the brick steps of a well-kept town house on Boston's west side. At the top of the steps, Aldrich Emerson took a moment to straighten his collar, then tapped at the door knock. Shortly, a petite, matronly servant cautiously opened the door, then sniffed indelicately as she announced, "Mistress Madeleine is awaiting you in the parlor."

Unlike his fair-haired first cousin, Aldrich Emerson was swarthy, his straight dark hair combed almost severely back from his forehead. But like his cousin, he could be brooding and silent, and the narrow gaze of his piercing eyes could be as intimidating as Grant's, if the mood so struck him. It was just such a silent look which first greeted Madeleine Vail that warm Massachusetts morning.

"Aldrich, your missive sounded urgent. What is on your mind?"

Aldrich's black eyes moved fluidly over Madeleine's petite form, over a small, oval face with which he could find no fault. She had drawn her light-brown hair back into a matching pair of mother-of-pearl combs and had dashed the most subtle of rouges to her pale features, a perfect match to her fashionable gown, with its peach bodice and green-and-peach striped skirts. She was lovely; he wanted to take her in his arms and hold her close, though he knew she would rebuff any such show of affection.

"I want you to know, Madeleine, that my agents have learned Grant's whereabouts."

Madeleine's eyes widened in surprise. She rushed to Aldrich, making no effort to minimize her nervous excitement, as her fingers firmly gripped the lapels of his jacket. "Where . . . oh, where, Aldrich? You must tell me where he is."

He smiled wryly, gently twisting her fingers loose from his jacket. "That, my angel, is information I do not intend to pass on. I just wanted you to know, and to appeal to you once again to be my wife."

Her rebellion instantly strong, she pivoted away, clenching her fingers together as she did so. "No . . . no, I do not love you."

Without pause, Aldrich was at her back, his hands gently gripping her upper arms in an attempt to caress them. "You did once, Madeleine. You loved me enough to give birth to my son!"

Shrugging away from his embrace, Madeleine moved a few feet away, then calmly turned back. "Yes, Dustin is your son, Aldrich . . . yours and mine." Emotion rippled her voice. "You were my love and my lover. Once . . . once we would have been married, and I am sure we would have been very happy together. But when you disappeared and I had no idea where you were, I married Grant. He is my love now . . . he is the only man I will ever love. Can't you understand, Aldrich, that he is my husband?"

Aldrich pressed his mouth into a thin line. "On that point, you are the only one who thinks so," he replied in frustration. "You have left me no choice . . ."

All color drained from her already pale features. "Wh-what choice is that?"

"Grant will die. I swear this to you."

In the three days since she had tossed herself from her horse, Delilah had not ceased to be surprised at the many changes that had taken place on the plantation. Even the attitudes of the slaves were different. In a meeting held two mornings ago between Grant and the slaves, Philbus, who had been so vocal about wanting to be a free Texas cowboy, now showed unrestrained enthusiasm in his new position as overseer at Shadows-in-the-Mist. Grant's show of confidence in him brought on moments of conscience in the burly slave as he remembered how easily he had lied to his new master.

Delilah watched the activities at The Shadows and made mental notes. Grant Emerson had devised a devious scheme. Without a doubt, he was aware of Philbus's lie, and appointing him overseer was his perverse way of bringing the slave's guilt to the surface. Just this morning, Delilah had overheard Grant announce to Mozelle that he was very aware of what was going on in the house. He had not defined his knowledge; there really had been no need.

Delilah was now faced with the same dilemma she thought had faced her within hours of entering The Shadows — how to extract herself from this embarrassing situation without losing face. On the other hand, she couldn't help wondering if Grant Emerson had been bluffing when he'd confronted the tight-lipped Mozelle only minutes after leaving his bedchamber. Delilah had arisen early, dressed, and had been sitting quietly by the window watching the stir of activity in the slave quarters when she'd heard Grant's bootsteps and the rhythmic tap of his cane. What could he have learned in the confines of his chamber that he had not known last evening? He had not acted in a peculiar fashion at dinner. Yet, a darkness had hung on his brow that she had not noticed before, as if a thousand questions were scattering his thoughts into a million splintered fragments. She'd noticed him watching her more intently, the moments of his silence longer, his smiles almost forced.

Since Grant had left The Shadows that afternoon, Delilah took advantage of her solitude to visit the graves of her parents. As she descended the hill and entered the grove of oaks separating the cemetery from the house, she was immediately surprised to see the ornate marble headstone announcing her father's resting place. Upon it was carved the words: "Angus Aaron Wickley . . . Delilah's beloved father." A gentle wind swept up from the bayou. Delilah felt the warm glaze of tears trace a salty path over the smooth curves of her cheeks. She'd left The Shadows too hastily to order a tombstone; who, then, had cared enough to mark her father's grave with such elegance? Had Philbus sold off a cow or two to afford the cost? Had Mr. Wells chosen this way to remember his lost friend?

It mattered not . . . only that it had been done. Quietly, she dropped to the ground and began pulling weeds from the base of the monument. Looking toward her mother's grave, she said, with the softness of a sad, thoughtful child, "Don't worry, Mother . . . I will take care of you, too."

After she'd completed the chore, she continued to

sit in the warm summer grass, her legs tucked beneath the cool cotton skirts of her gown. She'd gotten dirt beneath her fingernails and picked absently at them, her gaze fixed to her father's marble headstone. When melancholy choked in her throat, she looked upward to watch the southerly travels of cumulus clouds. The minutes became an hour . . . then two.

A veil of darkness began to drift down from the horizon. Only then did Delilah realize how long she'd been away from the house. She knew she'd thought a thousand thoughts, but she couldn't remember a single one. Had anyone missed her? Had supper already been put on the table? It really didn't matter; she wasn't hungry anyway.

As the shadows of the timberline began to deepen, Delilah suddenly sensed a human presence. Her heart should have stirred in alarm, but it did not. No emotion moved her, even as booted masculine feet approached somewhere behind her, then again paused. She recognized the man's gait . . .

Her fingers gently caressing the silky petals of a clover leaf, she looked up at Grant Emerson. "You know who I am, don't you?" she asked quietly.

"Yes." He replied with only a moment's pause.

Her tone did not change, "Then why haven't you run me off?"

"I saw no need. You were doing no harm. Besides . . ." His had fell softly to her shoulder as he continued. "I am curious as to your motives."

Could she so easily betray her wickedness? Could she admit that her purpose, if she could not find her father's gold, was to seduce him, marry him, and recapture The Shadows, as she had promised Angus Wickley she would? Could she bear to witness his shudder of disgust, his voice angrily ordering her off his land?

These past few days she had watched a man who hardly fit the description of "Yankee dog." He might well have been mistaken for a southern gentleman had one not known differently. Delilah sighed deeply. No, she could not bring further disgrace upon herself by betraying her motives.

Painfully aware of the silence that had fallen between them, Delilah shrugged his hand from her shoulder, even as she had wanted to enjoy its gentleness. "My motive, Grant, is a simple one. The Shadows was my home for many years and I missed it terribly. I am sorry I deceived you, but I merely wanted to spend a few final days here. Perhaps now I will be able to go on with life." Rising to her feet, she met his gaze, then dropped her eyes in her moment of shame. "I will pack and be gone before the night. Please, do not be angry with your slaves. It's really my fault for putting them on the spot the way I did."

"I don't blame them . . . Delilah." His eyes held hers in the failing light. He liked what he saw in her face: the gentle hue of shame upon her cheeks, the slight tremble of her mouth, the way her gaze dropped, then rose again as if she wanted to redeem herself but couldn't quite find the words.

Delilah attempted to step around him. "I'd better pack and saddle my horse—" she said.

Grant's hand shot out, gripping her upper arm. He didn't want her to leave Shadows-in-the-Mist. She belonged here . . . He could not allow her to leave, and yet he could not admit to her that he wanted her to stay. As her almond-shaped eyes quizzically held his gaze, he smiled a mirthless smile. "The horse is not yours, Delilah," he said. "It is the property of this plantation—"

112

"No! No!" She instantly cut him off, firmly pulling her arm free of his grip so that her hands could land upon her hips. "Bella is mine! She was a birthday gift from my father—"

"She is plantation property. If you want the horse, you must—" *She must what?* he wondered, his mind whirling at a rapid pace. *What chore could she perform that would be worth the value of the horse?* Stacking his hands upon the head of his cane, he continued to hold her angry gaze until the answer came to him. "You must work for me! The horse cost fifteen hundred dollars. If you want her, then you will pay off her cost."

How Delilah kept her composure she would never understand. She pivoted smartly away from him, her right toe tapping upon the firm earth. She wanted to hurl insults and degradations, to tell him how much she hated him. But she knew he would only be amused by her theatrics. "Fine, then!" she eventually replied. "Keep the horse. I've got two feet, and walking won't hurt me a bit." She lifted her chin arrogantly, so sure was she that he would let her take her horse rather than see her leave The Shadows on foot.

With the experience of five years of riverboat gambling under his belt, Grant had learned to recognize a bluffing woman. And even before that? How many times had Madeleine threatened suicide in her efforts to force him to stay with her? Grant shrugged his shoulders as if he really didn't care one way or the other. "Very well," he answered, "if that's the way you want it," then turned to begin his ascent of the hill toward The Shadows.

Delilah was quite taken aback. He had called her bluff! "If I were to work for you," she hastily called after him, "what would I have to do?"

Her sharply spoken words halted Grant's retreat. He did not turn back as he asked, "What are you capable of doing?"

"Well, I can't make beds worth a damn . . . and I can't cook worth a damn . . ."

Slowly, Grant turned back. "Do you normally speak in so unladylike a fashion, or do I simply bring out the worst in you?"

It pleased her to displease him so, and it simply fueled her enthusiasm at a time in her life when she had never been angrier. Crossing her arms, she continued. "I also can't pitch hay worth a darn . . . and I have no experience picking cotton."

Without warning, Grant's left hand darted out and snatched one of her wrists. She was too surprised to protest as he pulled her close to him, dropping his cane so that he could grip her other wrist. "You've told me what you can't do, Delilah Wickley, now tell me what you can—"

"Look at me," she responded flippantly. "If there is anything I can do with any competence at all, I'm sure an astute person like you will be able to guess what my qualifications are."

His eyes narrowed dangerously, even as his mouth curled into a rakish grin. He thought his angry quarry beautiful beyond description. "What I see in your eyes, Delilah Wickley, I've seen in the eyes of lusty black-haired Creoles wearing sheer red gauze and sitting in the parlors of brothels with more on their minds than sleep."

Had her wrists not been so firmly pinched between his fingers, she'd have slapped his face. He would like that, wouldn't he . . . to have her respond to his degradations like a common street woman? "I dislike you immensely, Grant Emerson. I would rather be dead than to stay here at The

Shadows in your employ."

"I do not believe that, Delilah," he whispered pulling her close. "I believe you would agree to stay if you were not so blasted hard-headed. I believe you would do anything to stay at The Shadows. Anything . . . even put up with me!"

Of course, he was right. She was a little miffed that he could read her mind so easily. When she attempted to extract her wrists, his grip tightened. Meeting his eyes, her mouth pinched as she continued the game of cat-and-mouse. "If you are going to kiss me, get it over with so that I may go on with whatever I must do." She spoke matter-of-factly, a ploy, he supposed, meant to rile him.

A smile turned up the corners of his full, masculine mouth. "Kiss you?" he responded with feigned surprise, wanting nothing more, indeed, than to taste the sweetness of her mouth. "I am merely trying to decide how to release your wrists without losing my head."

Her eyes widened. "Oh? You think I am a violent woman . . . that I will attack you? I assure you, Grant Emerson, that I am too much a lady to do something that cheap and common."

He pretended that he was safe to release her wrists. As his fingers loosened, however, she raised one of her pretty hands to slap his face, a move, because he had anticipated it, he caught in midair. "Too much a lady, hmm?"

His handsome face was ever so close to her own, an amused twinkle in his eyes, a smile playing upon his mouth. Her heart began to thump madly. Oh, what a traitorous body she possessed! She simply had to change the subject before she embarrassed herself by responding to his nearness with wanton abandon. Turning sharply away, her hand fell to the iron gate of the cemetery. "Who erected my father's tombstone?"

He retrieved his cane from the ground as her eyes scrutinized the monument. "Philbus mentioned that Mr. Wells had ordered its placement."

"That was very nice of him."

"Very nice, indeed. Now . . . about that horse, and your staying on at The Shadows?"

"I could keep the business ledgers," she replied almost absently. "You are right, of course. I would do anything to stay at The Shadows." Her head slightly turned, though he still could not see her eyes. "Even allow myself to become employed by a Yankee-Doodle gambler."

Grant laughed aloud, at which time she spun back to him, her eyes flashing fury that he found humor rather than insult in her response. "Yankee-Doodle gambler, eh?"

"What is so amusing, Grant Emerson?" she demanded of him.

He took one of her wrists and pinned it against his chest. "Miss Delilah Wickley, you can stick a feather in my hat any old day, and you can call it anything you please."

Though he again held her wrist tightly, his fingers caressed it, then moved up to intertwine among her own. Rather than respond to his challenge by jerking her hand away, she lifted her chin and asked in a tightly controlled tone, "Do I have use of my horse while I am working toward purchase of her?"

"If a bank held a mortgage on your home, wouldn't it allow you to live there while you made your payments?"

"I imagine that it would."

"There . . . you have your answer. Only . . ." He

felt confident releasing her wrist this time that she would not strike him. Though the fury was still in her eyes, it appeared more controlled. "I would be honored if you would occasionally ride with me. I could show you some of the changes I'll be making at The Shadows."

She liked the idea of his company, though she could not betray that to him. "If it is convenient to me, I might ride with you. In the meantime . . ." Her golden eyes mirrored her own inner conflicts. She wanted to be part of The Shadows, even as a mere employee, but she also wanted to be free to come and go, and to do so without his being aware of every move she made. If she wanted to take a midnight ride, she did not want him questioning her motives. She did not want Grant Emerson acting as her father and stifling her free spirit. Gathering her thoughts, she continued once again. "In the meantime, I would ask that I be allowed to reside aboard the riverboat while I am in your employ."

Grant was visibly surprised; if his own eyes were the mirrors of his soul, she would have seen disappointment. "You may have your own room at the main house—"

"But The Shadows belongs to you, not me. That may once have been my room, but it is now merely another room in your house. I would prefer the solitude of the riverboat until such time as you make other use of it. I assume that you will eventually make it seaworthy and take it to the waters? The last overseer we had lived there. Perhaps if you hire an overseer, you'll want him to—"

"I gave Philbus the job. He gave me no reason to believe he'll be wanting to live aboard *Bayou Belle*."

"Southern masters do not make one of their slaves overseer."

"Well, I'm not southern. That explains my deviation from tradition. Is it so disagreeable to you to see a slave in a position of authority?"

"Of course not," she responded indignantly. "My father had wanted Philbus to be the overseer, but he worried about what the neighbors would think. When our last overseer left us just before Christmas, Father was considering Philbus for the position—"

Grant clicked his tongue sarcastically. "But what would the neighbors have thought?"

"He'd gotten to the point where he just didn't care any more," she replied. A distinct chill traveled the length of her spine as she remembered her father's last years—the forgetfulness and eccentricities, the childish temper tantrums and moments of brooding silence. It had all started that night, that awful night their fast-moving wagon had plunged into the icy depths of Bayou Boeuf—

"Are you all right, Delilah? You suddenly look so pale." Grant's hand moved slowly forward, then dropped gently to her arm.

Nervously patting her hands to her cheeks to return a bit of color, she wondered how he could possibly notice her pallor. The veil of darkness had deepened all around them, the forest across Bayou Boeuf now looming over them like threatening tentacles. "I assume my occupancy of the riverboat will not pose a problem?"

Of course it poses a problem. I want you near me. But Grant knew he could not reply as his heart dictated. "If it is what you want," he said simply. "But you will take your meals at the main house, won't you?"

"I can cook for myself."

"But there is no need. Daisy and Mozelle always

prepare more than enough. I insist."

"Well . . . I never did like that uppity Trusdale. I'd rather not stay in the same house with him."

"He won't return from Wellswood right away. Mr. Wells sent word that Old Peck had died and asked to keep Trusdale there until he can replace him."

"Oh, I see." Now, for another excuse . . . But she could not come up with one so quickly.

"Will you take your meals at the main house?" He reiterated his request.

Delilah sighed wearily. Where she ate her meals was a miserably small matter. Would it detract from her strength to concede this once to the arrogant easterner? "Very well. But since you are now employer and I am your employee, it wouldn't be proper that we take meals together."

"That is foolish. I do not enjoy dining alone."

She pressed her mouth into a thin line. "I am employed as your bookkeeper, not as your companion, Grant Emerson," she replied cruelly. Her heart fell like a deadweight. She did not want to be caustic; she wanted to be warm and friendly . . . even sensual. She did not want him to dislike her; she would rather he desired her, filled his every moment with thoughts of her.

"But I insist that you take your meals with me," he responded, undaunted by her sarcasm. He realized that conceding even this one tiny matter was extremely difficult for her.

Was it her imagination or was there a sharp edge to his tone she had not noticed before? Was he now exercising his rights as an employer, or did he so look forward to her company that he would order it? And did she find the thought of dining with him so disagreeable that she would put up this ridiculous opposition? Looking up and catching the angry

119

glint of his flashing blue eyes, she conceded the tiniest of smiles.

"Very well, Grant. Let's call a truce. We will discontinue this challenge of wills and try to get along. If at the end of two weeks, we find we simply cannot accomplish that, I will go on my merry way and we need never cross each other's path again."

"And I will keep the horse—"

"Oh no—" Linking her fingers against the folds of her skirt, she again smiled. "I will steal the horse right out from under you—"

Stepping to her, Grant took her wrist, but gently this time. "Why are we quarreling?"

Her gaze lowered to the long, slim fingers massaging her wrist. "I'm not sure."

Without warning, his hand slid to the small of her back. A wanton tremble wracked her body; she wanted only to extract herself from his touch before he sensed that she was anything but displeased. But her body would not obey and she found her eyes connected to his.

Grant regarded her silently, his masculine desire for more than just her nearness painfully overwhelming and yet his own good senses warning him she would not be receptive to any show of affection . . . or desire. Her mouth appeared pale and moist . . . her topaz eyes invitingly, teasingly sensual. Before he could prevent his own traitorous actions, he dropped his cane and his hands circled her narrow waist. Her loose locks were wild and flowing in the delicate wind whipping up from the bayou. She herself closed the distance between their bodies, and her soft, supple breasts burned through the material of his shirt, branding him with her own desire. Her fingers traveled the hard muscles of his upper arms and halted their tremulous caresses upon his shoulders.

Delilah was suddenly shaking like a child. What was she doing? Was she merely toying with him . . loathing him . . . or was her heart guiding her every movement? His chiseled features softened and invited the silky caresses of her fingertips. His hooded eyes absorbed the darkness of the bayou, and in that moment, the breath of space between them became nonexistent as he claimed her trembling mouth in the fiercest of kisses. His fingers tightened through the thick, rich masses of her hair, and she pressed herself against him, unable to prevent her body's betrayal of the hatred she carried within herself for this loathsome, despicable man.

His nearness muddled her thoughts. Feeling his arms around her, caressing her sensitive flesh, felt so natural. She could die in his arms that very moment, and feel that her life had been fulfilled . . . almost.

She had never enjoyed more than a kiss and a man's arms wrapped around her. She had never sensed the overwhelming masculine desire she now sensed in Grant's arms. His body was like granite against her soft one, his chest an iron-hard expanse of flesh to which she molded as though she belonged there. His mouth traveled the delicate column of her throat . . . lower . . . lower. Her head tilted back so that she could enjoy the sensation of his soft breath against her flesh, the swelling mounds of her breasts that could hardly be contained by the scant fabric of her gown.

Then, only then as she realized she wanted more in his arms than she had ever experienced before, did the strength return to her with brutal force. She tore herself away from him, half staggering against the hard iron of the fence, and dragged the night air deeply into her lungs in an effort to quell the volcano erupting within her. Scarcely able to see his features through the masses of hair that had invaded her face, she lifted her skirts and fled from him . . . fled the traitorous desires that burned through her body.

She did not look back, even in spiteful challenge when he called her name, like a father might call to a wayward child.

Eight

Delilah stood on the roadway, at a point where Bayou Boeuf almost touched the ribbon of well-traveled darkness. She knew that it was cold and stormy and yet she did not feel the icy rain penetrate her. Momentarily, the foggy silence was disturbed by the rumble of wagon wheels approaching from beyond the realms of her dream. Then came a voice, far away, altered by fear yet still familiar.

"But, massah, dey ain't nobody a followin' us."

Her father! Dear Lord, there was her father! Could Angus Wickley, half beating the harness horses into a frantic pace, have heard the declaration of his slave Lathrop? Delilah reached out for him as the wagon fled past, but her hand touched only the cool glass separating her from the happenings before her. But even as she was held back, her father's thoughts became her own. He had to keep his gold from falling into the hands of the outlaw bunch gaining on them in the distance and to protect the two children hiding beneath the tarpaulin in the back of the wagon. One of those little girls was Delilah. How could she be in two places at one time?

Driven on by fear, the sting of the frigid December rain, and the haunting calls of the bayou, Angus lost all sense of time and distance and reason.

With the heavy midnight darkness upon them, Angus Wickley reined the team into a stand of live oaks, then hopped down from the seat. "Help me, Lathrop," he demanded. "Hurry, man, get the shovel and the box."

"But, massah, dey ain't nobody back dere. An we's almo.
home."

"But I am here, Lathrop. Don't you see me? Deli
lah is here?" Had she actually spoken the words.
Lathrop continued as if he had not seen her, stand
ing there in the darkness, viewing their franti
movements.

The almost maniacal gleam in his master's dark
eyes against the dusky arch of moss-enshrouded
oaks did not go unnoticed by the slave. In the next
few moments, the two men dug a hole between the
roots of the largest of the oaks and were scarcely
able to position the treasure-ladened iron box before
the sides of the hole sank in on top of it. Behind them,
muffled by the blinding storm, the sobbing of the two frightened young girls could be heard. Angus cursed inwardly.
Why had he allowed Delilah and Lathrop's daughter Daisy
to accompany them on this trip? Why couldn't he have left
both young girls both tucked safely in the arms of their
mothers? Tossing the shovel into the back of the wagon, Angus folded back the tarpaulin, revealing the delicate features
of his amber-eyed daughter, the rich cascades of her chocolate-colored tresses in disarray across her gently heaving
shoulders. She held fast to her young friend, Daisy, whose
tear-stained face pressed tightly against Delilah's. "Do not
weep, children. We are almost home."

Delilah could see nothing but her father's loving face, like
a beacon of hope, against the darkness of the night. "Papa,
we are so frightened."

Touching his fingers briefly to her cheek, he smiled, repo-
sitioned the tarpaulin and quickly jumped to his seat beside
Lathrop. Once again, the harness mares stirred into action,
clambering onto the road that would take them home to
Shadows-in-the-Mist.

Angus had driven the exhausted team half a mile against

*the sheets of icy rain when he was sure gunshots exploded
beneath the thunderous midnight skies.* "They're upon us,
Lathrop!" *he screamed.*

"Dey ain't nobody dere, massah," *the slave exclaimed, defeat lacing his voice like a lost battle.*

*As Angus beat the reins frantically against the team, they
ran out of control, blinded by the storm and the heavy darkness of night, until they plunged into the rain-swollen currents of Bayou Boeuf.*

Delilah shot up from her sleep, her body
drenched in sweat, her fingers raking at her throat
in an attempt to dispel her nausea and fear. *Dear
Lord,* she thought, desperately searching for a glim-
mer of light in the midnight darkness. *I was
there . . . I was there on the roadway, a mute witness to it
all. I knew what Father was thinking. And Lathrop! I
heard his thoughts, too, inside my head just as if they were
my own. I felt the freezing water drawn into the lungs of a
terrified little girl. And dear Lord! I saw them bury the
gold! I know where it is!*

Tears streamed down her face as she tried to
quell her emotions. She could almost smell the
darkness pervading the large, airy cabin aboard
Bayou Belle, almost grab the grief she felt, as though
it was a tangible thing dangling just within her
reach.

Her hands shaking out of control, she somehow
managed to strike a match and light the lamp beside her.

Despite the midsummer night's sweltering heat,
she shivered. She didn't want to be alone. She
would even have accepted the company of the cool,
detached Grant Emerson, who had quietly evaded
her these past two weeks. He was a strange man—

teasing and affectionate one moment, silent and brooding the next.

Swinging her feet to the deck and shaking herself, hoping to drive away the painful memories her nightmare had caused to surface within her, Delilah felt for her robe at the end of her bed. Pulling it on, she took up the lamp and made her way to the large dining room that could easily seat thirty guests. Her father had added a Franklin stove to the front end of the elegantly furnished room and two matching brocade divans and side chairs. Delilah liked the room, with its regal columns against the walls and the carved wooden arches breaking the monotony of its ceiling. She set about stoking the kindling that was still alive in the Franklin stove, then discovering that the water in the kettle she'd placed there earlier was still hot. Within moments, she enjoyed a cup of honey-sweetened tea, then moved from the stifling heat into a breeze drifting along the deck of the riverboat. Across the lawn, the big house loomed against the horizon, where not a single light shone from within.

She had brought a small kitchen cloth with her and used its coarse fabric to wipe the perspiration from her neck and brow. Her robe fell open, betraying her gauze nightdress clinging damply to her slim form. She lowered the towel to absorb the beads of perspiration between her breasts. Lifting her eyes to view the fullness of the moon, she sighed deeply, wishing the dawn would come quickly and erase the gloom that had settled upon her.

When Grant Emerson saw her standing there, a chill sifted through his body. He stood quietly in the darkness of the timberline, his eyes following the stretch of moonlight across the bayou, which appeared to end at the edge of the rail where she stood, a goddess in the summer night. He did not mean to spy upon her, but he could not force himself to turn away. The sight of her against the silhouette of the riverboat caused him to tighten within.

Grant was bewildered by her resentment of him, a resentment with no visible cause except that he was now master of The Shadows. It was not his fault her father had lost the plantation, nor was it his fault Angus Wickley had died and his daughter had been forced to move. That had all happened before he'd come to Louisiana. He wondered if Delilah Wickley would have loathed any other man who might have purchased The Shadows.

He smiled to himself. He liked to think she wouldn't have gone to the trouble with another owner.

The scrape of a boot against a rock suddenly caught Delilah's attention. Grappling with the lapels of her robe, she narrowed her eyes, scarcely able to discern the dark outline of a man against the timberline.

"Who is there?" she called cautiously, preparing to flee to her cabin if the need arose.

Grant stepped out of the shadows, then moved toward the gangplank connecting the boat to land. "I didn't mean to startle you," he responded. "I couldn't sleep."

She narrowed her eyes as she watched his slow approach. Something was different about him . . . When he halted less than ten feet away from the gangplank, she realized the difference. "You're not carrying your cane, Grant," she said with visible surprise. "I thought you needed it."

He drew his lame leg up to a toppled bucket, then crossed his wrists upon his knee. "I have heard that every man needs a crutch of some sort. I thought the cane was mine."

"I would suppose that a man with your past *would* need some sort of a crutch — perhaps conscience or guilt, but certainly not a cane."

Since she could not possibly know anything about him, except what Ellie McPherson knew, he guessed that she was offhandedly referring to the death of Charles McPherson. "I possess neither of those," he replied. He would not confess the truth about what had happened aboard the riverboat. He and Ellie had made a pact so that she could save face among her neighbors. The events leading to Charles McPherson's death three years ago could only cause embarrassment for her if word got around; he surely would not divulge them. Drawing himself up once again, he prepared to leave. "I'd better get back to the house before we find a reason to quarrel."

Delilah was immediately sorry she'd been thoughtless. Grant had given her no reason to treat him so badly. "Would you care for some of Father's favorite brandy?" she asked in an attempt to make amends. "That might help you to sleep."

He smiled. "You've still got a bottle of his peach brandy? Mozelle said it was the best, but I could find none in the liquor cabinet."

"I'm afraid I pilfered the last bottle when I left the plantation," Delilah replied with a sheepish grin.

Grant watched her intently as he approached, his pulse pounding at the loveliness of her. Strands of her chestnut hair clung to her forehead and her lips were seductively, sensually, parted, as though the air she drew between them was an attempt to quell the fire within her. He liked to think he might be the reason for her state rather than the weather, but that possibility was a remote one.

"I'll take that brandy, Delilah, if it won't be too much trouble."

She shrugged her shoulders. "Horse feathers! What trouble could there be pouring a bit of liquid from a corked bottle?"

He traversed the gangplank and took his first step onto the lower deck of *Bayou Belle*.

"Shall I give you a guided tour?" Delilah asked in a soft, sultry voice. "The fee will be paltry."

He nodded, left speechless by the silkiness of her tone. As she opened the door leading to the main cabin, he saw the beads of perspiration dotting the smooth skin above the bodice of her robe. Noticing the direction of his gaze, Delilah's hand quickly rose. Grant fought to regain his composure. "After the tour, am I still invited for brandy?" he replied to her question.

"I said it would be no trouble," She repeated.

Soon, Grant was being taken through the decks and halls of *Bayou Belle,* to the cabin belowdecks, the roundhouse where, on a commercial riverboat, the men would have been lodged. She showed him the changes her father had made and, she took him into the long dining parlor which she confessed was her favorite room aboard ship. She did *not* take him to the cabin where she slept.

"What would people think if they saw me boarding the riverboat past the hour of midnight?" he asked.

"I'm sure, Grant, they would think we were having a romantic tryst. Of course, we both know better, don't we?" She spoke softly, sensually, her

129

fingers lightly holding the lapels of her robe together. Unconsciously, his eyes lowered to her long, slender fingers, then gazed beneath, at the moist ivory flesh she halfheartedly attempted to hide from him. Try as he might, he could not keep his mind where he wanted it. Crimson flushed his cheeks as he met her suspicious gaze. "I do hope it is brandy you want, Grant, and nothing more."

"If it was more I wanted, I'm sure I'd have to fight for it," he replied. Coolly, deliberately, she let her robe fall open, then made a dramatic pretense of grabbing for the lapels. Immediately, Grant took her wrists and held them to his chest. "What kind of game are you playing, Delilah? Your words are a seduction, your actions enticing. If you are attempting to stir my desires, then, my beauty, you are succeeding." Releasing her wrists and stepping back from her, he fought a smile as he gazed into her face. "Perhaps I should forego that brandy—"

"No!" She had not meant to speak the single word so sharply, and immediately softened her voice. "What I mean to say is that we've gotten off on the wrong foot and . . ." her eyes lifted shyly, "I really do believe we could be friends."

"Do you, indeed?"

Her bare foot shuffled back and forth beneath the hem of her gown. "We could try, couldn't we?"

Good senses dictated that Grant should remind her of how she had deceived him and lied to him, how she had attempted to form a mutiny among his slaves. He wanted to remind her, too, of the way she had so cruelly and falsely accused Ellie of going into league against her. But his heart reminded him that she felt she had a reason for all the things she had done.

He groaned inwardly, those good senses of his betrayed by an unreasonable heart. He hated himself for allowing her to crawl beneath his skin. He gritted his teeth. "I'll take that brandy," he replied tonelessly, "and toast a new friendship."

Friendship! That was not what he wanted from her! He wanted to taste the sweetness of her kisses, feel the fire of her soul, and enjoy the softness of her body molded to his own in frenzied rhapsody. Yes, that was what he wanted. All his life, he had been accustomed to having his wishes and desires granted to him at the precise moment the urge came upon him. But now, patience alone would win him the prize he sought. He wanted this fiery southern beauty who was obsessed with recapturing her father's plantation. As he moved back onto deck with her, he almost believed he would trade Shadows-in-the-Mist for one exquisite night in her arms.

Dropping into a wooden deck chair, Grant watched her shadowy figure move about. She disappeared for a moment as she fetched a lamp from her cabin where, to his disappointment, she must have taken a moment to loop the tie of her robe. He watched her take two small goblets from a pocket, pop the cork from the brandy bottle, and pour the golden liquid into them. When she turned, a goblet in each hand, her allure made it almost impossible for him to perform the simple task of breathing.

Leaning forward, he took the goblet from her and thanked her. Delilah sat in another chair and pulled her feet beneath the hem of her robe. A twinkle in his powder-blue eyes, Grant lifted his goblet. "Shall we toast that new friendship now, Miss Delilah Wickley?"

Delilah lifted her glass. "To better days, no more

quarrels, and smiles rather than frowns." Delilah looked at him as if she had something on her mind. He did not have to wait long to find out what it was. "Tell me, Grant . . . What if I were able to come up with enough money to buy Shadows-in-the-Mist at a considerable profit to you. Would you be inclined to sell it to me?"

Instantly, Grant remembered the morning in the mercantile and a pretty young woman being forced to sell her family jewels. "I really don't know. I've grown quite accustomed to the place."

"Horse feathers! You've been here just over a month. How can you grow accustomed to a place in so short a time?"

Grant's teeth flashed in a teasing smile. "Land is like a woman. If it makes you feel good, you form a bond right off. If The Shadows was a woman, I would be hopelessly lost in her arms. The first moment I saw her, I was seduced by her beauty."

An area of dirt compared to a woman? She would not allow the comparison to ruffle her feminine feathers. "Speaking of women, have you ever been married?" she responded.

The question made his blood run both hot and cold at the same time. Beyond the bayou, the hoot of an owl ricocheted through the darkness. "That is a haunting sound, isn't it?" Grant said, in an attempt to change the subject of conversation.

Delilah, however, was intrigued by his discomfort. "Have you?" she repeated.

He looked up with a feeble smile. "Have what?"

"Been married."

Grant downed his brandy and stood up. He could not allow her to see how it prickled him to be interrogated about something so disagreeable. "Yes, I've been married."

She had believed him to be a bachelor. She took the empty goblet he handed her. "Did your wife die?"

"No."

"Did she divorce you?"

"No."

"Did you divorce her?"

"No."

What other ways were there out of a marriage? "Oh, I . . . Well, then, I must assume you are still married?"

"Assume what you will."

Delilah smiled reflectively, flames dancing in her golden eyes. She was not sure why he suddenly seemed so hostile. "I see . . . The woman is married but not the man?"

She had certainly touched on a most disagreeable aspect of his life. The very thought of Madeleine Vail made Grant's skin crawl—the way she had played on his gentlemanly honor, then had used tears and feminine despair to win his sympathy and drag him to the altar. Extricating himself from the clutches of the scheming woman had almost proved fatal. He still bore the scar of the razor-sharp letter opener she had driven into the back of his shoulder during one of her rages. His only guilt was having to leave Dustin, though the little boy was not his natural son, in the care of a madwoman. Thank God Madeleine's faithful housekeeper was there to supervise her mothering.

"I see you are not answering, Grant."

Startled by her feminine voice in the silence, Grant felt his nerves jump. A little voice inside him warned him not to respond too hotly to her chiding, because she might become annoyingly persistent. In order to quell his silent rage, he again smiled, though it was so stiff he was sure his face would crack and fall apart. A dull ache knotted inside. "I did not have a happy marriage. It was one of convenience, and I thank God it is over." He turned toward Delilah, his hands hanging limply at his sides. "Strange how I can go for a walk because I cannot sleep, be invited by a very beautiful woman to have a brandy aboard a riverboat, and eventually leave with my nerves more frayed than when I left my house," he remarked.

Just as Delilah stood, a burst of warm wind flooded the deck and snuffed the light of the oil lamp. Surprised by the sudden darkness, her foot caught on the edge of the chair and she fell forward, landing full against Grant and nearly sending him toppling over the rail and into the current of Bayou Boeuf.

She knew that her cheeks were awash with color and was thankful for the concealment of darkness. "I do apologize for my clumsiness," she said, attempting to extricate herself from his grip.

But he did not release her; rather, his hands at her back drew her closer to him. "I believe that everything happens for a reason, Delilah. You were meant to be in my arms."

Delilah's heart pounded; she was sure her blood had come to a boil and was searing through her veins. Her legs suddenly felt weak and she was sure she would loose her footing and fall, despite the security of his embrace. She wanted to feel his iron-hard muscles beneath her fingertips, to enjoy the warmth of his breath upon her cheek. But was her body's betrayal stronger than her hatred for him? She was suddenly a flurry of nerves and conflicts. She wanted to wrench herself free of him and give him a good piece of her mind, and yet an ache within her kept her a willing prisoner in his arms. She was enchanted by his touch, wanting him in a way she had never experienced.

He was a Yankee-Doodle dog, a rogue gambler . . . but she wanted to be part of him, now, without delay and the constraints of clothing separating them. She was pleasured by the very thought of being with him . . .

As though he had read her thoughts, Grant's full, masculine mouth descended to capture her willing, seductive one. His masterful caresses awakened a flurry of turmoils within her. Should she stop him while there was still time? But the words would not come. As she felt herself being eased back against the hardness of a deck lounger and the damp gauze of her gown was catching on a splinter, her robe an aggravating barrier now being dropped to the floor, she felt the torrent of his kisses, his tongue teasing its way between her teeth, his hands at the small of her back, easing downward to squeeze her firm buttocks, the hardness of his groin against her abdomen.

But no, she could not do this, not within three hundred yards of her parents' graves. What would her father think? He had raised her to be chaste and moral . . . to save herself for marriage.

Without warning, she gasped and scooted out from under him. Even in the darkness of the moon-bathed deck, the current now gently rolling beneath them, she could see the surprise in his crystal-blue gaze.

"What is wrong, Delilah?"

"I—I cannot do this."

"Why the hell not?"

Delilah shook her head to clear her thoughts. "It isn't right." She could still feel the searing flashes of pleasure flooding her veins and she trembled violently, hoping to expel the vicious betrayal within her.

Anger rose within Grant. His hands balled into tight fists. "Dammit, Delilah, you do not do this to a man. A tease is the worst kind of woman!"

"I — I did not encourage you — "

"You did not stop me!" He reached for her, his hand grazing her breasts as it captured her wrist, though she seemed not to notice. "Do you know what most men would do to a woman who does this?"

She attempted to extricate her wrist but he would not allow it. "Take her by force," she answered. "But . . ." Her eyes clouded in a mixture of apprehension and, he was not sure, was it fear . . . or desire? "You would not be so ungentlemanly, would you, Grant?" With her free hand she retrieved her robe and drew it between their two bodies.

He wanted to stand, but the pain in his loins would not allow it. He slumped back, his eyes closing. "I wish to hell I was everything you think I am! If you were a virgin before my visit aboard this blasted boat, you wouldn't be after!"

His doubt as to her state of chasteness gave her strength where none of his other words had. She shot to her feet, wresting her hand away from his brutal grip. "How dare you insinuate that I am — am — "

"Promiscuous? How do I know that you're not?"

"No man has known me. No man!"

He looked down at her, trying not to drown in her loveliness. His voice took on a tone of indifference. "Well, I don't know that, do I?"

Delilah would not allow the devilishly handsome Yankee to stir her passions. "Nor are you likely to find out, Grant Emerson."

Coming to his feet, he swept her into his arms, a move she did not protest. He held her close, his mouth touching her flushed features ever so softly. "One day, Delilah, one day you will . . ."

When his words trailed off, she shot at him, "Will what? Be your latest conquest?"

"No, my wild southern beauty . . . I will be yours—" She did not protest his gentle kiss, though his smile prickled the anger within her. But when his smile faded, and his look became serious, she knew that his arms—no matter how hard she fought him—were her destiny.

When she looked at him, her eyes were soft and warm. And mirrored in the depths of his own gaze she saw where she wanted to be.

Part Two

Nine

"You simply must let me go, Grant," she ordered, though not a single note of sincerity marked her words.

"Do you really want me to?"

A shale of lightning flashed on the horizon, momentarily bathing the deck of the riverboat in light. That morning, Philo had said a summer storm would come upon them within twenty-four hours. In the many years Philo had been at The Shadows, Delilah had never known him to be wrong when it came to the weather. "You'd best get back to your house. You'll be caught in the storm."

"It is too hot to storm. Answer me, Delilah . . . do you really want me to let you go?"

With a halfhearted push, Delilah put distance between them. She stooped to retrieve her robe and quickly pulled it on, though she was sure he had managed to drink his fill of her scant attire during the brief interlude of light. Large, steady drops of rain began to spatter then upon the deck. "What did I tell you, Grant?" she said with feigned annoyance. "You will be soaked through to the bone by the time you reach the house."

He drew his hands to his slim hips. "I believe I could bear a cool rain, after what you did to me," he replied.

"I did nothing to you!" Even as she spoke sharply, she wanted to hurl herself into his arms and feel his gentle hands span her waist. She wanted to feel the alien desires flood her body, the awakening of hidden pleasures.

How astute he was, for scarcely was she aware of his movements before she was being pulled back into his arms as though he had guessed her scandalous thoughts. His mouth dipped to her own, touching it with such gentle kisses, they were more like teasing whispers. "You are beautiful, Delilah. I will never forget the first moment I saw you—" Dark shadows mixed with the flash of lightning gave her face a strangely haunting glow. As the rain pelted upon them, Grant's glazed eyes drank in her loveliness, his iron-hard chest cushioning the rise and fall of her firm, small breasts. "I wanted to take you in my arms then."

"Pooh . . . I was lying upon the ground covered in grass and dirt—"

Dare he tell her about that morning in the mercantile? Would it spoil the moment of her willingness and her surrender in his arms. She was a proud young woman . . . she would not want to know he had overheard such an embarrassing moment. "I did not see grass and dirt. I saw a wild beauty aching to be loved . . . to be touched and held and nurtured by a man's adoration. I need you in my arms."

"I—I—" Where was her strength when she so desperately needed it? She did not want to be a giddy, stammering girl. She wanted to avert her gaze, wrench herself away, kick him in the shin, and scream insults and degradations at him. But the woman inside her wanted to be held and loved and needed by this tall, virile man whose very touch stirred her to depths of desire. In a moment that seemed like a thousand hours she recalled all the joy and happiness that had touched her life . . . but never could she remember feeling as happy as she did now, even soaked through to the bone in the deluge of rain. She felt as if Grant's arms had been made exclusively to hold her and awaken her passions, his body formed by the gods to complement her own. She felt that his searing kisses could not possibly be enjoyed by another, and that his eyes could glaze in passion for her and her alone. So he was a Yankee and a rogue gambler—he could not have chosen where he would be born, he could not quiet his adventurous heart.

The sudden intensity of his gaze snapped her from her thoughts, and the currents pulsating throughout her body pulled her like a magnet toward him. Rain dripped from the tip of his nose onto her cheek; his clothing, heavy and clinging, touched her cool skin. She wanted him . . . oh, how she wanted him! Still, her rebellion was as strong as well-forged steel. "You do know that I hate you," she whispered. "Surely, you must know that."

"I know," he whispered in return. "But I plan to change that." His mouth dipped again to her own, claiming the trembling prize. "Shall I withdraw into that blasted house up there . . . or shall I stay?"

Delilah squirmed against him. She should laugh in his face and order him away, tell him again how she loathed him. Her mouth parted, but she was unable to say those things. Rather, she waited for his mouth to press again to her own, an answer to his inquiry as readable as a spoken invitation.

The rain stopped as suddenly as it had begun. Taking a moment to remove his boots and soaked jacket, Grant approached and held her close for a moment. She enjoyed the musky, manly scent of him.

How easily he picked her up in his arms, cradling

her gently, the flashes of lightning guiding him as he moved along the deck and into the cabin where he knew she slept. He could not count the nights he had walked past the riverboat and seen that one dim light shining from within, wanting to go to her but held back by the uncertainty of her loathing. But that feeling existed no longer. She had claimed to hate him, but her luscious mouth, and her heart, were not speaking the same language.

Feeling the softness of the mattress and her bed coverings beneath her body sent a rush of panic through Delilah. She scooted to a sitting position and her hand moved to his shoulder. "I am wet. I don't want to soak my bed," she explained. Then, more truthfully, "No, no, that is not it. I—I'm sorry, I cannot do this." She pressed at her forehead as though it pained her. "Don't you understand, Grant? I want The Shadows, I would do anything to get it back . . . even—" Her moisture-sheened gaze lifted to his shadowed one.

"Even make love to me . . . perhaps even marry me, but require a prenuptial agreement making The Shadows community property? Then, I imagine, your plan was to make me so miserable that I'd sign over my share and hightail it for the East."

Her lips parted, her surprise naked before him. "Yes, I *would* go that far. The idea must sicken you."

He smiled, his hands slowly inching up her calves, then catching the hem of her bed clothing to take it with him in his travels. "Then begin your strategy, my southern beauty. I am receptive to it."

Her hands landed upon his, halting their progress. Delilah saw how calm he was, even with his eyes dark with passion, how his chest rose in long breaths against the fabric of his silk shirt. "Though you questioned my word before, I tell you again that I am a virgin," she suddenly blurted out, though she knew not

144

the reason why. If she wanted to quell his intentions, her declaration might only make her more desirable to him. A man would want from a woman what no man had enjoyed before.

"Then, my enchanting Delilah, I will take you places where you have never been before."

Her pulse raced wildly, a strange mixture of dreaded anticipation and wickedly wonderful delight mixing within her. She had never felt like this—the heat rippling through her rain-soaked body, the fervid intensity of her breathing, the way her flesh almost leaped to meet his hands as they moved deftly over the silkiness of her thighs. She wanted to be free of her gown, to rip the barrier of his shirt down his muscular arms and feel their flesh meld together in frantic rhapsody.

Grant's eyes sparkled. So hot was her skin beneath the droplets of rain and his searching hands that he could hardly give credence to her claim of virginity. Still, he could not bear the thought that another man might have touched her like this. He wanted to believe she was an untouched treasure, with mysteries and secrets waiting to be discovered. With a throaty groan his hands rose and entwined through the rich damp masses of chestnut hair.

"This is the last moment, Delilah. If you do not stop me now there will be no turning back."

She knew she should push him away. But even if The Shadows was to be her reward for rejecting him, she knew she could not. She wanted to be in his arms, beneath him, conquering and being conquered by him. She had never shared more than baby kisses with any other man; she wanted to know the passions of man and woman together . . . and the moment was right.

"No, I will not stop you—"

His mouth claimed her own, silencing her words. Then he pushed himself up and slowly, methodically removed his wet shirt, watching the movements of her eyes as they gazed over him. He rested a moment on his knees and Delilah wondered if his hip was bothering him. But he was not carrying the cane.

Rather, Grant himself wondered if he should remove himself from her, leaving her untouched. She was young and homeless, except for the lodgings he had offered her. Was he taking advantage of a woman at her most vulnerable? But even as conflicts tugged at him, he reached out to take her in his arms, pulling her against him. "Get rid of this, Delilah—" In one fluid move, her robe joined his shirt upon the floor. As his mouth sought her own trembling one, her body stiffened. Though guilt flooded him, he knew he could not deny himself the sweetness of this treasure.

Passion burned brightly between them. If Delilah were indeed a virgin, he had to build her passions to a point where there was no turning back, but his body was like an explosion that could not be contained. His fingers moved beneath the scant material of her gown at her shoulder, halting as she whispered her fear.

His mouth brushed each of her exquisite, translucent eyelids, the small throbbing pulse at her temple. "There is no need to be frightened. I will try not to hurt you." His fingers again began their travels, and the sight of her lovely breasts were his first rewards. When she shyly attempted to cover herself, he took her hands and held them to his chest. "Don't, Delilah. You have nothing to be ashamed of. No man will appreciate your beauty the way I do." Easing her to the soft covers of the bed, he drew her hands up to each side of the pillow beside her head and twisted the water from her hair. His hips straddled her; she could feel the hardness of him through the thick fabric of his trousers. Her hair was a wild disarray; she tossed it to free her mouth for his offering, his gentle caresses, then the almost brutal possession of his kiss.

When at last his mouth descended to capture one of her ivory breasts with its rosebud peak, Delilah drew in a quick breath of air. She could almost feel the heated convulsion building within her slender frame. What was this man doing to her? What was he doing to make her want more than she could imagine in her wildest dreams? The tingle in her breasts, teased by his kisses, surged throughout her, until her lungs threatened to explode with a want she had never before experienced. Unconsciously, her body arched upward, pressing against his searing caresses and willing them to go lower — to plunge beneath the material of her gown twisting at her waist as she frantically sought to escape from it.

Grant suddenly released her fingers. When he pushed up, Delilah watched him coyly from beneath the fringes of her golden eyes. When she heard the clink of his buckle and saw the movements of his hand at his waist, her eyes darted to take in his sharp features — his full, sensual mouth, his glazed, powder-blue eyes. She could not bring herself to witness him undressing, though she wanted to. She knew only that, with scarcely a moment's passage, his hard, naked form rested against her and his hand moved beneath the filmy gown to ease it downward.

With a gentle nudging he slipped between her silken thighs, his hands moving fluidly up from her knees, along the curve of her thighs and hips and plunging into the small of her back to will her to him. His kisses trailed over her passion-sensitive breasts and the small, throbbing pulse in her neck. She felt his hardness against her thighs and, without conscious awareness of her movements, felt her knees drawing

147

up to hug his slender hips. At that moment, he pushed up again, his hands masterfully caressing her in places that had never enjoyed such exquisite attention. Panic and wondrous anticipation seized her from within, and a small moan escaped her.

"Don't you want me, Grant? she softly asked him when his movements ceased.

"God, yes," he replied. "I just can't get enough of looking at you—" With a low growl, he dropped to her and drew her roughly into his arms. His left hand lowered, darted over the soft, flat plane of her abdomen, and his fingers found the treasure he was seeking—moist, warm, begging for his attentions. He almost wished there was not a question of her virginity so that he could fill himself with the urgency paining through his body. She was ready for him; he could tell.

When at last Delilah felt the pressure of him against her—there—her body stiffened, even as her long legs wrapped around his hard ones in delightful anticipation. When he gently rocked back and forth, scarcely allowing himself to enter her, she wondered if this was all there was to lovemaking. But as his hot body suddenly dropped to hers, he plunged deeply into her, and his mouth covered her own, drinking in her cry of pain. For one brief moment, she thought her insides were being ripped apart by the brutality of his thrust.

Wrapped within the heat of her, Grant kissed away the tears before they lost themselves in her hairline. His full, moist mouth caressed every burning inch of her face, his fingers wrapped through the strands of her wet hair. But the pained convulsing of her body instantly stilled, and her mouth lifted to accept his kisses with trembling desire.

"I will never hurt you again, Delilah." Emotion moved his voice. "I swear—"

148

As her hips moved timidly upward, to accept him fully, Grant continued his own search for fulfillment. His cadence, at first slow and methodical, soon erupted into hard thrusts. He drank in her tiny gasps, caressed her lovely eyelids, returning again and again to her full, sensual mouth and the teasings of her tongue.

Her firm breasts were like a brand against him, her mouth honey sweet against his, her long fingernails gently raking across the muscles of his back. He was unaware that the rain had begun again with brutal force and of the pounding of the riverboat on the storm-tossed currents of Bayou Boeuf.

For Delilah, the ecstasy of this, her first moment of lovemaking, was an experience she did not want to end. His pace matched the strength of the storm claiming the night, his eyes like the pale flashes of lightning upon the far horizon, his arms like those of the mighty oaks surrounding The Shadows-in-the-Mist. He plunged deeper and deeper still, his rhythm matching her own, his arms wrapping around her to pull her to her side for a moment before her back thrashed again to the mattress. She felt wild and wicked in his arms, her teeth nipping playfully at him as their joining reached a pinnacle of power and possession. Something wonderful was happening deep within; gripping spasms and pulsations she was sure he could feel with that part of him inside her. Then, with a long, low groan and a seizure of rapid thrusts, she was filled with sweet wondrous liquid fire, and he collapsed in an exhausted heap upon her.

So, this was lovemaking . . . Her life before this night suddenly felt wasted and empty. With the body of Grant Emerson—a man she had sworn to hate—covering her own in the aftermath of ecstasy, Delilah felt that she had been reborn just moments ago in his arms.

Momentarily, his breathing slowed and he moved to her side, his fingers brushing back the tangled locks of her hair, half dried by their shared moments of passion, lying upon her forehead. Then he took her chin and coaxed her gaze to his own. "Are you sorry, Delilah?"

She chuckled softly. "Yes, I am sorry . . . sorry I have never done this before."

His mouth gently grazed her own. "That, I am not sorry for. I could not bear the thought of another man being with you . . . like this." As he spoke, he wrapped a lock of her hair around his finger. "Have you ever noticed, Delilah, the tight little curls fringing your hairline when you are damp from exertion?"

"That is from the rain, not the dampness of passion," she said, smiling as her fingers eased across his waist. "Now . . . don't you think you should dress and return to your house before dawn breaks?"

He arched a pale, copper-colored eyebrow. "Oh? Love me and kick me out? Is that the plan? I thought . . ." His mouth brushed her cheek, "that I would sleep here with you."

She shot to a sitting position, knocking him to his back. "No, you cannot do that. What will the slaves think?"

Grant halted her attempts to cover herself with the sheet. "Don't ever worry about what other people think of you, Delilah. All that matters is what you think of yourself."

Her senses absorbed his masculinity, his questioning gaze holding her own as he awaited a response. All at once, she was only vaguely aware of her nakedness; after all, hadn't they just made wicked, wonderful love? And wouldn't it be foolish to try now to cover herself? Still, she *did* care what Mozelle would think if

150

she knew what a hypocrite she was. She had sworn to hate Grant Emerson, and to ruin him, but she had lain in his arms in splendid ecstasy. If Mozelle knew, she would never let her forget her vow of eternal hatred.

"Please, Grant, I am not ready for anyone to know. If it were to get around, I would have a terrible reputation. I don't feel like a hussy, but people would think I am."

"You are no such thing, Delilah."

Her gaze lifted coyly. "Then what am I . . . now that I have made love to you?"

He wanted to respond, "My woman," but was not sure how she would react to that. There was still a fierce independence within her, and a stubbornness he had never seen in another woman. One day, though, he would speak those words to her, and she would be receptive to them. He was that sure of himself.

"Well, I certainly cannot say you are merely my friend," he said in due time. "For the moment, we will not worry about what label to attach to you." Swinging his feet to the floor, he retrieved his trousers and began pulling them on. "I will respect your wishes and go home to my own bed. When he had pulled on his shirt, leaving it unbuttoned down his torso, he pulled her into his arms at the edge of the bed where she knelt. She had pulled the sheet up between her legs and was holding it protectively to her. "Don't worry, little angel, you are safe for the time being." Putting space between them, his fingers rose to caress her flushed cheek. "Will you ride with me in the afternoon?"

"It might be raining."

He looked out the window across the half-light of the cabin. "The moon is free of its cover of darkness. The storm is over."

"If I finish my work at the ledgers, I might."

"Good. I'll see you then."

"You will be gone most of the day?"

"I . . ." He hesitated. "I am riding into Alexandria with Ellie."

"Oh . . ." Her mouth pinched into a fine line. "Have a good trip."

He laughed good-naturedly. "You are not jealous, are you?"

"Horse feathers!" Quickly retrieving her robe, she pulled it on. "What you do is your business."

When she stood, he pulled her into his arms. "You *are* jealous. I like that."

With a childish "harrumph," she extracted herself and turned away. "You'd better go," She did not look at him; she suspected he was smiling. When she heard his bootsteps on the planked floor of the outer deck, she hurried after him. Midway along the gangplank, he turned. "When will you be back?" she asked.

The darkness of the night hid his slight smile. "Before our ride, Delilah. Anything else?"

Her hand lightly caressed the peacock-blue wood rail separating her from the man she had just lain with. As he left, she found herself wondering when they would again share another night of passionate magic. She longed for the moment she would be in his arms once again.

Jealous! Pooh! How could he accuse her of such an insecurity! He had known Ellie McPherson for three years. Surely, if he'd had any interest in her as anything other than an acquaintance, a further relationship would have developed. Delilah turned dreamily, caring not that her robe fell open. She felt confident that when Grant wanted to be with a woman again, that way, he would come to her.

* * *

The last crack of lightning had dragged Philbus from his bed. It had been close; he feared that the silo in the east pasture had been struck. A dim red aura shimmered on the horizon in that direction.

Leaving Mozelle asleep, he dressed, pulled on his boots, and moved toward the stable. Saddling his gelding, he soon moved cautiously through the muddy trails westward on the bayou.

He could see from a distance that the silo had, indeed, been struck. By the time he reached the pasture, he met up with Joby Cade, one of the slaves from a neighboring plantation. Nothing much could be done; the fire, high in the silo, was almost extinguished by the steady downpour of rain.

"What brings you out, Joby Cade?"

"Miz Anna thought it was one of our silos."

The two men sat atop their horses in the rain and watched the progression of the fire. "Miz Anna and Miz Violet still at each other's throats?" Philbus asked. The bickering of the two cousins was notorious along The Boeuf.

"Naw, they tryin' to git along, since Massah St. Cyr took to his bed. He's been feelin' a mite poorly."

When the fire had died out, Philbus unfolded his arms and one of his large hands landed full upon Joby's shoulder. "I'd best be gittin' back to Mozelle, fo' she be thinkin' I's meetin' a wench out here."

Joby Cade laughed. "You do that. Lovey might be a thinkin' the same thing of me."

The two men mounted their horses and rode in different directions. The St. Cyr plantation shared a common bond to the one now owned by Grant Emerson. Shadow Marsh and Shadows-in-the-Mist had both borrowed part of their names from the haunting ribbon of shadowy bayou connecting the two plantations.

A few minutes later, Philbus set the gelding on a steady pace toward The Shadows. But in a particularly narrow and treacherous turn in the trail, the big gelding lost its balance, slid on its haunches, and gently deposited Philbus on his buttocks beside the trail.

A little annoyed, Philbus fought for his footing, hoping to capture the reins of the horse before it high-tailed it for home without him. But the spooked horse bolted from him in the darkness and Philbus heard its plodding hooves fading in the distance. "Lawd! Blasted hoss. I's gonna whop his hide when I gits home."

His bed was a good half-mile away. Getting his bearings in the darkness, Philbus moved off the trail, taking a shortcut through a stand of pines. But he'd hardly moved a hundred yards before his boot caught in the root of a tree, sending him facedown in the dirt.

Scraping the mud and pine straw from his face, he cursed inwardly. His eyes stung and his mouth was full of debris from the ground. When, at last, moonlight sifted through the trees, giving him a clue as to his intended direction, he planted his palms firmly upon the ground on either side of his body, preparing to push himself up. But as his eyes readjusted to the predawn darkness, his movements ceased.

There, not two feet away from his face, was a partially exposed human skull, a dark, ragged hole where an eye might once have been.

Ten

Wringing her hands in a nervous frenzy, Mozelle was pacing the foyer when Grant entered the house. "Massah . . . Philbus rode out 'bout an hour ago an' his hoss jes' come back widout him. We's fierce worried." She rushed the words so quickly her breathing came in gasps.

"Why was he out this time of night?"

"Big crack o' lightnin', massah, suh. Philbus be thinkin' maybe de silo be struck. His pa an' a couple others rode out alookin' fer him. Jes' want ya to know, massah, so ya's don't be thinkin' Philbus run away."

A moment of darkness hung on Grant's brow. It annoyed him that the slaves had attached a label of cruelty to him simply because he was not a native Louisianian. "Why on earth would I think that?" he responded irately.

"New massah, don' be knowin' us folks like'n Massah Wickley. Philbus, he got real stubborn heart, but he ain't got no fool notions of runnin' away an' gittin' de hide whipt of'n 'im."

Annoyed, Grant turned back to the entrance. "I think what we have to worry about is Philbus being hurt."

Instinctively, Mozelle's fingers closed over his forearm for a moment. "Massah . . . massah, please, if'n

155

Philbus hurt, let me tends to him an' gits him well. Don't be a sellin' him off 'cuz ya might be thinkin' he's worthless. Please, massah—"

"Blast!" He pivoted back, his eyes so dark they might have taken on a new dimension. "Why do you constantly have to make me out to be a heartless villain? I'm damned sick of it!"

Though she was almost left speechless by his outburst, she would have attempted to apologize. But her new master gave her no opportunity. The front door slammed resoundingly and his bootsteps faded across the gallery and down the steps.

Moments later, Grant entered the stable and led his horse into the walkway. When he retrieved his saddle from its usual place, a young slave emerged from the darkness of the tack room, rubbing his eyes. "Massah wants Hank to be a saddlin' his hoss?"

"I can take care of it. Bring me the horse Philbus rides."

The boy scratched absently at his head. "Grampappy take it wid him when he ride out, massah."

"Who's your grampappy?"

"Philo, massah. He be's my grampappy."

Grant recalled Daisy mentioning to him that Philo's daughter, Clara, had died two years before. Philbus and Mozelle had no children, so the spindle-legged boy standing a few feet from him must be Clara's son. His voice softened; he'd always had a soft spot for orphans. "Go on back to your bed, Hank."

The boy turned to leave, his fingers still digging at the tight curls matted with straw.

Grant had just mounted his horse and emerged from the stable when the men came riding up. A mud-caked Philbus edged the gelding to Grant's side. "Massah, I found somethin' out yonder in de woods

156

what ya needs ta be aseein'."

"Whatever it is can wait until morning. Are you all right?"

"Jes' took a tumble from dis clumsy old hoss. What I found can't wait, massah. Bodie . . ." Philbus turned his attentions to another slave astride his horse. "Git a lantern from the stable fer me."

"What did you find, Philbus?"

Philbus slowly shook his head as he again faced Grant Emerson. "Found somethin' too awful to name, massah. Ya's just have to see fer yo'self."

Shortly, four mounted men, including Grant, were riding to the west. None saw Delilah emerging from the riverboat.

She had heard the men's voices, strangely out of place for that time of morning when the loudest noises were usually the chirps of crickets. Failing in her attempt to intercept the men before they rode out, she joined Mozelle on the gallery. "Where are the men going?" Delilah asked,

Mozelle shrugged her shoulders. "Don't know, Missy. Philbus say he found somethin' awful out yon in de woods and dey all ride out thataway."

"Something awful . . . they weren't more precise?"

"Naw'm." Mozelle crossed her arms loosely beneath her ample bosom. "Was my eyes deceivin' me, Missy, or was de massah comin' from de direction of de riverboat?"

Delilah mentally slumped, though her voice remained firm. "You were certainly mistaken, Mozelle. If he was near the boat, then he was spying upon me."

Narrowing her eyes, her full mouth pressed tightly. "Ya's lookin' a might peculiar, Missy. Dem cheeks all ashinin' like dey's been pinched. Like dey's been kissed and fluffed all over."

157

Silence. Delilah knew if she reacted too hotly, the perceptive Mozelle would assume she was right. Thus, her tone remained calm and slightly sarcastic as she replied, "I do declare, Mozelle. Knowing how I feel about that horrid, self-centered Yankee, how can you tease me so?"

"I 'spect I know how ya feel, Missy, but we won't quarrel 'bout it, will we?"

Delilah brightened. "I sure could go for a cup of cinnamon tea."

Mozelle turned toward the house, expecting her former mistress to join her. "Sho', Missy, jes' so long as ya don't go snoopin' about de massah's house ag'in."

In the kitchen, Delilah could hardly keep her mind on Mozelle's small talk. She was curious about the mystery that had dragged the men from the plantation and wondered what could be so important that it couldn't wait until morning.

Grant waited for Bodie to approach with the lantern before he got down on one knee beside the shallow grave. Crossing his wrists upon his raised knee, he studied the grisly sight. A small, perfect hole between the eye sockets was a clear indication that the man — or woman — had been murdered. But why, when, and by whom?

Except for Bodie, the other men were standing back. After long moments of scrutiny, Grant exposed more of the skull and the gruesomely grinning mouth with all of its front teeth missing. His movements caused the head to detach from the spine, and it rolled slowly across the mud. "Dat man's gonna come up out o' there an' haunt us fo' sho'," one of the men whispered gruffly.

The man had been dead long enough for the bones to be clean of any remains. "Any of you boys have a sack?" Grant asked. "We're going to take him back."

"Jesus Lawd!" The urgent exclamation was uttered by the same man.

"Need a spade, massah?" Philbus asked.

"He's practically lying on top of the ground," Grant replied. "Just bring me a sack. I'll get him up out of here."

Over the next few minutes, as Grant exposed a skeleton almost as tall as he himself was, he was fairly certain, from the rotting remnants of clothing and accessories found in the grave, that it was indeed a man. A large-caliber firearm almost fell apart in his hands, and what was left of a wallet contained a few coins, only one in good enough condition to bear a date: 1850. Whoever the fellow was, he couldn't have been killed more than six years before. Half an hour later, the skeleton lay full length upon a thick bed of wet leaves. Gathering canteens from all the men, he was able to clean the bones well enough to notice small things that might possibly lead to identification. The bones of the man's left arm were shorter than the right arm, almost dwarflike, and a twisted leg bone indicated that he'd suffered a serious injury at some point in his life.

As he somberly began placing the separated bones into the sack Philbus had handed him, he detected a rattle inside the skull. Momentarily, a small, cylindrical bit of metal fell into his hand—the bullet that apparently had killed the unfortunate fellow. He dropped it into the pocket of his trousers.

After he had tied a length of twine around the sack, Grant stood up. He would have handed it to one of the men, but he could see that every one of them was spooked. Then, from the ground, something gleamed in the last flickers of the lantern. He bent and picked up a round object to which a length of chain was attached. Except for one small patch midway up the chain, what appeared to be a watch and fob was tarnished and pitted by the length of time it had spent in the ground. His fingers sank through the mud at the back, feeling what might possibly turn out to be engraving, and a solid clue to the man's identification. Loosening the ties of the sack, he dropped that most crucial piece of evidence in with the skeleton.

"One hell of a night, eh, boys?" he remarked as he mounted his horse.

"Sho' is, massah," Bodie replied, and the others muttered beneath their breath.

It was almost four o'clock. The sun would rise in just over an hour and another long day would begin at Shadows-in-the-Mist. After her tea, Delilah had returned to the riverboat to bathe and don a comfortable day dress and then went to Mozelle's kitchen to await the return of the men. She was anxious to learn details of their discovery, but a little apprehensive, too. First and foremost in her mind was something that might reflect badly on her dead father.

When, at last, several horses were heard approaching at the stable, Mozelle and Delilah both moved out to the porch. Moments later, Delilah speculatively eyed an obviously exhausted Grant Emerson approaching the house. With the mystery about to be disclosed, she did not even think about their love-making earlier that morning. That part of her night was like a dream, and she wondered if it had truly happened.

His boot had just touched the first step when Delilah asked, "Well, Grant, what is it?"

He continued to climb the steps, then looked from Delilah to Mozelle and back again. "Let's have a cup of coffee. I'll tell you all about it." To Mozelle, he said, "You may be excused from your kitchen duties if you wish to tend your husband."

"Was he hurt, massah?"

"Just a couple of scraped elbows."

Moments later, when Delilah and Grant stood together in the foyer, he attempted to pull her to him. "I just want to know what you've found, Grant."

"Not even a hug?" he asked, his voice almost admonishing. He viewed their lovemaking that morning as an indication that a little hug would certainly not be out of line. Why was she being so standoffish? When she stiffly remained outside his grasp, his hand stretched out to her. "If not a hug, then company over a cup of coffee?"

Delilah wanted to be in his arms, to be held close and caressed and kissed. It was all she could do to pretend her detachment. "I'll keep you company . . . if you're going to tell me what you found!"

Grant chuckled, clasping his hand across her shoulder as they walked. "Delilah, you're as skittery as a wild kitten. I might even begin to believe you are responsible for what we dug up in the woods."

She suddenly felt weak. She would have fallen, except for the strength of his hand holding her up. Soon, she sat at the table, and Grant was pouring them both a cup of coffee. He soon took a chair across from her.

He sat forward and took a sip of the steaming hot liquid. "What did you find?" Delilah blurted impatiently.

A quizzical look arched his brow. "Find? What do you mean?"

Anger sharpened her voice. "Tell me now, Grant!"

He did, without a moment's delay. When he completed the last of the grisly details, he asked her what she thought.

Delilah knew a deathly pallor had touched her features. All she could think about were the frequent nights in the four months before his death that she had awakened her screaming father from his nightmares. What had he said? *He's dead, Delilah girl . . . didn't mean to kill him . . . gun went off . . . buried him in the woods.* She'd always thought, in his waking moments, that she'd convinced him he'd just had a nightmare. Could what she have heard been his conscience speaking . . . a desperate need by a man in failing health to confess his sins before God?

Becoming aware of Grant's scrutiny, Delilah shrugged shyly. "Many years ago travelers were attacked by Indians," she said. "He was probably a victim."

"He had an 1850 coin on him . . . and a gold pocket watch. Indians—anyone—would have taken his valuables. And Indians in these parts did not normally use guns."

Mention of the watch piqued her interest. She remembered her father's claim that he had lost the watch that had been his father's and his grandfather's before him. He had been sickened by the loss . . . Had it been six years ago?

"The remains of this poor man . . . is that what was in the sack you took into the stable?"

"It was. When I journey into Alexandria with Ellie today, I'll stop by the sheriff's office and find out what I should do with it."

"I wouldn't put too much stock in the sheriff," Delilah commented. "He's a high-handed planter who probably doesn't bother to learn the names of his deputies. You would be better to bury the fellow in the cemetery and forget about him."

Grant was sure he detected fear in Delilah's voice. "This doesn't sound like the Delilah I've heard so much about along the bayou. The kind, sensitive lady who has the admiration of everyone would never suggest burying a man without trying to learn who he was. Unless . . ." One of his strong forearms locked across the other on the table, "the lady knows something she doesn't want to get around—"

Delilah rose so quickly she upset her coffee. She made no attempt to clean up the liquid now dripping to the floor. "I don't know anything. Why would you think I had anything to do with that fellow's death? I—I was just a sixteen-year-old girl when he died."

Grant rounded the table and hugged her to him, despite her protests. "I was not accusing you, Delilah," he assured her. "I thought perhaps you knew something—"

"I don't know anything!" She wrenched her arms from him and turned away.

"Then tell me—" His hand moved toward her, then fell back to his side, "why you are so sure it was six years ago that he died? Why not last year, or two or three years ago?"

Delilah shut her eyes so forcefully, a pain dragged at her forehead. She prayed he would not notice her trembling. "You said he had a coin dated 1850 in his pocket. I just thought—" From the corner of her eyes she saw him digging into his left pocket.

Grant held his hand out to her. "Look at this, Delilah," he replied. "Here is a coin dated 1852. If I were killed and buried today, would you assume—if you dug me up in a couple of years—that I died in '52?"

She shuddered visibly. "You're being morbid. But I understand your point."

His mouth twitched in amusement. When his hands gently folded over her shoulders, she did not protest. "Just another mystery to solve. I'll wager, dear lady, that whoever killed the fellow was a vagabond who'll never pass this way again."

Her head of chestnut tresses fell gently to his shoulder. She tried to keep the worry out of her voice, but it was impossible. "I hope you're right. I wouldn't want to know that . . ." She did not complete the statement. "Would you mind if I did not work on the books today?" she asked instead. "I'd like to visit Dentley."

He had visited the Wells plantation just last week and had met the likable Thomas Jefferson Wells. "Are you going to ride Bella?" he asked.

"I promise," she laughed, "that I'll only ride the part I've paid for with my last two weeks' wages."

"Don't be racing my chattel against one of Wells's horses."

"Horse feathers! He sold Lecomte this past May. He was the only one who could have given Bella a real challenge."

"If he hadn't sold the horse to Mr. Broeck, I'd have bought him myself, since the locals were so fond of him. He only paid twelve thousand five hundred and the horse was worth twice as much."

"You'd have wasted your money. The poor soul had slowed down miserably the last couple of years. That's why Mr. Wells sold him." She had her reasons for wanting to ride over to Dentley, though she did not feel compelled to give Grant that reason. It would only start an interrogation, and she wasn't up to being questioned.

"He'd slowed down, huh? Is that why Bella could have beat him?"

Turning, she gently slapped her hand to his chest.

"Stop teasing me, Grant Emerson, and give me permission to take the morning off."

Even as she would have withdrawn her hand, he took it and held it lovingly. "Permission granted, my lady," he responded. "And I would hope that one day when you're out visiting, you'll add Ellie to your agenda."

Stubborn pride filled her. She had no reason to back down on her previous opinion that Ellie had known of the sale of The Shadows and had informed Grant Emerson of it. She missed Ellie, but she could not forget her betrayal of their friendship. If anything at all could mend the friendship, it was time . . . and enough of that had not yet passed.

"Ellie will be with you today?" Delilah asked.

"I said one day, not today." Cupping her face gently between his palms, he continued. "You are a very stubborn woman, Delilah Wickley." Then he drew her breathlessly close and his mouth lightly brushed her own. "Promise you'll take care of yourself and be wary of strangers."

Her mouth pinched in disapproval, yet she did not break contact. "Don't treat me like a child, Grant Emerson. After last night . . ." A coy blush rose in her cheeks, "you should realize I am a woman . . . and I can take care of myself," she added as an afterthought.

"Of course, you can—"

"And don't patronize me."

"I didn't mean to. I am merely concerned for you. But let's not banter quarrelsome words, Delilah."

Her voice softened. "I'm sorry. Perhaps I am just tired—"

"We both are. I have things to do today and cannot rest, but you should take a few hours before you go visiting."

"Perhaps I will."

He stood slightly back from her and drank in the vision of her. He sensed that she didn't seem to mind his close scrutiny; he was aware of her eyes holding his, almost giving permission for the bold pleasures he visually sought. In his imaginations, the material of her gown covered little more than the thin shift she had worn that morning . . . the same one he had removed from her. He could almost see the tips of her breasts pressing against the fabric, imagine the flat plane of her stomach and all her sensual curves.

Delilah loved the way he looked at her, his approval evident in the warm darkening of his crystal-blue gaze. His mouth was gently curved into a smile, as though he could not hide his admiration of her, and his fingers wrapped through hers and squeezed ever so tenderly. When he drew her to him and whispered, "You are a man's dream come true," she felt a sweep of relief. He had taken his pleasure with her in the predawn darkness and she had worried that he might now find her less attractive and might even begin avoiding her. But she did not see that happening, not if she interpreted his look correctly.

Abruptly, her eyes dropped as guilt flooded her. Was she really beginning to care for this tall, proud easterner, or was her ultimate goal still to recapture The Shadows, as she had promised her father she would. She didn't want to believe she was so cold and calloused, and yet she knew how determined she could be when she wanted something. A wild array of emotions tugged her from within. She truly wanted to believe that she would not stoop to prostituting herself in order to recapture her home.

"What is on your mind, Delilah?"

She looked up sharply. Had her thoughts been so visible? "Oh, I—I was just feeling the effects of so little sleep," she explained, managing the smallest of smiles. "I really must be going."

He didn't want her to leave. More than that, he didn't want her to visit any other plantation. He was selfish; he would rather she spent the day with him — and more . . . a lifetime. "Very well," he replied against the wishes of his heart, "but don't forget our afternoon ride."

"I won't," she responded, turning toward the door. Then smiling timidly, she offered a challenge. "Perhaps a race. Your old plug against Bella?"

"Perhaps."

Grant tucked his hands into his pockets as she turned with a swish of her skirts and disappeared into the early-morning sun. He sauntered toward the window and watched her as she exchanged a word with Mozelle, touched her hand gently to the head of one of the young boys who offered her a freshly picked berry, waved to Philo, who was already into his work as plantation blacksmith . . . Yesterday, he had seen her almost as a precocious child, today she was a warm, sensitive woman, one who had walked into his heart as though he hadn't built a barrier there after his marriage to Madeleine.

Why did he let thoughts of Madeleine blacken his mood today? He had enough problems with the gruesome discovery that had been made in the pre-dawn darkness. He would have to deal with that in the next few hours, but this afternoon he wanted only to enjoy an afternoon of leisure and uninterrupted pleasure in the company of the lovely temptress who had stolen his heart.

Outside the window, he watched her — the precocious child again — lift her skirts and break into a graceful run toward the riverboat where she had chosen to live. He smiled to himself. If he sold the blasted thing, she would *have* to move into the house.

Moments later, Delilah and Daisy stood on the bayou side of the riverboat, speaking in hushed tones.

"They's found them, Missy? Ya remember when yo' pappy was havin' them dreams, an' it skeert ya real bad. Well, they was somebody kil't, an' they's been found!"

"If my father had anything to do with it, it had to have been accidental," Delilah assured her, her brows pinching together. "Papa couldn't possibly kill anyone. He wasn't a violent man. Dear Lord, Daisy . . ." Delilah squeezed her friend's hands firmly between her own. "Your master has found Papa's watch. It was in the grave with that man. How could he have gotten Papa's watch if he . . ." She refused to finish her statement, but the possibilities crept through her shoulders in a cold shiver.

"Yo' pappy be gone now, Missy. Ain't nothin' ever goin' to hurt him again. What diff'rence do it make?"

"Papa's reputation will be tarnished. That means a lot to me, Daisy. Please—please . . ." she implored, shaking Daisy's hands vigorously, "you've got to help me get Papa's watch out of that bag of bones."

Daisy's eyes widened. She would do anything at all for her former mistress and friend, but this was asking a bit much. "Lawd, Missy, dey's a man inside dere wid de meat all scraped off. Ya's askin' me to put my hands in dere?"

"You've been feeding the kittens in the tack room every morning, Daisy. Please, no one will think anything about your going in there. But if I do—"

"They might think ya's just goin' fer Bella's saddle—"

168

Daisy lifted her eyes to her taller friend. All their lives, the two young women had helped each other, without any questions asked. But this time . . . "Naw'm, Missy, I ain't goin' to put my hands in dere wid dat dead man. But I'll sneak the sack o' bones over to you an' you can stick *your* hand in it."

Shaking her head in dismay, Delilah replied. "Oh, all right, you silly, superstitious ninny. But replace the evidence so that the casual observer will be none the wiser."

"Huh?" Daisy looked genuinely perplexed.

"Put some things in another bag," Delilah explained simply, "a bridle or a halter and hang it in the exact place where the bag of bones is hanging. You know that none of your people are going to bother it, and I'll put the bones back when I leave for my visit to Wellswood and Dentley."

"All right, Missy, but if'n de massah finds out, I's goin' to be whopt right good."

"He's not going to find out, and you know he wouldn't whip you. He's not that kind of man."

Daisy chuckled softly. "Didn't think I'd be hearin' ya sayin' nice things about dat Yankee-Doodle gambler, Missy."

"Hush, Daisy." Delilah clucked her tongue. "Now let's do what has to be done. You don't want your uncle's reputation tarnished, either."

"Whatever dat means, I reckon not, Missy." As the petite Daisy moved toward the steps, she lifted her clean white apron to wipe the sweat from her brow. "Lawd, Missy, we's grown up into women an' we's still gittin' into mischief."

Delilah's gaze drifted with the retreating Daisy. She and Daisy had been born on the same night, had almost drowned together in the same bayou, and now it seemed only right that they should conspire together. Still, guilt and worry pinched at Delilah's conscience. Grant trusted her, and she could well imagine how he would feel if he knew she was hiding still another secret.

Last night, she had been obsessed with recovering her father's gold. This morning, she was obsessed with protecting her father's name. She had little doubt that the death of that man was somehow related to the gold her father and Lathrop had buried that dark December night.

Delilah sighed. Last night the gold, this morning the death . . . and in the moments between the two, something wonderful had happened.

She was so torn inside that she didn't know which way to turn. She wanted the gold and The Shadows . . . she wanted to protect her father's memory . . . and she wanted Grant Emerson.

The danger of her own situation made her shiver.

If the game she was playing had rules, she was breaking all of them.

Eleven

In her nervousness about retrieving the watch, Delilah almost forgot the reason she wanted to visit Dentley, which was to talk to Thomas Wells, her father's oldest friend. She had to find out from the man who had known him best if Angus Wickley had been capable of murder.

So deep was she in her thoughts that when Daisy burst aboard the riverboat half an hour after leaving her, Delilah was sure she'd jumped high enough to touch the ceiling of the main cabin where she had gone to relax. She pivoted sharply.

"I got them," Daisy rushed the words. "Pert near got caught by ol' Philo. Lawd, Missy, take these here bones, fo' I faint!" With one wrist across the bridge of her nose for dramatic emphasis, she held the sack at arm's length.

"I swear, Daisy, I don't know what I'm going to do with you!"

"Take these bones! That's good enough fo' me!"

Delilah couldn't help but chuckle in spite of the seriousness of the situation. The twine around the sack had gotten caught around Daisy's fingers, and wrangling it from her proved to be something of a chore. Just as a wide-eyed Daisy might have wailed that the varmint inside had gotten her for sure, Delilah felt the separation of sack and flesh with such

171

force that she almost fell.

As if she sensed another presence, Delilah's gaze darted over the niches and crannies of the main cabin, which was furnished with discarded items from the house. Sunlight spilled in through the windows, speckling the walls with nervous dots of light and shadow. When she was sure that nothing more than the morning was looking in on them, she loosened the ties of the sack, then cautiously scooted her fingers between the coarse fabric and made her way to the bottom. Sinking into a chair as she did so, she heard the deathly rattle of the bones as the sack touched the floor and then her fingers oozed into the lingering dampness of small patches of mud. Imagining that the gold watch would be heavier than the bones, she eased along the bottom of the sack, raking her fingers back and forth. She couldn't remember ever doing anything more unpleasant in her life and closed her eyes, hoping the moment of nausea she felt would pass. "Where is the blasted thing?" she asked, looking toward Daisy. "You don't think he removed it, do you?"

Daisy had been watching her from beneath her half-closed eyes. "Lawd, Missy, I wouldn't know. Do ya know it was even in there to begin with?"

"I figured it was—" Suddenly, her fingernails tapped against something with a dull, hollow, almost eerie metallic sound. Her hand came up from the sack and the watch, with its short length of tangled chain, fell across her palm.

"There, I've got it." Relief was too mild a word for what she felt in that moment. "Return the sack to the stable—"

Daisy found her footing with the agility of a cat. "Naw'm, ya's said ya'd put it back yo'self—"

Delilah was too happy now that she held the one piece of evidence that could tie her father to the dead man to let Daisy's fear prickle her. "Very well, I'll return it."

"Better do it befo' Massah returns."

Delilah was surprised. "He has already left?"

"Yas'um . . . heard him say to Mozelle that he was havin' breakfast with Miz El, an' ya know she gits up real early-like."

She didn't like the idea of Grant being with Ellie. "Yes, I know" was all she could manage to reply. Strangely enough, she couldn't imagine Grant being attracted to Ellie in any way more than a friend, though she wasn't sure why. Ellie, though older than Grant, was a beautiful woman, sure to turn masculine heads.

"I'd better be mosyin' along, Missy," Daisy announced, kicking out at an imaginary stone. "Mozelle'll be screamin' an' hollerin' 'cause I ain't there to help with the kitchen chores. Ya'll be back fo' lunch, Missy?"

"I'd imagine, but I'll just take something from the cold box."

"Cold box empty, Missy. Massah, he tells Mozelle to share what was left over from the day among my people. Ain't he a nice man?"

"Papa did the same thing," Delilah snipped. "Or was *his* generosity just taken for granted?"

Daisy turned at the door, giving her former mistress a chastising look. "Yo' pappy was a true southern gent'lman . . . expect no less of him. But Massah Emerson, he be's a Yankee, an' we don't 'spect him to care 'bout nobody but hisself. He may not a been born on the bayou, but he's no less a gent'lman than yo' pappy. An' I think ya's beginnin'

173

to realize it yo'self, Missy."

Dropping the watch into the pocket of her dress, Delilah sauntered toward Daisy. She and Daisy had shared everything all their lives, and Delilah wished she could share her true feelings for Grant Emerson with her. She wished she didn't feel so compelled to quarrel with her friend, in order to hide those conflicting feelings that were tearing her apart. After all, didn't Daisy keep her up to date on her own romance with Lancie?

When Delilah did not reply to her bold observation, Daisy grinned and moved onto the outer deck. Viewing the silent Delilah within, she whispered, with apprehensive mischief, "Don't ya be forgettin' them bones, Missy."

Watching Daisy's retreat toward the main house gave Delilah the moment to study the aftermath of the early-morning storm. Everything was wet; the ground was thick and muddy. When she returned the bones, she'd better remember to remove her riding boots, lest someone see her tracks leading into the tackroom. She had no doubt she would be suspected when Grant discovered the watch missing. Dear Lord, she glumly thought, suppose he accused one of the slaves? Suppose he threatened to whip one of them to extract a confession from him? Delilah shook her head. No, she would never believe he was that cruel. If it came to that, she would have to confess, but she would not produce the watch and have her father's memory smeared across the parish, the state . . . and the hearts of everyone who had known and loved him.

As she turned toward her bedchamber, Grant dominated her thoughts. She could imagine him sitting in Ellie's tidy little parlor, enjoying tea and

Miss Mandy's famous blueberry tarts. She could imagine them engaging in small talk and . . . would he tell Ellie about last night? Surely, he wouldn't!

She sat on the edge of her bed, her thoughts running topsy-turvy through her brain, her fingers tightly linked together, and a painful emotion tugging a tidal wave from within her. Grant and Ellie . . . Ellie and Grant . . . the two of them sitting together, laughing, sharing small talk, gently touching each other for emphasis . . . Ellie's arm linked through his on the long carriage ride to Alexandria . . .

Did this ugly rage within her stem from jealousy?

No, she was too much a lady for that.

Wasn't she?

Four miles to the west, Ellie sat upon her divan, tears streaming down her face. Miss Mandy had not been able to console her, nor had Maden. When he had been unable to extract from her the reason for her tears, he had quietly shrugged his shoulders, left the house, and blamed his mother's unhappiness on "womanly things."

But when Grant arrived, it took only a few minutes for his gentle, masculine charm to open her heart. She took his hand and held it warmly. "You are such a good friend, Grant. And I don't know why you put up with me. I was cruel to ask you to keep secret the circumstances surrounding Charles's death. Perhaps selfish, too. What must people think?"

Grant tenderly caressed her hand. "I don't care what people think, Ellie. You and I know what really happened. That's all that matters. Now tell me

175

what is the matter?"

She shrugged delicately. "It's silly, actually. I was going through some letters and ran across one I received from Delilah when she was visiting her aunt in New Orleans a couple of years ago. In her letter, she said that nothing, save death, could end our friendship. And now, so short a time later, she will not speak to me and believes I am responsible for your ownership of The Shadows." The tears freshened in her eyes. "I miss her so much, Grant. I almost wish she had been right about me—that I *had* known about the eviction—so that I wouldn't feel so . . ." She grappled within for the right word, "wronged."

Grant's fingers lifted to brush a tear from her cheek. "These past two weeks I have seen a side of Delilah Wickley that she didn't want me to see. Just this week . . ." He paused, feeling a pang of guilt over the small lie, "I overheard her telling Daisy how wrong she had been about you. I believe that stubborn Wickley pride is keeping her from visiting you. But will you give her time to come around? I know she misses you, too."

Suddenly, their conversation was jostled by a burst of gunfire from outside. Both rose to their feet and would have darted to the porch had not Maden entered, patting at a smoking shirtsleeve. "Don't worry, Ma, the gun went off and the buckshot scattered through my sleeve." Seeing her worried expression, he laughed. "See? It ain't nothin'. Didn't even scrape the skin."

"I do wish you wouldn't be careless with your gun," she admonished with motherly tenderness.

Returning to their seats, Grant linked his fingers and rested his elbows upon his parted knees. "Shall

I tell you something to get your mind off our Miss Wickley?

"If it's possible," she answered.

Over the course of the following few minutes, Grant relayed the events leading to the discovery in the woods. When he finally finished, Ellie shook her head. "That is quite a story. I assume, then, that you plan to visit the sheriff while we're in town?"

"If you are still up to traveling. I brought the finest carriage from The Shadows for your comfort."

Ellie smiled. Because Grant was always so considerate of her, she wondered why they had never formed a relationship more intimate than just friends. "I have some shopping that simply must be done. If you can bear the company of a dour woman, I would like to go with you. You can tell me all about how our Delilah is doing."

Grant patted her hand. "You go and powder those red cheeks," he said. "I'll not be wanting people to think I am responsible for your melancholy."

As she rose, Ellie touched her mouth in a gentle kiss to Grant's cheek. "You are such a patient man, Grant. Give me but a minute."

Half an hour later, when the carriage was moving smoothly on the road alongside the railroad track, Ellie could hardly believe she'd been so unhappy. The morning was warm, but not unbearably so, the atmosphere less humid than one would have expected after the storm. Spanish moss, hanging thickly from twisted branches, glistened like silver against the fringes of Bayou Lamourie. Along the way, Ellie pointed out the place where locks would be built to control the flow of Lamourie waters into Bayou Boeuf. Passing miles and miles of rich, fertile

177

cottonfields compelled her to inform Grant that caterpillars had devastated the area crops back in '46.

"In other words," Grant laughed, "I shouldn't get too cocky about plantation life?"

"Or its perfection," she laughed in return, her prior melancholic mood charmed away by his company. "Things do go wrong, even in a life as tranquil as that provided by the plantations." Instantly, Grant visibly shuddered. "What is wrong, Grant?" Ellie asked.

"I don't know." His voice was low and distant. "I can't imagine the majority of the nation putting up with this way of life for much longer—the wealthy white planters . . . the unfairness of slavery. There is a rebellion against this cruel institution brewing in the North."

"Well, they cannot touch us here," Ellie said. "We are like two different worlds."

"We're not as different as you think," Grant replied. "Look there . . ." His tone brightened as he pointed out an approaching rider. "Isn't that Lancie?"

Glad of a diversion from the subject, Ellie cupped her hands across her brows to block out the sun. "I was wondering where he had gotten off to this morning."

Shortly, Lancie pulled the big gelding up to the halted carriage. Tipping his hat, he greeted them both. "Miz El," he then said, "got them new halters ya wanted fo' de mare an' colt. I tell Mistah Garrett to put 'em on yo' bill—"

"That's fine, Lancie," she replied. "When you return to the cottage, remind Maden to put linament on the sorrel gelding's leg—"

178

Lancie seemed reluctant to leave. "Sho', Miz El, I'll do that." He tipped his hat in parting. "Have a good day in town, ya hear?"

As Lancie coaxed the gelding into a lope, Grant flicked the reins at the mare. "You've got a new pair you haven't shown me?"

Ellie shrugged. "I promised them to Lancie. Every year he gets a bonus, and this year he wanted the mare and colt. Don't worry. I'll still give you first choice otherwise."

"I'm still not sure whether Lancie trusts me with you."

"Now, where did that come from?" Ellie asked. "Lancie is like an old mother hen. I keep telling him he needs a wife so that he'll have someone else to fret over."

"Has he shown any interest in anyone?"

"You know he has, Grant Emerson!" she gently admonished. "One of your own slave girls. I'm surprised you haven't caught him over there."

Grant laughed. "He asked if he could see Daisy, and I have seen him at The Shadows a few times. But he wasn't very forthright a couple of times. He tried to convince me he was checking to make sure the horses I purchased from you were settling down all right."

"Did he, indeed?"

"Daisy's the one he's interested in."

"The prettiest girl on your plantation, with the exception of our Delilah."

Grant nodded knowingly, even as the image of Delilah, and the memories of her soft flesh against him, filled his thoughts. He forced the images to scatter before Ellie sensed the true focus of his moment of silence. "You know," Grant mused. "Daisy

179

must be half Lancie's age."

"Neither Lancie nor Daisy seem to have noticed. I offered to buy Daisy from Angus last year, but he wasn't willing to sell her. The purchase price of her mother at auction was more than some of the strongest bucks at The Shadows. And, of course, Angus would not allow one of his slaves to marry a freed man."

"A buck is a male deer. I have *men* working at The Shadows."

Ellie had noticed the change in Grant's tone. She had not been aware of the extent of his hostility toward slavery. She wondered then why he had not freed his people . . . but the answer came instantly to her. He was not a native Louisianian and he had to change tradition very slowly. "I meant no disrespect in the way I referred to the men of your plantation, Grant."

"Forgive me. I know you didn't."

"Would you be willing to sell Daisy to me?"

"No!" He had not meant to speak the one word so sharply and instantly softened his voice. "But I will entertain the idea of setting her free and then she can do as she pleases. I'll discuss it with her when the time seems right."

The carriage turned onto the main thoroughfare to Alexandria, a well-traveled road flanked by hackberry and live-oak trees. The harsh gray skies of the morning had given way to a glow pulsating through the bank of clouds on the horizon. From the distance came a muted rumble of thunder, an omen that made Ellie remember Grant's carefully disguised forecast of a confrontation between North and South.

"The people of this area would frown upon your

freeing one of your slaves," she continued. "It has certainly caused Lancie his fair share of trouble. Besides, you cannot free Daisy, Grant, without causing trouble among your other slaves. They would not understand why you selected her. Would you . . ." Ellie drew in a quick breath as she smoothed down the folds of her dark-blue traveling dress, "entertain the idea of selling Daisy directly to Lancie?"

Grant didn't like the idea of having his plans dictated by the will of his neighbors, as Ellie's conversation suggested. "I couldn't give a damn what the neighbors think." That was not exactly true, but Grant did not amend his small lie. "I cannot imagine that my selling a slave to a freed black man would be viewed with any degree of tolerance, either. If Lancie is having a hard time now, imagine how it would be if he *owned* a slave of his own."

."Perhaps you're right, Grant. But I do wish you'd give it some thought."

Grant grunted his response. The silence that fell between them lasted for the rest of the trip. The mare clipped along at a steady pace, making good time. Within two hours, the outskirts of the village of Alexandria replaced the peaceful countryside of the bayou. Grant assisted Ellie down from the carriage on Front Street. "I have a few errands and will return for you in about two hours," he informed her. "Will that be sufficient time for your shopping?"

"I believe you're in a hurry to return to The Shadows," she replied, with a pretty laugh.

He shrugged absently. "I did ask Delilah to ride with me this afternoon. Of course, if you need to stay in town longer, I'm sure she will understand."

There were still times that Ellie resented Grant's attention to Delilah. She was also a little miffed that, after three years, he had finally found a reason—that being Delilah—to stop using the cane. *Please, please, stop struggling with these jealous emotions!* she quietly chastised herself. *You are only a friend to him. Delilah is the woman he wants. He has made that abundantly clear.* "Two hours is plenty of time," she replied after a moment, forcing a timorous smile. "Could you pick me up in front of Garrett's?"

Reboarding the carriage, he tipped his hat and lazily said, "Your wish is my command, my lady," and flicked the reins upon the mare's haunches.

Sixteen miles to the southeast, Delilah had just returned the bones to the peg and scattered the bridles and halters in the other sack when Philbus entered the tackroom. When his look narrowed accusingly, she snipped at him. "I can't find my black bridle. Have you seen it, Philbus?" When he still did not answer, she asked in her same brittle tone, "Well, what is wrong with you? Shouldn't I be here?"

Though he was sharing a look between her stocking feet and her boots set neatly upon the floor, he made no comment. "Ya's can be jes' 'bout anywhere ya wants to be, Missy. Massah says ya got free run o' de place an' we's to be, uh, what was dat word—a-com-mo-da-tin'. I be *accommodatin'*, Missy, if I knows what ya be wantin' me to be accommodatin' wid."

"You could help me find my bridle, Philbus," she replied.

A large hand extended and a crooked index finger pointed to the other side of the tack room. "Right dere on dat peg, where it always is, Missy."

A sheepish grin met his suspicious gaze. "Well, I was just curious about that bag of bones. Can't I be curious?"

"Ya's can be jes' 'bout anything ya wants to be, Missy, but don't ya be messin' wid dat dead man."

Delilah sat on a small stool, pulled on her boots, and began lacing them. "If I have free run," Delilah obligingly reminded Philbus, "then I should be able to look in that sack."

"Ya don't want to be doin' dat, Missy. Ain't a sight a lady needs to be a lookin' at."

"Horse feathers!" Standing, Delilah turned sharply to retrieve her bridle. "Just because I'm a woman doesn't mean I don't have a strong constitution."

Philbus enjoyed bantering with his former mistress. "Don't know about yo' constitution, Missy," he countered, "but I remembers when ya's a little tad of a thing an' yo' mammy tried to make ya eat oatmeal an' ya's screamed and thrashed and threatened to lose yo' stomach all over de table if'n ya was forced to eat it. Remember dat, Missy?"

Only now did Delilah allow herself the indulgence of a smile. "Think about it, Philbus." She wrinkled her nose. "Oatmeal. Do you like oatmeal?"

Taking the bridle from Delilah so that he could tend her waiting horse, he released a deep, throaty laugh as he turned. "Naw'm, sho' can't says I do." Delilah followed him into the stable walkway. "Ya know, Missy," Philbus continued, "if'n ya's goin' over to Mistah Wells to talk to Swainie—"

Delilah instantly cut him off. "Why do you think I'm going to see Swainie?"

A firmness settled into Philbus's gaze. "Swainie

183

was de one with Massah Wickley de night dey buried dat man out yon in de woods. Din't ya know dat, Missy?"

His statement shocked Delilah. If she had not dropped to the small keg where Philo usually sat, she was sure she would have fainted. "Will you tell me what you know about this, Philbus?" she questioned.

"Ya'd better tell Swainie to keep his mouth shut, Missy," Philbus replied. "I don't know why dat man got hisself dead, but I know how, an' de las' I seen of him he was wid Massah Wickley and Swainie. Dey rode off from here, an' 'bout midnight I hear a single gunshot. It'uz December, I recall, an' I got up an' waited outside in de bitter cold. Presently, I see Massah Wickley and Swainie ridin' in, but I hid so dey wouldn't see me. Massah was white as a sheet an' Swainie, he real quiet. Never did find out 'xactly what happened out der, but whatever it was, Swainie's de only one alive to tell 'bout it. I b'lieve dat's why Massah Wickley sell off Swainie to Mistah Wells. Massah knew dat if Swainie talked bad 'bout a white massah to *another* white massah, he's liable to get his back tore up real good."

"Mister Wells does not whip his slaves," Delilah reminded him. "Besides, why would Father wait five years to sell Swainie and his family?"

Massah knowed he was sick . . . might'a even knowed he wuz goin' ta pass on. Maybe he done it ta protect ya's, Missy. Sho, Mistah Wells don't whip his slaves," Philbus agreed dryly, "but he an' de massah, dey real close friends. Mistah Wells be making a 'ception if'n one o' his slaves talk about his friend what be's dead an' in his grave now an' can't defend hisself." Philbus turned back and finished saddling

Delilah's mare. "Ya best be tellin' Swainie to keep his mouth shut, Missy," he said again, handing her the reins. "Yo' pappy was a good man, an' dat man what's got kil't and buried out yon in de woods, he weren't nothing but po' white trash!"

"Do you know who he was?"

Philbus shook his head. "Don't know, Missy. But I hear yo' pappy says to him that they'll see he leaves de Shadows so's he won't be diggin' fo' de gold that 'uz buried on dis land. I jes' remember, Missy, dat one o' dat man's arms, it 'uz all shriveled up like it shouldn't ought to be hangin' dere."

Delilah stood beside her horse and accepted Philbus's linked fingers beneath her boot to assist her into the saddle. She sat astride her horse and looked down at the burly slave. "You won't be telling anyone else any of this, will you, Philbus?" she said quietly.

"Ain't said nothin' in six years, Missy, an' won't be sayin' nothin' now. 'Sides, I's jes' guessin' what happen't out yon in de woods. I's can be all wrong . . . but den, I's could be right, too. I's jes' don't know."

"Maybe I will have a word with Swainie." Delilah was worried. This mystery might implicate her father. Though nothing could harm him now, there was still Swainie to worry about. The law would frown upon a slave—even one doing the bidding of his master—who had knowledge of a white man's death. Yes, she had to talk to him, tell him to keep anything he might know to himself.

As Delilah coaxed the mare onto the trail leading toward the bayou, she felt a heaviness of heart. Too much was happening too quickly—her father's death and the loss of The Shadows, finding herself without a home, losing Ellie's friendship, slipping into Grant Emerson's life with the boldness of a hungry she-cat, then taking him to her bed and loving it.

Now, there was the matter of this ugly mystery dredged up by an innocent storm. She wanted justice to be done, to see the poor man properly buried, but she also wanted to protect her father's memory . . . and the very much alive Swainie.

For the time being, her nightmare—and her convictions that she knew the location of the missing gold—were far from her mind.

Twelve

Grant could have gotten more cooperation from a snail than from Sheriff Leroy Stafford. He merely grunted his responses, promised to look into the missing persons files and told Grant to "bury the poor fellow proper." He did not seem interested in the description of the remains as he reluctantly reduced them to writing, the watch, or the caliber of handgun the man had carried. Grant felt the sheriff really couldn't have given a damn that someone might have met a violent death.

At the bank, Grant picked up parcels of mail Hugh Penrod had been collecting for him since his last visit. Among them was a letter from Madeleine. Gritting his teeth, mentally reminding himself that he could do nothing about the woman's outrageous pursuits but to ignore them, he stuck the letter into an inside pocket and visited around town, paying the bills of local merchants and suppliers. His mood was as black as last night's storm.

At just past eleven he picked up Ellie at Garrett's and together they journeyed to the Exchange Hotel for lunch.

"Do you suppose my packages will be safe?" Ellie asked.

Grant looked up and down the busy street, instantly spying a barefoot boy resting against a store-front. When he had gotten his attention, he asked if the boy wanted to earn a dollar?

The instant reply was a very enthusiastic, "Yes, sir!" as he dashed to his feet and Grant's side before another boy could beat him to the job.

"When the lady and I come out of here, if all her packages are still on the floorboard, I'll give you that dollar."

The freckle-faced boy smiled, revealing a wide space instead of front teeth. "Mister, if you want, I'll make sure there's a few extra packages there when you get back."

Grant laughed, tousling the boy's red hair. "I don't think that'll be necessary."

He and Ellie moved toward the dining room of the Exchange Hotel. "I hope you'll tell me over lunch what happened at the sheriff's office," she said.

"You really don't want to know," he responded. But over the course of their lunch, he did, in fact tell her what had transpired. At first opportunity, he changed the subject to something more general and soon began to enjoy Ellie's company for the first time that day. But behind his easy smiles and congenial voice, Ellie detected deep thought, and she imagined that they were sixteen miles away, with Delilah Wickley.

"You're anxious to return home, aren't you?" Ellie said.

He shrugged. "I'm beginning to like it out there. It's a beautiful land—"

"It isn't the land," she chuckled. "It's Delilah Wickley. She has eased her way beneath your skin, hasn't she, Grant?"

"She does keep me on my toes. I would—" Grant stopped abruptly when he noticed a man had approached and stood beside the small table. His arms were crossed against his belt and the stench of him was almost painful. "What do you want?" Grant asked, wanting to be quickly rid of him.

"I hear from the sheriff you found some dead bones out on your place."

"What is it to you?"

"My old lady run off with a panhandler a few years ago. Might be he knocked her in the head and buried her out yonder. Need to know so I can rightfully take up with the old lady I have now and be signing a marrying certificate since she's knocked up—"

"It was a man we dug up, not a woman. Sorry to disappoint you." The man grunted and turned to walk away. "Who was *that*?" Grant asked Ellie.

"He's a Brady. His brother Luther is overseer at the St. Cyr plantation, but I've heard rumors he's about to be discharged because of cruelty to the slaves. He's even worse than Buckeye, the one you just met. It's no wonder his wife ran off. The foolish girl didn't know what she was getting into when she answered his advertisement for a wife. She should have stayed in the East."

Humor laced Grant's look. "Don't tell me Good Ol' Boy Buckeye couldn't find a wife right here?"

Ellie laughed. "In these parts, Grant, no woman in her right mind marries a Brady. Now . . ." Her fingers linked for a moment beneath her pert chin. "Are we going to begin our journey home so that you can meet your other obligations?"

If Grant had ever suspected Ellie's true feelings for him, it did not reflect in his thoughtless reply. "Our Delilah is not an obligation. She is a pleasure, even when she is naughty."

Grant did not see the glint of green fire in Ellie's eyes, nor could he possibly perceive that the long car-

189

riage ride to Lamourie Bridge would be as silent as death.

Taking a diversion to Wellswood, the plantation of Montford Wells, brother of the man she had planned to visit, Delilah had dismounted just as Thomas Jefferson Wells was descending the steps to his own waiting horse being held in place by one of his brother's slaves. "Miss Delilah Wickley," he greeted, removing the hat he had just pushed back from his brow. "What brings you to Wellswood?"

Delilah allowed herself to be hugged by her father's good friend. "I came by on the hopes that you might be visiting Lucie this morning." Silence. She allowed a moment to pass before she continued. "Something happened last night," she proclaimed, forcing a note of mystery into her voice. He was, after all, on his way out of his brother's house and he might consider her visit ill timed and not worthy of his delay. "I need to talk to you about it."

Her wording evoked the proper response. Looking toward the slave, Thomas Wells said, "Take my horse and Miss Wickley's into the stable. I'll be a few minutes."

Shortly, he and Delilah sat in the shade of the gallery and another slave was bringing a tray of lemonade. "Now, Delilah, what is this all about?"

In a rush of words, she told him what had happened, omitting the story Lancie had told her that morning or that Swainie might possibly be involved in the man's death. She also did not admit the recovery of the watch that she had stolen from the sack. "Do you think my father could have . . ." The words did not come easily. "Committed murder?" she ended quietly.

Perplexity and surprise mixed in the gentleman's

eyes. "Murder, Delilah? Good Lord, no! Why would you think such a thing?"

She shrugged guiltily. "I . . . Of course I don't think he was. I just needed to hear it confirmed by the man who knew him best. The grave *was* found on land belonging to The Shadows. It would be logical that one might assume my father had something to do with it."

"That part of the woods is accessible to anyone passing through. And no man in his right mind would even suspect your father."

Silence again. Delilah wondered how Thomas's conclusion might change were he to know about the watch and about her father and Swainie being the last people to be seen with the man. But the facts should not matter, only that Thomas knew her father well enough to conclude that he could not be guilty of murder. Delilah allowed herself to smile. "Thank you, Mr. Wells, for relieving me. I know my dear father is out of harm's way now, but I was worried about the investigation that might be made of this. I wouldn't want even the least bit of suspicion to fall on him. I loved him so."

"As we all did," Thomas replied. Taking her hand, he patted it fondly. "Now, you enjoy that lemonade Queenie brought out to you. I've got to get back to Dentley."

"Would it be all right if I ride over and visit a few minutes with Swainie?" Delilah asked.

"Of course," Thomas was well aware of Swainie's popularity at The Shadows. He had never understood why Angus had sold the family. "He's doing carpentry work in the quarters this morning. You might want to speak to Lucie before you leave Wellswood. In fact, I will wait and ride back to Dentley with you."

191

Shortly after Thomas and Martha Lucie had married, Lucie, as everyone called her, had been thrown from a horse. Since that time, she had not been normal and conversing with her was extremely difficult. Delilah had been one of the few people Lucie actually seemed to recognize at times, perhaps because she had always been patient with her. "Of course. I wouldn't think of leaving Wellswood without seeing Lucie," Delilah replied, lifting her hand in response to the gentleman's nod. "And thank you for waiting for me." She moved across the gallery and gently knocked on the door. Presently, Jeanette Wells, the wife of Montford, who cared for Lucie, answered the knock.

The pretty dark-haired woman smiled. "Come in, Delilah. I believe Lucie knows you're here."

If Martha Lucie Wells was even aware of her presence that morning, her blank stare did not indicate it. Delilah spent a few minutes with her, then shared parting amenities with the Wellswood household.

Moments later, she rode beside Thomas Jefferson Wells, chatting pleasantly during the course of the short trip. When they parted at his plantation home, Delilah sauntered along the short length of road leading into the slave quarters. She quickly located Swainie working on the roof of one of the cabins. He seemed surprised to see her. "Missy, what ya doin' here?"

"Mr. Wells said it was all right to visit with you," she responded. "Swainie, something was found in the woods last night and we have to talk."

That declaration brought him down from the roof immediately. He untied the sleeves of his shirt from around his waist, pulled the garment over his sweaty torso, then motioned to a grove of oaks where there were several hand-hewn chairs and half-barrels. He sat only after she had. "What's on yo' mind, Missy?" he asked, wiping perspiration from his brow with a square of muslin. After she had related the news of the discovery and her conversation with Philbus that morning, he asked, "Did ya tell Massah Wells, Missy?"

"Of course not!" Delilah shot to her feet. "He is a very honorable man and, regardless of his friendship with my father, he would cooperate with the authorities if it came to it. I don't want you to get into trouble, Swainie. I just want to know what happened that night."

Swainie tightly linked his fingers. Normally, he would have stood in deference for his former mistress, who was also standing, but his knees felt as limp as weeds. His dark eyes eventually looked up to meet her own waiting ones. "Missy, I swears befo . . ." He stopped short of saying, "God Almighty", then quietly continued, "that Massah Wickley didn't kill dat white trash. And neither did Swainie," he added as an afterthought. "Sho', they was a shot fired, but when dat man threatened Massah, he jes' pushed him off him, I seems ta recall. Dat fella, he cussed and raved like a madman, then he got back on his hoss, jes' as alive as you and me."

"But my father's watch was found in the grave," Delilah reminded him, returning to her seat. "Can you explain that, Swainie?"

Swainie slowly shook his head, his sinewy body swaying with the movement. "Lawd, Missy, I can only think dat white trash stole yo' pappy's watch. Massah was fierce mad when he run him off'n The Shadows, an' they was a scuffle between them befo' Massah smacked him down. Dat fella, he must'a twisted yo' pappy's watch loose when dey was ascufflin'. But, I swear, Missy, he was alive when Massah

193

an' Swainie left him. If I's lyin', let de Lawd Almighty strike me dead!" Even as he spoke, he looked heavenward, fear darkening his eyes.

"Do you know who the man was, Swainie?"

"Naw'm. Remember he tells Massah his name when he rode up to de Shadows, but I don't recall."

"Do you remember what he wanted?"

"Sho', Missy . . . he was askin' Massah fo' permission to dig fo' dat gold. Massah run him off once, but he come back real late at night and roused Massah from his bed. I hear dem arguin' real loud-like an' I goes to see if Massah need me. Dat's when Massah, he says to saddle two hosses, 'cuz we's goin' ta see dat white trash leaves de Shadows."

"Why did he come back so late?"

"Massah thinks he wuz plannin' to steal a good hoss, 'cuz he was fierce mad at Massah fo' runnin' him off. His was limpin' real bad. Well, Massah, he feel sorry fo' dat mis'able ol' hoss, so he tells me to put it in a pen and bring de mule an' he traded de mule fo' de hoss. Dat hoss still over dere, if I rightly remember—big ol' gelding Philbus likes to ride."

"Good Lord." She was thinking that they should get rid of the horse, but that would be like prying the breath out of Philbus. She'd get a fight out of him if she even suggested it. But she stopped to think. If a fair trade was made . . . the horse for the mule . . . then there would be no harm done. Still, she would feel better if she got a second opinion. "What do you think about the horse, Swainie? Should I ask Philbus to get rid of it?"

"Philbus, he real fond o' dat hoss, Missy. Be sort a' like pryin' apart a couple a' dogs in—" He looked up sheepishly. "Sorry, Missy. Don't mean no disrespect."

Delilah was pacing back and forth as if she could not gather her thoughts. "Swainie, you've got to swear you'll say nothing about this," she whispered harshly.

"S'pose somebody start askin' questions, Missy?"

"No one is going to ask questions. And Philbus is not going to say anything about that night. For heaven's sake, don't volunteer any information!"

"Lawd, Missy . . . I tells ya dey ain't nothin' ta hide. Dat man, he was alive. Don't ya believe me?"

"Of course I do." Actually, she wasn't sure. Though she had never known Swainie to lie, she prayed that he was not doing so now. She did not know whether he harbored bitterness toward her father for selling him and his family to Dentley. Would he tell a different story to take revenge against her father even at the risk of his own life? "Swainie, you do know what a difficult decision it was for Father to sell you, don't you? He was trying to save The Shadows—"

"Sho' I do, Missy." Swainie was well aware of the real reason his family had been sold, but he had no intentions of telling Delilah Wickley. He couldn't tell anyone the reason, not if he wanted to live . . . not if he wanted to protect his family against being sold again.

Delilah was sure she detected bitterness in Swainie's voice. "Would you like the new owner to talk to Mr. Wells about buying you back?" she asked.

He turned slowly. "Naw'm. Massah Wells a real fine massah. We's like it here. Sukie, she real happy workin' in de big house, an' Massah Wells, he don't make the little'uns work in the fields until they's at least nine. We's know how Massah Wells is goin' ta treat us. We don't know 'bout Massah Yankee-Doodle—"

"He's a good man. The people at The Shadows have no complaints."

For the first time since Swainie had climbed down

from the roof, a grin crept across his face. "Sounds to me, Missy, like ya'll be changin' yo' mind 'bout Massah Yankee-Doodle. I hears ya be fierce mad when he buy de Shadows."

The betrayer within her rebelled. She wanted to scream her denials, to assure Swainie that she hated Grant Emerson every bit as much as she had a month ago, but the words just wouldn't come. She also did not want Swainie to see the crimson creeping upward into her cheeks as she remembered the moments she had shared with Grant just last night. She quickly turned away. "Horse feathers! I merely tolerate Grant Emerson."

He chuckled, the sarcasm hardly suppressed. "Sho', Missy."

"Oh, Swainie!" She tried to present her anger as she turned back, but found herself laughing instead. "You think what you want. It makes no never mind to me."

In the next few moments, Delilah reaffirmed the need for discretion concerning the night the man had died and soon gave her goodbyes. As Bella strained against the bit, fighting for control over the will of her rider, Delilah tried to feel relief, but felt only a raging disappointment. Angus Wickley had never been the same after the wagon had plunged into the bayou that dark December night a decade ago. A man more prone to cruelty had emerged from a delirium that had lasted several weeks. A man who had never severely punished his slaves had soon begun locking an infractor in the toolshed for days at a time. He had once struck out in rage when one of the slaves had talked back to him, and another time he had let the apples rot on one of the trees rather than let some poor whites "poach" them. Still, the times that he had been kind and tolerant far outweighed his bad moments. But those moments would be most likely remembered.

Could a man so unpredictable of mood have committed murder?

By the time Bella entered the trail on Bayou Boeuf leading to Shadows-in-the-Mist, tears streamed down Delilah's sun-warmed cheeks. When she reached the curve in the trail fringing the spot where the skeleton had been found, she reined Bella into the dark, dank glen where scarcely a single ray of sun could penetrate the overhanging foliage. The ground beneath the thick blanket of rotting leaves and pine straw was like a pit of mud. Though she was frequently close to being unseated by a stumbling Bella, she soon found the empty grave and sat atop her horse, staring into the long crevasse as though she expected to find something—anything—that might exonerate her father. But she found nothing and, expelling a weary sigh, coaxed the mare back toward the trail.

Five minutes later she reached the grove of oaks where, in her dream, her father had buried the gold. Two of the trees had recently been felled by an axe and chopped up, leaving a considerable tangle of branches and mounds of neatly stacked logs, aging for winter fireplaces. Dismounting and tying Bella off, she moved through the debris, kicking at the ground and trying to find the spot where the box might have been buried. She knew it was there, just as surely as she knew her own name.

It might be inaccessible to her right now, but once the debris had been cleared away—

Again, she sighed.

Was she dreaming silly dreams? Settling upon a log, her wistful eyes staring all around, she let the time pass by, as if she had a thousand years of it in reserve.

* * *

When Grant returned to The Shadows at just past one in the afternoon, he tried not to show his disappointment that Delilah had not yet returned. "She didn't show up for lunch?" he questioned a worried Mozelle.

"Naw, suh, massah, suh . . . befo' she left she say she be back befo' lunch. An' ain't seen nary hide nor hair. Right worried, massah. Don't like her ridin' that high-steppin' fo'-legged beast her pappy gave her fo' her birthday las' year."

That declaration, Grant was sure, was meant to make him feel guilty for requiring her to pay off the cost of the mare. He kept a deceptively straight face. "I'd better ride out and see if I can locate her." Slapping his hat to his head, he turned and marched out the door. His limp was more pronounced, an unconscious betrayal of deep worry. "Philo! Philo!" he yelled across the spanse of yard separating house and stable. When the old gentleman emerged from the darkness within, Grant bellowed out at him. "Fetch my horse from his stall, will you?"

Philo, who had never heard such urgency in his master's voice, did not dally. Moments later, he watched Grant dig his heels into the mare's sides and disappear onto the trail. "Massah sho' in a hurry," he mumbled to himself. "Must be worried 'bout Missy."

As he returned to his chores, he mumbled his approval of Missy and the new master "likin' each other a real fierce bunch."

When Delilah heard the rider approaching on the trail, she immediately drew herself up. Had the rider not been Grant, she might have been dismayed that her solitude had been interrupted. Even from the distance of a hundred yards, she saw the relief sweep over his face as she filled his vision.

She jumped down from the log just as he dismounted his horse. "You didn't come all this way just looking for me?" she asked in a sultry tone.

"Mozelle sent me out," he fibbed, a grin sliding off his face. "She was worried about you."

A coy look met his gaze. "And you weren't?"

"Of course not. I was just worried about my chattel," he replied, cutting his look to the fifteen-hundred-dollar mare.

She could tell by his voice and half-cocked smile that he was teasing her. "You were worried about me, too," she argued without feeling. "Worried that you might have to work the ledgers yourself."

"Ma'am," he drawled, as he approached and took her arms to draw her close. "I had a big old ache inside wanting to see your purty features again. Truly, ma'am, I am enamored of your charm and your sun-kissed beauty."

She tried to suppress her grin, but couldn't quite accomplish it. "Pooh! Grant Emerson, don't you toy with my affections with silly, insincere flatteries, and in an almost convincing southern manner at that!" Her gaze lifted, holding his own for a long, warm moment. She wanted to ask about the visit to the sheriff's office and know what he had learned. But she couldn't appear too eager. She wanted to know how Ellie was doing. But the words wouldn't quite form.

"Don't you want to know about my morning?" he murmured as if reading her thoughts. Even as he awaited her response, his hands circled to her back to draw her close.

Delilah nodded her head, her hands moving timidly around his waistline. "You can tell me about it if you like." She deliberately spoke with indifference. Wrapped in Grant's arms, a glorious wave of security swelled within her. Why did he make her feel like this—warm, and yet not uncomfortably so . . . excited, and yet not anxious . . . wanting to be loved fully, and yet satisfied to simply have his arms embracing her as his whisper-soft breath played upon her cheek. The tangle of emotions tugging her within was itself like a blanket of mystery and intrigue.

Then she recalled he'd told her that he'd been married. Because she was still not sure how, or *if*, the marriage had ended, she gently extracted herself from his arms, shivering as she did so, because she had made love to him before the issue was resolved to her satisfaction.

"Don't you want me to touch you, Delilah?" he asked.

"Someone might ride by," she responded, though she really didn't care if they did. "Besides, you are going to tell me about your morning."

The long ride to Alexandria and back, and now the few minutes he had spent on horseback, had aggravated his hip. He moved past her and fell lazily against the log to draw his leg up. "Sheriff didn't seem too interested to me," he finally said. "Reluctantly agreed to send out a list of missing persons."

Delilah was surprised. She had expected Sheriff Stafford to pursue the matter with enthusiasm. "He isn't going to investigate?"

"Didn't say he wouldn't, but pretty much hinted that if I wanted to investigate, to be his guest."

"What are you going to do?"

Grant crossed his arms, his eyes grazing over her. "I'm going to do as the sheriff suggested and bury the fellow proper."

200

"That's all?"

"I might make a few notes and do some checking around myself. The sheriff may not be concerned, but I am."

He seemed so adamant to solve the mystery. All of her worries rushed full force upon her. When she threw herself into his arms, she met his perplexed gaze. "I missed you, Grant. Can't I show it?" she explained.

He appeared doubtful. "Scarcely two minutes ago you were worried about someone seeing us together," he reminded her. "Now, you lift your guard? What are you afraid I might find out?"

"Nothing . . . nothing. Enough of this nonsense!" She smiled, even as deception and diversion pulled at her heartstrings. "I'm sure, Grant, that it would be something other than my guard you'd rather I lifted?"

He did not have to feign his shock; it was genuinely reflected in the rich, crystal depths of his eyes. "Delilah Wickley!" He clucked his tongue several times, even as his hands stole around her waist. "You *are* trying to change the subject!" Though his tone was harsh, the look of feminine wickedness molding her pretty features made him smile.

"Shut up, Grant Emerson, and kiss me."

He grinned boyishly, expelling a chuckle. "You are toying with my affections—"

"So? Do you, or do you not, want to kiss me?"

Pulling her close, feeling the hot brand of her breasts against his shirt, his eyes raked over the gleam of her golden eyes, her pert nose, her full, luscious mouth slightly parted. God! What control he must have to take this moment to study her, when all he wanted was to feel her mouth against his own, the curves of her soft, sensual body pressed against his

201

taut frame. When her leg boldly lifted and pressed against his thigh, he could no longer delay her sweet kiss or deny the artful travels of her fingers as they locked through his hair.

"I'm hungry for you, Delilah."

She responded with only a whisper of space between their mouths. "I'm hungry for food, Grant."

"Not for me?" he bantered huskily.

Her mouth touched upon his own once again. "Food first . . ." she whispered in between her short, teasing kisses, ignoring the painful wrenching of her stomach, "then . . . perhaps dessert."

Thirteen

Grant realized what Delilah was doing only when she artfully glanced across the ridge of his shoulder, as if looking for a reason to extricate herself from his arms. His mind wandered back in time for a moment, trying to recall the last words he had spoken before their playful bantering had begun. Ah, yes! *What are you afraid I might find out?* So, that was what she was working so ardently to avoid. Her seduction and brazen caresses against him had been simply to get his mind off "the mystery," as the whole of his plantation had labeled the grisly discovery.

"Why, you little flirt. You're trying to charm away the subject of last night, aren't you?"

Delilah gave him a coy look. Rather than respond, she announced haughtily that she was starving. "Could we return to The Shadows?" she asked.

He gripped her arm firmly. "Not until you tell me what you know about the body in the woods."

She pressed her mouth petulantly, her arm folding up in an attempt to loosen his hold. "Ain't no body in the woods, Grant." She looked around, quietly amending, "Well, nobody but us living folks."

She had not expected her response to anger him, but that is exactly the reaction she got. His tanned features became even darker against the pale golden fringes of his thick hair. Flipping his hat back from his forehead, he barked, "You know damn well what I mean, Delilah—"

"Why are you so angry?"

"Because you know more than you're letting on, and I hate secrets—"

"Do you, indeed!" Her own violent reaction came as a surprise, even to herself. "You are the one who killed Charles McPherson, but the details surrounding it sure have been kept a deep, dark secret! You're the one who claims to have been married, but you won't even tell me how, or if, the marriage ended! This—this mystery wife," she continued her thoughtless attack, "could be just as dead as Old Bones and buried in a dank place just like the one you dug him out of—"

His mood had not been particularly good the whole day. The feisty miss standing before him now certainly did not help to improve it, especially with accusations that he could very well be a murderer, and twice over. "As far as Charles McPherson is concerned, you—and anyone else on the bayou—can think what you like. As for the subject of *my wife,* I don't see what business it is of yours!"

"You can say that . . . after last night?" She whispered the words harshly.

Though he really wasn't sure why, she had infuriated him. He released her arm almost as if he found her repugnant. "Last night . . ." He turned sharply away, then slowly turned back to face her, his mouth widening into an ugly smirk. He wanted to hurt her, to pay her back for the wicked deceptions that had been the foundation of their relationship from the very beginning. He had been amused by it before; now he was in no mood to indulge her wickedness. "I took to the bed of a very pretty trollop," he continued momentarly. "What red-blooded American male wouldn't, given the chance?"

Scarcely a second passed before her hand bristled back and met his cheek in a stinging blow. His head jerked to the side, and she was sure she'd hurt herself more than she could possibly have hurt him. He did not look at her; if her tears were for his benefit, he did not invoke his privilege.

"Perhaps I shouldn't have said what I did," she said, a painful lump in her throat, "either about Charles or your wife. But I also do not deserve to be called such a filthy name. Until last night, I had never been touched." Her words erupted into sobs. "You can keep Bella. I am leaving The Shadows, even if I have to walk!" She moved swiftly toward her horse, the thick, tangled masses of her hair brushed by a summer wind, her chin held high and proud despite the slump in her heart. She was not sure exactly what had provoked the quarrel, but she was certainly not willing to back down. True, she had slung the first insults, but he had certainly slung the most degrading. How dare he call her a trollop!

Grant had immediately regretted his thoughtless outburst. He thought her anything but a trollop! She was the woman he wanted to share his life with—not a woman like the crazed Madeleine Vail . . . not a gentle woman like Ellie. He wanted Delilah Wickley, wanted her deceptions, haughtiness, womanly passions, and provocative innocence. He would gladly trade The Shadows for her promise to stay with him forever.

But even as he wished to call her back, the powerful mare was kicking up dust in its hasty retreat onto the trail.

Damn! he thought. Why couldn't the truth about Charles be told? And why couldn't he have told her the truth about Madeleine . . . and a dark-haired boy named Dustin, who had just last month turned six years old.

Thinking of Dustin made him think of his cousin, Aldrich. It had been several months since one of Aldrich's threatening letters had reached him. Had he forgotten his vendetta? Was he, even now, wedded to his love, Madeleine, who had given birth to his child? Had Aldrich finally forgiven him?

Grant pressed the heels of his palms against his throbbing temples. He hated that his ugly past was catching up to him. If he could not be truthful with Delilah, he could not expect her to love him as much as—God, yes! As much as he loved her. He had fallen in love with her that morning in the mercantile, even before he had known her name.

"I can't let her leave!" He spoke the words viciously, his unsteady gait quickly closing the distance separating him from his horse. *I'll have to tell her the truth about Madeleine,* he thought, drawing himself into the saddle. *And about Charles.*

Delilah did not go directly to The Shadows. Rather, she coaxed Bella on a steady course past her late father's plantation and soon entered the trail taking her to Lamourie Bayou. No one could have been more surprised than Lancie when she dismounted halfway between Ellie's cottage and the stable.

"Lawd, Missy, let me look at you!" he exclaimed, taking the reins of her horse. "I can't believe ya's really here."

"You should feel nothing but disgust when you look at me," Delilah responded.

Confusion creased his brow. "How that be, Missy? Ain't like ya's a ugly ol' bug or somethin'. Why, ya's still so dang purty ya make me feel all swimmy-headed."

Just then, one of Lancie's old hunting dogs bounded from the stable, followed closely by Maden. The young man grinned his pleasure. "Missy, you come to see my ma?" he questioned, pulling his hat down from his head.

A jab of shame pierced through Delilah. "If she'll see me. I wouldn't blame her if she refused."

"You done Ma a terrible wrong, Miss Delilah," Maden replied with gentle chastisement.

That was something he hadn't needed to point out. "Well, we'll just have to see which of us has more character now," Delilah replied.

"Huh?" mumbled the two men in unison.

Delilah smiled timidly. "Never mind. Tend my horse, Maden, while I check if your mother will see me."

"Sure, Miss Delilah."

Ellie had seen Delilah ride in. Since she had spent that morning in town with Grant, she wondered if the reason for her visit was a reprimand. Had her young friend laid claim to Grant Emerson and did not want Ellie spending time with him? Or had she come to apologize? Certainly, Ellie would never forget the harsh words Delilah had spoken to her in her hotel room that cool March morning.

Whatever the reason for Delilah's visit, Ellie suddenly found herself a bundle of nerves. She stood in the shadows of the foyer, watching Delilah talk to Lancie and Maden, but when Delilah suddenly turned toward the house, she quickly moved across the parlor, to look out a window overlooking Bayou Lamourie.

Delilah's footsteps shortly came across the gallery along with a light rap at the front door. When Ellie could not bring herself to answer at the second series of raps, Miss Mandy appeared from the kitchen and was the one to face Delilah. "Why, Missy," the matronly woman greeted. "Sho' has been a while since you visited us here. Come on in, Missy . . . don't know where Miz El took off to—" Upon entering the parlor, with Delilah a step behind, a very surprised Miss Mandy spied the lady of the house maintaining her vigil of silence by the window. "Oh . . . Miz El, thought you was off somewhere. Should I bring some tea?"

"You might ask our visitor" came Ellie's cool response. She couldn't forget all the sleepless nights and the painful moments spent these past few weeks. She couldn't forget that morning, when she had once again succumbed to tears because of Delilah.

"Tea would be nice," Delilah replied, taking the servant's hand. "How are you feeling today, Miss Mandy?"

Her eyes saddened. " 'Bout well as can be 'spected, Missy. Thank ya fo' askin'."

Delilah was reluctant to release her hand and be left alone with Ellie. Despite the bravado she had displayed just moments ago, she now felt weak enough inside to collapse. Certainly, she had not expected Ellie to welcome her as a long-lost friend, but she also had not expected her tone of indifference. The hunger she had felt at not having eaten all day now disappeared.

It was all Ellie could do to maintain her control, to stop herself from turning, closing the distance between them, and drawing Delilah into a warm embrace. Rather, her tone remained deliberately cool. "What brings you this way, Delilah?" she asked.

"I need to eat a great big slice of humble pie, Ellie." Delilah replied. When Ellie turned, a tearful Delilah continued. "I have no right to expect you to forgive me, and I won't blame you if you refuse. But I have to tell you how wrong I was, and how sorry I am that my hateful accusations have spoiled our friendship."

Ellie's eyes narrowed suspiciously. "Why now? Why today?"

Delilah had reasoned out all of the whys in her horseback ride along the bayou. She was going to leave The Shadows today, if she could implore some good soul to drive her into Alexandria, and then she was going to board a steamboat and begin her journey to New Orleans, where her great-aunt Imogen lived. Before she left the place she loved, and the people who were so dear to her, she had to leave no stone unturned in amending her past wrongs. For that reason, she stood before Ellie, in the neat parlor of the cottage where she had been born.

"Why not now?" Delilah replied, rather than answer Ellie's queries. "This is something that should never have happened, and I should never have let so much time pass before seeking your forgiveness. If I do not have your forgiveness, at least I have made the effort to seek it."

Ellie had linked her fingers so tightly together that pain shot into her wrists. Unlinking them, she smoothed down the folds in her paisley gown, then straightened her lace collar. "I don't know what to say, Delilah."

"Please say you'll forgive me, Ellie. I promise never to ask for anything ever again. I promise . . ." A deep sigh whispered throughout the room, "that you'll never have to see me again."

Ellie quietly surveyed her friend, allowing the last

words of her promise to sift into her brain, like a slow-acting poison. What was Delilah saying? Dear Lord, was she going to leave the bayou without even looking back? Ellie didn't like the prospect of that and quickly walked closer to Delilah. "Are you leaving The Shadows, Delilah?"

"Yes. Grant and I cannot get along, so I have decided to visit my great-aunt in New Orleans."

"Imogen? Has she invited you?"

"I have had an open invitation since Father's funeral," Delilah replied. "Please, Ellie, you must give me an answer."

Unwillingly, Ellie's gaze strayed over Delilah's face and her windswept hair. "Of course I forgive you, Delilah," she replied. "I know you didn't mean it—"

"But I did mean it . . . at the time. That is why I need your forgiveness. I know now that you couldn't possibly have known about the foreclosure. I was angry because a Yankee had purchased my father's plantation, and I took it out on you. Oh, Ellie, Ellie . . ." Delilah hugged her older friend, "I have missed you so much. All the times when I wished I'd had someone to talk to, it was always you I thought about. Oh, forgive my horrible pride! Time is a more precious thing to waste than gold."

"Please don't leave, Delilah. You could stay here at the cottage. There's plenty of room."

Drawing back and taking Ellie's hands, Delilah laughed without mirth. "No, I would be too close to Grant Emerson. I need to get away—"

"From him?" Ellie frowned severely. "A woman does not run from a man she hates, Delilah . . . only from a man she loves, and who might possibly love her."

Delilah attempted a smile. "Don't get your hopes up, Ellie. He despises me as much as I do him. Why,

210

he even called me a trollop."

"Grant wouldn't do that," she argued without feeling.

"Perhaps the Grant you know wouldn't. But the one I know did. I have always brought out the worst traits in a man. Your Grant is no exception. But I was not without fault in our confrontation," she humbly admitted. "I accused him of murder, twice over."

"I hope one of his 'victims' wasn't my husband Charles."

Tears of humiliation and shame burned in her eyes. "I'm afraid that he was. Oh, Ellie . . . Ellie, he has every right to think badly of me. I've done him such an injustice." She wanted to tell Ellie about taking the watch from the sack, but she dared not. Ellie was a woman of honor. If she felt that what Delilah had done was wrong, she might decide to tell Grant.

So, when Ellie coaxed her to the divan and began chatting to her about other things—anything to change the subject—Delilah was sure she detected a small spark of jealousy in her friend. In the hour and a half of their visit, during which Miss Mandy served a lunch of beef sandwiches and baked potato wedges, Ellie made no pretensions in her desires to avoid discussing Grant Emerson. By the visit's end, Delilah had no doubts that Ellie McPherson was in love with the man in whose arms she had made sweet, wicked love.

With one matter behind them, and another still ahead, Delilah hoped her friendship with Ellie would survive the ravages of this romantic triangle. Perhaps when she had put two hundred miles distance between them, Ellie and Grant could get together.

Sitting atop her horse at midafternoon, Delilah promised her friend that she would never say anything to hurt her again. "I promise."

The faintest smile touched the corners of Ellie's mouth. "Never say never. We are all human."

"And we will always be friends. When I am living in New Orleans, will you come for a visit?"

"Of course, I will. I am very fond of Imogen."

"And . . ." Delilah's eyes dropped. "One day will you tell me . . ."

When she did not finish her statement, Ellie coaxed her. "Tell you what?"

"About the circumstances of Charles's death?"

Ellie frowned her dismay. "Grant had made me promise that I wouldn't."

"Then will you tell me one thing?"

"If I can."

"Did Grant kill him?"

Maden and Lancie were approaching from the carriage house. "We'll talk about it another time," Ellie replied in a harsh whisper.

Delilah swore beneath her breath at the untimeliness of their approach, though it did not show on her face. She smiled. "You two are just in time to see me off."

"We'll be seeing you more often, Miss Delilah?" Maden asked, enthusiasm etched into his smile.

"I'm afraid not. I'll be traveling to New Orleans this week." When Maden could hardly mask his disappointment, she added, "But I'm sure I'll be visiting from time to time."

Lancie's deep voice broke a moment of silence. "Ya take care of yo'self, Missy, ya hear?"

By the time she aimed Bella toward the trail, tears stung Delilah's eyes. A strange array of feelings enveloped her: anger, jealousy, loneliness, uncertainty. Would she ever settle down and find a place in life?

Great-aunt Imogen had once promised to line up worthwhile gentlemen to escort her about town. But could she ever allow another man into her life after she had been with Grant? The memories of last night feathered into her consciousness—his hard, male body pressed to her soft one . . . the lusty growl from his throat as his mouth sought her own in a fiery kiss . . . the sensual travels of his hands over her sensitive flesh. A frustrated sigh touched her mouth as she coaxed Bella into a lope, caring not a whit that the branches and twigs surrounding her snapped against her tender flesh. She wanted only to return to The Shadows, collect her personal belongings, and sweet-talk someone into driving her into Alexandria.

Patting the mare's thick neck, Delilah leaned forward. "I'm sorry, Bella," she whispered against her windblown mane. "You'll have to remain with that blasted Yankee dog!" Again, she sighed, a fresh flood of tears stinging her eyes. "But you don't have to be lonely. My heart will be with him, too."

Grant had ridden into The Shadows as if he had a posse on his trail. "Where is Miss Wickley?" he yelled hoarsely as Philo emerged from the stable.

"Missy, she ain't come back," Philo replied, taking the reins of Grant's horse.

Grant's eyes narrowed. "What do you mean, she hasn't come back?"

"Jes' what I says, massah. 'Scuse me, Massah, don't mean no disrespect. When Missy rides that high-steppin' mare, she ain't likely to show up till dark, or past. I sends some o' de boys out a lookin' fer her . . . she be out der sum'weres."

His hand dropping to the old gentleman's shoulder, Grant allowed himself to smile. "No I'm afraid she's angry with me. She'll come back when she's cooled off a bit."

Philo shook his head as he contradicted his master.

213

"Don't know 'bout dat, massah. Oncet, she mad at her mammy 'cuz she wouldn't let her go ridin' wid one o' dem wild Hankins boys what be's po' white trash here an' abouts, and she go out on de bayou in a pea-row an', Missy, she fall asleep and get caught in a naughty current and ended up down round Cheneyville. Hunert men or so out lookin' all night fo' Missy. So, massah, if'n ya made Missy mad, she might not come back till de mornin', jes' so's ya'll worry 'bout her."

"We'll just see about that," Grant replied matter-of-factly. "Give the horse a bit of grain, will you, Philo?"

"Sho', massah."

Grant had moved a dozen or so strides toward the house when a horse stirred dust on the road. He turned, expecting to see Delilah approaching. Rather, a big, barrel-chested man sat atop what might possibly have been the biggest horse Grant had ever seen. The man, dressed in a long overcoat, halted a few feet from where Grant stood. "Mister Emerson?" Grant nodded. "I'm Leroy Biggs, deputy sheriff of Rapides. Sheriff Stafford sent me out here to collect some remains—"

"The sheriff didn't seem too interested this morning when I saw him," Grant cut him off. "Why the change of heart?"

"Had some time to think about it. If a murder was committed, he wants to get to the bottom of it. Going to take those bones over to Doc Miller for a full report. You goin' to turn over them bones, or do you want me to return with a warrant?"

Grant's agitated gaze stirred across the thick, scrubby face of the deputy. "You can take them. It'll save me the trouble of having to rebury the fellow."

The man dismounted and followed Grant toward the stable. Momentarily, they entered the tack room

214

and Grant snatched the sack down from the peg to hand it to him. "Is that all you'll be wanting, Deputy Biggs?"

Sweeping his long coat back, Leroy Biggs pried the ropes loose from the bag, bent to one knee, and looked in. Then he looked up at Grant with a toothless grin. "You tryin' to pull somethin', Mr. Emerson?" At that moment, he laid the sack open, exhibiting the array of bridles and harnesses inside.

Grant's gaze sunk to the assortment of leather and metal bits. "What th—" Drawing his hands to his hips, he called crossly, "Philo . . . come in here, will you?" When the slave stood in the doorway, Grant looked straight at him. "Where's that bag we brought in from the woods last night?" he asked.

Philo had never seen his new master's eyes looking so dark and intense. He was suddenly apprehensive. "They was dere, massah. Philo ain't seen nobody foolin' round in here what's not s'posed to be. I swears, massah."

"Are you pulling something here, Mr. Emerson?" the deputy asked again, raking his fingers absently through the contents of the sack.

"You wait out at your horse," Grant replied. "I'll get to the bottom of this."

Bloodshot eyes suddenly cut to the waiting Philo. "Maybe I better talk to the old nigra myself—"

"You'll speak to no one except me!"

Leroy Biggs looked at Grant narrowly, then got to his feet. "I'll wait, mister, but I'd better leave here with that bag of bones."

Grant and Philo stood silently inside the tack room. Grant's eyes scanned the room with every peg, halter, saddle, and accoutrement contained within its sixteen-foot walls. When, at last, he heard the shuffle of boots and hooves on the earth outside, he turned to the slump-shouldered Philo. "You must remember who has been in here this morning. It is very important —"

Philo scratched his head. "Well, dey was Philbus, but I was wid him de first time an' he jes' got his saddle, den dey was Daisy, an' she jes' put some scraps out fo' dat ol' wild mama cat wid de kittens what lives beyond dat wall der. Den dey was Missy, when she —"

Grant's head snapped up. "Delilah Wickley was in here?"

"Sho', massah, but I heard her talkin' to Philbus whilst she was lookin' fo' her bridle. An' dey weren't nobody else but me, massah, an' Philo wouldn't a teched dem der bones, even if I's paid to tech 'em."

"You get a couple of boys from the quarters, and go over the stable real good. And I want to talk to Philbus."

"Yas suh, massah . . ."

Grant's control astounded even himself. Someone at The Shadows had stolen the bag containing the murdered man's bones, and someone was going to have to own up to it. He suspected Delilah, but there was always the possibility that one of the slaves was attempting to protect someone — one of their own or their former master . . . someone. Slowly, Grant devised a plan in his mind. He turned to the old man. "Philo, if that sack isn't found by sundown, I'll make some big changes on this plantation."

Confusion marked the old man's brow. "Changes, massah?"

"Changes!" he repeated without detail. "Perhaps I have placed too much trust in your people . . . and especially in Philbus." Guilt was like a dagger in Grant's heart as he moved to the outside where Leroy Biggs waited. Philbus was the one he least likely suspected of taking the evidence, though he might have turned a blind eye while someone else had. "I'll have the sack found by sunup. You needn't wait around."

Leroy Biggs slid his hat to the scant remains of his greased-back hair. "I have a few people to see along the bayou, and I'll be back. You better have that evidence for me, Mister Emerson."

"I'll have it." His conviction did not come from the heart. Actually, he did not hold out much hope of the bones being found. Whoever had stolen it away had done so for a reason, a reason that might mean the difference between life and death. He was infuriated that he had placed enough trust in Philbus to make him the overseer and for his generosity that same man might have allowed Delilah to take crucial evidence in a crime. He would have to rethink that decision. Perhaps he had been trying too hard to win the trust and confidence of these people and they were laughing at him behind his back.

He stormed into the house, surprising Daisy as she set the dinner table. "Let me know when Miss Wickley returns," he bellowed, then moved quickly toward his bedchamber on the second floor.

At the resounding thud that had marked the master's return home, Daisy sighed. "Lawd, I knowed Missy bein' round this here house was goin' ta make Massah meaner'n a rooster!" she mumbled.

Then she smiled to herself, thinking that if her former mistress could make him that mad, she could also use her feminine wiles to calm him down.

After all, she'd seen the condition of Delilah's bed aboard the riverboat when she'd changed the sheets that morning after her departure. She couldn't have done that much damage all by herself.

217

Fourteen

Deputy Biggs returned at three o'clock in the afternoon. Since the skeleton had not been found, a fuming Grant Emerson ordered the Sheriff to leave the plantation. "I'll be back with a warrant, Emerson," Biggs threatened, turning his horse toward the neutral grounds of The Boeuf.

Grant had just sent word to the fields that a meeting would be held among the plantation slaves when Delilah rode in on her lathered mare. Taking the reins as she dismounted, a still ruffled Grant roughly chastised her. "Why the hell do you ride a valuable animal into the ground? Have you no sense at all?"

"I guess I don't!", a frustrated Delilah shot back. "For your information, I attempted to walk the horse the last three miles, but she refused to be held back!" The white lather against Bella's gleaming black body appeared as clouds against a stormy sky. Snatching a rag from Philo's stool, she began briskly rubbing the mare, ignoring Grant as he removed the saddle and blanket. The silent tension between them was unbearable and reinforced Delilah's decision to leave The Shadows. She would not subject herself to such a despicable man. "Since I am leaving," she said after a moment, "and I am

218

not taking the horse, I would like my wages for the past two weeks."

"Cash wages will be only half what I would have applied toward your purchase of the horse. I'll pay you thirty dollars for the two weeks."

"That will be enough," she mumbled, "to get me far away from you."

Grant gritted his teeth. For a moment their gazes locked . . . Delilah's cool and controlled, Grant's narrowed and hateful. When he unexpectedly grabbed her wrist and pulled her to him, he was surprised by the rapid pounding of her heart against his chest. Did anger throb there beneath her heaving breasts, or was it something else?

"I wish you were my prisoner," he hissed between his tightly clenched teeth. "I'd chain you to a bed . . . which is where you do your best work!"

She could see by his lethal look that he was daring her to slap him, and she refused to give him the satisfaction. When an ornery smile crept onto his mouth, she reevaluated that decision, but only for a moment. "Well, I tell you, *Mr.* Emerson, when I leave here, I'll practice that art with a wide array of men. If you think I was good last night, try me again in a couple of months when I've had plenty of practice!"

"Don't be vulgar!" His roughness relaxed into a gentle embrace. "I'd kill any man who touches you!"

Her eyes narrowed in humor, even as her mouth pressed sarcastically. "Why? You don't want me? Don't you remember? I'm a trollop."

The sight of her exquisite face beneath the mid-afternoon sun made his body tighten painfully. He wanted to drag her to the nearest bed and love away her boldness and her rebellion! He wanted to

219

claim her with brutality, and yet speak the tender endearments flooding his heart. Why did she stir such a befuddling array of emotions within him?

When he spied Daisy approaching, Grant released her. "You've just been granted a reprieve," he whispered.

"From what?" Delilah retorted, her gaze cutting to Daisy's worried features. "The whipping post?"

"Worse . . . Me!"

Aware of their harsh bantering, Daisy paused a few feet away, waiting to be recognized. Grant turned his gaze to her, "Massah, will Missy be havin' supper with you?" she asked.

"You might ask her that question."

Delilah had taken up Bella's reins and now turned toward the stable. "I had a late lunch," she responded across her shoulder. "I'll not be having supper."

"A late lunch with who?" Grant queried, arching a copper-colored eyebrow.

Just before she and Daisy merged into the darkness of the stable, Delilah paused and half turned back. "That is none of your business," she responded. She wanted so much to tell him of her reunion with Ellie, but she knew it would give him immense pleasure and that was the last emotion she wished to produce in him.

"As long as you are working for me, everything you do is my business," he hissed, though she was no longer in sight.

"That relationship has terminated," she reminded him from the stable. "I am no longer your employee."

Grant swore under his breath, turning so that he would not be tempted to answer her. As he moved toward the big house, he called across his shoulder, "Don't take anything from the plantation that does not belong to you, including my horse!"

"And you leave my wages on the desk so that I can collect them!" she called just as crossly. "Blasted man should get off his high horse!" she mumbled when he was out of hearing range.

A low rumble of laughter erupted from Daisy. "Lawd, Missy, the way ya carry on with the massah, I swears they's love abrewin' between ya."

"In a pig's eye!" she grumbled, her voice cracking with irritation. "His ego sticks out all over him! Who could love such a man?"

Confusion creased Daisy's brow. "Ain't never seen no ego, Missy. Lawd, ya musta seen more of him that I has."

Recalling Grant's harsh tone, Delilah shuddered visibly. She did not bother to explain to Daisy what ego was, but let her think what she wished. "What on earth has riled his feathers so?" Delilah asked, not really expecting an answer from her friend.

"Don't ya know, Missy?" Daisy asked, backing away from the mare prancing in place and twisting Delilah within the circle of her reins. "Ya's s'posed to return the bones to the peg, an' ya didn't, Missy. Ya promised that ya would!"

Delilah had been turning in place, attempting to extricate herself from the leather bindings surrounding her. She ceased her movements. "What do you mean? I did return them—"

"Naw, ya didn't, Missy. They's gone an' Massah's right mad."

"I did!" Delilah argued firmly, releasing the reins to extract herself from them. "I swear, Daisy, I put them back before I went on my ride."

221

Daisy shook her head. "Well, they's gone. If'n ya didn't take 'em, don't know who did. Massah's called us all together at seven this evenin'. Betcha', Missy, he's goin' ta put one of the bucks under the whip till somebody tells where them bones are."

"He wouldn't do that."

"He's mighty riled, Missy."

"He seems to be more angry with me. Did you tell him about my having the sack this morning?"

Shock registered in Daisy's dark eyes. "Lawd, no! I ain't a wantin' to be whopped up fo' helpin' ya, Missy. I keep my mouth shut real tight. An' ya don't—" Suddenly someone called Daisy's name sharply. Mozelle stood at the kitchen entrance, her hands drawn to her hips.

"Ya git in here, Miz Uppity High Yella. Ya's s'posed to be de cook, an' I is doin' all de work!"

Daisy shrugged apologetically as her gaze lifted to that of the taller woman. "I'd best git on in, Missy. Mozelle's, she's liable to have a cow if'n I don't."

"I'll come say goodbye before I leave."

"Yeah, Missy . . . I hear the two of ya, an' I s'pect ya leavin' fer sho'." Again, Mozelle called, her voice even harsher than before. Turning toward the house, Daisy waved. "See ya later, Missy."

Left alone once again, Delilah sought out Philbus, who was scouring the tack room and thinking that perhaps the bones had simply been overlooked.

"Philbus?"

"Huh?" Startled, he turned. "What is it, Missy?"

"It's about your horse. Swainie says it belonged to the dead man. You've got to get rid of it."

"Naw'm!" he immediately challenged her. "I trade my ol' mule fair an' square fo' dat hoss, an' I been

222

ridin' him for pert near six years or so, an' I ain't agonna git rid of him. Ya better git dat notion plumb out o' your head, Missy! 'Sides," he reasoned, "if'n nobody's come lookin' fo' dat man an' his hoss for dees six years, I don't reckon nobody ever will!"

Delilah nodded. "Swainie and I both guessed that you'd feel that way. Very well . . . you keep your horse—"

"Fully intend to," he cut her off, turning back to his search. "Good day to ya, Missy."

The mere suggestion that he get rid of his horse had hit a sore spot. Delilah turned and silently left him to fret about it.

Grant's restless footsteps carried him between his bedchamber and the study on the first floor several times before he eventually settled down upon his bed. Tucking his hands behind his head, he stared absently at the ceiling. Blasted woman! he thought, wishing she were more reasonable, yet in the same moment remembering the exquisite wonder he had enjoyed in her arms. He closed his eyes and might have fallen asleep if Mozelle's fat old cat had not suddenly pounced upon him. He cursed the beast without feeling, then watched it settle at the foot of his bed with its head resting against his boot.

The unbearable heat was not relieved by the breeze wandering in through the open windows, and the thin layer of perspiration became an adhesive between his flesh and his shirt. When it popped out in beads across his brow, he tore the shirt down his arms and dragged it across his forehead. The lids of his pale-blue eyes eventually closed, and he fought for a moment of calm within the confines of the room.

Beyond the window, he could hear the occasional snicker of a stabled horse, and farther past, a flock of startled widgeons cutting the wind. Philo's rhythmic hammering at the anvil suddenly broke the tranquility, followed shortly by the grunting of a sow in a pen at the quarters. Children's laughter could be heard like a soft, low song, and he took a moment to wonder what they had to be happy about. There was nothing humorous in slavery.

His fingers suddenly clutched at his hair and he felt that he might split apart at the seams. Damn! How could life fall apart in one day!

A knock sounded at the door. "What is it?" Grant called without opening his eyes.

"Monsieur, do you need my service?" Trusdale replied.

"Not now, Trusdale. I just want to rest." He didn't care much for Trusdale. or his attitude of superiority. When Montford Wells, pleased with the French Negro's temporary service at Wellswood, had hinted that he'd be interested in purchasing Trusdale, Grant was not sure why he had balked.

The manservant's monotone voice pierced the thick wooden door. "Does monsieur need a bath drawn?"

"Not right now."

"A tray of brandy, monsieur?"

Grant was a little annoyed by Trusdale's persistence. Although he was simply trying to be efficient at his job, Grant wanted to be left alone. "Later, perhaps," he called. "Let me know when it's seven o'clock."

"Very well, monsieur."

Grant didn't know why he chose that moment to remember the letter he had stuck into his pocket that morning. But he shot up, swinging his boots to the floor. When he did not see his jacket in the room, he remembered that he'd slung it across the seat of the carriage. Usually, before leaving the carriage, Philbus gave it a good inspection. Perhaps his jacket had been given to one of the servants. Rising, arching his back to relieve the tension gnawing at him there, he moved toward the door and the corridor. He met Trusdale coming out of one of the rooms.

"Have you seen my jacket?" he asked politely.

"Which one, monsieur?"

"The one I wore this morning . . . the gray one."

"No, monsieur. Perhaps it is downstairs. Shall I check for you?"

"No, I need to get out," Grant replied. "I'll find it."

Moments later, he emerged from the house, noticing at once the sun in its slow, late-afternoon descent. His entrance into the stable brought Philo to his feet.

"Have you seen my jacket?" Grant asked him.

Philo moved quickly toward the carriage. "Massah left it here," he explained. "Philo was gonna give it to Daisy to bring to de big house."

Grant took the proferred garment. As he turned back to the house, he spied the tall, willowy form of Delilah Wickley moving slowly along the upper deck of the riverboat. He watched her descend the main stairway, turn left on the lower deck, then exit the boat over the gangplank. She seemed to take a deliberate course, around the pond and toward the cemetery. When she slowly sunk into the hill's descent, he, too, moved in that direction.

When at last he crept into the shade of an oak, he noticed that she had changed into a pale-yellow gown, simply made and yet elegant in the way it clung to her curves. She had dropped to a cool patch of ground between the graves of her parents and her fingers absently caressed the delicate petals of the clover in which she sat.

A strange stillness suddenly settled upon the evening as he watched her golden eyes flirt among the flora and fauna, occasionally lifting to study the peaceful marble headstones of her loved ones. How could she appear so tranquil, so elegant and so at peace, and in the next moment be a boiling volcano of raging passion?

Delilah was at a distance of about fifty feet with her back turned to him, and yet he could envision her thoughtful features and the melancholy downcast of her eyes. Suddenly, a colorful butterfly, flitting among the clover, perched upon her shoulder, causing her to reveal her lovely profile to him. She smiled admiringly, her hand moving toward the tiny, miraculous life so trustingly lit there.

Grant began to move across the soft cushion of ground separating them. His eyes followed the flighty movements of the butterfly as the whisper-soft tendrils of its legs wrapped around Delilah's finger. He paused just out of touching distance of her.

"It's beautiful, isn't it?" she sighed, turning her head just enough to see him from the corner of her eye. "When I was a little girl, my mother had an old calico cat she called Sweetie. Several days after the poor beast was viciously killed by a pack of dogs, my mother was working in her flower garden. Everywhere she moved, a beautiful butterfly—

226

with vibrant colors just like Sweetie's—flitted along with her as she did her chores. When it lit upon her shoulder, Mother told me it was Sweetie's spirit, coming to say farewell. Then it just flew off into the wind, never to be seen again."

As Grant regarded the beauty of her, his body longed for her nearness. She was such a puzzle to him that sometimes he didn't know what to say or do when he was in her presence. Her moods were so unpredictable. "Why do we quarrel, Delilah?" he asked after a moment, the emotion in his voice causing her to turn. When she moved, the butterfly commenced its journey among the flowers dotting the patches of clover.

"I don't know." If she was still angry with him, it did not reflect in the softness of her reply. "It is a shame, isn't it, when two adults cannot be civil with each other for more than a few minutes at a time?"

She did not move as he approached and dropped to his knees at her back. Tenderly, his hands went around her shoulders and held her close. "You must know I don't want you to leave The Shadows, Delilah."

"But we cannot get along—"

"We could give it another try." In the back of his mind, he suspected her of taking the skeleton, but he didn't feel that this was the time to bring it up. Convincing her to stay at The Shadows was much more important to him than anything she might have done. "Perhaps I say things I shouldn't, but you also behave as if you do not like me . . . not even a little bit."

Delilah caught her breath as his words sifted into her ear. His musky scent assailed her delicate senses and, unconsciously, her head fell back to rest against his shoulder. "You are right," she responded after a moment. "I can be a little snip sometimes." She did not protest as his fingers lowered and touched her silky skin just above the bodice of her gown, then rested there unobtrusively.

"You're a devil of a girl, Delilah," he gently laughed his response. "How could a man not like you? How could he not . . . grow to love you?"

"Horse feathers!" Her laughter joined his own. "Look at the two of us, Grant? One minute we are at each other's throat, slinging vicious names—"

"And stinging blows," he added without argument, a grin raking his handsome features.

"The next . . . we are like this, enjoying each other. You do enjoy being with me, don't you?"

"As much as I enjoy a damn good steak!" he continued the playful chiding. Delilah turned, allowing herself to be warmed by his gaze, her mouth easily surrendering to his own seeking one. When the merest breath of space existed between them, he whispered, "Let's call a truce, Delilah. Stay at The Shadows, and when I act like a self-centered, egotistical rogue, simply mount Bella and ride off for a while. I don't want to fight with you any longer."

"Then you are surrendering?"

"If you wish."

Her mouth pressed petulantly. "I like to win my battles, Grant."

"Then . . ." His hands outstretched, "take me your prisoner."

Her arms scooted along his beltline, then circled to his back. As the sun continued to descend, she was content to rest against him, her head against his shoulder, his rhythmic breathing touching softly against her hairline. Without realizing she'd intended to speak, she suddenly asked, "Am I really a trollop?"

Grant's grin stretched from ear to ear. "Ain't goin' to let me fergit that one, eh, purty miss?" he drawled, squeezing her to him as he wrapped his arms around her. "Now, tell this ol' man," he continued playfully, "that the purtiest little filly this side of The Boeuf is goin' to stay around."

She grinned shyly in response to his chiding. "I told Ellie that I was leaving."

His surprise was like an open book upon his face. "You did? When?"

"This afternoon. I rode over to see her. We—" She shrugged. "We made amends." When he did not respond, she continued quietly. "I don't know if she told you what I said to her that day, but I was wrong and I asked her forgiveness. A friend like Ellie comes along once in a lifetime, and I would never forgive myself if I'd lost her forever. Frankly, I wouldn't have blamed her if she'd run me off—"

"Ellie isn't like that."

"Yes, I know, she's one of a kind. Thank God she is a tolerant woman and understood my error."

"Have you changed your opinion?"

Confusion marked her brow. "What do you mean?"

"I know you were angry that a *Yankee-Doodle gambler* purchased The Shadows. Have you decided I'm not so bad after all?"

She slumped. "How—how did you know they— we—we're calling you that?"

He laughed. "I overheard Lancie use the unflattering description before he, too, decided I wasn't so bad."

"I must agree with him . . . you aren't so bad.

229

But you're still a Yankee and I've heard tell Yankees are an intolerant breed."

"Then punish me," he growled huskily, "and make me suffer. Stay at The Shadows and be an aggravating thorn in my side."

"Pooh!" Feigning indignation, she sat ramrod straight, prying herself from his gentle embrace. "I should punish you by leaving. That would make you think twice about treating me so badly."

"Think a lot of yourself, don't you?"

"More than you do, I suppose," she cooed, the unpleasant memories of the late morning as remote as the moon. She wanted only to enjoy his closeness, to hear the soft laughter in his voice. She wished the tender moments would go on forever. On the other hand, she wondered how long it would be before he said something to completely destroy the mood.

As she again relaxed against him, the sweetness of his breath whispered upon her cheek. She sighed wistfully, feeling the gentle massage of his fingers upon her bodice. She had feared after last night that he would lose a certain degree of respect for her, but she did not detect it in his gentleness. What a perplexing man he was, she thought, her sun-washed features softening as she smiled her own approval of him.

"Grant?"

"Hmm?" Lazy contentment pronounced the low, wordless sound. When she turned, she could almost see herself reflected in his eyes. When she said nothing, he chuckled softly. "It is very impolite for a lady to stare so boldly. It would certainly make a man wonder what is on her mind . . . and hope it was something delicious."

"I am wondering," she replied, "how I can agree to stay, without looking every bit the fool." Absently, her fingers closed over his hand gently resting against her bodice. "You know when I pulled that stunt on the trail, I did so because I hated you enough to wish you dead."

"And do you still wish me dead?"

She turned, surprised by his inquiry. "Of course not. Sometimes I wish . . ." Her eyes closed lightly, then slowly crept open. "Sometimes I wish . . ." she began afresh, "that *I* was dead."

Deep lines carved into his brow. "Why would you wish that? Are you so unhappy?"

"I don't know that I'm particularly unhappy. But I am not happy, either."

He stirred on his knees, and his hands roughly gripped her shoulders, drawing her back to him. "If you will let me, Delilah, I will chase away your melancholy. I can think of nothing more challenging than making you happy to be here . . . to be with me."

She groaned, even as her fingers lifted to encircle his wrists. "Why would you want that, Grant? I have been cruel and deceptive and secretive. You cannot possibly like me, let alone want to make me happy. And you cannot possibly trust me. Surely . . . surely you believe I am the one who stole away the sack containing that poor man's remains—"

"Blast it! I wish I'd left him buried out there and said nothing. He's causing more trouble than I'm willing to put up with."

"Then you don't think I took him?"

"I didn't say that," he responded without argument. "Frankly, I hope he doesn't show up. I'd rather concentrate . . ." His mouth brushed lightly

231

against her cheek, "on making you happy like I said I would."

"Let's not quarrel anymore, Grant. I promise to be open with you if only there will be no more quarrels. Though . . ." Eyeing him coyly, she continued on a softer note, "I've heard it is very enjoyable for a man and woman to make up following a good fight." With one swift move, she was on her knees facing him, her hands easing toward his own, her gaze all-consuming upon his face, her mouth graced by so faint a smile it was hardly there at all. "I want you to believe, Grant, that I had nothing to do with the disappearance of the sack." She deliberately did not tell him about removing the watch. "In the future, I promise not to do anything behind your back, and not to snoop in your house—"

"You've been snooping in my house?" He echoed her last words. "Whatever for?"

"Ammunition, I suppose," Delilah responded, shrugging apologetically.

"Did you look in the gun cabinet?"

She crinkled her nose. "Not *that* kind of ammunition, Grant. Something . . . more personal."

"Oh, I see." A half-cocked grin said much more than his words. "Something you might use to get me off my plantation, eh? Confession to some heinous crime that might get me strung up on the gallows? Perhaps you think I've deserted the military—"

"Horse feathers!" Lightly, she slapped at his good leg. "You look more like a gambling rogue than a soldier! And . . . no, I'm not trying to find something on you. I guess . . ." Her eyes dropped coyly, "I'm just nosy."

"I have nothing to hide." Again, he thought of the

letter in his jacket pocket . . . "If you want to snoop, then snoop."

"Aren't there letters from your . . . umm, wife, that you wish to hide?" she asked.

"I burn them," he replied, unaffected. "I have letters from a vengeful cousin that I also burn. So — snoop, little one, if it pleases your fancy, but I warn you, it'll bore you to tears." With graceful ease, Grant rose to his feet, then drew her up against him. "Come, let's get back. I have a meeting with the slaves and you, my snoop, you must get your sleep so that you can play tug-of-war with the ledgers in the morning. I brought a stack of paid bills back from Alexandria that needs to be posted."

As they walked along, his arm linked protectively around her waist, they enjoyed the last rays of the dipping sun together. For the first time since she'd talked her way into his life, Delilah did not worry who might see them intimately, lovingly embracing as they moved toward the house overlooking The Boeuf.

Somehow, she knew things would be different between them now. The quarreling was over and something new and wonderful would guide their destinies.

Nothing else mattered but that they were together . . . moving toward a point of no return.

Fifteen

And move they did . . . from sun-warmed days into passion-filled nights, until the summer passed so quickly, neither was really quite sure just when the transition into autumn took place. Grant hardly noticed when the cotton was ready to be picked in late September, and Delilah really didn't care. All she knew was that she was with Grant at Shadows-in-the-Mist, she was happy and deeply in love with the Yankee rake.

The latter realization was the beginning of Delilah's heartaches; it dropped a gloomy veil over what should have been sheer, joyous contentment. She could not forget her promise to her father: *I will get The Shadows back, Papa. I swear it on my life!* She was tormented by that promise, and torn by the turmoil of emotions tugging her within.

Though the weather was cooler, darkness did not fall until after seven. With Grant coaxed out to the field by Philbus, who was still secure in his job as overseer and excited over the rich cotton crop this year, Delilah saddled Bella and took to the night air, as Grant had enthusiastically recommended. After several minutes of riding, she ducked into a shady spot at a bend in Bayou Boeuf and dismounted. She was melancholy to the point of tears, and she knew she had a lot of dreadful thoughts to sort out.

She perched upon a fallen log and pressed her palms to the cool bark on either side of her thighs. She was suddenly reminded of the grove of felled oaks on the bayou, and the vision made her smile. She had been so determined that when the debris had been cleared up she would dig for her father's gold. Now, two months after the nightmare that had rudely startled her from her sleep, she hadn't given the booty a second thought. Grant's arms had been her reward—his passion, her treasure. Nothing mattered to her but being with him. Even Shadows-in-the-Mist had ceased to be important to her. She would live in a shack with him, if that was what he wanted.

Sighing wearily, she looked up, only now noticing her position. She was able to see any comings and goings on both the trail and the bayou but doubted anyone would be able to see her. The shadows were deep and haunting, enveloping her and cutting her off from the last glints of sunlight. Even Bella's dark form, still but for her nibblings at the ground, would be indistinguishable to the casual passerby.

The quiet was broken only by the rustle of a breeze through the trees all around her. Against the fringes of the clearing, the pale golden leaves of a wild wisteria, mingled with those of the white oak, paper-thin and shaped like open hands, rained to the ground, creating an almost hypnotic effect. A shuffling in the underbrush did not startle her; a raccoon, unaware of her thoughtful scrutiny, moved absently across a dry patch of ground along the bank, foraging for food. A soft plop in the shallow bayou current, probably a bullfrog, next caught her attentions. Her nose crinkled in distaste as she thought of the bayou residents catching the beasts in order to enjoy the delicacy of their hind legs, dipped in batter and deep-fried in lard. She would as soon eat a snail!

But she didn't care about frogs and snails and raccoons. Guilt plagued her, vicious tugs of loyalty between the memory of her father, her rashly spoken promise, and the exquisite joy she felt in Grant Emerson's arms. But was it love she felt for him? Or did she simply want to be mistress of Shadows-in-the-Mist, with a legally recorded certificate of marriage for proof—something she could lay upon her father's grave with gloating satisfaction? Would she use the Yankee to accomplish the purpose that had initially drawn her back to The Shadows? Dear Lord, surely this emotion swelling within was love. It was wonderful, sensual, exquisite. Being apart from him made her feel empty inside. Being with him brought a womanly glow she could feel from head to toe, and the gentleness of his arms around her made her tremble with desire. *It is love! Dear God, tell me it is love!*

Desperation surged within her like ice. She buried her face in her hands and tried to shake away the awful feeling. These past few nights, after their exquisite moments of lovemaking, something had always rested right on the tip of Grant's tongue, words he somehow had not brought himself to utter. She had a feeling she knew what he wanted to say, and though she longed to hear the words, she had to be absolutely sure she did not have ulterior motives.

He had been so good to her. Knowing how much she loved the riverboat, he had hired men in Alexandria to refurbish it, adding fresh coats of white paint and a brighter blue trim, sanding and painting balustrades and repairing a small section of rotting deck on its paddle wheel end. All the changes were aesthetic ones; no efforts were made to repair the cracked rudder or replace the blown boiler engine. Holes were patched in the smokestack, but only to make them look good. The large, airy cabin in which they shared their exquisite moments had been redecorated, with new furnishings ordered from New Orleans and rich blue-and-gold damask draperies and matching bedcoverings. Delilah and Grant knew *Bayou Belle* would never ply the gentle currents of The Boeuf, but it was their special place, and it deserved the attention it had gotten.

Bella snorted. Looking up, Delilah caught the shadowy sight of a rider on the north side of the bayou. She pushed herself up, moved the few feet toward Bella, and rose into the saddle. A short while later she left the mare with the young stableboy Hank and moved toward the riverboat.

She was surprised both to see a lamp lit in her cabin and Daisy emerging with a large box. " 'Bout time you got back, Missy. Massah, he's a pacin' the flo' awaitin' fo' ya to get back."

"I thought he'd ridden out to the field with Philbus."

"That's what massah *wanted* ya to b'lieve, Missy, an' why he sent ya off ridin' that high-steppin' critter. He's got a big ol' surprise awaitin' fo' ya." She held the box out to Delilah. "And this here be th' first, Missy. Massah says to help ya get into it, an' then ya's having a special dinner at th' big house with him . . . an' special ente'tainment, too!"

Delilah took the box, sat on the divan, and

opened it. She gasped at the sight within; a rose-colored satin gown with complementing jewelry — earrings and a necklace studded with exquisite opals and diamonds. "I—I cannot accept this." She stumbled forth the words.

"Sho' ya can, Missy. Lawd, I don't remember a time when ya's growin' up with yo' pappy and mama that ya ever had such a dress! I says ya make the massah happy an' wear it tonight, then if ya feels funny 'bout it, then ya's tell him ya can't keep it. What ya say, Missy? I got ya a bath drawn, warm an' bubbly, jes' the way ya like it."

Forgetting her personal dilemma for the moment, Delilah was almost sure she'd melted as she spent a very long half-hour bathing, dressing, and having her hair fixed by the chattering Daisy. When, at last, she scrutinized her appearance in the cheval mirror, she was pleased. She felt suitable for the romantic evening Grant had planned.

"Dear Lord!" She spoke the two words sharply, drawing her hand up to cover the necklace.

"What's wrong, Missy?"

"He's not . . . I don't suppose he's—"

Daisy chuckled exuberantly, guessing the subject of her attempted inquiry. "We's all got a bet goin', Missy," she confessed, leaning close as she added, "But don't tell the Lawd, 'cuz I think He considers it gamblin', but we all think Massah's goin' ta ask ya to marry up with him. Won't that be somethin', Missy, ya bein' back at The Shadows, jes' like ya said ya would!"

Tears flooded her eyes. "Don't say that, Daisy. He deserves someone better than me."

"Ain't nobody better'n you, Missy. I knows, 'cuz I been yo' bes' friend, 'most since we was born."

Sniffing back the tears, Delilah turned and hugged Daisy firmly. "And have I ever told you how dear you are to me? I wish . . ." Putting a breath of space between them, she finished softly, "that Grant would release you so that you could marry Lancie."

Daisy smiled her biggest smile. "He will, Missy. I feel it in my heart. An' Lancie's a patient man. He'll be there a waitin' fer me. I jes' knows it."

Delilah squeezed her hands. "Well, if you think I will pass inspection, shall we go to the big house?" Reaching down to gather up the voluminous frills and folds of the elegant gown, she moved toward the gangplank and the autumn darkness, almost positive she knew what Grant had in store for her.

Grant paced the parlor floor like an expectant father. Taking his watch from the inside pocket of his jacket for perhaps the hundredth time, he sighed deeply. Daisy had said it would take only half an hour to get her ready, and it had been well past that since she'd ridden in.

When at last he heard feminine voices at the gallery, he took wide steps to the foyer so that he could greet her personally. As she stepped into the light, the vision of her almost took his breath away.

The childlike way she held up the full, shirred skirts brought a smile to his mouth. But the way the bodice hugged her slender frame and womanly curves sent a river of steel throughout his body. The exquisite jewelry and dozens of hand-sewn pearls dotting the wide lace collar of the gown shone in the lights of the chandelier. She had drawn her hair up into a cascade of chestnut ringlets and wisps of tiny curls clung to her glowing ivory skin.

Delilah had never seen Grant looking so elegant, a ruffled jabot hugging his neck, his crisp white shirt in brilliant contrast against his black jacket and trousers. He had swept back his golden hair, trimmed neatly at his collar, leaving untouched the wide, thick sideburns against his firm jawline. Beneath the lights, his eyes seemed so pale a shade of blue that the color was hardly there at all.

"I am so glad you could make it to my party, my lady," he said, taking her hand.

"I am honored to have been invited, kind sir," she responded. "But you really must tell me, what is the special occasion?"

Grant squared his shoulders. "I plan to take the evening slowly and not lay all my cards out on the table. Now . . ." He favored her with a slight smile. "Will you consent to my being your escort for the evening?"

"Why, sir," she drawled, "it is my pleasure."

Over the course of an hour, they dined on pheasant and artichoke dressing, sipped white wine, and chatted pleasantly over small, unimportant things. But every time Grant's voice grew serious, Delilah quickly brought up another subject for conversation, until the only way he could quieten her was to draw her into his arms and cut his eyes to a doorway, his cue to Trusdale to take up his violin and his position as one-man orchestra.

"When did Trusdale return to The Shadows?" Delilah asked, a little disappointed to see the uppity fellow.

"This afternoon. Montford found a reliable man and no longer needed him. Though he did . . ." he continued, to give hope in her moment of disappointment, "offer to buy Trusdale."

240

She wouldn't let his return be a source of distress to her, at least not this evening. She had enough on her mind, wondering if Grant had something special planned for her.

When Grant swept her into his arms, Delilah could imagine nothing more wonderful, their gazes lovingly locked, their feet moving in unison with the music, his fingers pressing into the small of her back to draw her close. His manly aroma grazed her senses, his breath upon her cheek sweet with wine. Deliriously happy, and yet apprehensive of the reason for their celebration, Delilah whispered, "Such a wonderful evening . . . I hope it never ends."

"It has only just begun," he responded. "The night is full of surprises. Who knows what might happen next?"

"Are you ever going to tell me . . . why?" she asked, gazing into his cool, blue eyes.

"Why? The celebration?"

"No . . . why Jackson parted the Pontchartrain with redcoats," she chuckled sarcastically. "Of course, why the celebration!"

His feet ceased to move, but Trusdale continued to play. Grant took Delilah's hands, his gaze moving admiringly over the full length of her beautifully adorned body. "Because, Miss Delilah Wickley . . ." Dropping one of her hands, his own moved into an inside pocket of his jacket. He clutched whatever he had removed in the palm of his hand. "Miss Delilah Wickley," he began again, taking her left hand to slip a diamond ring upon her finger, "will you do me the honor of marrying me?"

Sheer horror glazed Delilah's golden eyes as her bejeweled hand curled into a ball. Shaking so vio-

241

lently she felt she would collapse, she turned, instead, and fled, leaving him in mute surprise in the dimming light of the dining room. Instantly, an equally surprised Trusdale ceased to play his violin.

"Monsieur caught his lady off guard," Trusdale said, hoping the explanation would ease Grant's mind. He could see that her flight had confused him.

"Perhaps I should go after her." Grant forced a smile. "I do need either a yes or a no, don't I, Trusdale?" Moments later, he found her at the end of the gallery, sobbing uncontrollably. She did not hear him approach and was caught unawares when his hands gently encroached upon her shoulders. "I hope these are tears of happiness," he whispered against her hair. Only now did he notice that she'd removed the ring and was turning it in a circle between her fingers. "You do not like it?" he asked. "We could choose another—"

"No . . . no, it is not the ring. It is beautiful. I—I—" She could scarcely control her sobs. "I don't deserve it, Grant. Though you are all I've ever hoped for, I think I was afraid of something like this. Dear Lord, what must you think of me?"

"What I think? Well, my love, I think . . . I know," he softly amended, returning the ring to her finger, "that I love you. Nothing else in the world matters, and I would hope the feeling is mutual."

She turned, exposing the full extent of her despair—her tear-reddened cheeks, her full, trembling mouth, the pain reflecting like mirrors in her eyes. "I cannot marry you," she whispered in response. "You must know that when I forced my way into your life, it was for the purpose of trapping you into marriage so that I would be mistress of The

Shadows. I swore on my father's grave that I would get the land back any way I could. How can you not be repulsed when you look at me? I am a despicable woman. Seduction . . . marriage for profit . . . I am the worst kind of whore!"

He eyed her sternly. "You have told me what you did and you have told me what you think you are, but you have *not* told me, Delilah, that you love me. That is what I want to know. Do you love me . . . and if you do, will you be my wife?"

The sobs began afresh as she slumped against his shirt, her fingers clutching the lapels of his jacket for support. "I do love you, Grant, but—how can you trust me? Although knowing me as you do, you cannot believe I would marry you for any other reason than my love for you and my desire to be with you always, to be your wife and the mother of your children? I just don't see how you can want me."

"But I do want you—"

"You've never even told me . . ." The sobs stilled. "Whether you are still a married man."

"I am not a married man," he echoed softly. "Will it make you feel better about me if I tell you the whole story?"

She gently nodded, against his shirt. He wrapped a strong arm around her shoulder and coaxed her to a wicker settee on the gallery. She sat beside him, her hands tenderly enfolded within his own, her eyes downcast, watching the breeze rustle against the crisp folds of her satin gown. She listened, first to the deep sigh he expelled, then to his softly spoken words.

"I have a cousin, Aldrich, who is a bit of snake. When I sold my importing business in New York, I returned to Boston, only to learn that Aldrich's betrothed was carrying his child and Aldrich was nowhere to be found. When two months had passed and we still had no word from him, I married Madeleine—against the wishes of my parents, I might add—in order to give her child the Emerson name. After the birth of the child, I had the marriage annulled, without disturbing the legitimacy of the child. This happened almost six years ago, Delilah, and I have put it behind me. My marriage to Madeleine was never consummated and was strictly for the benefit of the child."

"You didn't love her?"

A husky laugh erupted from him. "I didn't even *like* her. When I presented her with the annulment papers and turned to walk out, she plunged an ivory letter opener into my left shoulder. No, I certainly did not love her. I wanted only the protection of my family for the sake of the little boy, Dustin. Without a marriage, they would not have been able to intervene in the event of neglect."

"And what of Aldrich? Did he ever show up?"

Grant's mouth pressed into a grim frown. "He was representing the family at a funeral in Connecticut. When Madeleine wrote him of her pregnancy, he had immediately started the trip home in order to marry her. But he was arrested in a small town only thirty miles from Boston and prohibited by a sadistic marshal from sending correspondence to either Madeleine or the family. By the time he showed up some months later, Madeleine was married to me, and, by law, I was the father of her child."

"He must not have been very happy about that."

"He was furious. Death threats have made their way to me at least twice a year."

"Surely he could have married her and made matters right with the court, simply by admitting paternity."

"It could have been that simple . . ." Again, Grant frowned his dismay at having to relate the unpleasant story. "But to this day Madeleine swears to love me and will not consider marriage to Aldrich." He deliberately did not tell her of Madeleine's last letter, warning him that Aldrich had learned his whereabouts and was "coming after him." He was surprised that he hadn't made his appearance by now.

Delilah could only stare into Grant's eyes. She could see that he was telling her the truth; indeed, she could think of no reason that he should lie. Still, the fact that he claimed to love her and wanted to marry her filled her with such grief that she thought she would crumble away into nothingness.

Delilah stood briskly, clasping her hands as she paced before him on the planked floor of the gallery. "I—I don't know what to say, Grant," she said, halting her movements as she turned to him.

He stood, his palms easing beneath her satin-clothed elbows. "Say that you love me, Delilah."

She became vividly aware of the strength of him, of his tenderly spoken words, of an almost desperation in his voice as he solicited her feelings for him. They had not spoken of love before this night, though their tenderness toward each other had spoken it loudly and clearly. There was nothing Delilah wanted more in the world than to whisper again the endearment he so longed to hear and to hear it returned a thousand times over. But turmoil tugged viciously within her. Did she truly love him, with

245

all her heart and soul, as she had so eagerly confessed to him just moments before . . . or did she profess love simply to recapture The Shadows?

Because the answer did not come immediately to her, she turned and fled into the evening darkness. She was aware of the surprised call of her name, and yet she did not respond to it. She turned, caught the dark outline of Grant's form against the lighted window, and fled into the woodline toward her bayou sanctuary.

Soon, she slowed to a walk, feeling the burning of exhaustion inside her chest. Her thoughts were broken and scattered, her tears so bitter, her eyes burned like fire. During her flight through the short spanse of woods, the tangle of flora and fauna had torn the neatness from her hair. But she couldn't have cared less. She knew only that she had to put time and distance between herself and the tall, proud Yankee who would take her into his arms and his heart. She had to sort out her own tremulous feelings.

Grant would have fled after her if Daisy had not stepped out to the gallery and boldly pinched her fingers over his sleeve. "I knows Missy better'n anybody in this world, massah. Ya leave her be an' let her think this out, an' she'll be a comin' back right soon. Ain't goin' to do no good fo' ya to pressure her—"

"You were listening?" There was sharp rebuke in his voice.

"Na, suh . . . but can't close my ears when I happen to be near enough to hear ya two atalkin'. Missy, she's feelin' right poorly 'bout the way she

246

treated ya when she first got here. There's a big ol'
ugly monster named guilt grabbing Missy's insides,
an' she don't be thinkin' she deserves to have ya love
her. I thinks she does, massah, if I's can be so bold
as to say, an', massah, ya couldn't find a better
woman even if ya poured yo' own mold."

The frown left Grant's brow; his features relaxed
into a thoughtful cast. "You're some kind of lady,
Miss Daisy. I'll tell you what . . . if you're right
about your Missy, I'll—" His recitation ended
abruptly. Surprise would be more effective . . . at
the right time and the right place.

Daisy linked her fingers at her back and turned,
pausing when she reached the door to reassure him,
"Missy, she'll come round, Massah."

Delilah's flight had left him feeling cold and angry. "Blast it, Delilah," he mumbled, "why can't you
act rational?"

Delilah slumped into a sobbing heap. Oh, why,
why couldn't she come to grips with her emotions?
She knew, beyond a shadow of a doubt, that she
loved Grant. There were too many times she had
fretted over his short absences from The Shadows,
too many long, love-filled nights she had lain in his
arms and could imagine no more wonderful place to
be on the face of the earth . . .

*Oh, Grant . . . Grant, why couldn't you have been ob-
noxious and hateful? Fat and bald and repugnant. Why do
you have to love me? It could have been so easy . . . marrying you and taking The Shadows away from you. Making your life miserable and forcing you to leave. But no
. . . you have to be a kind, gentle man with the patience
and tolerance of a saint. Show me your faults! Make me*

*want to marry you for selfish reasons! Make me want to do
everything within my power to hurt you! Make me hate
you!*

Her fingers began tracing the seams of the lovely
gown Grant had purchased for her. How had he
sized it so perfectly? How had he described her pro-
portions to the dressmaker? How did he know that
particular shade of rose was her favorite color? Her
hand lifted to cover the exquisite jewels at her
throat. Were they a family heirloom, or had he purchased them especially for her? Were they a gift, or
only a loan? Oh, how would she ever still the rush
of thoughts making her feel dizzy enough to faint!

Life had been so simple before her father's death.
She had done her daily chores with childlike indifference, had taken her mare on frequent excursions
along the bayou, had visited Ellie, or Lucie Wells,
had assisted in difficult deliveries at the slave quarters, and had beamed with pride over a tiny face
brought safely into the world.

Now, life, though it was beautiful with Grant,
was difficult to cope with. She had brought about
the turmoil herself and now she didn't know how to
undo it. Grant deserved a wonderful wife, one who
would marry him for no other reason but love . . .
and though she felt she could give him love, she
wondered if other motivations still rested, like a
snake coiled beneath a rock, within the core of her
rapidly pacing heart.

Delilah knew there was only one solution. She
could not remain at The Shadows while she came
to her decision, with Grant looming over her emotionally and physically, awaiting her response. She
had to leave, for however long it took to reach into
her heart and hold the truth in her hands. She

could have no doubts when she gave Grant her answer.

Pushing herself up and raking the backs of her hands across her tear-reddened cheeks, she resolved to go to Imogen in New Orleans. She hoped her aunt still welcomed a visit. Two hundred miles and perhaps a couple of months might resolve her inner turmoils and conflicts. When she returned to The Shadows, she had to be sure that it was to Grant's arms she returned and not to the seven hundred acres of earth where a promise had been made over her father's grave.

Grant sat quietly on the deck of *Bayou Belle,* watching the shadow of the southern beauty emerge from the timberline. He had figured she would eventually return to the riverboat, rather than the big house. When she ascended the gangplank, then the stairway to the second deck, he came to his feet in the darkness. "I know you need time to yourself," he explained, watching the downcast reflection of her eyes in the dim light of the moon. "I just wanted to make sure you were all right."

Timidly, Delilah cast a look in his direction, noticing at once the halo of golden light surrounding the fringes of his hair. He had removed his jacket; his shirt was unbuttoned, exposing the thick copper-colored matting of his chest. "I'm all right. I apologize—"

His hand went out, touching her arm. "There is no need. I will give you this night alone to think. Tomorrow I hope you will have an answer for me." When she did not reply, he said softly, "Good night, then."

She immediately regained his attention. "The necklace, Grant? Do you want it back?"

He turned, the pain of her inquiry darkening his eyes. "I bought it for you and it is yours to do with as you please. You may even . . ." He managed a tiny smile, "throw it in The Boeuf if you wish. Now, good night."

She said nothing, but allowed him to move past her and down the main stairway. Swallowing the tightness in her throat, she watched him walk toward the big house, his limp more noticeable, yet his shoulders held squarely back. She wanted to call out to him, to confess her love for him before he distanced himself from her, and yet something held her back. She dreaded the night ahead, without him. She dreaded the morrow, when he would expect his answer.

She dreaded the demons fighting within her.

She dreaded what she had to do and held long within her heart the last glimpse of him as the darkness swallowed him.

Sixteen

Before the dawn, after a long sleepless night, Delilah began packing her canvas bag with a few garments and necessities. She knew that Grant would not arise until six, as was his usual custom, so by five o'clock she was coaxing Bella toward Ellie's cottage on Bayou Lamourie.

Ellie, an early riser herself, was surprised to see Delilah ride past the gallery and dismount at the stable, where Lancie took her horse. Fearing that something had happened, she met Delilah halfway between the cottage and stable. The despair written in her friend's face deepened her apprehension.

"What has happened, Delilah?" Hugging her younger friend to her, she entreated her toward the cottage. Shortly, they sat together on the divan in the parlor. "Is it Grant?"

Delilah's fingers brushed absently at the dust clinging to her riding skirt and nodded almost imperceptibly. "He asked me to marry him last night," she replied. "I—I simply must get away."

A moment of resentment burrowed up from Ellie's heart, though she quickly masked it. "Do you love him, Delilah?"

Moisture gathered on her lower lashes. "I love him dearly, Ellie. At least, I think I do."

"Why do you harbor doubts?"

With shame fragmenting her words Delilah told her friend of the promise she had made to her father, heightening her story with confessions of the guilt and regret she had felt these past few months she had spent with Grant. "How can I be sure, Ellie," she asked after the long recitation, "if I truly love him, or I just want to keep my promise to Father?"

"Your heart should tell you."

"But suppose I should marry him and realize that I don't love him? He doesn't deserve that kind of pain. Dear Lord, I don't see why he should even trust me, let alone want to marry me. I've deceived him and lied to him and he probably still believes I stole that silly old bag of bones, though he has let the matter rest these past few weeks. But Leroy Biggs and Sheriff Stafford are still worrying him about it and, though I am *not* responsible, I feel so responsible for his troubles. I just feel that I should get away and sort out my feelings for Grant. That is why I have come to you."

"If you stay here, Delilah, Grant will still come to see you," Ellie replied, misinterpreting her intentions. "He will not leave you be, if he loves you. And . . ." Gently, she shrugged, "I can't say that I would blame him. Love is a wonderful feeling, and he is going to want to be with you."

The soft gray mist of the morning invaded the large room through the gossamer curtains, momentarily capturing Delilah's attentions. She had scarcely noticed the lovely beginning of the new day on her four-mile ride along Bayou Boeuf and the trail taking her to Lamourie. Now, she wished she could enjoy it with Grant, who would soon be arising. "You have always been such a good friend to me, Ellie, and I have always been able to confide in you. I want to travel to New Orleans to visit my aunt Imogen, but I want you to be aware of my plans so that you will not worry." She removed the ring Grant had placed upon her finger and pressed it into Ellie's hand. "I want you to keep this for me, and if I do not return in two months, return it to Grant. You must swear on our friendship, Ellie, that you will not tell him where I am."

"Grant is my friend, Delilah. It is terribly unfair of you to ask me to lie to him."

Delilah sniffed back her emotions. "You don't have to lie to him. Just be evasive, should he ask."

"I just don't know—"

"Then I will have no choice . . ." Pain marring her brow, Delilah continued, "but to go someplace other than the one I have confided to you. Please, please, don't make me do that, Ellie. Keep my confidence—"

"I just don't understand!" Ellie's voice, soft just moments ago, suddenly became harsh and annoyed. "You could have traveled to New Orleans without telling me. I know you can take care of yourself. I would not have worried—"

Delilah's hand gently covered Ellie's. "Then who could I have kept in touch with? Who could have written to tell me how Grant is? I would not be able to bear the time apart from him if I could not know he is well—"

"This certainly sounds like love to me, Delilah."

Rising and approaching the window, Delilah looked out at the new face of the dawn. Somewhere from beyond the timberline came the long, clear, plaintive cry of a wild turkey. She shivered, then turned slowly to again face Ellie. Rather than respond to her observation, she asked if she had Ellie's word. "Will you keep my secret and let me know how Grant is doing?"

Ellie, too, came to her feet. A lengthy silence passed between them, each woman holding the gaze of the other. Finally, Ellie took Delilah's hand and gently swung it back and forth. "Though it does not set well with me, I will attempt to keep your secret," she said. "I will entreat Grant to give you time to sort out your feelings, and I will assure him of your safety." Tears swelled in Ellie's eyes. "But I will not see Grant hurt—"

"Dear Lord—" She knew for sure now. "You're in love with him? You're in love with Grant Emerson."

"Don't be absurd," Ellie nervously countered, "I am four years older than Grant."

"Does that really matter?"

"I don't! I don't love him!"

Delilah's gaze warmed. "Oh, but you do, Ellie. It is something one woman can see in the eyes of another."

The last vestiges of Ellie's denial crumbled before her. "All right! I care deeply for him, Delilah. But it is an affection that is not returned. And I care enough about him to want him to be happy. If *you* will make him happy, then so be it. I am not one to stand in the way of true love."

Delilah hugged her friend. "I don't know what to say."

"Say that you will come back. Say that you will not break Grant's heart. I couldn't bear it—"

"I can promise you only that if I do come back, it will be because I can confess my love for him, without any doubts as to its motive." Ellie offered no response. "Will you see that Bella is returned to

254

The Shadows tomorrow?" Delilah asked. "And would it be all right if Lancie drove me into Alexandria? I'll catch the first steamboat out for New Orleans."

"Of course he can. But why not return Bella to The Shadows today?"

Delilah suffered a sharp pang of conscience. "Because I do not want Grant to know I am gone until I am far away. Tomorrow, please?"

"Very well. But I don't like any of this."

At the moment, Delilah very much disliked herself even more than she disliked oatmeal. "I know you don't. And I wouldn't blame you if you never wanted to speak to me again."

Half an hour later, a very solemn Lancie sat beside her on the carriage seat, coaxing the mare into a trot. He said nothing; his silence sent a very clear message of disapproval.

Grant was surprised to find Bella gone from the stable. He called to the boy Hank, who appeared from the darkness of the stall he had been cleaning. "Did Missy ride out this morning?" he asked.

"Yas suh, massah . . . 'bout hour o' so ago."

"Did she say where she was going?"

"Jes' ridin', massah. Dat's all Missy say." Considering the matter settled, Hank turned back toward the stall with his heavy broom.

"Boy?" Hank turned back. "Did Missy look happy this morning?"

Hank shook his head. "Can't rightly say, massah, dat she looked happy. She 'uz real quiet-like."

A frown creased his brow, even while his gaze softened. "When Missy gets back, you make sure

Bella gets a good portion of sweet feed. How would you like to be assistant groom of the stable?"

Young Hank's eyes became large. "Massah, me?" Unable to suppress his glee, a grin spread from ear to ear. "I likes dat jes' fine, massah," he said and broke into happy songs.

Now that he was once again alone, Grant wondered where Philo was. Not seeing him sitting on the stool seemed rather peculiar and he wondered if the old gentleman was ill. But Mozelle would have said something this morning if that was the case, so he rested easy, thinking that perhaps Philo's chores had taken him away from the stable.

Seeing the simple-minded slave girl sitting at her usual spot, Grant halted a moment to observe her. The frog ornaments, some of glass and some of wood, seemed to have dwindled away. "Lose your frogs, girl?" Grant asked.

"Frogs, dey be in de box, massah," she replied, "sho' 'nuff."

Shrugging, he resumed his short trek to the stall where his horse waited. He would have to remember to ask Philo if some mishap had resulted in the girl's dim-wittedness. Saddling up, he was soon riding through the quarters. He waved to Granny, rocking on her front porch and smoking a corncob pipe, then moved gingerly through the children picking up fallen pecans on the roadway. He couldn't help thinking about his vivacious Delilah and wanting to be with her, to hear her answer to his proposal of marriage. But if she needed these few extra hours of solitude, who was he to deprive her of them? What did it matter if he was aching inside with anticipation?

He entered the meadow where cattle grazed, then

paused to look over the silo that had burned a couple of months before. Sitting atop his horse, he wondered how the badly damaged structure continued to stand. He looked around, hoping to catch the flowing chestnut-colored hair of the woman he wanted for a wife.

But he saw nothing, with the exception of the trees bending to a sturdy wind and gray-fringed clouds stirring overhead.

He did not see the rider submerged in the deep shadows of the timberline, watching him through hate-filled eyes.

Aldrich Emerson had seen his cousin ride away from the rich plantation on The Boeuf. He had planned to make his presence immediately known, but decided to enjoy a few minutes of cat-and-mouse beforehand. Seeing Grant's tall, well-proportioned frame, which showed no evidence of aging, made him grit his teeth in frustration. Even his thick golden hair had not thinned, as had Aldrich's. He had always envied his younger cousin his good looks.

He would have arrived on The Boeuf weeks earlier had it not been for a comely lady in Natchez who had diverted his attentions for the moment. Had she not been killed by a runaway freight wagon, he would probably still be in her arms. Lynette had been a beautiful young woman with frequent need for a man's intimacy. Such a waste! Aldrich thought, remembering his last glimpse of her mangled body upon the muddy roadway.

Despite his intense hatred for his cousin, Aldrich could not help but admire him. He had never failed at any endeavor undertaken, and today, might very well be worth half a million dollars. Aldrich had done some checking up on him in New Orleans last week, discovering a cache of bank accounts in his cousin's name with monies untouched in over two years. Whatever business Grant had engaged in, he had been very good at it.

When Grant eventually turned his horse away from the burned silo, Aldrich dogged him along the dark periphery of the woodline. His mouth curled into a malicious smile as he thought of the days and weeks ahead, when he would choose just the right moment to rob Grant of his wealth . . . and his life.

Grant halted his horse in the meadow and looked around. He had an eerie feeling he was being watched but could see nothing of the imagined interloper. Apprehension crawled through him; remembering the last time he'd felt like that, he half expected to feel a sharp letter opener pierce his back.

Prodding his horse ahead, he soon entered the trail through high grass that would open onto the cotton fields where Philbus and the other slaves were working. Perhaps if he whiled away his time in the fields, he wouldn't think about Delilah and the time would pass more quickly.

When he reached the field, he found two of the women preparing several chickens to be barbecued later in the morning. A stone pit, constructed for just that purpose, stood at the edge of the field. As he dismounted his horse, he asked the older woman, Luba, if he was invited for lunch.

"Sho' is, massah," she responded with a wide smile. "Udie an' me, we's goin' ta bake some fresh-dug taters, too, an' we's brung a big ol' pan o' peach cobbler dat Granny baked jes' las' night."

Grant liked these people very much. He never really thought of himself as their owner; he felt more like a friend. "I'll stick around until dinner's ready then. In the meantime . . ." His hands dropped from his hips, "I'd better get out here with the men and earn my keep."

The two women thought he was just kidding, expecting him to remount his horse and ride through the neat rows of cotton like lord and master of the manor. Rather, he tied his horse off with others that had been ridden to the field that morning and moved on foot into the ripe cotton.

Shock registered in the faces of the workers as he took up a cotton sack, drew it across his shoulder, and began plucking the bolls of cotton from their thick, thorny claws. Mumbling sounds drifted through the field and one of the men cautiously approached him. "Massah, dis ain't no kind of work fo' ya."

"If it's good enough for you, it's good enough for me," Grant replied without looking up. Cutting his thumb on one of the bolls, he emitted an oath and drew a handkerchief out of his rear pocket.

"At leas' allow me ta show ya how to pick de bolls widout hurtin' yo'self, massah."

"I think, Sebastian, that might be a good idea," he replied.

He had just resumed the job after Sebastian's instructions when Philbus rode up on his big gelding and dismounted between the rows. "Massah, somebody was a followin' ya, but when I tried to get close, he took off."

Apprehension again prickled in Grant. "I thought I was being followed," he replied. *Could it be my cousin?* he wondered, shrugging off the dismal prospect. "This is hard work! These blasted things don't want to let go of the bush."

"Ya don't need to be doin' dis type of work," he almost echoed Sebastian's statement. "Ya's makin' everybody feel real funny 'bout it."

Grant grinned. "Udie and Luba are preparing a feast fit for a king over there. I want to earn my share."

"Ya's can have anything ya want widout workin', massah."

"But it'll taste better if I earn it." Actually, he did not want to be idle, to fret over Delilah's absence . . . and her ultimate decision. As far as he was concerned, his future happiness depended on her answer. He could not imagine the rest of his life without her. "You'd better climb back on that horse," Grant continued after a moment, "and keep an eye out for the watcher in the woods."

"He hightailed it," Philbus reminded him, looming over him as if he expected him to faint from the exertion of work. "But I'll keep an eye out anyhow."

Less than an hour later, an exhausted Grant Emerson was naked to the waist like the other men in the field. Sweat ran in rivulets over his sun-bronzed flesh; the late-September sun was so hot that his head felt scorched through the thick fabric of his hat. He wanted to quit his work and seek a shady spot for rest, but was too embarrassed to give out before the rest of the pickers. Thus, he endured another three hours of the grueling labor, and was thankful for the aroma of barbecued chicken and baked potatoes calling them to the cooking pit.

During the course of the ample meal, Philbus told Grant that tomorrow was the day The Shadows was supposed to work on parish roads. "If'n we don't, the police jury be levyin' a fee on us," he explained. "Who do ya want ta send out, massah?"

"I got a notice the other day. Thanks for the reminder. I would have forgotten. Take as many men as are needed," he said. "We'll work a limited crew in the field tomorrow."

"Ya should put some o' dem young'uns to work, massah. Other planters, they's be workin' de young'uns."

"No!" He spoke the single word with harsh criticism. "I don't like to see children workin' . . . and I don't care what other planters do."

"Jes' niggers, massah — nothin' but yo' property, jes' like de plow mules an' de hosses."

Grant cringed from the sarcasm in Philbus's voice. He was the most outspoken of the slaves on the plantation; and that was the main reason Grant had given him the job of overseer. He spoke his mind without hesitation, just like his feisty wife, Mozelle. That was a freedom Grant felt all men and women had the right to enjoy, though Grant wished Philbus would be a little less vocal at times.

Rather than respond with anger, as his heart would have done, Grant's steely gaze flickered over Philbus as he repeated matter-of-factly, "We'll work with a limited crew. It's just one day."

"An' it could be one day closer to de rain dat could ruin the cotton dis year, massah. Come October, it'll be rainin' cats 'n dogs. Usually does."

"We'll beat the rain. I feel lucky this year." Anxious to change the subject, Grant asked if the children in the quarters got daily lessons in general subjects.

"Such as what, massah?"

"Reading, writing, arithmetic."

Philbus snorted in surprise. "Onliest stuff dees chil'ren learn is how to pick cotton, cut cane, and clean up after whites."

"I want them tutored."

"What fo', massah?"

"So they'll learn to say, 'the' and 'that,' instead of 'de' and 'dat.' So they'll say 'what for,' instead of 'what fo'.' That's why, dammit. Learning doesn't hurt anyone."

"Except you, massah. Ya start teachin' black chil'ren an' ya'll be dragged away in chains yo'self. Whites, dey don't want de blacks ta learn. Dey might begin to believe dey's pert near as good as dem white folks." He had deliberately emphasized the *dey, de,* and *dem* in his recitation. He rose, dropping his wooden plate into a pile with others. "Ya de massah on a plantation in de South," he warned Grant, "an' ya need ta git dem dang fool Yankee idees out of yo' head. It'll jes' make ya unpop'lar wid yo' white neighbors, massah, an' ya don't want ta be doin' dat, now do ya, massah . . ."

Grant climbed to his feet, cursing inwardly. He respected Philbus for speaking his mind—though he didn't particularly like what he said—but he felt that he should be free to do as he pleased, and to hell with the neighbors. He would not, however, quarrel with the man he had befriended these past three months. "I'm going to leave you to the fields," he began, untying his shirtsleeves from around his waist to pull the garment on. "Del—Missy was not at the house this morning and I need to be sure she's all right."

"Missy'll be fine. She carries a pistol in her saddle case."

Grant was surprised. "I didn't know that."

"Lots of things ya don't know 'bout Missy, but . . ." Only now did the moody Philbus allow himself to smile, "I reckon ya'll be findin' out a lot more 'bout her after ya make her yo' woman."

"So . . ." Grant mused, "Daisy's been talking."

Philbus laughed out loud, but there was little mirth in it. "Ain't no secrets wid dat Daisy around, massah. Ya's already made Missy yo' woman in one way . . . time to make her yo' woman in de other. If'n ya git her knocked up, massah, won't look good on de bayou in de uppity white circles, her spewin' a bastard baby—"

Grant's eyes fixed on the face of The Shadows' overseer. Rage seethed within him. "You know, Philbus," Grant said with forced civility, "I could grow to hate you." With that, he moved toward his horse, drew himself into the saddle, and galloped away.

At precisely the same moment Grant might have been dismounting at The Shadows, Delilah was sitting at the Red River Steamboat Company, waiting for the next departure. Having first checked the schedule, she knew she had a bit of a wait so had picked up a book of poetry at Garrett's Mercantile, where she had also sold another piece of her mother's jewelry. Mr. Garrett had gotten very generous in the prices he paid, and she was still surprised at the thirty dollars he had given her for the pearl necklace. She had not wanted to sell the piece, which had been one of her mother's favorites, but she didn't want to show up on her aunt's doorstep penniless.

She sighed deeply, thinking of Grant and wanting to be with him. She could think of nothing more wonderful than becoming his wife, and she hoped he would forgive her for running away. She had to make sure the feeling inside her was love. She already missed Grant and could not bear to think of the hurt he would feel at discovering her flight from Shadows-in-the-Mist. She hadn't even had the courage to tell him why.

She frowned darkly. Though she held her recently purchased book open upon her lap, she had hardly read a word, choosing instead to watch the comings and goings of passengers, of workers unloading produce on the dock, of the faint shadow of residents moving about on the Pineville side of the river. The Red River current seemed swifter this afternoon, the depths a deeper, murkier red, like mud after a summer storm.

How strange was life, she thought, remembering the carefree days at The Shadows, sharing her innermost secrets with Daisy and sealing the confidence with linked pinkies and childish giggles. Closing her eyes, her chin resting upon her balled hand, she could almost feel Bella's mane whipping against her face as she rode her into the wind along Bayou Boeuf. She could feel the strength of her powerful body against her thighs and hear the rhythmic clip of her shod hooves upon hard, well-traveled earth.

Now, she was a confused shell of a woman fleeing from a man because she didn't know if she loved him. She had once wanted nothing more than to hurt the Yankee who had purchased The Shadows, and now . . . she cringed inwardly at the thought of it. *Please . . . please, dear Lord, let my inner turmoils fly off into the clouds. Let me return to him because I love him and want to be his wife . . . and for no other reason.*

Suddenly, tears rushed upon her golden eyes, but she lowered her gaze and discreetly brushed away the evidence of her melancholy. It occurred to her that Ellie might break her confidence and send word to Grant. Even now, he might be rushing to Alexandria to intercept her flight. Would she want him to do that? Even as she mentally answered "no," she found herself watching the door, waiting for his tall frame to fill her vision, waiting to see his hand briskly rise to brush back his pale golden locks, waiting to see his eyes narrowed and angry, his mouth trembling with rage that she would dare to leave him.

Feeling perfectly miserable, she rose from the hard, uncomfortable bench, caring not a whit that her book fell upon the floor. She paced back and forth, wishing the time would pass and boarding would begin. Lancie had offered to remain with her until departure, but she had been so afraid she'd change her mind that she'd politely declined his company. Now, she wished he was here, convincing her that what she was doing was foolish . . . convincing her to face her problems and not run away.

But she really didn't feel she was running away. She felt that she was giving herself time—time to assure herself that by marrying Grant she was doing the right thing for the right reason. Besides, Aunt Imogen was getting on up in years, and as her only niece, she owed her this visit.

"Passenger's boarding for New Orleans . . . Pier Two—"

The company agent's absently droned announcement caused Delilah to start. Turning, preparing to retrieve her book and canvas bag, she paused and looked back at the door. No, he would not come. So accustomed to her riding off and spending many hours alone, he probably had not yet even missed her. She could board the steamboat and be halfway to New Orleans before he would become alarmed enough to send out a search party.

She gently closed her eyes for a moment, drew a deep breath and turned, preparing to begin a new—but she hoped temporary—life away from Shadows-in-the-Mist . . .

And the man in whose arms she had loved away long, exquisite nights on the riverboat rocking gently upon the currents of Bayou Boeuf.

Seventeen

When Delilah had not returned to The Shadows by four o'clock in the afternoon, Grant had made the rounds of the neighboring plantations and homesteads, inquiring if she'd been seen. He'd not been able to talk to Ellie, since she was in bed with a headache, and if Delilah had visited there that day none of those living at her homestead made any mention of it. He did not see the mare tucked away in a back stall of the carriage house.

It was almost as if Delilah Wickley had dropped off the face of the earth.

By nightfall, his concern deepened and by midnight he sent out a plea for volunteers from the neighboring plantations to search for the missing Delilah. Mozelle cried that she'd been thrown from the black voodoo demon she rode and was lying somewhere in the woods, crushed and mangled and unable to call for help. Daisy asserted her conviction that Delilah could take care of herself, and Philbus worried that the trusting girl had been spirited off to Texas by a good-fer-nothin' skunk.

Grant was sick with worry. Even as he barked orders from the gallery to mounted men carrying torches, directing them to different areas along the bayou, his insides crawled with apprehension and dread that he'd never see Delilah again. His mind raced frantically as he plotted her recovery from whatever disaster had befallen her.

By the time he mounted his own horse, every acre on both sides of the bayou was being covered by caring men who had watched Delilah grow up and who cared about her. If she was out there; they would find her.

Four miles to the west, a man named Tarpley Jenkins was dismounting his horse at Ellie's cottage, hoping to elicit the assistance of her son and handyman in the search for the missing woman.

Ellie had just slipped into a robe and taken the lamp Miss Mandy handed her when the fall of masculine boots resounded on the gallery outside. There, still pulling on his shirt and adjusting his suspenders, stood a darkly frowning Lancie, and behind him Maden and the Jenkins fellow from St. Landry Parish.

Lancie drew Ellie to the far corner of the gallery. "It's gone too far, Miz El. This here fella says dere's about two hundred men out in de woods along de bayou betwixt here and Cheneyville ahuntin' fo' Missy. What we's goin' ta do."

Ellie was furious that Delilah had put her in this position. She could not bear the thought of hardworking men out scouring the midnight darkness for a woman who was probably seventy-five or more miles away, safely tucked in the compartment of a steamboat bound for New Orleans. Delilah had not wanted her to tell Grant she was gone until tomorrow, but she simply could not allow this ridiculous farce to continue until then. "Lancie, ride over to The Shadows and tell Grant that I must see him immediately. Tell him it has to do with Delilah."

"Sho', Miz El. But what do I tell this fella here?"

"Tell him nothing. After I have talked to Grant, he will call off the search and all those poor men can go home to their wives and children."

"It sho' is goin' ta embarrass Mistah Emerson. He might not be able to face his neighbors tomorrow."

Ellie cringed at the thought of the repercussions. Rather than respond to Lancie's more than likely accurate observation, she lowered her gaze when she scooted past the man named Jenkins, then softly closed herself within her house. Miss Mandy stood in the foyer. "What's happened, Miz El?"

"Our Delilah!" she snapped, though not to chastise the dear servant who had inquired. "She gets me in one predicament after another, with her nasty little secrets and inability to face her problems!" Softening her voice, her hand fell to Miss Mandy's arm. "Grant will be visiting shortly. Could you make a pot of coffee?"

"Sure, Miz El. Maybe I better dig out that bottle of laudanum, 'cuz you's goin' to have to peel that po' Yankee off the ceilin' an' sedate him when you tell him what Missy done this time."

"You just might be right," Ellie responded, moving toward the bedchamber to change from her night clothing. Throwing herself down on her bed for a moment, she felt tears sting behind her closed eyelids. It had not been a particularly good day for her, culminating in the sick headache that still lay in wait at the base of her skull. She could physically feel it sharpening its claws for another attack, and she hoped she would be able to maintain some semblance of control when Grant arrived. In the hour she took to dress and calm down, she reluctantly accepted a small dose of the laudanum Miss Mandy offered her, and the headache waned a bit. By the

269

time Grant arrived, she felt almost lightheaded and, for the moment, her anger with Delilah temporarily went the way of the headache.

Hearing the familiar sound of Grant's bootsteps, she opened the door before he could knock. Even in the half-light, his annoyance was as plain as a noonday sun. "You called me away at a crucial moment, Ellie. What is this about Delilah?"

"Come in," she responded. "We'll talk about it."

"If you two have had another tiff," Grant said, entering the cool, lamplit parlor, "couldn't we discuss it after she's been found?"

"She isn't lost. That is what I want to talk to you about. I know where Delilah is —"

He turned sharply, taking her arms in a rough grip. "What do you mean? Where is she?"

Ellie tried not to respond to his painful grip, though she jerked her arm in a feeble attempt to loosen it. "I'm not at liberty to tell you where she is, Grant. But since you have called so many men out to search for her, I felt it imperative you know right away that Delilah has left The Shadows of her own accord and is not in any danger."

His arms dropped; suddenly, the sweltering heat within the cottage was unbearable to him and, giving her a somewhat beleaguered look, he stepped past her through the open door and moved the length of the gallery. When the hand of the silently approaching Ellie touched gently upon his shoulder, he shrugged it off.

"Please, let's talk, Grant," she implored him. "You must understand the position I am in."

"I know only that I considered you a friend, Ellie," Grant growled, "and you have done something this . . . this despicable! You must know how I feel

270

about Delilah! Why didn't you come to me immediately?"

In a rush of tears, Ellie collapsed to the thick cushion on the settee. She could not bear Grant's scolding. She could not bear the thought of his being angry with her. She cared so deeply for him; loved him . . . would give the world if her love was returned. But he loved Delilah and she was the woman he wanted. And Delilah was her friend. As painful as the request had been, she had made a promise to Delilah. Because of her loyalty, a dear, gentle man like Grant Emerson had changed into a raging bear before her eyes.

Half expecting him to draw back his hand and slap her, she was surprised when his fingers circled her wrist and drew her to her feet. Holding her gently in his arms, his hand rose to caress her loose hair. "Forgive me, Ellie. I would never in a thousand years want you to cry. We'll talk now, and you tell me everything. All right? Will you dry those tears?"

Unable to speak, she nodded gently against the warmth of his chest. She enjoyed being in his arms, even if he offered her no more commitment than comfort.

Aldrich had been dogging Grant all day and enjoying it immensely. Though he'd never been able to place himself at a vantage point to hear him clearly, he had asked one of the men in the woods what was going on. The man had responded that "Missy" was gone from the plantation. "She probably run off," he said. Believing Missy to be a recalcitrant slave, Aldrich had shrugged off the explanation and continued watching Grant from the

271

darkness of the woods. Thinking he was a member of the search party, none of the other men paid any attention to him.

Now, he sat in the midnight darkness, watching Grant embrace a beautiful dark-haired woman on the half-lit gallery of her house. He could not see that the woman was crying, nor could he hear the words they were speaking to each other. He knew only that they turned in each other's arms and moved quietly into the house.

So! His dear cousin had a woman, and from the looks of it they cared very deeply for each other. Aldrich gritted his teeth, infuriated as he remembered how Grant had robbed him of Madeleine and established himself legally as the father of her son. Thinking back over the years, Grant had always been popular with the women. His remarkable looks had turned many a feminine head. Aldrich did, however, get a gloating satisfaction in the fact that somewhere in the past, Grant had suffered an accident that had left him lame, putting a dent in his masculine perfection. He only hoped it was not a temporary impairment, caused by some silly mishap that would quickly heal itself.

A gentle wind caressing the tree tops suddenly invaded the narrow space in the woods where Aldrich sat astride his horse, robbing him of his hat. The movement startled the horse, which drew back on its haunches, crackling dry twigs and leaves. As Aldrich quieted the beast he'd rented from an Alexandria livery, a big black man emerged from the darkness of the carriage house and looked around. Fearing detection, Aldrich caught his breath and prayed that the horse would not give away his position.

Soon, the man returned to the carriage house, and a relieved Aldrich dismounted his horse to retrieve the lost hat. He imagined that Grant would be a while; surely he would want to satisfy the woman as completely as he intended to satisfy himself . . . He'd always been such a considerate bloke, believing a woman's sexual gratification to be as important as his own. As young men, the very drunk Grant had made such a declaration in the company of Aldrich and a half-dozen of his college chums. He'd been the butt of their chiding for several weeks thereafter.

Now, there he was, enjoying the favors of the beautiful woman in whose arms he lay, wrapped and warm and satisfied. Envy seethed within Aldrich; sure, he'd been able to attract beautiful women, but he'd always had to fight for their attentions, whereas Grant had not.

His position in the woods afforded him a good view of the dark waters of Bayou Lamourie scarcely a dozen yards behind the woman's house. Thunder suddenly gripped the northern horizon, which appeared as a silvery tapestry against the darkness, simultaneous with the scatterings of large drops of rain that ended almost as quickly as they began. Dark clouds descended to the timberline, then tumbled off into a hauntingly black sky.

He didn't mind waiting for his cousin to emerge from his night of pleasure. He'd waited a long time for his vengeance, and it was soon to be his.

Grant sat quietly on the divan, his elbows resting on his parted knees. He had allowed Ellie to tell him the happenings of the day and had not interrupted. But when she stopped short of telling him where Delilah had gone, his head snapped up with renewed anger flashing in his eyes.

"What do you mean, you can't tell me where she is? I demand to know her destination. It is my right!"

"And by what law do you exercise such a right?" Ellie calmly countered.

"By my right as the man who loves her . . . the man who would offer her his home and his future and want nothing but to be loved in return."

Oh, how dearly Ellie would have loved to hear those sentiments, but with her as the object of his affections and adoration rather than the flighty Delilah. "You really must return to The Shadows and call off the search, Grant," Ellie said.

He, too, arose. "I will not leave until you tell me where Delilah is—"

She faced him, boldness and determination mirrored in her gaze. "Then I hope you are prepared to spend many nights and days here, because that is something I will not reveal. I have told you that she is safe. I have told you that she needs time to think. But I will not tell you where she is. She asked for two months. The least you can do is give it to her."

"I love her, Ellie. And I do not want to spend two months without her."

A nerve twitched in Ellie's left eye. She pressed her lips together firmly, hoping to alleviate the anger she felt within. "Delilah spent most of her life being a carefree girl, Grant. I am sure . . ." She hesitated to continue, "that you have made her a woman. Give her some time to adjust to that new and demanding role."

"I've demanded nothing of Delilah. What we have together was as much her choice as it was mine." Anger boiled within him. Grabbing his hat from the divan, he moved toward the door. "I'd better call off that search, Ellie. But, you mark my word, I'll be back tomorrow . . . and the next day and the next day and the next after that . . . until you tell me where Delilah is."

For the first time, Ellie felt what might possibly be hatred for Delilah . . . and Grant, too. She felt that she'd been caught in the middle, and there wasn't enough loyalty to either of them to be worth the aggravation of it. Moving out to the porch with him, Ellie caught his arm just as he prepared to descend the steps. "Please do not be angry with me, Grant."

Turning, his voice softening even as the annoyance darkened his eyes, he took her warmly in his arms. "Tell me, Ellie . . . tell me where she is. If you care anything about me—about our friendship—you will not keep this vicious secret."

"I cannot," Ellie responded, maintaining her determination. "Give her time."

He pulled her close and held her, his hands moving gently over her arms, his mouth brushing her cheek as he entreated further. "If I promise not to go after her, will you tell me where she is?"

"No," Ellie responded simply. She suffered a sharp pang of conscience as he drew slightly back and smiled.

"I promise you, Ellie, you *will* tell me."

"No, I won't—"

Separating himself from her, he began to walk down the steps. "You will," he responded, his hand brushing over hers for a moment.

When his dark form was absorbed into the darkness, she sighed. "You're probably right, Grant," she said quietly. "I could not deny you anything."

Rather than trail his cousin back to his plantation, Aldrich spurred his horse to the northeast. It would take him a good two hours to reach his hotel room in Alexandria, where he had left his few earthly possessions. He had not considered that he would need much to accomplish the mission that had brought him to Louisiana, but now decided that a trip to a good haberdashery was required. He had a new plan of action and would need more than the modest traveling clothes he had brought with him. *An eye for an eye, a tooth for a tooth* . . . a woman for a woman—

Unless the lovely, dark-haired woman had a ring upon her finger, she was fair game. What better way to wreak his vengeance than to take Grant's woman, just as Grant had taken his six years ago? He would have to draw on his ample charm to beat his fairer cousin out of his prize.

Until he put his plan into action, Aldrich needed sleep; that was first and foremost on his mind for the time being.

When night had fallen, a mate had been sent ahead in a rowboat to affix lighted candles in cylindrical paper shields to scraps of lumber and weight them with stones. As the steamboat moved along the stretch of water laid out by the mate, the fascinated passengers, gathered on deck, peered into the gloom as the *Clarion* "ate up the lights."

Delilah was intrigued by the many requirements of running a steamboat on the Red River and into the bayous toward the Atchafalaya. She had watched the roustabouts punch long poles to the bottom to sound out the shallows. The *Clarion* was not the best boat for this stretch of waterway. She was unsuited, underpowered, deep-hulled like an ocean-going ship, and slow to answer the helm. Her pilot, whom she knew only as "Captain Billy," was something of a hothead, determined to reach New Orleans before the lighter *Rodolph*, a good two and a half hours behind her.

A scurry of activity erupted among the crew as the pilot pushed them ever onward, taking chances that a prudent man would not have taken. More than once they almost ended up in water too shallow to navigate, among clusters of snags and sunken trees that could possibly weigh a ton. But luck was on Captain Billy's side, because they continued to move through the thick red currents of the Red. At this pace, they might possibly reach New Orleans hours ahead of schedule.

Delilah sighed wearily, attempting to make do of the situation. Steamboats were not her preferred mode of travel—most travelers on them were men of coarse habit, recklessness, and uneducated mind—but it was a quicker and more reliable mode of transportation than a fancy carriage that could be waylaid on the road by bandits.

A high wind built up in the early evening, its gusts whipping smoke from the chimneys and flattening the tall grass on shore. Delilah struck up a friendship with another young woman traveling alone, and they enjoyed each other's company over dinner that evening. Afterward, when the mosquitoes got too pesky on deck, they retired to Delilah's compartment, to chat and make plans to spend time together when they reached New Orleans. There, Delilah gave the less fortunate young woman one of her dresses, simply because it matched her eyes. So pleased and tearful was Hilda Roswell that Delilah quickly brought up another subject—her aunt Imogen, who was a colorful and lovable character in old New Orleans.

"Your aunt Imogen, she will let you out unescorted?" Hilda inquired. She was not very pretty, much too thin and slumped as she walked, but she had kind eyes and a warm smile. "You're not like me, a raggamuffin of a girl. You look like a real lady. Do you have a man?"

"A very nice one, in fact," Delilah responded, allowing a sad smile to touch her mouth.

"Are you going to see him in New Orleans?"

"No, I left him behind. He is master of a plantation on The Boeuf."

"A master . . . heavens forbid! That is quite a catch, Delilah. Why isn't he traveling with you?"

She shrugged delicately. "He doesn't even know I'm gone. He must be furious with me."

"You run off?" she asked, astounded that a sensible woman would be so foolish. "Why?"

"He asked me to marry him and I'm not sure it is what I want—should do."

Hilda sighed with childlike annoyance, dropping against the pillow of the cot. "Oh, do tell me, Delilah, if he is terribly handsome—"

"He is, indeed, handsome," Delilah replied to the younger woman's inquiry. "He is tall and fair and his eyes are so pale a shade of blue that they look almost white—"

278

"Voodoo eyes," Hilda blurted out, jolting up. "My mam says eyes like that are voodoo eyes. Used to be, they'd have to be dug out to destroy the evil." Before Delilah could respond, Hilda's hand darted out to touch the rich, full cascades of her hair. "I wish I was pretty like you," she continued on a softer note. "I wish my hair was thick and full and my skin was clear like yours. Maybe I'd be able to snare me a good man."

The compliments embarrassed Delilah. "I think you *are* pretty, Hilda," she responded. "And you are still very young, much too young to be thinking about snaring a man."

"I'm pert near eighteen years old, I am—"

"And when I was eighteen," Delilah laughed her response, "I cared more about my horse than I did about men. I would just as soon have donned a pair of britches and taken to the woods than to attend the fanciest ball with the most handsome man in Louisiana."

"I don't believe you was no tomboy," Hilda responded, not sure that she should take her seriously. "You're too pretty to be a tomboy."

"But I was. I swear, sometimes I still am!"

As the moonlight was drowned out by the gathering of dark clouds, Delilah and her new friend bade each other good night and separated to their own compartments. Delilah had enjoyed the moments spent with Hilda Roswell; the heaviness of heart she had felt since the dawn had drifted off with the wind.

But when she found herself alone, all her sad, confusing thoughts returned with brutal force.

Despite the easy, rocking motion of the *Clarion*, Delilah could not sleep. She sat upon the small cot in her private compartment, her book perched upon her drawn-up knees, trying to read by the dim light that scarcely permeated the small area. Suddenly, the scalding curses of a crew member ignored the thin veneer walls and rushed into Delilah's brain. She was reminded of Grant; he might be venting his fury in just such a way, though she did not relish the idea of such ugliness escaping from so gentle a mouth, a mouth she could almost feel warmly pressing upon her own.

He must be very angry with her. She wondered if Ellie had kept her confidence, almost wishing that she hadn't. Delilah wondered if she had been too hasty in leaving The Shadows, and perhaps that uncertainty was the reason she could not sleep.

"We're slowing down. Fill her fireboxes, I want more steam!"

The masculine voice boomed through the still night air, followed by the low mutterings of other workers. Hearing the rush of bootsteps on the hurricane deck caused alarm to grip Delilah.

Just as she lurched up from her relaxed position, the boilers exploded with a resounding boom. A panicked Delilah pulled on her coat and rushed onto the boiler deck in time to see the hull disintegrate and half the upper works blow into the pitch-black sky, along with human bodies, iron chimneys, and various and sundry supplies that had, just moments before, been stacked neatly on the main deck. People rushed to and fro, crushing Delilah against the walls through which she could feel the heat of fire. With shrieks and sobs trembling through the night, people began slinging themselves overboard into the rushing currents of the Red River.

"Dear Lord," she mumbled, shock and disbelief glazing her eyes. A man's hand grabbed her wrist, pulling her along behind him. "Hilda! Hilda! she called with blind panic. As she was unceremoniously dragged along, the steamboat drifted into a sandbar, her paddle wheel sinking into the surrounding sludge. Some invisible force tore her wrist from the man's grip and she found herself tumbling into blackness, then into the treacherous current. It was just as well that fate took over; she wouldn't have known which way to jump anyway to escape the danger.

Her lungs bursting with tepid water, she managed to crawl along the sandbar, through burning debris and dismembered human remains, until the soft bank cushioned her sobbing body. She reached out to pull a child from the shallow water, but it was dead. Holding it to her, sobbing so bitterly she could scarcely catch her breath, she scooted along on her buttocks until the treeline loomed above her. There, against a bale of cotton that had been blow from the deck, she placed the dear little soul, his delicate features hauntingly illuminated by the flames consuming the *Clarion*. Then, something indistinguishable came flying through the air as another explosion rocked the boat, piercing her thigh. She screamed into the darkness —

And then became a part of it.

Part Three

Eighteen

Grant just stepped out to the gallery when he heard Philbus call to him. "Massah, ya's ready to ride over dem fields ya's thinkin' bout buyin' from Mr. Montfort?"

"I'll meet you out there about, say, half past eight," Grant responded. "I have a call to make this morning."

"To Miz El?" Philbus asked, shaking his head with disapproving calm. "Ya'd be better off givin' Missy time ta think, massah."

"I take it that Lancie has been over here this morning running his mouth?" Grant countered, the irritation like a growl deep within him. "I don't like gossip, Philbus. And I don't like anyone putting their noses in my business." Thinking back over the night, and the understanding with which the searchers had accepted his news, he imagined that he and Delilah Wickley were the talk of the town, so to speak. He didn't like it one bit, but there wasn't much he could do about it. Spreading gossip was human nature. "I'll meet you there," Grant reiterated, forcing a moment of composure. Philbus said too many things that crawled under his skin. He wasn't in a mood to give him satisfaction this morning.

He stood in the shady coolness of the gallery until Philbus had ridden out. Then he moved toward the stable, saddled his horse, and began the short ride toward Ellie's cottage on Lamourie. The Boeuf was strangely peaceful and quiet this morning, hardly a fisher on shore or a living creature detectable in the smooth current. It was rather like the eye of the storm, with the worst yet to come.

Four miles of brooding silence later, he was not surprised to see Ellie sitting quietly on the gallery, sipping a cup of strong chicory coffee. She knew him too well . . . and knew patience was not one of his virtues when it came to getting what he wanted.

"I was expecting you this morning," she announced with more vibrancy than she felt. "And you've wasted a trip. I told you everything I am at liberty to tell you."

His mouth locked into a grimace, his eyes holding her own in a challenge of wills. Dismounting, he propped his boot on the second step. "What makes you think I have not ridden over for a cup of Miss Mandy's coffee?"

"Because, Grant Emerson, I know you will pester me to death until you have your own way. I am not — I repeat, *am not* — going to tell you where Delilah is."

Grant dropped the reins of his horse and moved toward a settee across from her. "Oh, I see, Ellie McPherson . . . this is your way of getting me to visit more often. I have been paying so much attention to Delilah that you have felt slighted. Now you will make me beg for information on her whereabouts? What a cruel woman you are."

His very accurate declaration caused a rush of crimson to flood Ellie's face. She quickly set down her cup so that it would not drop from her trembling fingers. "You are a preposterous man," she countered, much more defensively than she had intended. "Your ego must be a terrible handicap."

Grant had absolutely no idea how close he had come to the truth. He had never considered Ellie any more than a friend, and assumed she felt the same about him. They often teased each other with playful indifference; Ellie had once explained that if people could not be childlike, despite age, they would grow old and die much more quickly.

Miss Mandy appeared to hand a cup of coffee to him. Before she could favor him with one of her warm greetings, Grant gently chided her. "Lord, look at you, Miss Mandy! Is that a new red bandana? You sure look good this morning!"

She feigned shock even as a smile creased her round cheeks. "Ya's teasin' me, Mistah Emerson. Ya's goin' ta make me blush somethin' fierce an' I'll have ta go hide some'ers until I's recover!"

When a chuckling Miss Mandy scooted back into the house, Grant returned his gaze to Ellie, his smile fading as he did so. "Did I neglect to tell you how lovely you look this morning?"

A smile turned up one corner of her pretty mouth. "And flattery will not get you the information, either, Grant Emerson."

"I can't get anything by you, can I?" he responded, adding a little cream to his coffee. Then his tone grew serious once again. "Ellie, I have to know where Delilah is. I will not be able to think or concentrate, or do anything worth a damn." Being able to admit this helped alleviate the anger he felt inside, though he wasn't sure why. "If you don't tell me, every time I hear of a mishap within a fifty-mile radius, I'll be worried that Delilah might be involved. Don't make me go through this."

"Nothing is going to happen to Delilah. She can take care of herself."

"That may very well be. But I cannot take care of

287

myself without her." Setting down his cup, pressing his knuckles beneath his chin with his elbows resting on his knees, he entreated further. "Without her, Ellie, I am a shell of a man. Without her, Shadows-in-the-Mist doesn't mean a thing to me. She belongs there with me, and I will not stop pestering you until you tell me where she is."

"And you will go running after her!" Ellie countered with anger. "I know you, Grant."

"I will not argue, because you're probably right. More than likely, I will go after her and bring her back. It is only a matter of time before I know in which direction to go, because if you won't tell me, someone will—"

"No one else knows where Delilah is."

Grant settled back, then absently tucked his thumbs into his waistband. "I imagine that Lancie and Maden know."

Shock registered, though she said nothing.

"I'll check the hotels in Alexandria, the train station, the ticket office on the dock. I'll check the liveries to see where she left her horse and go on from there—"

"The horse is in my stable."

A copper-colored eyebrow arched. "Indeed? Then I assume Lancie or Maden drove her to her destination?"

"Assume what you wish."

"I've never seen you like this, Ellie. I don't know why you're so determined to keep us apart. Why don't you enlighten me—"

Ellie shot to her feet and moved across the gallery at a frisky pace. "I have important things to do, Grant. I cannot sit here all day and quarrel with you. You do what you must to find Delilah. You will get no help from me."

All of a sudden they were like two strangers, cautious, suspiciously eyeing each other, half expecting a knife-wielding arm to dart out from the cover of a long black cloak. Grant climbed lazily to his feet, returned his hat to his head, and drawled with uncharacteristic sarcasm, "Sorry to have bothered you, Miss Ellie. I'll be moseying along before you fetch your gun and run me off. Don't let me keep you from all those important chores." As an afterthought, he added, "And I'll take Miss Wickley's horse back to The Shadows."

Ellie's heart fell like an anchor. "Grant, please don't be angry with me—"

He brusquely cut her off with a "Good day, Miss Ellie," then tipped his hat as he briskly descended the steps, retrieved his horse, and moved toward the stable.

Tears flooded Ellie's eyes. She did not want the charming Yankee to leave angry, yet she could not call him back. To do so would be to expose her weakness and vulnerability.

Actually, Grant was not as angry as she imagined. He went through his morning regimen with little thought of Delilah or of Ellie's stubbornness. He looked over the acreage with Philbus and decided its value was well within the price range Montfort Wells was expecting. The Shadows was a small plantation, just over seven hundred acres, and the new purchase would double its size. Other area plantations were still considerably larger, but Grant considered quality, rather than quantity, the true worth of a place. He would expand in the future when land became available.

After he'd checked over his finances, he sent for Philbus. Before he could explain the reason for the summons, Philbus made an announcement. "Dat wench Daisy, massah, has took off to de woods with Lancie. Ya want me to fetch her back?"

"She'll return," Grant replied indulgently.

"Sho', massah, after she's flopped dis way an' dat wid dat free niggah an' whelped his young'un—"

"It isn't any of your concern," Grant snapped, handing a sheet of paper, folded in thirds, to the outspoken overseer. "Take this to Montford Wells."

"Yas, suh, massah," Philbus replied.

After the burly man left for Wellswood with the written offer, Grant retired to the study to look over the ledgers that had been neglected for a couple of days. With tender reminiscence he touched his fingertips to the entries Delilah had made . . . the smooth, flowery lines of her pen that made his heart ache with want of her. Why couldn't she have come to him in her moment of indecision? Didn't she know that he would have understood, and given her whatever time she needed? He would have left her alone, had that been what she wanted. There had been no reason to run away.

He groaned his outrage. Damn Delilah! Damn Ellie! Why did they have to keep their vicious little secrets!

He slammed the door with a resounding thud, a warning to the house servants to leave him alone, then attacked the ledgers with a vengeance. By the time he had dwindled away the piles of receipts and shipping invoices and had begun to post the bank drafts, half the afternoon had passed and his stomach crudely reminded him that it needed a meal.

He hadn't realized how black his mood had become; even the outspoken Mozelle had refused to invade his private, angry sanctuary by announcing dinner.

A light rap sounded at the door. Trusdale pushed the door open and peered in. "Monsieur, I would not have disturbed you, but you have a visitor."

"Who is it?"

"I do not know, monsieur. He wishes to surprise you."

"Just what I need," Grant mumbled, forcing civility for the sake of the good-natured servant. "I'll be out in a minute. Make our mystery guest comfortable, will you?"

"*Oui, monsieur.*"

As the servant took his leave, Grant called out to him. "Did that blasted girl return, Trusdale?"

"Miss Daisy?" Grant nodded. "*Oui . . .* she is back where she belongs."

Grant swept back his hair with such force that he might have been pitching hay. He was in no mood for company, and this interloper, whoever he was, had only prickled his mood further. Straightening his shirt, and tucking its loose tails into his waistline, Grant turned toward the corridor. His hungry stomach would have to wait until he'd gotten rid of the unwanted guest.

Though he'd half expected him to show up for the past few weeks, Grant's eyes still registered shock when they settled on the tall, thin form of his first cousin. His gaze darted warily over Aldrich Emerson's hip, where a gun might hang, then to the oversize coat where a rifle could be concealed. Though he saw neither weapon, he did not let down his guard.

"Are you not happy to see me?" Aldrich asked, stretching out his hand as he walked toward Grant.

Cautiously, Grant took his cousin's hand. "Considering that you've threatened my life a dozen times or more, I will reserve judgment."

"We are cousins, Grant. You should take my

moods lightly."

"This one has lasted five years," Grant caustically reminded him.

In a moment of very tense silence, Grant studied Aldrich slightly. Though he seemed thinner, as did his honey-brown hair, he had hardly changed in the six years since Grant had last seen him. They had never really gotten along; they had quarreled as boys, and they had quarreled as men. No matter what one did, the other never seemed to approve. And now, if he had not come to follow through on his threat, what had brought his cousin these many miles to see him?

"You are wondering why I am here, aren't you, Grant?"

A quizzical eyebrow shot up. Rather than respond, he asked if Aldrich would care for a brandy.

"I'd rather a whiskey if you have it. Have you already forgotten that it is my preferred liquid nourishment?"

"I remember only," Grant countered politely, "that you once drank me under the table . . . and we had only a few bottles of brandy." He sidestepped toward the liquor cabinet, refusing to turn his back to his cousin. When he had poured the drinks, he handed the whiskey to Aldrich. "How did you find me?"

"I thought you were in New Orleans. I checked banking records and learned that you'd deposited funds in one of your accounts in the name of this plantation. I did some—"

"Banking records are supposed to be confidential."

"—Further checking." Aldrich finished the interrupted statement, then quickly gulped the whiskey. "When a man wants information, there is always someone willing to provide it, for a price."

"And why did you go to all this trouble, if not to

292

kill me?" Grant turned a suspicious eye to his older cousin. "Yesterday when I was riding, I thought someone was following me. Was it you?"

"It was," Aldrich replied truthfully. He turned into the light, betraying the severity of the scars upon his gaunt cheeks, the result of a bout of smallpox as a child. "Did you get your slave girl back?"

Thinking that one of the servants had mentioned Daisy's absence, he replied that his manservant had said she was back. Grant felt rather like a hare trapped against a butte by a cougar. He still had not turned his back on his cousin. "Now . . . tell me what brings you here?"

"I told you, we are cousins, and I would like to get this messy business behind us. We could get along—"

"We never have in the past. What makes you think we can now?"

"We are no longer boys, Grant. We are men who have made mistakes. It is not your fault that Madeleine will not have me—"

Grant poured another whiskey into his cousin's empty goblet. "Are you saying that you are willing to let bygones be bygones?" A moment of silence whittled away at Grant's nerves. He had too many problems to have to worry about his cousin's motives right now. "I asked you a question, Aldrich."

Aldrich's already thin mouth thinned even more. "I am willing to let old wounds heal. It is as our fathers would wish it."

Mozelle quietly approached, waiting to be recognized. Grant's eyes turned to her. "Daisy, she finally come back to de kitchen," she said. "Would you care for a late lunch, massah?"

"You mean, Mozelle, that I have been forced to endure hunger simply because you did not want to prepare my lunch?"

293

"No, massah, I had yo' lunch fixed, but ya was in such a mood, I didn't think ya'd be wantin' ta be disturbed. 'Sides, ya don't much take to my cookin'."

"Bold wench . . . she should be whipped," Aldrich mumbled.

Grant merely smiled. "She has a right to speak her mind. And it's true, I don't take to her cooking at all."

Mozelle was suddenly furious. With unthinking boldness, she shot back. "Fo' ya info'mation, massah, it be's me what's been fixin' yo' meals since de midsummer, not dat uppity Daisy. She jes' been takin' de credit, 'cuz she don't know how ta cook herself! Can't even cook a pot o' water widout burnin' it!" Shocked by her outburst, Mozelle clamped her hand over her mouth. With tears burning in her eyes, she turned and fled toward the kitchen.

"I would assume that you're going to whip her now. No master would put up with a hotheaded nigra."

"I told you, she has a right to speak her mind. And it's just as well she did. I've been giving Daisy credit for what Mozelle has been doing. That is unfair."

"You just don't change, do you, Grant?" Aldrich snorted, exhibiting a thread of the intolerance Grant remembered so well in him.

"I guess I don't. Now—" He stretched out his hand. "If you are not in a hurry to leave, won't you join me for lunch?"

"I'm famished myself. You know that notorious Emerson appetite . . ." Just as they entered the dining room, the ancient grandfather clock in the foyer chimed the hour of three. When Grant started like a man struck, Aldrich laughed. "Thought it was my knife plunging into your back, eh, Cousin?"

"The thought did occur to me," Grant somberly replied.

Over lunch they caught up on matters of the Emerson family scattered throughout New England, and both men avoided the subject of Madeleine Vail. When the child's name came up, it was in accordance with the appropriate antics of a child his age, rather than his role as Madeleine's son. "You know," Aldrich began without discernible malice, "he may be your son in the eyes of the law, but he looks just like me."

"I agree," Grant replied. "The last time I saw him at my father's house — and he was only two — it was like seeing you again." A moment of revulsion shivered through him as the image of Dustin's mother crept into his mind. Although, thus far, Aldrich had conducted himself as nothing less than a gentleman, Grant couldn't help but wonder if Madeleine's persistent refusal to marry him had sent him South to wreak his vengeance. "Why don't you remain at The Shadows as my guest, Aldrich? We could get to know each other all over again. Perhaps . . ." He smiled for the proper effect, "we might even begin to like each other."

Just at that moment, Daisy entered the dining room and held something out to him. "Miz El's boy jes' brought this over, massah."

When she curtsied, then turned to leave, Grant called her back. "I've decided to return the kitchen duties to Mozelle."

Daisy rolled her eyes heavenward. "Thank you . . . thank you, massah!" she responded, and scooted toward the kitchen with the news. She had been worried sick that the new master would learn that Mozelle had continued to prepare his lunchés because she herself couldn't cook worth a flip.

As he read Ellie's short missive, a frown pressed upon his forehead. Eventually, he looked up, meeting his cousin's steady gaze. "Will you excuse me? I have something to do."

"No trouble, I hope?"

Grant quickly folded the note and stuck it into the pocket of his shirt. "I hope not. Please avail yourself of the house. The servants will provide you whatever you need."

Within moments, Grant was coaxing his horse onto the shady trail toward Lamourie. He hoped Ellie had merely had a change of heart, but her note had sounded much too urgent for that. So worried was he that the bayou and the woods passed by in a blur, and when he entered the clearing where Ellie's cottage sat, he could scarcely remember traveling the four miles distance. As he dismounted, Ellie was almost running to meet him. Her eyes were red and swollen from crying, and the anguish upon her features so visible that fear flooded into Grant's rapidly pacing heart.

"What has happened, Ellie? Is it Delilah?"

"I—I don't know, Grant. There was a steamboat explosion on the Atchafalaya last night. The news just came down the bayou. Dear Lord, Delilah boarded a steamboat yesterday afternoon in Alexandria. I'm so afraid she might have been on it."

"Where the hell was she going?" Grant growled, allowing anger to suppress the mixture of fear and dreaded anticipation clawing at his insides.

"She was going to visit her aunt Imogen in New Orleans for a couple of months—"

"Has anyone confirmed that she was aboard?"

Ellie dropped her eyes. "No . . . I just have a dreadful feeling."

Grant's fingers circled her arms and held fast. "We wouldn't have to worry about this, Ellie, if you'd told me where she'd gone. I could have intercepted her and brought her home. Dammit! Dammit!" he growled again, releasing Ellie as if he'd suddenly found the touch of her repugnant. He turned away

296

and swept back a stray lock of hair. "Do you have a map of the rivers?" he asked. "I've got to find out what happened to her—"

"No, I don't, but . . . shouldn't we first make sure she was aboard?" Ellie sensibly asked.

"Of course I'll do that. Do you think I'm stupid?" He moved toward the stable and stood there alone, his shoulders trembling and his hands drawn to his hips. When Ellie approached, a tearful Grant turned and held her close. "God, I don't know what I'll do if I've lost Delilah. I don't even think I'd want to keep The Shadows." Then he drew back, wiped away the evidence of his grief, and remounted his horse.

When he had disappeared onto the road taking him northwest toward Alexandria, Ellie collapsed into a sobbing bundle upon the cool earth.

Maden, who had watched their exchange from the darkness of the carriage house, approached and dropped to his knees before her, taking her hands. "Don't worry, Ma," he said softly. "Our Miss Delilah will be all right."

"I know, but Grant hates me," she sobbed. "I cannot bear it."

Maden had silently borne his suspicions all along. His mother was in love with the Yankee who had always treated her with the affection of a brother.

He didn't like seeing his mother in pain.

It made him hate Grant Emerson.

Grant felt sick at the pit of his stomach. He blamed himself; had he not asked Delilah to marry him, she would not have felt the need to flee. But mentally and emotionally castigating himself would not solve the problem. He forced calm upon himself and saw very little of the countryside as he quickly closed the distance to the village of Alexandria. He prayed to God he would find her sitting serenely by a window at the Exchange Hotel, watching the steamboats lined against the riverbank, and thinking that perhaps she had been a little hasty in her decision to leave. Yes . . . God yes, let him find her there, safe and secure and warm, waiting for him to come for her.

But he did not find her at the Exchange Hotel. He learned at Garrett's Mercantile that she had sold another piece of her mother's jewelry. "Funds for a trip to New Orleans," she had explained to John Garrett. Grant's heart sank a little. When he dismounted his horse outside the small office of the Red River Steamboat Company, he dreaded approaching the ticket office; he didn't want confirmation that Delilah had, indeed, been aboard the ill-fated steamboat.

"Yes, what can I do for you?" a small, church-mouse-thin man asked Grant without looking up at him.

"I need information about a passenger on an afternoon trip—"

The man looked up then, peering at Grant over the rim of his spectacles. "Yesterday, sir?" Grant nodded. "The *Clarion,* sir?"

"I don't know. The passenger was Delilah Wickley—tall, chestnut-brown hair, pretty—"

"I know Miss Wickley, sir." Silence. Grant mentally attempted to peel the apprehension from his heart. "Miss Wickley was aboard the *Clarion.*"

"Were there casualties?" Grant asked.

"A good number," the man replied. "Perhaps I should summon my manager to talk to you."

"No . . . just tell me where survivors were taken."

"All survivors were brought back to Alexandria."

"Have you names?"

A dark-clothed man approached from the right. "May I help you, sir?"

Grant turned. "I want the names of the survivors of the accident yesterday."

"Come this way." Grant was taken into a small, cluttered office. When the gentleman sat at a desk, he fumbled for a sheet of paper. "Tell me the name you are looking for." he asked Grant.

"Miss Delilah Wickley."

The man quickly scanned the short list. "No, I'm sorry. Her name is not here."

"Do you have a list of the dead?"

"Not yet, it is still being compiled."

A tremble raked across Grant's jaw. "When . . . when will the list come in?"

"I expect it anytime."

Grant moved toward the door. "I will wait outside. Please, will you let me know if her name is on the list?"

The man grimaced. "Are you kin, sir?"

"I will be her husband. And that makes me all the kin she has, sir."

In the outer office, Grant caught a boy up by the collar. "Do you do jobs for a fee?" he demanded.

"Yes, sir," said the boy.

"Is this boy trustworthy?" Grant asked a company employee.

"As trustworthy as they come," said the man. "He's my son."

Grant's hand moved from the collar. Bending to one knee, he asked the slightly built boy, who might be ten, though it was hard to tell if he knew where Shadows-in-the-Mist was located.

"Yes, sir. Sure do," the boy confirmed.

"You see that bay gelding out there? I want you to take him back and tell Philo to saddle up a horse named Bella. You bring her back to Alexandria—and don't you wind her, hear—and I'll give you five dollars."

"Yes, sir!" the boy looked across at his father. "Can I go, Pa?" he asked.

"Go on, son," the man replied. "I'd do it myself for five dollars."

Grant watched the boy leave on his horse. He knew in his heart that he'd have to go after Delilah, and Bella would be a much more reliable horse for the search. He sat back to wait, both for word of the victims, and for the return of the boy.

Nineteen

Lyle Bishop moved quietly through the woods, occasionally dropping to one knee to listen for the soft crunch of a deer moving over fallen leaves or a squirrel barking fiercely at an interloper into its private domain. He needed to bring a meal home, and the forest had not been cooperative that morning. Toward noon, he purchased a line of trout from a local Biloxi Indian and began the five-mile trek to his small cabin on Spring Bayou.

Half an hour later, he stopped by the homestead of Widow Lamont, leaving the two largest fish for her supper. Since her husband had died last year, he had seen to her needs and interrupted her long moments of solitude with regular visits. This day, he sat in one of two rocking chairs on a sturdy porch built over the water, and together they enjoyed the peace of the bayou.

"What for do you waste your time on an old woman?" Marie Lamont asked, for what might have been the hundredth time in the past four weeks. She sucked on a pipe that had been her husband's, blowing the smoke in circles. "You are a handsome young man, Lyle. Your Louise has been gone for nigh on to three years and you need another woman to keep your cabin clean and satisfy your needs."

"I'm only twenty-nine," he replied, favoring her with a smile. "I imagine it'll take a while to find another

301

woman as good as Louise." His dark, weathered skin might give one the impression of an older man, his thick black hair peppered with silver and an unkempt beard hiding his natural good looks. Deep lines at the corners of his eyes testified to a hard life of dependency on the bayou and a jagged scar from his temple to the line of his beard gave evidence of its brutality. He considered the scar a mark of triumph; the man who had ruthlessly attacked him one dark November night lay moldering in his grave these past four years.

Cutting his visit short, Lyle soon said his farewells to the friendly old woman and resumed his journey to his own homestead. He walked over high rolls of earth and along the edges of the bayou, through stands of bent cypress. A lover of nature, he paused to admire the purple blossoms of verbena and the tangles of yellow-petaled black-eyed Susans cascading over woodland slopes.

He had just watched a mourning dove as it fell to the ground and lay still as if stunned, to distract Lyle's attention from its empty nest, when he caught sight of an unfamiliar texture against the dark, rotting ground of a shady dell. Readying his gun in the event of ambush, he moved steadily through the thick stand of white oaks and hickories, brushing at brambles that would have caught and torn his flesh.

He stooped over the still form, almost too stunned to move. Never in his years on the bayou had Lyle expected to encounter such a lovely vision — smooth ivory skin and chestnut-colored hair so thick and tangled his fingers got caught in their rich depths as he tried to disengage muddy strands from her face. And what a face it was! he thought, drawing in a breath he was almost sure would be his last. Even though she was unconscious, she looked vibrant and alive, her cheeks rosy, her mouth full and slightly parted, her eyelids almost translucent. Her gown was torn, with both dried and fresh blood staining the left side of her voluminous skirts.

As he tried to position her so that he could find the source of the bleeding, he was overwhelmed by her womanly curves. His eyes fixed to the soft, alluring swells of her breasts against the tight bodice of her gown brought a rush of crimson into his bronze cheeks.

Soon, he found the wound, along with a short, ragged bit of metal still protruding from her thigh. He was in a quandary; should he return to Marie Lamont's cabin, which was only a quarter mile back through the woods, or take her to his own cabin, an hour's distance away?

Picking her up, careful not to disturb her wound, Lyle stood for a moment in the gloomy dale. He turned first in the direction of Marie's cabin, then toward the trail that would ultimately empty into the clearing where his own secluded cabin sat. Then he looked down on the unconscious features of the exquisite creature cradled in his arms. Was he willing to share her with Marie during her convalescence? No . . . He turned in the direction of his own cabin, his gun and line of fish slung against his back, his bootsteps confident upon the earth. Delilah was light against him, like a crippled butterfly finding a final roost.

By the time he entered his cabin, the cool of the late afternoon had descended upon the bayou. Within moments of lowering her gently to the only cot in the cabin, his large hands were wiping away the mud and the muck that had collected upon her in her blind travels through the woods. He saved the wound for last; it would require very careful surgery. He prayed the sharp piece of shrapnel had not pierced an artery. He wouldn't be able to help her then, except to give her a peaceful place for her eternal rest. In that event, she would have the best company in heaven — his wife, Louise, and their little daughter, Enid.

Lyle Bishop had heard about the explosion aboard the *Clarion* on the Atchafalaya, and though she was probably one of its passengers, he could not imagine how she had traveled so far through the woods on her own. He wondered how she could even have walked, with the pain of the metal embedded in her leg. That she had managed the distance gave some evidence that perhaps the bone had not been pierced.

Over the course of a half hour, his hands worked with the skill of a surgeon as he carefully extracted the metal fragment, then cleaned the wound with whiskey and applied a poultice of hickory bark and jimsonweed. He thanked God for her unconsciousness; she would never have been able to bear the pain of the surgery. He would not have been able to offer her enough whiskey to produce the proper effect, since he had just enough in the cabin to keep the wound clean during the healing process.

He removed her dress and undergarments, reveling in the beauty of her nakedness and shamed by his own physical responses, and put one of his bed shirts on her. After he'd eaten his meal of fried fish and boiled potatoes, he washed the remnants of her gown and intimate garments as best he could in a wooden tub out back. After they had been dried by a brisk wind that had blown up, he sat down on a small stool to mend the many tears. All the while his gaze kept cutting to her sleeping face.

That night, he slept on a pallet on the floor. Several times he thought he heard her moan, but when he crawled to her bedside, he saw her still and pale, his imagination playing tricks on him. A steady rain fell in the early-morning darkness and he set about placing pots and pans beneath the drips he expected. He'd not had a good enough reason to get on the roof and fix the leaks, but the young woman lying across the room now gave him that motivation. He would get out at first light and make the cabin safe, secure, and warm for her. She needed him to take care of her, and he would not do it haphazardly.

As dawn cast an arch of shadows upon the cabin, Lyle was climbing a rickety ladder, a bucket containing nails, small pieces of smooth tin, and jars of pine resin firmly clutched in his right hand.

When he had finished the task, he sat quietly upon the roof for several minutes, watching the awakening of the day: a lightning flash of gray as a rabbit darted into the woods, a wild turkey strutting boldly among the pines, the rays of the sun glittering upon the silver leaves of a raintree. Against the bayou, palmettos bent to touch the shore and a heron hovered low, caught a small fish from the slowly moving current, and glided back into the trees.

To the left, beneath a small elm Louise had planted herself, were the graves of his wife and their daughter. They both had taken ill and died within a week; it hardly seemed so long ago, three years of grieving and seeking solitude as he had wallowed in self-pity. Except for a casual traveler or a hunter, he'd had no visitors at the cabin since the gathering at the funeral.

Until last night.

Drawing a deep breath of the new day, Lyle climbed down the ladder, entered the coolness of the cabin, and checked on his patient. She was breathing easier this morning.

For the next few minutes, Lyle washed up the few items he'd dirtied preparing his breakfast that morning, straightened the cabin, and drew back the frayed cotton curtains hanging at the small windows. When the lady awoke, she would not want to meet the gloom of the simple cabin.

He took up a book, volume two of *The French Revolution*, a history by Thomas Carlyle. He'd taken more than six months to read the first volume and hoped to complete the second by the end of the year. This morning he'd read scarcely a half dozen pages when a single phrase — *He is an acrid distorted man* — compelled him to remember his father and the brutal years of his childhood. His father had been such a man — brutal, distorting — caring not a whit about his wife and children, gathering his coins to buy a bottle of cheap whiskey rather than the flour needed to bake a loaf of bread for his family, brutalizing those closest to him without the least provocation. Lyle shivered; looking toward the sleeping woman, he wondered what kind of life she had lived.

He wondered if she was being missed. He wondered if men were out scouring the woods for her. Surely, such a beauty would not be forgotten.

Grant Emerson had garnered some hope from the fact that Delilah's name had not been on the list of dead. In such a tragedy, there was bound to be some confusion, omissions, and oversights, and he prayed that his Delilah had been a favorable victim of one or the other.

The boy had returned with Bella just minutes after the list of dead had been made available. Since then, Grant had ridden at a steady pace through the night, frequently plunging into thick woods and skirting treacherous bogs. A steady rain in the predawn hours had driven him to the cover of a stand of white birch, where he had huddled beneath his bedroll and the tarpaulin within which it had been wrapped.

He felt so alone and isolated, the terrain unfamiliar to him, and the uncertainty of what he would find at the end of the line tearing at his gut like a starving cougar. He wasn't sure how he'd managed it, but he caught a few hours of sleep before the little voice inside woke him. The rain had stopped and his tethered horse showed renewed spirit after filling its belly in a large patch of wild clover.

An hour more into his journey, a kind old gentleman offered him coffee, bacon, and biscuits at his campsite. "Do you know about an accident eastward on the river?" Grant inquired.

"Not on the Red . . . but hear a steamboat exploded on the Atchafalaya, oh, 'bout ten, twelve miles from here. You headed that way, mister?"

"Yes," Grant replied.

"Fella travelin' back to Alexandria said it was a real bad sight. Still scrapin' pieces of bodies out of the tree-tops. Sure you want to see that, mister?"

"I had . . . family aboard," Grant responded, gulping a morsel of food and feeling sick inside. "Got to find her."

Despite an obsessive need to reach the carnage on the Atchafalaya, Grant lingered at the old man's camp and enjoyed another cup of coffee. He dreaded the sight awaiting him; dreaded learning that his beloved Delilah might be among the dead. Tears flooded his eyes, but he turned his head, expelling a forced cough to regain his composure. When he stood, he was unable to suppress the tremble rocking him from head to toe.

"I'd better be going, mister. Could I pay you for the meal?"

"No, sir. One day I might be the one stumbling upon you, and I might need a meal. I'll warn you, mister, that if you got money on you, you might hide it in your sock or somethin'. There's all kind of riffraff on the river that'd be more'n willin' to take it from you."

Grant forced a smile. "I can take care of myself. Thanks for your hospitality."

"Enjoyed the company," he replied matter-of-factly, sipping at a third cup of strong coffee.

Mounting his horse, Grant raised his hand in farewell, then entered the trail fringing the south side of the

Red River. A brisk breeze swept over the water, cooling the nervous perspiration that had gathered on his brow. He tugged his hat down further over his sun-colored hair, feeling a wild impulse to drive his horse into the water and allow the current to suck him under. Had he not had so much respect for the life of the mare Delilah loved so much, he might have done just that.

Just under two hours later, Grant came upon the encampment of men working the steamboat accident. A few men snatched a few moments of rest while dozens of others sifted through the debris. What was left of the *Clarion* appeared as a child's broken toy, rammed bow-first into the mud by a bullish schoolboy. Off to the left he saw bloodied pieces of canvas covering the victims.

"Have you come to help out, mister?"

Seized by the horror of the sight, Grant did not at first hear the man's inquiry. When it was repeated a second time, he started. "I am looking for a passenger."

"Survivors sent back to Alexandria. You can look through the bodies over there if you've got a stomach for it."

Grant, weak and trembling, turned toward the canvas-covered forms. "There's a lady over there—" the man brusquely said, pointing to a wooded area, "who was found wandering in the woods."

"Thank God!" The words tumbled out before Grant could warn himself it might not be his Delilah. Turning, feeling a sickness in the pit of his stomach that threatened to unfoot him, he moved precariously through the debris toward a shady wood. A woman sat with her back to him, a blanket drawn across her head and hanging in limp, damp folds over the wooden crate upon which she sat. But the dress—God, the dress, he had himself purchased it for Delilah! He reached out, gripping her slim shoulder, "Delilah, thank God—"

Instantly, the haggard features of Hilda Roswell turned to him. She smiled timorously. "I am sorry, sir, I am not—" Her eyes narrowed with recognition as she recalled Delilah's description and the proud gleam in her eyes as she had spoken of her man. And he had the voodoo eyes she had so innocently described to her. "You're her man, aren't you? Miss Delilah's plantation master. She told me about you."

The disappointment darkened Grant's gaze, even as he managed a comforting smile for the young survivor. "I am Delilah's man," he replied with husky emotion. "Do you know where she is?"

Hilda set down the cup of coffee from which she'd been sipping. "I was tossed against the rail as the *Clarion* was sinking. I saw Miss Delilah crawl upon the bank and I tried to call out to her. She . . ." Hilda's tearful gaze dropped. "I saw her pull a dead child from the water and place it on the bank. Then . . ." Her gaze lifted, betraying to Grant the full extent of her grief, "I heard her scream, an awful, pained scream. When I was able to free myself from the wreckage, I managed to crawl to where I had last seen her, but she was gone. I went into the woods and called for her, but—oh, forgive me, sir— I couldn't find her. I searched everywhere and that is why I didn't travel back to Alexandria with the survivors. I was trying to find your Delilah, and perhaps I would have if one of the men hadn't found me and made me come back here. She's out there somewhere, sir, hurt and alone and afraid. Please—please, won't you find her? She was so kind to me. She . . ." Hilda's trembling fingers smoothed down the folds of her damp and crumpled dress. "She gave this lovely gown to me. She said it matched my eyes so beautifully that it was a sin for anyone except me to wear it."

Grant had not been able to suppress the moisture that formed in his eyes during Hilda's recitation. "Where will you being going, miss?" he asked, his brusqueness meant to diminish his emotions. "I'll be happy to let you know when I have found Delilah."

"New Orleans. I live on Rousseau Street in the Carrollton District . . . number 14. Thank you, sir. I will not rest easy until I know your lady is safe and well."

Tenderly, Grant's fingers brushed at the wisps of brown hair the blanket had not held back. "What is your name?"

"Hilda, sir. Hilda Roswell."

"Is there anything I can do for you? You must have lost everything. Do you need money?"

"I will be all right, sir. The steamboat company will compensate me for my pitiful loss."

"I will have Delilah write you personally."

He did not want to leave Hilda Roswell sitting there alone, but he had to continue his search for Delilah. When he mounted his horse and moved southward into the woods, he found himself surrounded by the quiet desolation, both of the forest and of his heart. He felt empty and alone, and he could not envision the warmth and pleasure of holding his beloved Delilah in his arms ever again. Instinct alone drove him onward, into the bleakness of the morning; in his heart he felt that he had lost her forever.

Delilah allowed a moment for her eyes to adjust to the flood of light within her enclosure. She felt as groggy as if she'd just drunk several gallons of her father's peach brandy and could hardly manage to lift her hand to her face. Where was she? Aboard the ill-fated *Clarion?* In a strange forest? Was she dead?

As her vision began to lose its foggy edges, she turned her head, allowing the form of a seated man to gain some degree of clarity. He slept in a rough-hewn rocker, his head back against a pillow, his thick, masculine features scruffy and yet gentle. She felt the throb of pain in her leg. When she attempted to sit up, the pain sharpened, and a groan erupted from her mouth.

Lyle Bishop instantly lurched forward, his gaze turning to hold Delilah's still-foggy one. "I am terribly thirsty," she said, weakly, and with a sudden burst of energy from the man, a ladle of water was being held for her. She felt the tenderness of his hand at the back of her neck as he tried to help her. Having quenched her thirst, she looked down at the thick muslin shirt covering her form and disappearing into the blanket drawn across her legs. She managed a small smile. "I do hope your wife . . . or your mother, changed me into this—"

Lyle arched his dark, shaggy eyebrows. "I'm afraid not," he responded. "I live here alone."

Her face crinkled with disapproval. "Well, I guess it couldn't be helped. My dress and coat were a terrible mess as I recall."

"No coat." Rising, he approached a table and picked up her dress. "I washed and mended it. I'm afraid it'll never be the same."

"You mended it yourself?" she asked, astonished.

"When a man lives alone, he learns to do just about everything. I can even cook a pretty fair meal, if you're up to it."

She stretched out her hand and waited for Lyle Bishop to take it. "If my memory serves me correctly, my name is Delilah Wickley," she said. "I seem to recall that I was involved in an accident—"

Lyle took her hand with pleasure, then dragged up a chair and sat down beside her. "I found you unconscious in the woods. If you were aboard the steamboat that exploded on the Atchafalaya last night, you somehow managed to travel a very long way on foot—"

She fought for recollection. Her last memory before opening her eyes to see the kind face of the man sitting beside her was of lying on a muddy riverbank. What had happened to Hilda . . . or had she even existed? What had she been doing aboard a riverboat—

Why wasn't she at Shadows-in-the-Mist, keeping her father in line? No . . . no. She shook her head, trying to sort out her foggy thoughts. Her father had lost the plantation and then he had died. But she still lived at Shadows-in-the-Mist. How could that be?

"Are you all right, Miss Wickley?"

"I — I don't know." She met his concerned gaze. "My thoughts are terribly muddled. I can't seem to recall why I was on the riverboat, or where I was going."

"You've had an ordeal. Don't worry . . . you'll remember after a while." He patted her hand in a comforting gesture. "Just be happy that you've remembered who you are."

"Oh, dear —" She tried to raise herself from the cot, but the pain caught in her leg and she quickly rested back on the pillow. "How rude of me . . . I did not ask your name."

"Lyle Bishop at your service." Catching the direction of her gaze upon the form of her leg beneath the blanket, he assured her that it had seemed a serious wound. "But once it is healed the scar will hardly be noticeable." He spoke with confidence.

"Horse feathers . . . I am hardly worried about having a scar."

Lyle gave her an easy smile. "You should be concerned. You are a very beautiful young lady and it would be a shame to have your beauty marred."

Such flattery embarrassed Delilah. "Well, Lyle Bishop, where is that meal you said you were a master at cooking up?" she said to change the subject.

"I can cook up a meal that'll curl your toes, Miss Wickley." They joined each other in laughter. "I'd better fire up the oven before you wither away into nothing but skin and bones." Before he reached the door, beyond which he would gather wood for the stove, he turned back. "Do you have a husband, Miss Wickley, or someone I should try to get word to?"

Again, puzzlement rested upon her brow. "I don't think so. I'm just not sure. I know that my father is dead, and I believe my mother is, too." Behind the foggy vortex of her innermost thoughts, a vision fought to surface. It was like someone — a man, she was sure — was walking toward her, but he was only a dark form against a bright, blinding light. "Who are you?" she whispered to herself, and when Lyle cast a look in her direction, she explained, "Just talking to myself. It is probably one of my many bad habits."

"I do that, too, but . . . I'm usually the only intelligent person in the room to talk to. You're here now."

She smiled in response to his kind words. When the late afternoon outside the cabin had swallowed him whole, Delilah sank back against the feather pillow.

So she would not have to grapple with the worry of what she could not remember, she began looking around the cabin. A few glasses and china plates were stacked neatly on open shelves above a trestle table with heavy knobbed legs; a quaint, colorful quilt covered most of the wall above a table with two chairs tucked neatly beneath it; a portrait of an elderly man and woman hung over an overstuffed chair, and beside it a small side table bearing the daguerrotype of a woman with a small girl sitting serenely upon her lap.

A snapping chill descended through an open window, causing her to pull the blanket over her shoulders. She sat huddled there, one leg drawn up and the other, uncomfortably wrapped with bandages, straight along the edge of the narrow cot.

When Lyle returned, he started a fire in the stove and began preparing fish and potatoes to be steamed. Delilah watched him in silence. He was a tall, massively built man, and yet he moved with the grace of a much smaller person. His kind eyes reminded her of Hilda, though she wasn't sure why. So many things weighed heavily on her mind. Why was she able to remember so vividly a woman she had known for only a few hours and not be able to picture the face of the man who tugged so gently on the threads of her heart?

"Is everything all right?" Lyle asked, noticing her worried expression.

"Yes, but . . ." She shrugged as if it really didn't matter. "There is someone—a man—who I feel I really should remember, but I just can't. It is like he is standing on the other side of a wall. I know he is there, but I can't see him. Do you think it might be just a dream? A figment of my imagination?"

"I am sure if he was someone important, you would remember."

In the next few hours, all of her efforts to remember were for naught. She had enjoyed a good meal with the kind Lyle Bishop, they had played several games of backgammon, at which she'd beat him three of the four games, and he had carried her out to the porch so that she could watch the setting of the sun.

A golden tapestry across the far horizon kept tugging at her memories. She remembered eyes the pale hue of rain-washed ink and a full, masculine mouth whose touch upon hers she could almost feel.

Why, then, couldn't she remember the man himself?

Twenty

After spending three days scouring the woods for some trace of Delilah, a very discouraged Grant Emerson came upon a small trading post at a clearing on Spring Bayou. There, he purchased a straight razor, soap, and two new shirts, though not of the quality to which he was accustomed. He was determined not to leave the area until Delilah had been found, even if he had to rough it in the woods.

Also in the trading post that morning was a burly man purchasing ladies' dresses, lavender water, and a brush and comb set displayed in a velvet-lined box. Grant and Lyle Bishop exchanged glances, then continued to stroll among the various and sundry items being offered for sale. On the wide counter Lyle eventually added a bottle of whiskey and three yards of white cotton to his purchases; Grant added dried beef and a half-dozen biscuits to his items.

When Grant left the post some minutes later, he found Lyle Bishop rubbing his hand over the sleek neck of his horse. "Quite a horse, isn't she?" Grant said.

"Finest animal I've ever seen," Lyle responded, his smile scarcely noticeable through his scruffy facial hair. "Where does a man get a horse like that?"

"Actually the horse isn't mine. Belongs to a lady friend." Politely, Grant extended his hand. "Name's Grant Emerson."

Lyle did not hesitate to take the proferred hand. "Lyle Bishop . . . You're not from around here, are you?"

"I have a planation on Bayou Boeuf, about two days from here—"

Silence. All at once, Lyle Bishop felt uneasy in the presence of the stranger. Surely he had not come here without cause. Should he ask his reason, or should he just go on his way? Curiosity was a burning ember inside of him and he had to know what he was facing. "You just passing through?" Lyle asked, his hand gently rubbing Bella's muzzle.

"I'm looking for someone—a woman who was aboard the *Clarion* when it exploded on the Atchafalaya."

Lyle's heart fell like a deadweight. "Looking too far east, ain't you?"

"I may be." Grant had always considered himself tall, but beside the much taller and massively built Lyle Bishop, he felt almost insignificant. He was slightly intimidated. "I'd better be on my way," he said, then took the reins of his horse and galloped away on it.

Even as a seed of guilt began to grow deep inside him, Lyle Bishop smiled. The man with the fancy, high-stepping mare was moving in the opposite direction of his cabin on Spring Bayou . . . the cabin where he had left the lovely Delilah Wickley quietly stitching a sampler his Louise had begun two weeks before her death.

He didn't want to lose her to the handsome stranger . . . at least, not yet.

And perhaps never.

Aldrich Emerson was enjoying the luxury of his cousin's house on The Boeuf. Several days ago, Grant's woman had sent word to the household that their master had been "called away on business" and, Aldrich had

316

not been able to pry any information from the servants. He was stunned at the loyalty his cousin had won from these people in the few short months he had owned the plantation. He was also a little irritated that they treated *him* like an unwelcome interloper. They prepared his meals, because their master would have expected it, and saw to his comfort. But beyond that he couldn't even draw them out in conversation. And they certainly did not obey his orders. He'd never in his life seen so many noses stuck up in the air.

This morning, Aldrich bathed and dressed in his best suit, saddled one of Grant's finest horses, and turned eastward onto The Boeuf. Perhaps he would be able to get some information from the woman, Ellie.

Aldrich grinned to himself. Who was he trying to fool? He couldn't care less where his cousin had gone. He reveled in the timeliness of the business venture that had taken Grant away from The Shadows and prayed he wouldn't return anytime soon. He had come to The Boeuf to kill his cousin. Now, he wanted only to see him have to live with the same pain and humiliation he himself had lived with these past few years.

When he rode into the clearing where Ellie's cottage stood, the big man who worked for her emerged from the carriage house carrying a gun pointed toward him. "I am Aldrich Emerson, cousin of the master of Shadows-in-the-Mist," Aldrich hastily announced. "I am paying a social call on your mistress."

"Miz El ain't my mistress," Lancie growled. "She's my employer." Just at that moment, Ellie McPherson emerged from the house and stood on the gallery. "Don't ya git off dat hoss," Lancie warned, "until I sees if Miz El wants ya to be visitin' her." Lancie sidestepped to the gallery, as one might sidestep a skunk, spoke in muffled tones with Ellie, then returned, motioning to Aldrich with his gun. "Miz El says ya's welcome to visit a spell . . . An' I'll be a keepin' my eyeballs on ya, mister," he added.

A slightly ruffled Aldrich dismounted, allowed Lancie to take the horse into the carriage house, and turned toward the gallery where the lovely, dark-haired woman stood. As he ascended the steps, he removed his hat and held it to his chest. "Good morning, Miss Ellie. You'll have to forgive me . . . I don't know your last name."

"McPherson," she replied, offering her hand. "Please, do call me Ellie." She had not smiled; the face was strangely blank as she spoke. "You are Grant's cousin? *The* cousin from New England?"

Aldrich laughed pleasantly. "The very same, Ellie. I assume you have heard all about the problems my cousin and I have had."

"Grant has spoken to me about them," she admitted. "He deeply regretted the circumstances that led to your estrangement."

Aldrich looked toward the circle of settees and chairs at the end of the gallery. "Might we sit and chat a spell?" he asked.

"Miss Mandy, could we have some coffee on the gallery?" Ellie called into the house.

Aldrich stretched his wiry frame before settling onto the larger of the two settees. Ellie sat across from him in a wicker rocker, her fingers resting gently in the folds of her skirt. "What has brought you to the cottage?" she asked after a moment. "Did someone at the plantation tell you that Grant would be here?"

Aldrich looked surprised for a moment. Then, as if realization suddenly clicked in his brain, he said, "Oh, I'm sorry. Didn't Grant tell you I was here? He was called away on business the same afternoon I arrived and offered me the comfort of his home. I have been there for the past three days." Chuckling good-naturedly, he continued. "The servants at The Shadows will scarcely even give me the time of the day. I was feeling a trifle lonely, so I thought I would visit with you. I do hope you don't mind."

"Of course not." A frown settled upon Ellie's face which she immediately chased away with a smile. "Did Grant tell you about me?"

"He said you two were very close." His gaze did not betray the small lie; Grant had told him nothing about Ellie . . . and for good reason, Aldrich surmised. He wanted to keep the pretty thing to himself.

Momentarily, Miss Mandy brought out a tray bearing two cups, bowls of sugar, and freshly skimmed cream. As she set it down on the small table between the two people, she cut Aldrich a careful, appraising look. "I don't think she likes me," Aldrich said when she returned to the house.

"Grant said the same thing the first time he visited. They—she and her son, Lancie—are very protective of me. They try to guard against troublemakers . . ." With a sweet laugh, she continued. "And anyone who hails from farther north than Shreveport is considered of dubious character."

"Well, I will certainly try to improve my image, Ellie."

Ellie McPherson was very taken with the debonair Aldrich Emerson. He was not at all what she had expected, considering the stories Grant had told her about him. He was charming, witty, and very handsome in his own way. "Have you met any of the other neighbors on the bayou?" Ellie asked. She really wasn't sure what to say him; his steady, admiring look had somewhat flustered her.

"I have to admit, Ellie, that I really don't enjoy riding alone, so I haven't ventured out until this morning." Silence. His even features relaxed and a moment of thought pressed his brows together. When her questioning gaze met his own, he continued, though somewhat hesitantly. "I was just wondering, Ellie . . . Would you care to go riding with me? I noticed some fine riding horses in your pen, and . . ." Now, he was the one to be flustered. "You do ride, don't you?"

"I do." Ellie smiled. "If you'll give me a moment to change into something appropriate, I would enjoy a morning ride."

Aldrich Emerson made Ellie feel giddy, like a schoolgirl, and his easily offered compliments brought a pretty rush to her features. He almost made her forget the passion that grew within her for Grant. It was, perhaps, because of Grant that she was so attracted to his cousin. Her feelings had been rebuffed for three years. What better way to punish Grant for his lack of attention than to encourage the development of a romance between herself and his worst enemy?

Aldrich, too, had not expected to be so attracted to Ellie. When that first morning's ride had transgressed into a daily event — something that she boldly encouraged herself — he almost felt that he could grow to love the soft-spoken, kind-hearted Ellie McPherson. Enjoying her company every day for the following week, he met most of the planters along The Boeuf. Their visits lasted well into the night and when, at last, he ventured to take her in his arms and kiss her, he was surprised, and a little wary, of her reception. He had expected some degree of hesitancy; she was, after all, a well-bred southern lady.

That she was receptive to his attentions pleased him very much. He had only to play his cards right, and she would forget all about Grant.

His plan was working to perfection. He had only to bide his time and pray for Grant to remain away. Ellie McPherson would be his.

"What are you thinking, Aldrich?"

His hands spanning her tiny waist, her arms about his neck, he met her soft gaze in the soft light of the gallery. "I am thinking how happy I have been this past week, Ellie. I never thought it possible that a woman like you existed."

"But . . ." Her eyes lowered coyly, "didn't you love Madeleine?"

"I loved her very much," he replied truthfully. "But she is hotheaded and temperamental. You are gentle and good-hearted. You are the kind of woman a man hopes for when he is ready to settle down." Ellie extracted herself from Aldrich's embrace, turning away to face the moonless night. She was at odds within. She had enjoyed Aldrich's company, and his attention to her, but she had known him only a week. The serious tone of his voice made her feel uneasy, even as she harbored an unspoken obsession to make Grant think twice about having rejected her as a lover. In a matter of moments, Aldrich's hand fell gently to her shoulder, coaxing her back to him. "Did I say something wrong, Ellie?"

"No, Aldrich, you say all the things a woman loves to hear. I simply am . . ." Gently, she shrugged, "not sure you should say them to me when we have known each other so short a while."

"I didn't mean to make you feel uncomfortable. Please forgive me. Do you want me to leave?"

Dear Lord, Ellie silently cried, *I cannot keep harboring hopes that Grant will love me. Even if Delilah is dead, he will not want me. He considers me nothing more than a friend.* Timidly, she looked up, taking Aldrich's hand and bringing it against her warm cheek. "No, please don't go." She had been so lonely. It had been more than three years since she'd been with a man, and the deep yearnings within her for intimacy were almost too painful to bear. She wanted from this tall, quiet-spoken man what she had never gotten from Grant. She wanted love . . . she wanted to feel the warm and tender awakening of feelings too long suppressed. "Stay with me, Aldrich."

321

His forehead creased. "Stay with you? But what about Grant?"

"What about him?"

"Then what about your servants, Ellie? When I am still here beyond the setting of the sun, I can feel the mental pitchforks digging into my back."

Ellie laughed, the delicate inflection like a whisper on the September wind. "Miss Mandy's brother, who lives in New Orleans, accompanied his master on a business trip to Alexandria. She and Lancie are visiting him. As for my son, he is spending the night at Dentley, taking care of a colicky horse."

"You mean, Ellie, that we have the place all to ourselves?"

"Just you and me — and them thar horses and chickens." She laughed her reply. "What do you say, Yankee? Have a brandy with a lady?"

"How could a man refuse?" Aldrich replied, drawing her against him.

Together, they moved into her large, comfortably furnished parlor, where they shared a brandy, then danced in each other's arms, Aldrich's throaty humming providing the only music. "Your hands are so small," Aldrich murmured against the thick fringes of her hair. Then he took hold of the scarf holding back her auburn locks and untied the bow. "There, how lovely your hair is against my hands." His mouth sought hers, caressed it, teased it until her body was hot and flushed against his own, ignoring the threads of their clothing to warm him through.

His kisses traveled over the slim column of her throat and his hands rose to roughly take the shoulders of her blouse and pull it down her arms. Her body surrendered to his boldness, her full, sensual breasts heaving against his searching mouth. She cared not that he had uncovered her and that her blouse dragged across her elbows, nor did she try to prevent him from easing her back to the wide divan. She knew only that he wanted her . . . that he would not reject her as Grant had done. He found her beautiful and alluring. He looked at her as a woman, and his hands boldly skirted her passions, bringing them into full bloom. His fingers eased beneath the waist of her gown and slipped it and her underthings under her buttocks and down her legs. When he shifted, relieving himself of his trousers, and the hardness of his groin pressed against the juncture of her thighs, she did not want another moment of foreplay, of painful teasing. She wanted to feel him inside her, possessing her, taking from her what Grant had not.

As Ellie's fingers dug painfully into his shoulders, Aldrich positioned himself to take her. How voluptuous she was, her breasts full and hot against his mouth, her body almost scalding hot against his own. *I am taking what is Grant's,* he thought wickedly, his hands easing beneath her buttocks, his slim hips coaxing her thighs to fall apart for him.

She gasped when he entered her; it had been so long . . . Then they moved together, slowly and beautifully, clinging to each other as if their happiness depended entirely on their union. The thrill Ellie felt encompassed her whole being. This was the man she wanted, not Grant. This was the man who could awaken her passions, not Grant.

His frantic pace within her scorched the very depths of those passions. She would gladly be his woman, if he wanted her. She could hardly remember her lonely life before him, and could not envision the future without him.

When at last they lay in exquisite fulfillment, their bodies moist and hot one against the other, Ellie drew a deep, trembling breath and her her hands circled his still-clothed shoulders. "You must think me a wanton hussy," she murmured.

He rested his chin gently between her breasts. "I think you are a treasure . . . and I am a very happy man."

"Do you love them and leave them, Aldrich Emerson? The ladies, that is?" she asked.

"Not unless they run me off."

Her eyes crept open and a smile graced her luscious mouth. "We have solitude, we have the night . . . and my bed is boringly comfortable."

"Then shall we make it exciting?"

He uncovered her, pulling up his trousers as he did so. It pleased him that she made no move to cover her nakedness. He offered his hand to her and she did not hesitate to take it. As she shook off the last remnants of her crumpled clothing, she allowed him to take her up in his arms.

He moved through the corridor as though he knew the way to her bedchamber.

There were many hours of darkness left; many hours to love away the long Louisiana night.

Grant sat quietly against the tree, his knees drawn up, exchanging his side arm between his hands as he stared into the hypnotic flames of the campfire. It had been ten days since he'd begun his search for Delilah, and he'd still found no trace of her.

He hadn't eaten in two days, nor shaved in four. His eyes were bloodshot from lack of sleep and he felt a gnawing tension eating its way through him. Having journeyed back to the trading post on Spring Bayou, he would replenish his supplies in the morning and begin the trek back to Alexandria. Perhaps the steamboat company had gotten some news on Delilah.

Throwing his pistol to the ground between his boots, Grant groaned. Damn her! Damn her for doing this . . . for getting herself into this mess! Hadn't she realized how much he loved her? Couldn't she have trusted him enough to let him help her work things out?

He would never forgive her.

He would never stop loving her.

But it was time to face the grim realization that she was gone forever.

Delilah's skin was hot and dry. A deeply concerned Lyle Bishop bathed her forehead in cool water, but in her delirium she brushed his hand away. The wound in her thigh was a dark, purplish red and he feared that infection had set in.

She'd been doing so well, he thought, again returning the cool cloth to her forehead. *What will I do if she dies?* he thought in panic. *Why didn't I tell the man who was looking for her that she was at my cabin? Perhaps she would not have taken this turn for the worse if I had been honest enough to allow her to be taken to a proper physician!*

Delilah's eyes darted rapidly beneath her translucent eyelids. Her fingers dug deeply into the bedcovers, and all of Lyle's efforts to pull the blanket up over her were met by delirious rebellion.

"Grant . . . Grant . . ." she mumbled, slinging her head back and forth, the damp tendrils of her hair clinging between Lyle's fingers as he tried to quiet her. "Grant, I'm sorry . . . I'm so sorry . . . Forgive me—"

"Delilah!" Lyle spoke her name harshly, his palms pressed hard against her face. He did not want to hear another man's name fall from her lips. "Delilah, wake up!"

Her eyes crept open, and her pain was naked before him. "I'm sick, Lyle," she sobbed.

"I know," he responded. "I don't know what to do for you."

Tears flooded her eyes. "I need Grant."

"Who is this man Grant?" But Lyle knew; he recalled

the man at the trading post who had casually introduced himself.

"He is the man who loves me . . . the man I love. He will make me feel better," she replied, coaxing his hands away from her face.

"Not unless he is God," Lyle shot back, jealousy seething within him. "He will not make you feel better!"

Her fingers rose, then closed weakly over his sleeve. "Please, Lyle, you must take me to Grant. He is out there searching for me—"

His lips parted in surprise. He had said nothing to her about meeting the man at the trading post, of his declaration that he was searching for a missing passenger. No one else had been to the cabin in the past week. How could she possibly know he was searching for her? "Be still, Delilah. You are making matters worse—"

"I want Grant. Please . . . please . . ." Her voice became whisper soft as a foggy darkness washed over her. "I need Grant. I need—"

Silence. Her breathing was dangerously erratic, her skin so hot he was sure it would burst into flames. Lyle grabbed at his hair, feeling the urge to pull it out by the handful. How could he have been so stupid! He was no doctor. He had probably contaminated the wound when he'd extracted the jagged metal piece and might possibly be responsible for her death.

He had not meant for this to happen. He had wanted only to take care of her and enjoy her company. He had not wanted her to get sick, and he certainly did not want her to die. Should he do nothing, and pray to God she recovered? If she died, should he bury her? No one would be the wiser? If he sought help for her and she died anyway, would he be accused of murder?

He was in a quandary. Things could have been so simple. Seven days ago she had been sitting peacefully in the chair by the fireplace, completing the needlework his Louise had begun. She'd even felt well enough to prepare supper two nights ago. They had laughed and read to each other from one of the few books he owned, and they had talked for hours on end. Though she had told him about her life before this past summer, she had said nothing of the man named Grant. Now, she was lying helpless upon the bed, exhausted by the mere calling of his name and her pleas to be with him.

Linking his fingers beneath his bearded chin, Lyle did something he hadn't done in three years. He prayed . . . prayed for the answers to his dilemma. He closed his tear-moistened eyes and asked for God's help, bitterly remembering the last time he'd asked God for anything. But he had lost Louise and Enid, despite his prayers. Since that somber morning when he'd buried his loved ones, he had only cursed the Almighty and had begged him to take his own life as well.

Delilah had given him no indication that there was anyplace else she would rather be. She had seemed to be happy at his cabin in the woods, and he had harbored the hope that perhaps she would like to stay. When he had found her in the woods, he'd felt that an angel had been sent into his lonely life to brighten his days. He simply could not understand how things could go so wrong in so short a time.

He watched her sleeping face, deathly pale and still. He could not let her die. Rising from the stool, he moved quietly across the room toward the door. When he stood in the cool of the night, he found his hatchet and moved into the woods. He would build a travois, and in the morning, he would take her to the trading post. Perhaps her man would be there.

Overhead the night sky was a deep blue-black and the air heavy with humidity. He hoped it would not storm before the dawn, but in the event the weather was not favorable, he decided he should build a frame for the travois, upon which he could tie a tarpaulin.

After he had tied together the basic frame, he gathered gray moss from the trees fringing the bayou, some of it trailing for more than a yard before touching the ground. When he had enough to form a comfortable mattress, he covered it with a blanket. From his position in the darkening light of the cabin porch, he watched the sleeping Delilah through the paneless window. She had not stirred.

But she had not died, either.

He found hope in that.

Twenty-one

The following morning, a driving rain required Lyle to use the frame and tarpaulin he had constructed for the travois. Having placed the half-conscious Delilah gently upon the mat of Spanish moss and tucked several blankets over her, he began the short trek to the trading post. He wasn't sure what he would do with her once he got there, but he knew he could not keep her at the cabin, where she would certainly die. The old woman who ran the trading post was rumored to be a healer; she had saved Paw McCullough's gangrenous arm when an educated sawbones would have amputated it. Perhaps she would put together one of her concoctions and save Delilah's life.

When an exhausted Lyle entered the clearing shortly before dawn, he found the post dark and uninhabited, though he could see the shuffling figure of the proprietress through the window of her living quarters at the rear. Pulling the travois under the overhang of the porch, he dropped against the wall, his breathing as heavy as the stormy black skies overhead. He removed his hat to wring the rain out of it, then pulled back the tarpaulin to check Delilah's pulse. It was shallow, her skin still hot and dry, but she had stayed dry on the journey to the trading post.

He was sick at heart. He wanted to remain with

her, reassure himself that she would recover, and yet at the same time, he wanted to flee into the woods so that he would have no knowledge of her death. If he left now, he could return to his miserable solitude at his cabin down the bayou and be none the wiser.

Easing himself on to his knees, Lyle pulled back the tarpaulin just enough to touch his mouth in a gentle kiss to Delilah's forehead. "Forgive me, Miss Delilah Wickley," he murmured against her feverish brow. "If I had told your man a week ago where you were, perhaps you would not be so sick now. But . . . I will leave you in the care of the Widow Pitney, and I am sure your Grant will return for you." He smiled sadly. "Forgive me . . . I must leave you now."

If she had heard him, she gave no indication of it. She was deathly still, the only visible movement the flutter of her thick eyelashes. Placing a final kiss upon her brow, Lyle let the tarpaulin fall, rose to his feet, and turned toward the same dark trail from which he had emerged scarcely five minutes before. He did not look back; tears sheened his eyes and emotion rocked his shoulders.

Grant had scarcely enjoyed more than an hour of sleep during the stormy night. He was cold, wet, and hungry when he reached the trading post just as the sun was rising over Spring Bayou. He sauntered onto the porch at the same time a latch on the inside of the door was being lifted. Momentarily, the proprietress, a woman whose width possibly matched her short stature, allowed the cool morning to seep into the trading area. She was surprised to see the tall outline of a man against the backdrop of live oaks and elms. "Ye're early today, mister," she said by way of greeting. "Hope I didn't keep ye waitin' long."

"I just arrived," Grant replied. "A bit of a storm we had last night, eh?"

Looking toward the travois that had not been there the night before, the Widow Pitney wondered what Grant had brought for trading. Probably pelts, since he had gone to the trouble of protecting them from the weather. Casting him a sideways glance, she thought he really didn't look much like a trapper. "Come on in, mister. I've just brewed a pot of strong chicory coffee. Biscuits, too, if ye've got a hollow in yer gut."

"I've got a hollow something fierce." Grant lightly chuckled his reply. Then he felt guilty for responding with humor, when he had such an ache in his heart. Entering the trading post, where a large black stove had already heated the interior through, he was soon sipping hot coffee and eating biscuits coated with butter and honey. He hadn't realized he was so hungry until he picked up the fifth biscuit. "Mighty good," he said, watching the woman straighten merchandise on the counter. "What am I paying for such a satisfying breakfast this morning?"

Her wide smile revealed toothless gums. "Five cents a half-dozen. Reckon ye're working on the sum pretty good, eh, young fellow?"

"I reckon so," Grant mumbled.

"So, young fellow, what'll ye be wantin' to trade yer goods fer?"

A moment of deep thought darkened Grant's brow. He quickly gulped the last morsel of biscuit. "What do you mean?"

"Yer travois outside . . . ye brought goods fer tradin', didn't ya?"

"The only things I brought were me and my horse," he responded.

"Ye don't say, young fellow? Well, mayhap another

fellow left it there, then had personal business in the woods."

A movement from the porch made Grant stiffen, but it was only a large, wolflike dog pacing across the porch. "Your dog?" asked Grant.

"I feed him sometimes, but he belongs to the woods." Suddenly, the beast started growling and barking—short, fierce barks that were almost painful to the ear. With an annoyed grunt, the old woman moved around the end of the counter and toward the porch. "Blasted old whelp prob'ly smells them skins," she mumbled, taking up a broom in her travels. Momentarily, the animal yelped, though more from surprise than the abuse, since only the bristles fanned his backside. He trotted halfway across the clearing, then stood looking at her as if she'd suddenly lost her senses. Grant picked up the sixth biscuit, determined to get his full five cents worth.

"Lordy me!" the proprietress suddenly exclaimed. "Look at what we have here?"

Grant saw the old woman standing in the doorway leaning over and peering into the darkness of the tarpaulin. "What have you got there?" Grant asked.

"Just another stray," she responded, clicking her tongue. "Every time they're hurt or wounded and nobody wants to be bothered, they end up on my doorstep. The folks round here—even the Indians—think I got nothin' better to do than whip up concoctions. If it 'uz an ol' dog, I'd just knock it in the head, but . . ." She looked up at Grant and smiled, "reckon I better see what I can do for this pretty little thing."

An involuntary shudder passing through his body, Grant moved toward the travois and the old woman's side. He knew what he hoped to find beneath the cover, and yet he was afraid to consider the possibility. There had been too many moments when he had prayed, and his prayers had not been answered. Then he paused, his feet refusing to move forward, almost as if they had developed a mind of their own. It would be too much to hope for to see his beloved Delilah lying there.

When his gaze met the subject holding the woman's attentions, he felt that his senses had been rudely snatched away and sent hither and yon. He did not at first move; he was sure his flesh had suddenly turned into stone, unyielding and unresponsive. Was that his beloved Delilah, lying still and lifeless and wan beneath the rain-soaked tarpaulin? Allowing some degree of reasoning to return to him, his fingers began a shaky journey toward the pale features of the young woman.

When, in stunned disbelief, his fingertips brushed her hairline, then felt the hot flush of her cheeks, he could not speak. When the proprietress said, "Pretty, ain't she, young fellow?" he could not respond. He knelt, trancelike, beside her, his pale eyes gazing over her as if he expected her to disappear, like a fog recoiling from the fringes of a winter bayou.

The Widow Pitney's elbow gently dug into Grant's shoulder, and his senses returned with dizzy force. "My God, I've been out here for ten days looking for her. I've traveled a hundred miles up and down the bayou, along the Red and the Atchafalaya."

"She's what brought ye out, young fellow? Ye been lookin' fer the pretty miss?" When Grant failed to respond, she spoke with more firmness. "Well, ye'd better bring her to the back, and we'll see what we can do for her."

Grant had carried Delilah a hundred times, in their moments of teasing affection . . . their moments of intimacy . . . but when he did so now, he was alarmed at how much lighter she was. She was already so slim that the loss of a single pound could not possibly be healthy for her. Her head fell limply against his shoulder as he straightened, and her arm fell, her slim hand hanging limply as he followed the Widow Pitney to her living quarters in the back of the trading post. When he laid her on a large bed covered by a clean quilt, the widow immediately put a cool cloth upon her forehead.

She saw Grant's worried expression. "Now, don't ye fret, young fellow. She's alive . . . ye should find some hope in that. Now ye go on out to the front, and let me take care of your missy."

Grant had searched for Delilah for so long that he did not want to leave her now. He quietly conceded that she would be better tended by the woman, who seemed to know what she was doing, so he reluctantly turned and moved toward the curtain separating the two rooms. Just before he emerged into the trading area, he looked back at the still form of his beloved Delilah, drew a ragged breath, then let the curtain fall, cutting off his view of her.

The minutes passed. So that he would not go crazy wondering what was going on back there, he began straightening things that did not need straightening, popping a dust rag at bare shelves, drinking several cups of coffee, and waiting on the several customers who came in. When the Widow Pitney emerged into the trading post more than an hour later, she met the gaze of a very worried man.

"She has a wound on her leg. I cleaned out the infection and cooled down her skin with whiskey. Can't say yet if she's going to live—"

"I have to be with her."

When Grant started to step past the widow, she took his arm, halting him. "Yer little missy can take all the time she needs to get well, young fellow. I've

334

got another cot back here in a little room where I can sleep tonight."

"I will compensate you for your kindness," he offered quietly.

"The only thing I want, young fellow, is to see the pretty lass get better. Ye keep her skin cool — there's a bowl of whiskey back there on the table — and when her fever breaks, ye'll need to keep her warm."

Moments later, Grant pulled up a chair beside the bed and took Delilah's slender hand in his. The widow had changed Delilah into an oversize white bedgown and had placed a shawl across her shoulders. She appeared so innocent and so completely helpless. Tears moistened his eyes as he wondered where she had been these past ten days. He saw the gown she had been wearing lying across another chair. Someone had obviously mended its many tears. But who? He had talked to hundreds of people in the time that he'd been searching for her. No one had seen her. Could it be possible that he had missed talking to that one person who had found her? He was fairly certain he had covered the entire population of the region. Was it fate that had kept him from crossing paths with the kind soul who had helped his dear Delilah?

All through the day Grant sat beside her, watching her still features for some sign of movement, only halfheartedly eating the meal the Widow Pitney brought him in the early afternoon. They spoke very little when she checked the wound shortly before six that evening and changed the bandage. The wound had seemed so small; Grant could not understand how it had spiraled Delilah into the darkness holding her captive.

Night fell. The Widow Pitney retrieved a few of her necessities from the living area and informed Grant that she had one of the customers take care of his

335

horse and had put her in the pen. She dropped her hand comfortingly to his shoulder, then moved toward the small room where she would sleep that night.

Grant had noticed a few small improvements in Delilah: her fever had broken and her breathing was not quite so erratic. She had moved her head a little, and though she'd not gained consciousness, she'd emitted a small moan, as if some degree of conscious pain was sifting into her dark little world. Exhausted, his back aching, Grant pulled off his boots, then eased onto the bed to rest against her. A single lantern kept the room in dim light, a golden circle keeping them within its warmth and glow. Grant touched his mouth gently to her forehead. "My love will bring you back, Delilah," he whispered. "My love will take care of you." Then he drifted off into a deep sleep, with Delilah and his hopes and dreams to keep him company.

Despite her nagging worry for Grant and Delilah, Ellie had bowed to Aldrich's insistence that she journey with him into Alexandria that day. There, they made a round of the shops, dined at the Exchange Hotel, and opened a new account in Aldrich's name at the bank. While Aldrich did other personal business about town, in the time she spent alone, Ellie inquired at the steamboat company if any word had been received about Delilah. None had, but she did not give up hope.

She had known Aldrich less than two weeks, and yet she cared very deeply for him. She was not sure why she had not told him about Delilah when he had been so curious about Grant's life on The Boeuf. Perhaps she was still a little envious of Delilah. She had managed to win Grant's love, when she herself wanted it. Would Delilah be able to turn Aldrich's attentions away from her, also? She knew that, inevitably, Delilah would return to The Shadows and that Aldrich would meet her, but until that happened, she wanted Aldrich all to herself.

Though she cared deeply for Grant, she really hadn't considered taking another husband. But the presence of the tall, debonair, and very charming Aldrich Emerson made her reconsider. Were he to ask her, this very minute, to be his wife, she was virtually certain what her answer would be. She could imagine him waking up in the morning, pulling on a gray satin smoking jacket and sitting down in the overstuffed chair in the parlor. She could imagine their exchange of small talk, of endearments and assurances, and making plans to spend the day together. It was all very beautiful, and it gave her hope for a happy future where it had seemed rather bland before.

That evening, Aldrich was strangely silent on the return trip to Lamourie Bayou. He kept the carriage horses at a steady pace, looking neither left nor right as the distance to Ellie's cottage quickly closed.

Because of his thoughtful mood, Ellie had not expected Aldrich to invite himself into the cottage, as he had done on most evenings they had spent together. But he hopped down briskly from the carriage, took her hand and drew it into the crook of his arm, then escorted her onto the gallery. When at last he dropped to the settee, holding her hands across the small table, she quietly asked him what was wrong.

"Fear," he said shortly, his dark eyebrows meeting in a severe frown.

"Fear?" She echoed the one word he had spoken. "Fear of what?"

"Fear of having my hopes dashed," he responded huskily. "Fear of being rejected—"

"And who has rejected you?" Annoyance sifted into

337

her voice. "Surely not me. We have had a wonderful time together, Aldrich. I have been happy with you these past ten days. You have filled a painfully lonely void in my life—"

"And have you been happier with me than you have been with Grant?"

"Grant?" Across the table, she placed her palm softly against his clean-shaven face. "My moments with Grant could never compare to my moments with you. Since my husband died, Aldrich, no man has touched me . . . not the way you have. I don't know why I feel so comfortable with you, but I do. You're a wonderful man. And I think Madeleine is a fool for not accepting you when she had the chance."

Aldrich arched a dark eyebrow. "And what about you, Ellie? Will you accept me?"

Ellie was further annoyed by the approach of Lancie. "What is it?" she crossly asked the man.

"Jes' wanted to ask Mistah Emerson if he'll be headin' back to de Shadows this evenin'."

Both Lancie and Maden were aware of the moments Ellie had spent with Aldrich. They did not approve, though they had silently indulged her indiscretions, often spending the nights that Aldrich was at the cottage as far away from it as both could get. Ellie was too lovestruck to care what they thought about her relationship with Aldrich. She was a grown woman and they had no right to interfere in her life. "Will you need the carriage this evening?" she asked Aldrich.

"Not unless you're planning to run me off, Ellie," he responded.

"Mr. Emerson will be staying over," she said to Lancie. "You may take care of the horses." When Lancie left to see to his task, Ellie returned her attentions to Aldrich. "Now . . . back to the subject of our feelings

338

for each other. Aldrich, what are you trying to say?"

A tug of loyalties warred within Aldrich. He hated Grant, and because of that hatred, he wanted to take his woman. Yet, a part of him cared very deeply for Ellie, even envisioned a happy future with her. Had he met Ellie under different circumstances, he had no doubt that he would have fallen in love with her, for no other reason but that she was beautiful, warm, and sensitive. Her questioning gaze met his own in the darkness of the gallery. "What I am trying to say, Ellie, is that I . . ." He hesitated, drawing upon his inner strength and determination to disrupt Grant's life and make him miserable. "I love you, Ellie," he confessed quietly. "It doesn't matter that we have known each other so short a while. I could know you for months or years — until we are old and gray — and I could not love you more than I do this very minute."

Ellie seemed to wither within. She wanted to hear those endearing words, "I love you," and yet she was fearful . . . apprehensive. Could she repeat the endearment and be as sincere as he seemed to be? She avoided looking directly into his eyes. "I don't know what to say, Aldrich."

"Just tell me how you feel. If you cannot confess to loving me, I will wait. I will give you all the time you need, Ellie. I came to The Boeuf to see my cousin and to make amends for past wrongs, then go on my merry way. I did not expect to meet a wonderful woman like you. But if you cannot give me an answer because of Grant —"

"He has nothing to do with it." She had not meant to speak so abruptly and, certainly, she did not want to appear defensive when the subject of Grant came up. Softening her voice, she continued. "Though I feel incredibly young, I am thirty-six years old, Aldrich."

He laughed sardonically. "And I am the same age, Ellie." Grinning, he pointed to his hair. "Do you see any gray hairs? Do I have that many wrinkles? And you, Ellie, when you look in the mirror, do you see age? When I look at you, I see beauty and youth. When I am in your arms, I feel vibrant and alive, like a giddy schoolboy enjoying a first crush. God, Ellie! You do that to me. And . . . blast!" He suddenly shot up from his seat. "I want you to be my wife. And I pray to God that you want me as a husband."

Ellie suddenly felt dizzy. She squeezed Aldrich's hand. "You do surprise me, Aldrich," she whispered. Her gaze dropped, even as he lowered to one knee before her. "I just don't know what to say."

His hand went to an inside pocket of his jacket. Slipping a ring on to her finger, he pressed a kiss to the back of her hand. "Just say yes, Ellie. Say yes, and I will make you the happiest woman on earth. Say no, and I will go away, no hard feelings, though I will surely leave my heart with you."

A rush of emotions tore her asunder. She had been happy with Aldrich, but was that enough to sustain a lifetime relationship? And was she truly ready to give up on Grant? Suppose that Delilah was . . . No, she could not think that. Delilah could not be dead. She would return to The Shadows and she and Grant would be married. In that moment, as the realization of where she stood in Grant's life struck her like a brutal blow, Ellie knew that if she were to find happiness of her own, it would be as Aldrich's wife. Thus, she sniffed back her tears and forced a timid smile. "Yes, Aldrich, I will be your wife."

Aldrich wanted to deny that the feeling inside him was happiness. He wanted only to enjoy the gloating satisfaction of accomplishing his revenge on his cousin. Taking Ellie in his arms, he gently caressed her back. "You have made me very happy, Ellie. Let us be married as soon as possible—"

"We should wait until Grant returns—"

"No." Drawing back, he forced a smile. "Let's not wait, Ellie. The sooner we marry, the sooner we can begin our lives together as man and wife." Aldrich could envision nothing so personally rewarding as seeing the look on Grant's face when he announced that he was married to Ellie. Ah, how sweet to the tongue was the taste of vengeance! "What do you say? Let us be married right away?"

"If it is what you want," she softly conceded.

"What *we* want," he amended.

"Yes, soon, Aldrich."

Closing her eyes, she allowed him to wrap her in his strong embrace. She tried to force back the tears, but they burned behind her eyelids. Drawing in a deep breath, she soothed her emotions with silent assurances that she would be happy with Aldrich . . . as happy as she could have been with Grant had he loved her rather than Delilah.

Delilah attempted to shake off the foggy darkness surrounding her, but it held on with vicious pincers. She remembered very little of the past few days. Actually, she wasn't even sure if she was still alive, though she reassessed her mortality when she became aware of gently expelled breaths against her cheek and a light snoring mingled with the sounds of an awakening day.

When she tried to move, pain wracked her body. A heavy, masculine arm rested across her waist and a thick, netlike covering had become twisted around her shoulders. She felt as though she might smother between the covering and the body pressed warmly to her own.

Outside a small window — she imagined that was the source of the cool, refreshing breeze — an orange haze began to drift across the horizon. She opened and closed her eyes several times, hoping to sharpen her vision so that she could see who rested beside her. He seemed strangely familiar; she even felt comfortable against him, as if she belonged there.

When, at last, her vision gained some clarity, she was both surprised and wary to see the sleeping face of Grant Emerson, the man she had been running away from when the accident had occurred. She wondered what had happened so that she now lay in his gentle embrace. She remembered Lyle Bishop and the days she had spent in his cabin. She remembered suddenly becoming ill and the terrible pain that had shot through her body every time she had tried to move. And she vaguely remembered a softly whispered prayer. Had it been Lyle's . . . or Grant's?

She looked around at the large, modestly furnished room, finding it unfamiliar to her. Where was she? This was not Lyle's cabin. It was not her aunt Imogen's house in New Orleans. It certainly was not the big house at The Shadows or the quaint lodgings aboard the riverboat she had made her home these past few months.

"Grant?" She thought she had spoken his name, but no sound left her mouth. She attempted to speak his name again. "Grant?" Still no sound. Frustrated by her moment of weakness, she tried to stir against him. That, too, met with failure.

What did it matter if she could not make him notice her? She relished the nearness of him, bathed in the warmth of him. If she had indeed fallen ill, he would be her cure and, when he eventually awakened, his smile would be all the assurance she needed that he was happy to be with her.

342

In the moments that she waited for him to stir, her almost imperceptible shrugs managed to loosen the twisted shawl and release the arm that had been pinned against her side. She felt terribly hungry; if she had taken a turn for the worse, that was surely a good sign of recovery. She was also very thirsty. Seeing a bowl and ewer on a small table across Grant's shoulder, she wished she could get to it. Then she drank deeply of his strong, masculine features and her thirst became nonexistent. She needed . . . wanted . . . nothing but Grant. He was all the nourishment her body required. In his arms she would get well.

When a short, stocky woman suddenly emerged from the cover of a curtain, Delilah cast her a timid glance. When the woman approached the bed and bent over her, Delilah favored her with a tiny smile.

"Ye're awake, little missy?" the woman asked.

Delilah nodded. "I'm a little thirsty. Could I have some water?"

"Yer man wouldn't fetch it for you?" the Widow Pitney asked.

Delilah gently shrugged. "I haven't been able to stir him. He must be very tired."

Without warning, the widow's hand slapped firmly at Grant's shoulder. He lurched from his sound sleep. "Wh — what the hell?" he mumbled, pressing his palms to his closed eyes.

"Yer missy was thirsty," the widow admonished. "An' ye wouldn't wake up and notice her."

Stirring into full wakefulness, Grant gaped down at Delilah. Were those her warm golden eyes smiling up at him, her fingers, resting on his sleeve just moments ago, now traveling playfully up his muscular arm? With doubt darkening his face, his hand moved, stopping just short of her smiling features. Then, as if he was pained by the hesitation, his

343

fingertips brushed across her pale cheek.

He could not speak; rather, his arms circled her shoulders and drew her up against his chest. Even as the Widow Pitney continued to shake her finger in admonishment, he held her close, tears sheening his eyes.

He had his beloved Delilah back in his arms where she belonged.

A frown pressed upon his brow. *Where she belonged?* She had fled from him! Did she even want him?

He needed to ask, but somehow he just couldn't seem to find the words.

Twenty-two

Aldrich and Ellie were married the following Saturday morning. The day was cool with clear skies, a day perfect for a wedding. Ellie, however, would have gone through the ceremony with tears pressed upon her cheeks if she had let the memory of the heated confrontation with her son and Lancie that morning ruin her special day. Maden had threatened to leave home if his mother married Aldrich Emerson, a man she had known less than three weeks, and Lancie had said that he and his mother would seek other employment in the parish. "You do what you must!" a tearful Ellie, standing in her cream-colored wedding dress, had snapped. "None of you has any right to interfere in my life!" Then she had joined the preacher in the parlor, to go over last-minute details of the ceremony.

Ellie was sure that Lancie would have followed through on his threat if his mother hadn't refused to leave. "After all," Miss Mandy had said, shrugging in her casual way, "Miz El, she's got a right to do her own choosin'! She don't try to tell us what we's should do with our lives an' we ain't agoin' to tell her what to do with hers. Now, you spoiled rotten boy, Maden, and you Lancie, my only boy you leave Miz El alone!"

A furious Maden had immediately packed and moved to Dentley, where Thomas Jefferson Wells had not long ago offered him a job working with the horses. Ellie felt that once her hotheaded son had cooled down, he would return. And, of course, she would take him back. She didn't know where she would find a man to take care of the horses the way Maden had, nor could she imagine life at the cottage without her only child.

That evening, as she lay in her new husband's arms, she couldn't imagine being happier than she was that very minute. The wedding had gone without incident, and the few guests she had invited had seemed to thoroughly enjoy the small banquet Miss Mandy had prepared for them afterward. She had no doubts that Aldrich was going to be a wonderful husband and a joy to be around for the rest of her life. When she had been Charles's wife, she had felt insignificant, subservient, and insecure. With Aldrich, she felt special, like a woman with the whole world at her feet.

But even as she made love to her husband that night, a very dark guilt eased into her conscience. She wished they had delayed the wedding until Grant and Delilah had returned, and she was still a little confused by Aldrich's urgency that they not wait a single moment. She almost felt that she had done something sneaky. Silently, she prayed that Grant and Delilah would not be angry with her for omitting them from this very special event in her life. No, Delilah would be happy for her. She had to be honest with herself. It was Grant she was worried about. They had been very close friends—*just friends;* the thought still caused her to frown—and she could not bear his unhappiness with her.

As if it really mattered.

She had Aldrich now, and she was happy.

* * *

That morning in the tidy little cabin on Spring Bayou, Ellie was as far from the minds of Grant and Delilah as the moon. The Widow Pitney, complaining that the cot upon which she had offered to sleep was wreaking havoc on her back, had put the two young people up in the cabin a hundred yards farther down the bayou, where her son and wife had lived. It had stood vacant since they had moved across the river into Mississippi last year and Grant found it a perfect haven for Delilah's recovery. They had been happy there because they were together, and each day had seen her more improved. This morning, she had actually rushed onto the small porch to greet him upon his return from the trading post.

"Did you post my letter to Hilda?" she asked brightly, tucking herself beneath his arm as they moved into the cabin. "I do hope you brought something to eat. I'm starving!"

Grant laughed. "Yes, love, I posted your letter to Number 14 Rousseau in the Carrollton District, New Orleans, and I brought you . . ." He dropped a basket onto the table and pulled back the checkered napkin, "hot buttered biscuits, honey, bacon, and boiled eggs. And might I be granted the privilege of saying these good meals the widow fixes for you sure look nice on your bones?"

"Are you saying that I'm getting fat?" she asked, feigning indignation.

"Even if you were as wide as the dear old widow," he whispered against her cheek, "I would love you just as much."

"So, you *do* think I'm getting fat," she continued, cutting him a reproving glance.

He laughed as he picked her up so that her feet no longer touched the floor. "You cannot pick a quarrel with me, Delilah Wickley," he warned her. "You said you would consider telling me today where you were

347

when I was looking for you."

Her eyes dropped coyly. "I told you . . . nothing happened. He took good care of me. If he carried me to the Widow Pitney's, it was because he did not know how to help me."

"I have told you, Delilah, that I will not bash the fellow's head in. Has it ever occurred to you that I might want to thank him for what he *was* able to do for you?"

"No, I do not believe that." When his eyes narrowed hurtfully, she continued with haste. "I'm sorry. I don't mean to be cruel. But you were very angry that I had been taken to the trading post and simply left there in so ill a condition I could have died."

She was right, of course. He was still angry about it, and if he knew the identity of the man who had done it, he probably *would* bash his blasted head in. Perhaps he should forget about it, and simply be happy that she was alive and well and in his arms today. "All right. But one day, I want to know the identity of the man."

"When you've cooled off, perhaps. But I really don't see what good it will do." Drawing a long, deep breath, she eased into his arms, forgetting, for the moment the aroma of the biscuits in the napkin-covered basket. "When will we return to The Shadows?"

"I thought you wanted to travel on to New Orleans to spend time with your aunt Imogen," he said in surprise. "Now, you are wanting to return home? I thought you wanted time to think . . . and to decide whether you loved me for myself and not for the land—"

"Horse feathers!" Lightly, her fingers grazed his chest, unpopping the top button of his shirt as they did so. "I know I love you. If you want to sell The Shadows and move me into this cabin, Grant Emerson, I will be happy so long as I am with you. You are my love, and I will go wherever you go."

"And suppose I wanted to return to New England? Will you go with me?"

Her stunning gold gaze turned up to hold his own. "You asked me this a few days ago, Grant Emerson. You wouldn't move to the East. Don't you remember what would happen to a southern lady if she was to be taken farther north than Virginia?"

" 'She would whither and die,' " he mocked her words of that prior occasion, " 'like a magnolia bloom fallen from the tree.' " Actually, he would never consider selling The Shadows. For the first time in his life, he felt a sense of belonging somewhere. He not only wanted to spend the rest of his life at The Shadows, he wanted to expand it into the richest plantation on The Boeuf.

And he wanted Delilah Wickley at his side—his love, his wife, and his companion for life. Without her, the plantation meant nothing to him. Without her, life was meaningless.

Twilight had just fallen over the cool October evening. Sliding the widow's cream-colored shawl onto Delilah's slim shoulders, he coaxed her out-of-doors to watch the last glint of blue drop below the horizon. The beauty beckoning from beyond the bayou—the velvet night and star-studded sky—drew the breath from Delilah's body. Wrapping her arm around Grant's waist, she stood for a moment in the clearing and swept her gaze over the majestic night. Far away, banjo frogs joined in a haunting chorus and a haze washed over the bayou like a softly stirred wind. How happy she was, tucked beneath Grant's protective arm, his cheek resting ever so gently against her chestnut-colored hair, and his rhythmic breathing in chorus with her own.

"Are you still angry with me for leaving the plantation without telling you?"

"It was something that should not have happened, but . . . no, I am not angry with you. I like to think I'm an understanding man, and I realize you did what you felt you had to do. I only hope that you harbor no more doubts about your love for me."

She squeezed herself to him, her hand rising from his waist to stroke the pale blond fringes of his hair. "Make love to me, Grant."

Grant smiled to himself. Even though she had seemed to be her old self these past few days, complaining not even a little about the wound, he had not pressed her on the issue of intimacy. He wanted to be with her that way, but he had not wanted to appear selfish. He knew that when she was ready, she would be the one to bring the subject up. He couldn't, however, pass up the opportunity to tease her. "Make love to you, Delilah? I really don't think you're ready for that. We should give your wound a few more days to heal."

"Horse feathers! My wound is just fine." She gently shrugged against him. "If you no longer find me attractive —"

"Well, you *are* getting a little chubby —"

With feigned shock, she turned into his arms, her eyes blazing. "Grant Emerson, I do hope you're teasing me!"

"Why, darling, I wouldn't dream of teasing you until you are fully recovered."

"You *are* teasing me, you rascal. I can see that smile behind those big blue eyes. If you don't make love to me this very night — this very minute, in fact — I just might go on to Aunt Imogen's and allow her to set up those courters for me —"

"And I'll toss them into the Mississippi, one at a time." He laughed the threat. "Come . . ." Picking her up in his arms in one swift move, he turned toward the cabin; "I will show my little beauty how very much I want her."

It seemed to Delilah that scarcely a moment had passed before he was easing her onto the bed with its oversize quilt and large, fat pillows. He began removing his clothing. When she sat up and started to untie the stays of her bodice, his hand closed over hers, halting their movements. "Don't . . . I would like to do that myself—"

Her full, sensual mouth molded into a seductive smile. Her palms flat upon the bed and her knees drawn up, she watched him as he undressed—the broad expanse of his chest with its thick, curly copper-gold hair, his slim waist and narrow hips . . . the full, male part of him that would oh so soon join to her . . . the slim, muscular columns of his legs. When her eyes lifted to his own smiling ones, she knew that he was very aware that he pleased her.

As she held his gaze, transfixed, his knee fell to the bed. With one foot still on the planked floor, his fingers rose to deftly undo the stays of her gown. When, at last, his hands eased beneath the fabric to expose her shoulders, she felt the cool rush of wind through the window ply across her flesh. Then his hands lowered, cupped her firm, small breasts, and his mouth lowered to capture one pink rosebud. Easing her to her back, her proud, impassioned Yankee rogue covered her slim body.

When Delilah cupped his face between her palms, he lowered his lips to capture her parted ones, his hands roughly kneading her breasts. His mouth was hot against her own, his breath gentle and sweet, his body so enflamed that she almost felt the surrender of her own flesh. Her hands moved to the back of his neck to hold him close, and when his mouth trailed from hers, nipping playfully at her chin and down the column of her neck, she thrust her breast against his seeking mouth. His torrid possession scorched her like a brand and when his hands slipped beneath the waist of her dress and coaxed the offending fabric over her legs, she tried not to respond to the tiny prickle of pain as his fingers grazed her half-healed wound.

But he had noticed the brief drawing of her brows and his movements suddenly ceased. "Did I hurt you, love?"

"No, Grant. I care about nothing but being with you. The only pain you inflict is in taking so long—"

With a low chuckle, he again dropped to her. When her hands lowered to his narrow hips, he positioned himself between her silken thighs. He cut his gaze to the beauty of her legs lifting to wrap around his own. His passion-sheened eyes met her own languorous ones, and when her mouth puckered, his own caressed hers in the gentlest of kisses, his tongue darting to the sweetness beyond. He wanted her so badly that he ached from head to toe.

"Are you ready for me, love?" he asked in a husky whisper.

Rather than respond with words, her hips rose so that the hardness of him pressed against her. Before he could position himself to enter her, her hand lowered to gently guide him. Her boldness brought a twinkle to his eyes, and a tiny moan escaped her as the utter pleasure of him deep inside her enveloped her. Now that he was where he had wanted to be, he lay still, enjoying her, his hands working miracles over her flesh, his mouth teasing her breasts into hard peaks that ached for his caresses. A cool wind from the open window wrapped around them, but they felt only the rapidly surging heat of each other. Delilah was almost certain she would embarrass herself with desperate pleas if he did not begin to move within her.

Almost as if he had read her thoughts, his hips began to move, slowly, oh so slowly at first, then quicker, urging her to meet his masterful pace and blend into the exquisite blanket of sweet torment with him. Though the skies outside were clear, she was sure she heard distant thunder, or did it come from within her own body. She was sure she had seen a flash of lightning, or was it merely the passionate glaze of his eyes.

Together they moved into a netherworld of glowing light and siren songs, where nothing existed but the two of them. He plunged deeper and deeper still, and she found that she could scarcely meet his rhythm and pace. So rough was he that it flamed her skin with a primitive desire that again tore a moan from her mouth. In that moment, she sought his kiss and dragged her hands roughly down his shoulders to hold him close to her. Then it came, the explosion deep within her that momentarily drove away the frenzied sound of her own rapid heartbeat.

When at last they lay in wondrous fulfillment, Delilah wondered how she could have ever considered fleeing from him. She belonged with him, in his arms, being held and possessed by him . . . loving and being loved by him. Her life was not meant to be lived, unless it was lived with him.

When he was able to gain some physical control, Grant raised his head. "I did not hurt your wound, did I?" he asked.

"Wound?" she echoed. "What wound?" His chuckle warmed her. "Oh, Grant, now that you know I am well and able to travel, let us return home."

"I guess we had better," he responded. "There is no telling what my cousin has done to the place."

Delilah frowned. She hadn't been too happy to hear that Aldrich had located Grant. She only hoped he was not lying in wait, planning his revenge for what he might consider past wrongs. She wanted to return to The Shadows, but she wanted just as much to be far away from Aldrich Emerson. "He wouldn't harm you, would he?" she asked after a moment.

"He said that he was wrong to feel as he did. I really don't think he is planning revenge. Besides, he might already have taken off by now. He came to visit me, he said, and if I was not there, what purpose would he have to remain?"

"But you spent only an afternoon with him. If he wishes to make amends, he would want to spend more time than that."

Gently, Grant eased himself from the warmth of her and lay the length of her slender body. "I can think of better things to discuss than my cousin," he said.

"Such as?" she queried.

"Our wedding plans." Suddenly, he lifted his head and his right hand went down to roughly grapple with her own. "That reminds me. Where is the ring I gave you? I just realized I have not seen it!"

She laughed softly. "I left it with Ellie. I told her that if I did not return within two months, she was to give it back to you."

He snorted with annoyance. "That would have been humiliating."

"Don't worry," she teased affectionately, touching her mouth in a tender kiss to his forehead, "I will get the ring back. You needn't fret."

Moving so that she could see his features illuminated in the light of the one lamp, Delilah dropped her head against Grant's chest. She was still heady with passion, and scarcely felt the rhythmic thump-thump-thumping of his heart against her ear. How much she loved this man. He was all in the world she wanted, and to envision the rest of her life with him was to envision sheer joy. Delilah Emerson . . . How wonderful it sounded in her thoughts. Mrs. Grant Emerson.

"Oh, I do love you, Grant," she whispered, the happiness she felt vibrating in her voice.

"And what has brought about this?" he chuckled good-naturedly, tightening his grip around her shoulders. "Still thanking me for a damn good tumble?"

"I just don't want you to forget that I love you. Even when we quarrel, I want you to know how much I love you."

His eyes smiled even as his mouth pressed evenly. "Oh? And you are planning that we will quarrel often?"

"Often enough to keep boredom from setting in," she teased. "Just think how much fun we shall have making up after a darn good quarrel. Oh, Grant, let us return to The Shadows tomorrow. The widow will sell you the bay gelding and I won't mind riding it."

"But Bella is your horse. *I* will ride the gelding."

"See how easy it is for us to quarrel?" she pointed out. "Even over who will ride a silly old horse. We're going to have a wonderful, exciting life, Grant," she cooed. "You and me, at Shadows-in-the-Mist—"

"And, hopefully, in a few years, half a dozen little Emersons—"

Her eyes were bright with surprise. "A half-dozen! Then you will have to give birth to the last three or four yourself, because I won't. I'd imagine that two little Emersons, if they are anything like their father, will be quite a handful."

Together, they laughed, joked about having two pairs of twins, and fell asleep in each other's arms.

Tomorrow they would return to Shadows-in-the-Mist.

And soon they would be married.

Pierre Neville moved at a steady pace along Bayou Boeuf below the village of Cheneyville. As night darkened the sky, he dismounted his well-traveled mule, built a fire, then settled into his bedroll beneath a towering oak. Again, he took from his shirt pocket a bulletin he'd swiped off the marshal's desk in Baton Rouge and his gaze raked over the crude description written in Sheriff Stafford's scribble: *Skeletal remains found by Mr. Grant Emerson of Shadows-in-the-Mist Plantation . . . Description, provided by Emerson: male, approximately six feet in height, withered right arm, chip in right femur bone caused by old injury, bullet hole midforehead . . . grave uncovered by storm.*

It had been a stroke of luck that Neville had been in the marshal's office that day. He'd journeyed into the city to file trespassing charges against a neighbor with whom he had a running feud and had been sitting patiently at the desk, awaiting the return of the man who would take his report. There it had lain, for all eyes to see—a description that could only have been that of his younger brother, Paulie. Frankly, he had wondered why the Alexandria sheriff had cared about learning the identity of the victim. Most people considered the Nevilles poor white trash.

The bulletin sent by Sheriff Stafford had further advised that the remains had "disappeared." Disappeared? thought Pierre, gritting his teeth in outrage. Well, somebody had better assist in relocating Paulie Neville, so that he could be returned to the farm and buried with the other family members who had died.

Pierre Neville thought back to that warm spring day more than six years ago that he'd tried to talk his younger brother into staying on the farm. He might as well have been talking to the wind for all the response he got. But the adventurous Paulie had heard a crazy tale of a fortune in gold hidden somewhere on a central Louisiana plantation, and he had wanted to find it, pay off the mortgage on the farm, and settle down with his family and his new young wife. Pierre had watched him ride off that day, and he never saw him again.

Of course he'd always wondered what had happened to him, even thinking that perhaps he had found his gold and gone off to San Francisco, or some exotic port, to enjoy the wealth and make a new life for himself. Though Paulie had never been one to desert his family, Pierre had not wanted to consider the alternatives.

Now, Pierre had in his hand almost sure proof that his brother was dead—murdered . . . shot between the eyes and buried in a grave so shallow that rainwater had uncovered his remains.

Shadows-in-the-Mist . . . That was where Pierre would begin his search. That was where his brother's remains had been found, and there he would hopefully find the culprit who had killed him. There, somewhere on the vast, rich land of a fancy, sidewinding planter, he would find what was left of his brother and bring him back home for burial.

And if the gold that had gotten his brother killed had not been found, he wouldn't leave without it. The Nevilles had paid a high price—the murder of one of their own—and if anyone deserved the gold, it was his family.

Tucking the bit of frayed paper back into his pocket, Pierre sunk down into his bedroll. Closing his eyes, he soon drifted off to sleep, dreaming of a fancy plantation, a murdered brother, and a cache of gold that could be a new beginning for a poverty-stricken family.

Twenty-three

Storm clouds menaced the willow-lined channel of the Red River where Grant and Delilah sought solace for the night. Delilah tucked herself into Grant's arms to enjoy a peaceful sleep. Except for the occasional cry of a bird, the silence was solid. At midday tomorrow, they would reach Alexandria, and in the afternoon, their beloved Shadows-in-the-Mist would greet them.

Delilah sighed deeply, snuggling her face against Grant's chest. He had built a lean-to, over which he'd slung a tarpaulin, in the event of the rain an old Indian had forecast earlier in the day. It appeared inevitable, rolling across the horizon like a log pushed down a steep hill, but Delilah felt protected in Grant's arms. Nothing could touch her, not even the droplets of rain she could hear splashing into the swift currents of the river.

The sky abruptly became the color of copper and a heady wind blew up. Delilah tucked herself closer to Grant, using his body as a blanket against her. How soothing was the gentle rhythm of his heartbeat against her ear. She could lie beside him like this for the rest of her days and enjoy no deeper peace.

The wind began to shriek fiercely through the woods, rising and falling, shaking the timber as if a giant, invisible fury had been unleashed on the river. Despite the vicious slashing of the rain, the tarpaulin and the thick foliage of evergreens overhead kept them dry.

As the storm continued to snarl its outrage, Grant suddenly took Delilah and pulled her across his body, covering both of them with the blanket. "What are you doing?" she asked, trying to be indignant, but affectionately dropping her forehead against his cheek instead.

"The storm attacks us with such ferocity," he chuckled hoarsely, "that it makes me want to make love to you, Delilah."

She said nothing at first as she felt his hardness against her abdomen. "You can do nothing, Grant Emerson," she finally whispered seductively, "if you keep it in the barn."

"Delilah Wickley!" He feigned shock, his hands rising to roughly grip her shoulders. "You're becoming more of a hussy as each day passes." His surprise became genuine as her fingers scooted beneath his waistband, popped the buttons of his trousers, and freed his hips. Dropping her knees to each side of him and readjusting her skirts, she wasted no time in lowering herself over his masculinity, her muscles contracting over the fullness of him. He groaned his pleasure, and his grip became rougher over her shoulders, dragging down to massage her breasts through her blouse. "But you're a hussy . . . who very much . . . pleases me," he stammered the words.

Arching her back as she sat up, Delilah allowed the blanket to fall away. She wished she could feel the rain beating against her face and her flesh. She wished they could make love with the storm fiercely encircling them and drawing them into its torrent.

She wished the tarpaulin would toss hither and yon and make this night unforgettable.

Grant looked into her eyes, watched the tiny smile curl her mouth and her breasts move against his rough caresses. When his fingers curled the sleeves of her blouse downward, she bent, offering her breast to his moist mouth. Then she began rocking gently upon him, enjoying the fullness of him, feeling his hips rise and fall with driving force to impale her again and again. Their frenzied movements took away their breaths in unison, and when she sought the feel of his mouth against her own, she was not sure how much longer she could hold back the delicious culmination of her own pleasure.

Her face flaming, she enjoyed the sheer wanton pleasure of her body molded to his. His low growl, as he moved quickly toward his own explosive culmination, blended into her soft moan as their mouths locked and his tongue darted into the dark sweetness she had offered him. When, at last, their passions came together as one peak of pleasure, she collapsed atop him. Her body tingled with searing joy.

"I think you just raped me, you saucy little wench," Grant weakly growled.

"Oh, . . . and you tried so hard to escape," she shot back. Shifting her hips so that his manhood slipped from the honeyed warmth of her, eliciting a groan from him at the separation, she smoothed her skirts over her long, lithe legs and fell against him. Her eyes lightly closed against his chin, she felt the movement of his hands as he covered himself. "Can we sleep now, Grant Emerson?" But even as she spoke, the echo of his light snoring grazed upon her forehead. A smile touching her mouth, she moved her hand onto the expanse of his chest, to feel his heartbeat against her palm. "Yes, my love, sleep," she murmured, closing her own eyes and quickly joining him in slumber.

Pleading that he had to stay at The Shadows and look after business in his cousin's absence, Aldrich finally convinced his new wife to make the temporary move with him. She did not feel comfortable in Grant's house and was quick to relay her displeasure to Aldrich.

"Don't you think," Aldrich explained, "that if Grant were going to be gone a long time, he'd let someone know? He'll probably be back any day now. It will not hurt us to stay until then."

"I suppose," Ellie responded.

"And do you truly believe he would deny you access to his house?"

Ellie looked up, a little puzzled. "I can think of no reason in the world why I should be given access to Grant's house in his absence."

Aldrich, holding her close in the foyer, clicked his tongue. "You refuse to admit that you and Grant were . . ." He stopped short of completing the sentence with the word he wanted, "lovers," and substituted instead, "were very close."

"I have not denied that, Aldrich. But you are my husband now. And I plan to be a very good wife. We have our own place to take care of."

"Lancie will hold down the fort," he said, then took her hands and held them warmly. "Now, you make yourself comfortable and I'm going to ride out to Grant's fields and see how the picking is going. It is the least I can do for my cousin."

"Very well. I brought some needlework with me." When he moved onto the gallery, Mozelle approached. Ellie met her thoughtful gaze, wondering what was on her mind.

"Miz El, I don't mean ta be cruel, but . . . ya know what I's think?"

"And what is that, Mozelle?" she politely responded.

"I think Mistah Aldrich married ya because he thought ya was Grant's woman. I think he married ya to spite the massah, cuz Massah married his woman up yonder in Yankeeland—"

Her mouth trembled and her fingers linked so tightly together they hurt. "So . . . you don't mean to be cruel, Mozelle?" she said. "You could have taken a whip to me, and you couldn't have hurt me more. You know, I don't think I like you anymore."

"Now, don't be like dat, Miz El—"

"Please leave me, Mozelle."

Her mouth gaped; the lady had always encouraged freedom of thought. "But, Miz El—"

"Please, just leave!" Tears sheened Ellie's eyes. She bit her lip, trying to cease its trembling. Just as Mozelle would have disappeared, she called out to her. "Mozelle . . . how do you know about the other woman in New England?"

"I overhe'erd Missy talkin' to Daisy one day. She was tellin' her 'bout it," Mozelle answered.

"You haven't told anyone else what you think about my marriage to Aldrich, have you?"

"Naw'm. I likes ya too much fo' dat, Miz El." Then her gaze held to the smooth, varnished floor, she moved out of Ellie's range.

In wistful thought, Ellie moved slowly into the parlor, where she sat at the end of the divan and drew her elbow up to its plush arm. Grant filled her thoughts. Of course he had told her about the quarrel with Aldrich and the misunderstanding that had led to his marriage to Madeleine Vail. They had discussed it at length many times. Ellie also knew that, until just a few weeks ago, Grant had continued to receive letters from Madeleine, sent by his family since they had honored Grant's request not to tell her where he was. She knew that Grant accepted the letters only because he wanted to be kept apprised of the child's progress and any problems that might arise where he would need him. To this day, she was aware that Grant still sent money to Madeleine to help in the support of the boy who was, by law, his son.

Should she give Mozelle's cruel and thoughtless statement any credence? Would Aldrich go that far to seek revenge against his cousin? Surely, he would not use an innocent woman. And why would he think Grant would care? Her relationship with the handsome master of Shadows-in-the-Mist had never evolved past friendship. If Grant thought his cousin had changed for the better, he would be pleased that he had taken her for a bride.

Now that she thought about it, on several occasions Aldrich had left the impression that he considered her to be closer to Grant than she actually was. Did Aldrich believe she and Grant were lovers? Was that why he had courted her, proposed to her, and insisted on marrying so quickly? Did he look forward, with a cruel pleasure, to seeing Grant's face when he announced their marriage?

Dear Lord, thought Ellie. *Please don't let it be true. I could not bear the humiliation if he simply used me in so sick a manner in order to seek vengeance against his cousin.*

No! Aldrich had married her because he loved her.

And for no other reason.

Doubt was as thick inside her as the nausea that suddenly threatened to ruin her day.

* * *

The following morning, the bank of the Red River was a glittering maze of broken branches and leaves. Grant and Delilah had risen early, eaten what was left of the dried beef and boiled eggs the Widow Pitney had packed for them, and resumed their journey to Alexandria. The storm had turned the trail into a ribbon of treacherous mud, and several times the clumsy gelding Grant had purchased from the widow almost lost its footing. Ten miles into its journey, it slid down the bank of the Red River, neatly depositing Grant in the shallow current. He sat there cursing the beast and trying to separate his body from the mud that was more like a glue.

Sitting atop Bella at a bend in the trail, Delilah laughed so hard that painful knots gathered in her chest. Trying to stifle her giggles, she watched the darkness of ire spread across Grant's features. But as she again tried to stop her laughing, the big gelding nibbled playfully at Grant's cheek. Flicking his finger at the beast, he grinned ruefully. "I ought to drown you, you worthless critter!" he thundered. When he tugged on the reins, the horse pulled back, and Grant maneuvered out of the mud and began moving precariously up the bank, his eyes holding the gaze of the amused Delilah. "And you, too, woman! You'll pay for ridiculing me!"

"Oh? And what, pray tell, do you plan to do to me?"

Again, the mud dragged him down and he stopped moving, hoping that he would not slide back into the water. "Throw me a rope, Miss Delilah Wickley," he growled out the order, "and tie the end around the pommel." She made no move, but sat there looking at him. "Have you suddenly grown deaf, you wicked little tart?"

"Oh, I can hear," she teased him unmercifully, "but you have to say please."

He turned his head to look up at her, forcing a dark frown upon his brow. "Please," he shot the single word. "You are certainly asking for it."

Several moments of silence followed. Then Delilah untied the rope from the rawhide and threw it down the bank toward Grant. When, at last, she was backing Bella into the timberline, she watched Grant's tall, mud-coated form slowly ascend the hill. When he stood firmly on the trail, she dropped the rope from the pommel.

When she made no move to approach him, his powder-blue gaze turned fully to her, assessing her as he might a man with a weapon pointed at him. Until his mouth spread into a grin, she was not sure of his mood. Now, she nudged the horse up to his side.

Without warning, his hands dashed out, grasped her waist, and she was forcefully unseated from her horse. He sought a rough kiss, spreading mud across her face. "What are you doing, Grant Emerson!" she shot at him. "You are going to get me dirty!"

"Laugh at me, woman," he growled with feigned ire, "and you suffer the consequences!" By the time he finished wrestling with her, ignoring her halfhearted protests and threats, she was as muddy as he was. Then they fell together to the ground, their laughter blending together in harmony.

"Look at me, Grant! I'm a mess!"

"You look beautiful," he said with affection, flicking a clump of mud from her pert nose.

The love shone like a beacon in her golden eyes. Slipping her arms around his shoulders, she held him close. "Our whole life is going to be like this, isn't it, Grant? Playful and teasing and affectionate. Let us never grow old. Let us always stay young at heart. If we want to tousle in the mud, then let's do it . . . even if we're ninety years old, walking with canes and our lips sunk in because we have no teeth!"

He laughed deeply. "I hope that's not too apt a description of us in fifty or sixty years."

Neither had heard horses' hooves on the trail, but suddenly they became aware of three mounted men looking down on them, their horses halted half a dozen yards from where they sat, embracing like giddy children. "You two all right?" a tall man asked.

Grant pulled himself to his feet, taking Delilah's hand to pull her up with him. Instinctively, his hand went to his side arm. "The horse lost its footing and slid down the bank," he explained sheepishly. "We're all right."

Suddenly, one of the men prodded his horse closer, lifted his head, and exposed his features beneath the overhang of his hat. "Miss Delilah Wickley? Is that you?"

She narrowed her eyes, fighting for recognition. Then it came to her. "Mr. Garrett . . . what are you doing away from your mercantile?"

"Looking for you," he said, tipping his hat, then looked at Grant. "And a good day to you, Mr. Emerson. It looks like you've accomplished what a hundred men haven't been able to do. When Miss Wickley's name was not on the list of survivors or of the dead, the steamboat company called for volunteers. We've been searching for nigh on to two weeks now."

"I appreciate it," Grant responded.

Delilah was surprised that John Garrett would go to so much trouble. His life was his mercantile, and he'd spent very little time away from it. "Who is running your store?" Delilah asked.

"My sister Mary and my wife. I wouldn't be surprised if they've put me out of business by now." John Garrett looked toward Grant. "You're a mess, Emerson . . . you and the lady. But you can travel back to Alexandria with us."

Though they would rather have traveled together, just the two of them, Grant and Delilah accepted the offer. Every mile or so, John Garrett or one of the other men discharged a gun three times into the air, the signal to let the men know Delilah had been found and to come in from the woods. By the time they reached Alexandria, there were more exhausted men milling around the steamboat company than passengers and dock workers.

There, an equally exhausted Delilah gave her account of her adventure, then she and Grant took a room at the Exchange Hotel to bathe and change into clean clothing before journeying on to The Boeuf.

Two very happy people began the last leg of their return shortly after one o'clock that overcast October afternoon.

Ellie had fretted to the point of tears, wondering if her beloved Aldrich had ulterior motives in marrying her. That first night beneath the roof of The Shadows, she had made love to Aldrich almost mechanically; her heart had not been in it, and he had noticed the lack of sincerity in her responses to him. Though he had questioned her—and though she wanted to tell him what worried her—she had said simply that the excitement of their marriage had caused a minor illness, a malady that would certainly leave her before the passing of another day.

That morning, a very worried Aldrich went down to breakfast, leaving her alone in the bedchamber to nurse her illness. He sat where Grant usually sat, his fingers drawn to his chin in thoughtful silence. Mozelle entered and quietly set a plate of food in front of him. "Do you know what is wrong with my wife?" he asked, fearing that the bold-tongued slave had said something to upset her.

"Naw, suh, Mistah Emerson. I reckon she's jes' real anxious to see Massah an' Missy—"

"Missy! Missy!" he snipped, sitting forward in his chair. "Why would my wife be anxious to see some blasted slave wench!"

Mozelle expelled a surprised laugh. "Slave wench! Missy? Missy, she be de fine white lady Massah be wantin' to marry up wid him. Missy be de reason Massah gone these pas' two weeks . . . to find Missy an' bring her back to de Shadows where she belongs."

Aldrich stood so quickly his chair fell over backward. His eyes were narrowed hatefully, his teeth clenched so tightly the muscles of his jaws contracted beneath the strain. "What do you mean? Ellie—my wife—is the woman Grant loved—"

Again, the bold Mozelle laughed. "Miz El, Mistah Emerson? Miz El, she be jes' a friend to Massah. Why, I reckon they ain't even kissed a li'l peck on de cheek in dees years dey knowed each other. It be Missy—Miss Delilah Wickley, she's de massah's love. Jes' 'fo she left de Shadows, Massah asked her to marry up wid him. But Missy, she be so confused inside, not knowin' fo' sho' whether it be de massah or de Shadows what she loved de bes', so she run off

368

to make up her mind. But Massah, he'll be bringin' Missy back an dey's bound to be a great big weddin'. That's fo' sho', Mistah Emerson, what'll be happenin' when de massah brings our sweet Missy back!"

"I don't believe you," Aldrich hissed, folding his arms across his chest to hide the trembling of his hands from the slave. "Nobody has mentioned this . . . this Delilah Wickley. Not you, not any of the other slaves, not anyone I've met on The Boeuf, and certainly not Ellie. If she was so anxious to see this woman, why did she never mention her?"

Mozelle's dark eyebrows shot up. "Sounds like a big ol' conspir'cy ta me, Mistah Emerson. Reckon nobody here an' 'bouts—including Miz El—figgered Missy was any of yo' business. O'cou'se, Mistah Emerson, reckon ya'll be real happy to hear 'bouts yo' fav'rit cousin havin' a real sweet love, jes' like you an' Miz El have now. Jes' think, Mistah Emerson . . ." She continued in her sarcastic tone, "if ya's an' Miz El would'a jes' waited, they's could'a been a double weddin' ceremony . . "

Aldrich drew back his hand, preparing to slap the servant, but he dropped it to whisper harshly for Mozelle to get out. When she hesitated, he barked at her. "Get out, I say, or I'll take a whip to you!"

Mozelle, shaking her head, moved from the dining room, mumbling that "ya don't own me, Yankee-man, an' ya'll not be takin' a whip ta me."

Aldrich was blinded by his own spinning fury. He gripped the edges of the table so firmly that it could almost have crumbled in his hands. This could not be happening. The slave was lying! There was no Missy, no Miss Delilah Wickley. She'd made it up. All along, she had seen why he was courting Ellie McPherson and she was trying to dampen his triumph over his hated younger cousin. Yes, yes, of course . . . that was it. The slave Mozelle was lying through her blasted teeth!

He turned first toward the stairs that would take him to the chamber where his new wife was reluctant to awaken. He could ask her about this Delilah Wickley but—he cringed inside—was he ready to know that he'd been made a fool of, that his cousin had bested him once again? How could this have happened? Could it be true that such a beautiful woman could be no more than a friend to the handsome Grant Emerson? Could it be possible that he was yet to meet his cousin's true love—this phantom, this Miss Delilah Wickley.

The pain shooting into Aldrich's wrist compelled him to loosen his grip on the table edge. He wanted to rise and walk away, but he felt weak. He wanted to saddle a horse, ride away from The Shadows and not look back, but he had the obligation of a new wife. Could he desert her the way Grant had deserted Madeleine Vail?

He would not stoop to his cousin's level. He had made Ellie his wife, and he had a duty to her.

Slumping back in the chair, Aldrich's heated gaze pierced the fabric of the gossamer at the long window and caught the movement of a cat on the windowsill. A wife . . . he had a wife. He had ridden into Louisiana a free man, bent on revenge against a cousin who had wronged him, wanting only to accomplish that and return to New England, minus the burden of one despicable relative. But now he had a wife . . . a new kind of burden.

He had married Ellie for all the wrong reasons, and now he realized that, despite all, he loved the dear woman.

She was anything but a burden. Ellie was the

woman he wanted to spend the rest of his life with, in whose arms he wanted to love away the long nights. She made him forget the fickle Madeleine Vail.

He had married Ellie to get revenge against his cousin.

But now he loved her.

Which was stronger . . . his pride or his love?

How could he extract himself without losing face? And without losing Ellie? All the hatred he had borne for Grant suddenly flew off with the wind. He wanted only to enjoy Ellie, and to love her.

Damn his blasted pride! He could not let Grant get the best of him again!

Aldrich finally gained the strength to rise from the chair. All sounds of an active morning suddenly drifted off, leaving a stillness and silence as deep as death. He choked on the heaviness of the air within the room, like an oven without doors, a prison from which he could not escape. He felt the vicious, painful pounding of his heart, then the sheen of heat that suddenly burned his eyes. *Pluck the miserable bastards out!* he thought, digging his palms against them. *Dig them out so that they will not see Grant's triumphant gaze as he realizes the folly his stupid cousin has made! Dig them out so that they will not bear witness to the pain in Ellie's eyes when she realizes she has been so viciously used. Dig them out! My heart is blind! Why then, shouldn't my eyes be?*

"Ya's all right, Mistah Emerson?"

His hands jerked away from his moisture-sheened eyes. Slowly, as if emerging from a hypnotic trance, Aldrich's eyes turned to Mozelle. "Why shouldn't I be all right?" He barked his response, hoping to dispel the emotion boiling within him. "Don't I look all right?"

"Ya look sick," she replied truthfully. "Ya didn't touch yo' plate."

"I'm not hungry. Take the plate away." He ground out the words, then took long strides to the gallery and quickly descended the steps. He had to get away, go for a ride somewhere and think. He had to be alone. At the stable, he met Philbus emerging with his large gelding trailing behind him. "Who is Delilah Wickley?" Aldrich barked.

"She be the lady yo' cousin Massah Emerson's gonna marry up wid," Philbus responded.

"Why haven't I been told about her before?"

His ugly tone was beginning to anger Philbus. He drew a deep, calm breath before sarcastically responding, "Well, Mistah Emerson, I don't rightly recall ya askin' 'bout Missy befo'. Now ya knows who Missy is. What be de big fuss?"

Storming past him and into the stable, Aldrich bellowed an oath at Philbus and dragged a mare out of her stall.

Aldrich disappeared into the tack room in search of a saddle, and a thoughtful Philbus, scratched at his scalp beneath the rim of his hat. "Crazy Yankee-Doodle dog . . . sho' can git a burr up his butt!" he muttered.

Twenty-four

The two horses tied to the back of the rented carriage made it move at a slow pace, but that was all right with Delilah. Her arm tucked gently into Grant's, she enjoyed the afternoon, frequently waving to the Negroes in the cottonfields or simply watching the flurry of activity on the bayou. Men in their pirogues, a boat easily tipped over by inexperienced users, brought in their fish from the fertile depths of the water.

She looked down at the new frock she was wearing, its tight-fitting mauve velveteen bodice complementing the voluminous rose-and-blue plaid skirts. Mr. Garrett had sent it over from the few garments on his ladies' rack at the mercantile, "a welcome-home gift," he had explained. She was still a little surprised at his change in character. He was usually a gruff, staid man with very little to say, and now he was treating her as a long-lost daughter. The new dress had come with a matching parasol, but she didn't need to use it on this cool, overcast day.

Soon, they were moving onto the road alongside the railroad track, the last stretch before reaching Ellie's cottage. Delilah was anxious to see her friend and, of course, retrieve the diamond ring she had left in her care. As they neared the cottage, a shiver ran the length of Delilah's spine.

"Are you cold?" Grant asked.

"No . . . just excited," she explained. "I feel as if I've been gone a year, rather than just a few short weeks."

"You are anxious to see Ellie, aren't you?"

"Oh, yes, I've missed her so!" A frown knit Delilah's brows. She remembered the look on Ellie's face when last they had talked, when she had realized that Ellie was in love with Grant. Was there any way to relay her happiness without Ellie thinking she was smearing mud in her face? Dear, dear Ellie! Delilah could not understand why a good man had not snatched her from her lonely life at the cottage. She deserved so much, and life had been terribly unfair to her.

They finally entered the road leading to Ellie's house. Grant halted the horse at the carriage house and jumped down. Simultaneously, Lancie emerged from the darkness and Grant could hear the clip of horses' hooves just beyond. Lancie was wearing the black apron he always wore when shoeing the horses.

"Good afternoon, Lancie," Grant greeted.

"Lancie, I'm back," an excited Delilah called, waving her hand. She dropped it abruptly when she noticed his hard look and unsmiling face.

"Aft'noon, Mistah Emerson . . . Missy. Glad to see ya's all right."

Confused by Lancie's lack of emotion, Delilah looked toward the cottage, expecting Ellie to emerge and welcome her home. "Is Miss Ellie at home?" she asked.

"Naw'm . . . she's over at de Shadows."

"What is she doing over there?" Grant asked.

Lancie shrugged. "Why don't ya ride on over dere, Mistah Emerson, an' find out fo' yo'self."

Grant refused to be annoyed by Lancie. He jumped up to the carriage seat beside Delilah and flicked his reins at the horse. Moving back to the road, he turned the carriage eastward on the bayou.

"What do you suppose is wrong with Lancie?" Delilah asked.

"Frankly, I couldn't care less. As long as I've known him, he's had a chip on his shoulder. I don't know why Ellie keeps him around."

Delilah let the subject drop. Perhaps he'd had a disagreement with Daisy or was frustrated by the fact that she was a slave and he could not take her as a wife. Then again, perhaps he was just being ornery, as usual.

Forty-five minutes later Delilah found herself surrounded by the happy faces of the slaves at Shadows-in-the-Mist. With hugs shared all around, and a proud, and amused, Grant looking on, Delilah told them about her adventure and the steamboat explosion. Finally, when she was able to extract herself from the excitement, Delilah took Mozelle's hand as they moved toward the big house. "Lancie said that Miss Ellie is here, Mozelle. Is she?"

Mozelle's long, drawn out, "Uhhhh-huuuh, Missy. She be here, po' thing!" caused a knot of apprehension in Delilah's chest.

"She isn't sick, is she, Mozelle?"

"Might as well be. Life's gonna be a real drag fo' po' Miz El from here on out. Po' thing!" she whispered in her same harsh tone.

Daisy skipped up to Delilah as she prepared to mount the steps. "Did ya hear 'bout Miz El?" Daisy asked, a smile widening her face, then disappearing as her gaze met the narrow, disapproving one of the older slave at Delilah's side.

"Ya jes' shut yo' mouth, Miz Uppity High Yella!" Mozelle growled at Daisy. "Miz El will tell Missy about it herself, if'n ya don' mind!

Daisy very seldom responded to Mozelle's insults. However, with Delilah looking on, always the sympathetic friend, she turned away, feigning hurt feelings. "Don't go away, Daisy," Delilah called after her, extending her hand and waiting for Daisy to take it. She clicked her tongue at Mozelle. "Why do you have to be so mean to her?"

"Harumph! Look at dem ol' droopy eyes on dat gal. She's jes' tryin' to make ya feel sorry fo' her."

"Well," Delilah responded, "it worked. I swear, I just don't know why you two can't be friends."

"She's jes' mad 'cuz Massah made me de head cook," Daisy sniffed.

"An' I was de one doin' all de cookin', too, Miz Uppity Britches!"

"Hush, you two." Delilah couldn't help but laugh. "Such carryings-on. Both of you can go fight it out somewhere. I'm going to find Miss Ellie."

"She's up in de yella room, Missy. Ain't come out o' dere all day long."

"What's wrong with her?"

Mozelle's head took slow, deep nods. "She'll be tellin' ya, Missy. I reckon she'll really be needin' yo' friendship now. Needin' it mo'n ever befo'."

Delilah's brows pressed into a thoughtful frown. "When Grant—the master—comes to the house, will you tell him where I am?" She rushed into the house, nearly running into Trusdale in the foyer. She apologized to the manservant.

"It is all right, mademoiselle," he responded, bow-

376

ing grandly. "I am so pleased to see you . . . and all in one piece."

She smiled. "Thank you, Trusdale . . . I think." Then she turned, her wide skirts bouncing at her feet as she rushed up the spiral stairs. She tiptoed toward the yellow room and rapped gently upon the hard wood of the door with her knuckles. No response was immediately forthcoming. "Ellie . . . Ellie, are you in there?" she called. She heard noises within, then slippered feet upon the planked floor. The door came open so quickly that Delilah stepped out of the alcove where she had been waiting.

Ellie's startled look immediately erupted into a smile. She drew Delilah into her arms and embraced her warmly. "Oh, Delilah . . . Delilah, you're back. And you're all right. Dear Lord, I was so worried about you!" Taking her hands, she rushed her into the bedchamber. "Please, you must tell me all about your adventure."

Delilah sat on a daybed beside Ellie. "I think, Ellie, that it is you we should talk about," she said, frowning. "I have the impression that something is wrong, but everyone is silent. Are *you* all right? You're not ill, are you?"

A very shamed Ellie dropped her gaze, and Delilah was sure that tears glowed in her eyes, though she quickly sniffed back any show of emotion. "You might as well know, Delilah . . . I—I . ." She hesitated, trying to collect her thoughts. "I married Grant's cousin, Aldrich." Showing her the ring upon her finger, she continued quietly. "See, it is almost as pretty as the one Grant gave you." Reaching deeply into the pocket of her gown, she drew out a handkerchief, unfolded it, and handed Delilah her own ring, which she took and immediately put on her finger. "I've kept it close to me, always, so that the first thing I could do when I saw you again was return it."

"Thank you, my good friend." When Delilah looked up, her gaze sadly met Ellie's. "I've never known you to be so impulsive, Ellie. Do you love Aldrich Emerson?"

Ellie stood, pivoting sharply toward the window. She wrung her hands nervously together. "Yes, it was impulsive," she said, "and . . . yes, I do love him." When Ellie suddenly burst into tears, Delilah quickly gathered her into her arms. "I've always felt that I was young at heart, Delilah," Ellie sobbed. "But now I feel like a foolish old woman!"

"You *are* young, Ellie. You're young and beautiful and—" Drawing back, taking her older friend's hands in her own, she continued. "A new bride should be happy, if, indeed, you love him—"

"Oh, yes . . . yes, he's charming and debonair and so very sensitive to my needs. He is considerate and treats me like a true lady—"

"Then what is the problem?"

Attempting to quell her emotions, Ellie moved back to the daybed and defeatedly dropped to it. When Delilah joined her, she resumed. "I am told that he may have married me because he believed I was Grant's woman and . . ." she shrugged, "what better way to get revenge against a cousin you hate than to take his woman . . . the way Grant took Aldrich's six years ago."

"Who would have even suggested such a despicable thing to you!"

"Who do you think? Our Mozelle."

Delilah clicked her tongue. "Why do you listen to her? She can be so hateful sometimes." Delilah had

378

not yet met Aldrich, but she had heard things about him, and nothing nice. But could even a devil of a man do something so cold and calloused to a woman as good and gentle as Ellie McPherson? Delilah didn't want to think so. "Have you talked to Aldrich about this? I'd be willing to bet he would be shocked at such a suggestion," she said, hoping to give Ellie some hope.

"I haven't mentioned it to him. I'm afraid of his answer. If he seduced me and married me only because he thought he was taking me away from Grant, I don't believe I could bear the humiliation."

"Good Lord . . . didn't anyone tell Aldrich about me? Didn't anyone tell him that Grant had asked me to marry him?"

Ellie managed a small, tremulous smile. "I'm afraid that no one, including the slaves, has given Aldrich the time of day. I did not mention you to him because I was afraid . . ." She hesitated, then began again. "I was afraid we had lost you. And I was afraid that Aldrich would not be as interested in me if he knew you—a younger, more attractive woman—might be returning to The Boeuf." The clip of masculine boots suddenly sounded in the corridor. Ellie took Delilah's hands. "Please . . . please don't tell Grant!" she pleaded.

"About your marriage? I don't think it is fair of you to ask that."

"No . . . about my suspicions as to Aldrich's motives. I do not want to cause trouble between Grant and his cousin." Again, the knock sounded at the door, more firmly this time. "Please, Delilah."

Delilah reluctantly agreed, and moved toward the door. When she pulled it open, Grant was leaning in the alcove.

"You two ladies gossiping?" he asked. "About me, I hope."

The way he so easily sauntered into the bedchamber made Delilah wonder for a moment if he was used to conducting himself so casually in Ellie's company. She turned just as Grant hugged Ellie.

"I see you have found our girl," Ellie said pleasantly. "I was getting so worried."

"Are you all right, Ellie?" Grant asked.

"Poppycock!" She sharply spoke the single word. "Of course I am all right. If you are wondering why I am at The Shadows —"

"You are always welcome here," Grant cut her off, opening his arm to Delilah, who stood quietly by. "I gather that you have met my cousin, Aldrich?"

"Yes, I've met him," Ellie answered quietly. "In fact . . ." She forced a bright smile that did not radiate from her heart, "I married him this past Saturday."

He stared blankly at her, as if he had failed to comprehend her words. Then, as the news fully dug in, a grin stretched across his face. "You married Aldrich? My blasted cousin?" When she nodded, he said, "Hell, this calls for a celebration!"

Ellie flashed Delilah a warning look. "Aldrich and I would love that. But let's wait until after you and Delilah have been married. Perhaps we could have a get-together here at The Shadows and invite all of our neighbors."

"That's a good idea," Delilah agreed. "Isn't it, Grant? We could dance all night —"

Though the women spoke lightly, Grant noticed the tension. There was something they were not telling him, but he was too much a gentleman to press the issue. He couldn't imagine how his somber cousin had worked so quickly to win Ellie's love, and now that he stopped to think about it, he didn't have a comfortable feeling about their marriage. If anything was wrong, he would learn it later, when he was alone with Delilah.

He felt an urgent need to talk to Aldrich. He had spent only those two hours with him before he'd been called away to deal with the crisis of Delilah, and he had his doubts about Aldrich's sincerity in marrying Ellie.

Grant was suddenly aware of the silent stares of the two women. "I guess the past few weeks have drained my strength," he explained. "I would like to find my cousin, chat with him a bit, then rest for a couple of hours before dinner. You will be joining us, won't you, Ellie?"

"If you would like."

He took her hand as he prepared to depart. "Delilah and I . . ." he said as his other hand moved fluidly forward and grasped Delilah's, "would be honored. Wouldn't we?"

"Of course. Perhaps I will have the chance to meet your cousin . . . our dear Ellie's new husband." Sharing brief amenities, the two women soon heard Grant's retreat down the corridor.

"Thank you for not saying anything—" Ellie said.

"Horse feathers! We are friends. I honor the request of a friend. You know that. Now, I will rush over to the riverboat, freshen up, and return to spend the remainder of the afternoon with you. We have a lot of catching up to do."

Touching her mouth in a gentle kiss to Ellie's cheek, Delilah left her to her thoughts.

Grant untied Bella from the back of the carriage

and mounted, riding off before the advancing Philo could intercept his retreat. He wasn't sure in which direction to search for his cousin, but he felt he had to make the effort. Thus, he turned eastward toward the cotton fields. Aldrich had always enjoyed the chance to be authoritarian; perhaps he was out there barking orders to the pickers.

Grant had progressed halfway across the meadow where the silos stood when he saw the shadow of a horse grazing at the edge of the woods. Turning Bella in that direction, he soon hovered over the form of his cousin, leaning against a tree and chewing on a bit of straw.

"Out looking for me, eh, Cousin?" Aldrich asked in a mocking tone.

Grant dismounted, then drew his boot up to a fallen branch. Crossing his forearms upon his knee, he bent toward Aldrich. "In view of the length of my absence, quite frankly I'm surprised to find you still hanging around."

"I've been busy," Aldrich said shortly.

"So I've heard. You went and married Miss Ellie. I hope it is because you love her."

Aldrich gritted his teeth in rage. He came fluidly to his feet, flicked the dust and dead grass off his backside, and turned to face his cousin. "Why else would I marry the lady?" He ground out the question.

"It wouldn't be because you thought *I* loved her, would it?" Grant responded. When Aldrich failed to answer, Grant made a sardonic pretense of straightening his cousin's lapels. Then his eyes narrowed dangerously and the grip tightened. "If you do anything to hurt Ellie—"

Scowling, Aldrich peeled Grant's fingers loose.

382

"And what will you do, Grant. What *could* you do?"

"I guess I could do nothing. But I care for Ellie and I do not want to see her hurt . . . and especially, I wouldn't want to be the reason for it."

"Isn't it true that you have a woman of your own?" Aldrich forced himself to ask the question. "Why should you be worried about Ellie?"

"Yes, I have a woman. She and I both care very deeply for Ellie."

"Are you going to marry this woman?"

Grant's eyes narrowed. "I am."

"What's wrong, Grant?" Aldrich hissed, his hands clenching at his sides. "Wasn't my Madeleine enough woman for you?"

"You know damned well why I married Madeleine. If you had been there, it wouldn't have been necessary—"

"Well, I was in jail!"

"So you said." Grant turned back to his horse, hoping he could avoid any further confrontation with his cousin over this old issue. Just as he prepared to remount the horse, he turned. "Just tell me . . . do you love Ellie?" he asked Aldrich.

Of course I love Ellie! Aldrich thought to himself. But pride would not allow him to admit it to Grant. He had come to The Boeuf for revenge, thought he had accomplished it, and now he learned that all of his efforts had backfired. True, he had gotten a beautiful wife out of the deal, but he still had not been avenged. Grant could not get away with taking Madeleine away from him.

"I asked you, Cousin, if you love Ellie!" Grant harshly repeated the question.

"Of course I don't love the woman!" Aldrich lied with a malevolent grin. "I now must worry about how to get her off my blasted back!"

Without warning, Grant lunged across the short span of space separating them, startling both horses into retreat and landing full against an equally startled Aldrich. They hadn't come to blows since childhood, and Aldrich could not remember such black fury, even then, in the eyes of his cousin. Grant pinned him to the ground, straddled him, and drew back his right hand.

Then, just as he might have struck him a mighty blow, Grant dropped his hand. "Damn." He muttered the single word.

"Go ahead," Aldrich challenged. "Though you were younger, you used to beat the daylights out of me when we were boys. Don't you think you still have it in you?"

As if he'd suddenly found Aldrich repulsive, Grant pulled himself away and came to his feet. "You're not worth it, Aldrich."

"You hate my guts, don't you?" a frowning Aldrich asked him.

"Of course . . . I always have." Grant drew his hands to his narrow hips. "And thanks to you, Cousin, we both must walk back to the house."

Aldrich linked his fingers behind his back and sauntered in a slow circle around Grant. Then he paused, turned to him in a sharp military pivot, drew back his hand, and hit Grant across the face. "You cannot ignore this insult. I demand satisfaction!"

"Satisfaction for what?" Grant asked, rubbing the wound.

"You took Madeleine away from me and legally established yourself as father of my son. I challenge you to a duel."

A short, brittle laugh followed. "We are not stupid boys, Aldrich, playing stupid games! Dueling between men is illegal, and you know it."

"It doesn't matter. I plan to kill you, and I don't care what happens to me thereafter. Your blood will satisfy me!"

"You are a crazy son-of-a-bitch, Aldrich. If you want a duel, then so be it! In the morning—dawn—right here in this field."

Just at that moment, the clop of horses' hooves drew closer. Grant looked around. There on his big gelding sat Philbus, holding the reins of a prancing Bella. "Ya was ridin' Missy's hoss, Massah Emerson?" he asked. Then he grinned widely. "De boy Hank rode out to tell us ya's an' Missy wuz back at de Shadows." He handed the reins to Grant. "Where be yo' cousin's hoss?" he asked.

"Probably back at the stables by now." Grant mounted the nervously pacing mare. "Let's go Philbus. My hotheaded cousin can walk back!"

Philbus did not care at all for Aldrich Emerson, but he still felt a little strange, a slave riding back and a white man walking. "Massah wants me to give Mistah Emerson his hoss?" he asked in a hushed tone, leaning toward Grant.

"No!" Grant sharply responded.

When the two mounted men were out of hearing range of the one on foot, Philbus informed Grant that he heard the end of his talk with Aldrich. "Ya ain't really gonna meet yo' kinfolk in a duel, huh?" he asked.

"I will, unless the hotheaded bully has cooled off by the morning." Grant's sudden roll of laughter could be heard by Aldrich, who was a quarter-mile behind them now. "When we were boys, Philbus,

Aldrich used to challenge me to a duel at least every other day. He'd always give me my choice of weapons from the pair of dueling pistols his father had shaved the firing pins off of, and I would always choose the one to the right. Though the weapons were already useless, Aldrich would go to the additional trouble of rigging my weapon to fall apart when it was 'fired'."

"An' ya fell fo' dat every time, massah?" Philbus asked, surprised that his Yankee master would be so gullible.

"Of course." Grant shrugged. "I thought it might come in useful when I grew up."

A wide grin spread the width of Philbus's dark face. "Oh, I see, massah. In de mo'nin' when Mistah Emerson offers ya's first choice, ya's 'll choose de one on de left . . . jes' opposite o' when ya was boys."

"No . . . I'll choose the one on the right."

Philbus pinched his brows, confused. "Ya should'a learnt yo' lesson by now, massah."

"You see, Philbus," Grant explained. "I *did* always choose the pistol to the right. Aldrich will realize that, as a grown man, I will reason that since I always chose the one on the right, I will now choose the one on the left, because I will *expect* the right pistol to be rigged. He will then rig the pistol on the left and I will choose the one on the right, just like when we were boys. He won't be expecting me to do that."

Shaking his head, Philbus laughed heartily. "Lawd, massah, ya got yo' kinfolk all figgered out, ain't ya?"

"I hope so, Philbus."

"An' ya's gonna kill yo' cousin in de mo'nin. Sho'

386

is gonna hurt Miss Ellie, massah, to lose her second husband so quick-like."

"I wouldn't kill him, Philbus. Do you really think it would be gentlemanly to kill a man who is armed with a worthless weapon?"

"He'd do it to you," Philbus responded.

"That's why I am a gentleman," Grant mused, "and he is not."

Ellie and Delilah both rushed off the gallery and met Grant and Philbus as they rode in. "Did you find your cousin?" Delilah asked with a worried frown.

"He's walking in."

Philbus pulled his horse away. "I'll see if the horse he was riding came in."

Grant nodded, returning his attentions to the two women as he dismounted. He hesitated to meet Ellie's gaze, fearing she might see the worry in his eyes. Rather, he drew the two women under his arms to each side of him and moved toward the house. "I'm famished. Let's see if Mozelle has dinner ready."

"Where is Aldrich?" Ellie asked.

"He'll be along presently."

"Did you talk to him?"

"Some. Philbus came along and I decided to ride back with him to catch up on plantation business."

Ellie's gaze moved over the retreating ground beneath their feet and she almost shrugged Grant's arm off her shoulder. "He doesn't love me, does he?" she asked after a moment.

Grant halted so quickly that both women outdistanced him several feet before turning back. "He said no such thing, Ellie," Grant responded with irritation. "And I will not get involved in any quarrel between the two of you."

Ellie's emotions were already in shambles. Bursting into uncontrollable sobs at Grant's sharp rebuke, she turned and fled into the house. An annoyed Delilah lifted furious golden eyes to him. "Now, why did you have to talk to her in that tone of voice?"

"And I will not quarrel with you either, dammit!" Grant huffed, then turned and moved toward the stable, his limp more pronounced.

"Where are you going, Grant?"

"To talk to a horse!" he barked without turning back. "They might kick the shaboogies out of you, but they don't quarrel!"

Twenty-five

That evening at dinner, four people sat around the table, tense but civil to each other. Very little food was consumed during the three courses Mozelle and Daisy served. Ellie's nerves were on edge all day and she was first to bow out of the evening. "When will you join me?" she asked Aldrich.

Although he had sharply retorted, "Don't become a nagging wife!" his heart had wrenched in pain at his thoughtless verbal attack. He wanted to call her back, fold her into his embrace, and apologize, but he would not do so in the presence of his cousin and the woman named Delilah. If he'd been even the tiniest bit reasonable, he'd have realized that vengeance was nothing more than a black burden on a man's soul. If he didn't hate Grant so much, he might have been man enough to admit it.

That evening in the privacy of the cottage, Grant held Delilah close in the aftermath of love. He had not told her of the duel; there was no sense in worrying her if it did not come about.

"Grant?" His name so gently spoken startled him. Rather than respond, he pressed his cheek to hers. "Do you think that Aldrich loves Ellie?"

He frowned into the darkness, thoughtful for a moment. "I must be losing my mind, Miss Delilah

389

Wickley, but I really believe he does. He's just too blasted stubborn to admit it."

"Did he admit that he married Ellie because he thought she was your woman?"

"He did make such an admission. And I do believe that was his initial intention."

Delilah's rapid breathing marked a moment of apprehension. "Do you think he will seek vengeance against you?"

Grant's laugh was so insincere he was sure she had seen through the facade. "Aldrich is a blowhard. If he makes a threat, my precious, I assure you it will be an empty one. Did I ever tell you that when we were children I was the one who always won the battles with fists? He won the duels, but only because he cheated."

Silence. Delilah was well aware he was avoiding something. "Ellie said she is going back home in the morning . . . with or without Aldrich."

"You'll keep her here, won't you, love?"

Recognizing the urgency in his voice, she tried to see his profile against the evening dark. Had it not been for the faint scatterings of moonlight through the gossamer curtains spilling upon his golden hair, she would have seen little more than the shadow of his face. Something was wrong; there was just enough light to see the trouble in his pale-blue eyes. But she could not bring herself to press him and possibly annoy him. Rather, she said softly, "I love you so much, Grant, that I could not bear to lose you."

"And what has brought on this pensive mood?" he chuckled.

"I just wanted you to know how I felt. You do love me, don't you?"

"No, Delilah . . . I spent two weeks out in the boondocks searching for you, picking burrs out of my backside, and sleeping in swamps because I enjoyed the adventure." Softening his voice, he continued. "Of course I love you, my little southern beauty. Don't I have my ways of showing it, even if I don't say it all the time? Now . . ." His kiss touched upon her forehead, "go to sleep. We all have a busy day tomorrow—"

"What are we doing?"

"I've got three weeks of catching up to do," he answered. "And you, my sweet, have ledgers needing attention."

"Back to that, Grant Emerson. I thought now that I was your fiancée, you wouldn't make me work for the horse."

"The horse is yours, Delilah. But as lady of the manor, you have certain duties, and one of them will be the ledgers."

"Oh, so that's it!" she teased. "You're marrying me in order to get a free bookkeeper."

"And a companion, bed partner, and cook and bottle washer."

She let his teasing go without comment. "Grant, could I ask for something special as a wedding gift?"

"Besides the horse?"

"Besides the horse. Grant, I would like for you to give Daisy her freedom so that she can marry Lancie."

"But she'll leave The Shadows. Could you bear it?"

"She'll leave The Shadows, but not my heart. I want her and Lancie to be happy and together, the way you and I are. Besides, I will see her often.

Surely they will take a place at Ellie's. You know, Grant, it puzzles me sometimes that Lancie is so protective of Ellie. I know that at one time he had dreams of moving to the West, possibly California, and yet he stayed on at Lamourie, he and his mother."

"It is not unusual for a man to feel a sense of loyalty to his employer."

Delilah shrugged delicately against him. "It is more than that—"

"Didn't Ellie's father own Lancie and his mother?"

"Well, yes . . . he freed them both upon his deathbed."

"There, you see, he stays on because of loyalty to Ellie and his respect for her late father."

Delilah was not convinced, but with a softly uttered, "Perhaps," she let the matter drop. "And Daisy? Will you give her freedom so that she and Lancie can marry?"

Grant squeezed her to him beneath the warm covers of the bed. "Very well," he said after a moment, "if that's what you want."

She threw her nakedness across his own, sending the covers here and there. "Grant, thank you . . . oh, thank you."

He rolled to his side and positioned himself between her slender legs. "Blast it, girl . . ." he growled, moving to possess her for the second time that night, "if I'm ever to get a good night's sleep, I'll have to sleep alone." When she rose against him, he impaled her, rested within the intoxicating warmth of her for a moment, then aroused her pleasures as he quickly took his own.

* * *

Aldrich tucked himself into a small alcove of the bedchamber where Ellie slept. Opening the case containing a fancy pair of dueling pistols his father had given him, he picked up one, then the other of the beautiful weapons. They were similar to the smaller ones he and Grant had dueled with as children, except that these pistols were lethal; those of their youth had been harmless.

He studied the weapons in fascination, noting their heavily engraved barrels and carved ivory handles. Momentarily, he placed them back into the case, one with its grip on the left and one to the right. Then, taking the powder and accoutrements from a special place made within the case for them, he began to load the pistols.

He remembered the way his cousin had always chosen the weapon to the right. He would not be that gullible now. Taking a small file from the case, he picked up the weapon to the left and began filing down the firing pin. When he had rendered it useless, he tucked it into its molded resting place and patted it lovingly. He could not wait to see Grant's face when he realized that Aldrich had, at last, gotten the best of him.

"What are you doing, Aldrich?"

Aldrich slammed the case shut so quickly he upset a goblet of wine. Turning his gaze to a very sleepy Ellie, he responded with annoyance. "Nothing. I was just sitting here thinking—"

"You've spilled something. I'll clean it up."

He flicked his wrist. "Don't worry about it. The maid will take care of it."

She tried to peer past him, but his body shifted, blocking her view. "What have you got there, Aldrich?"

"Nothing . . . it's nothing that would interest you." He approached and held Ellie to him, then turned her back into the bedchamber. "Come, let's get some sleep," he said. "Tomorrow—" A moment of apprehension seized him. "Tomorrow," he began again, "we need to return to the cottage."

"Have you decided that we will stay on at Lamourie, Aldrich? When we talked after our wedding, you said you were not sure."

The bed was within touching distance. Tenderly, Aldrich folded Ellie into his arms. "I heard a Mississippi lady say not too long ago that a southern flower wilts farther north than Jackson," he whispered.

"That is what Delilah says about Shreveport." Ellie laughed softly. "Are you saying that we will stay here?"

"Of course, Ellie." He smiled for her; a warm, genuine smile that reflected his love for her like a mirror. "You are everything in the world a man could want, Ellie, and I am happy to be your husband. When we were in Alexandria, I deposited enough money in an account to double the size of your estate, if you wish—"

"Oh, Aldrich . . . you do love me. You truly do!"

"The money reassures you?" he asked in a surprised tone.

"To the devil with the money. Your confessions of happiness reassure me. I was afraid you had married me because you thought I was Grant's woman."

His startled gasp immediately became irritation. "Did Grant or that Wickley woman suggest that to you?"

"No, of course not."

"Did you mention to them what you—"

"No, I didn't," she easily lied. She could not bear the thought of angering him, not when he seemed in so loving a mood. She cared only that he was her husband, and he had confessed to love her. Perhaps her fears were for naught and that evil-tongued Mozelle needed to learn some degree of self-control. It was no wonder very few people liked her.

Aldrich eased his wife back to the bed, then gently covered her with his body. Combing his fingers through her thick, soft hair, he touched his mouth in a loving kiss to her own. "Are you convinced now, my darling, of my love for you?"

"Oh, yes, I am so happy that you love me, and that you and Grant will make amends and be friends—"

His breath suddenly caught, his fingers ceasing their tender movements through her hair. "I did not say we would be friends, Ellie. I never said anything like that. What he did was wrong. I cannot forgive him—"

"Did you love Madeleine that much?" she asked, a note of distress in her voice.

"He took my son, Ellie. By Massachusetts law, Dustin is Grant's son, not mine. That I can never forgive him for."

"But—"

A rapidly stolen kiss took away her response. "Hush, little wife, let us not quarrel," he said, his eyes sweeping over the beauty of her. "We are newly wed and there are more important things to put our energies into."

Without prelude, without the foreplay she might

have enjoyed, Aldrich threw off his clothing with a groan of annoyance and hastily possessed his gentle southern wife. She did not protest his roughness, nor his lack of sensitivity to her own needs, but moved with him toward the pinnacle of pleasure he would enjoy alone this time.

She knew only that something deep, persistent, and troubling was on his mind. When at last he filled her with his seed and collapsed atop her, she held him close, fearful that she would lose him almost before she had grown to love him fully.

In the hours of darkness they lay together, a very silent Ellie rested beside her husband, knowing he was awake but hesitating to disturb his own thoughtful silence. She wondered what was troubling him so much that he could not sleep.

Aldrich could not come to grips with the dilemma aching through his body. Though he had courted Ellie and won her for deceptive reasons, he loved her as he had never loved another woman, even Madeleine Vail. But he hated Grant, hated him with a passion that could not be quelled by common sense. Grant had been their grandfather's favorite grandson. He had been treated with love and understanding by his father, when Aldrich had received only mental and physical abuse from his own. Grant was the one the women had been attracted to; they had scarcely noticed Aldrich. The family had catered to Grant and had all but ignored Aldrich.

Grant had taken his son. Dammit, he had taken his son! It was unforgivable and, despite his love for Ellie and the desire to spend the rest of his life with her, he could not let Grant get away with stealing his son.

Even if it meant destroying himself, he would destroy Grant.

Tomorrow, at dawn, he would take aim and put an end to his lifelong adversary.

Lancie sat quietly beside his mother's bed. When she had not prepared his supper that evening, he went to the back of the cottage to check on her. There, he had found her in bed, complaining that she had a sick stomach; but now he was not so sure it was as simple as that. Her breathing was so shallow as to be nonexistent, and even his harsh whispers were slow to arouse any response in her. Only once did she speak. "I needs ta see Miz El, son," she had said.

"But I cain't leave ya by yo'self, Mamma," he had explained, taking her limp hand.

When the slow beat of horses' hooves suddenly reverberated through the cottage, Lancie shook his mother's shoulder. "I'll see who dat is, Mamma, an' I'll be right back."

A wave of relief washed over Lancie when he saw Maden dismounting at the carriage house. Before Maden could explain his late-night visit, Lancie bounded off the steps and ran toward him. "Maden, ride over to de Shadows an' fetch Miz El. Mamma's real sick."

"Miss Mandy's sick?" he questioned, then asked in a hard tone why his mother was at The Shadows.

"That don't matter now. You jes' get over dere an' fetch her."

Hopping back on the horse, he immediately spurred it to the east. "I'm on my way, Lancie," he yelled hoarsely, then galloped away from the home he had shared with his mother.

Maden was sure the young filly he rode could have given the famous Lecomte a run for his money. He covered the four miles of midnight darkness between Lamourie and The Boeuf in record time and, none too soon, drew the mare to a rude halt at the gallery of the large plantation house.

"Ma . . . Ellie McPherson," he shouted, deliberately refusing to call her by her married name. Within seconds, a light came on in the foyer, quickly spilling through the windows onto the gallery in wavering shadows.

A sleepy Daisy, dragging her heavy robe about her, stepped out to the gallery holding the one lamp. "Who dat be makin' all dat noise?"

"It's Maden, Daisy. Fetch my mother. Miss Mandy's taken ill and needs her."

In the time it took Daisy to climb the stairs and get the message to Ellie, Philbus and Mozelle both appeared from their cabin and Grant and Delilah made a quick approach from the riverboat. "What's going on, Maden?" Grant asked.

"Glad to see you and Missy are all right," Maden said, taking Grant's hand in a firm grip. "It's Miss Mandy, taken ill, I came to fetch ma."

In her talk with Ellie that afternoon, Delilah had learned of Maden's disapproval of her wedding and of his move to Dentley. She had relayed the distressing news to Grant earlier in the night. He intended to speak to Maden about it, but this was not the proper time. Grant turned toward Philbus. "Will you ready a surrey?" he asked the slave. "The ladies will need it."

Scarcely fifteen minutes had passed before Grant was easing the harness mare into a trot toward Ellie's cottage. Delilah sat beside him, a tearful Ellie on the plush backseat. Though Miss Mandy had been sick for several months, and Dr. Miller had given very little hope for recovery, she felt personally responsible for the bad turn she had taken. If only she had stayed at the cottage with her . . .

Miss Mandy groped among the bedcovers for her son's hand. "I'm here, Mamma," he said, offering it to her. "Don't ya be frettin'. Maden's gone over to de Shadows to fetch Miss Ellie."

Her mouth pinched with disapproval as she tried to shake off the moment of weakness. "What fo' ya be botherin' Miz Ellie, son? She jes' got herself married an' she don't need ta be worryin' 'bout me."

A frown pressed upon his brow. He held his mother's hand to his cheek. "Don't ya remember, Mamma. Ya said ya needed Miz El. Jes' a little while ago."

Deep furrows took away the smoothness of Miss Mandy's forehead. She fought to remember. "Lancie, boy, ya knows yo' mamma's real sick. Don't think these tired ol' eyes'll be seein' another sunrise."

Tears flooded the big man's eyes. "Don't be talkin' like dat, Mamma. Ya gonna be all right."

"I been dyin' fo' nigh onto a year now, boy. Ya don't need to be tellin' yo'self no stories, when ya knows the truth." A sudden strength seized her hand, closing it firmly over her son's. "Ya gotta promise yo' ol' mamma, ya won't be telling Miz

Ellie about . . . well, you know. It'll jes' be embarrassin' Miz Ellie, an' hurt a whole lot o' people. It won't be doin' nobody no good."

"No, Mamma, I won't be tellin' nobody—"

Miss Mandy closed her eyes, pressing out the tears resting there. "What Miz El's pappy did so long ago, Lancie, ya don't need ta be bringin' it up—"

"Mamma . . ." Lancie spoke sharply, despite the emotion quivering in his voice. He turned his mother's hand over in his own. "Miz El, she ain't never goin' ta know that we has de same pappy," he promised her. "I swears it on my grave, Mamma—"

"Better swear it on mine," she cut in softly, " 'cause it'll be dug yon on the hill fo' tomorrow's out."

Tears streamed down Lancie's face. Rather than argue with his dear mother, Lancie dropped his forehead to her shoulder, sobs shaking his massive frame.

Moments later—he had not heard the approach of the surrey outside—a woman's hand was closing over Lancie's shoulder. He looked up, meeting Ellie's rueful gaze. "She's real sick, Miz El," he whispered with emotion.

"I know," she responded quietly. "Let me sit with her. Maden is riding for Dr. Miller."

"He said jes' last week she'd lived past her time fo' dyin', Miz El. What makes ya think—"

"Miz El?" Miss Mandy's feeble voice touched her to the heart. When Lancie stood, Ellie took the chair he'd abandoned. Taking the servant's hand, she held it warmly between her own, eliciting a small smile. "Miz El, I sho' hopes ya happy with yo' own Mistah Emerson—"

"I'm very happy. Now . . . shh, dear." Miss Mandy always wore a scarf to bed, to keep her hair neat while she slept. Ellie began to smooth the graying wisps escaping around the fringes of the thick fabric, then touched her fingers gently to Miss Mandy's cheek. She felt warm, but not feverishly so. Her breathing was alarmingly shallow, as if it would cease at any minute.

"Miz El, Mistah Grant an' Missy, they come over with you?"

"Yes, they're in the parlor. Would you like to see them?"

"Sho' would, Miz El, if'n ya don't mind."

"Of course not." Rising, Ellie's hand dropped briefly to Lancie's. How could she know when her tear-sheened gaze met his own that she was looking into the eyes of her half brother? "Let's make a pot of coffee, Lancie."

"Yas'm, Miz El," he responded. Lancie thought nothing of the way Ellie's hand moved into the crook of his arm. She had never seemed to recognize the distinction of the classes—of slave and owner, or black and white. As long as Lancie could remember, she had always treated him like family.

He smiled to himself. Didn't life have its funny little twists and turns?

Since the household had been turned upside down, Daisy dressed and began her clean-up chores just past midnight. The master's cousin was sitting in the parlor, drinking whiskey and brooding miserably, and Daisy surmised that her master

401

would want someone to keep an eye on him in his absence. Besides, she was worried about Miss Mandy and wouldn't be able to sleep until word had reached the house. Philbus had ridden out just a few minutes before, to stay at the cottage to await word, then bring it back to The Shadows. Everyone on the bayou loved Miss Mandy. She'd heard the old-timers say many times that she had been the favorite of Miss Ellie's father.

While Aldrich Emerson was out of his suite of rooms, Daisy went to see if he had made one of his usual messes. She had never seen a man who could do something as simple as writing a letter, then leave a mess that would take an hour to clean up. She slipped into the suite, ignoring the disheveled bed and moving straight into the alcove where Aldrich spent a lot of his time. There, her eyes made a disapproving sweep over the spilled wine and soiled papers upon the desk. Mumbling to herself, she took a cloth from the pocket of her white apron, bent to one knee, and began taking long swipes at the spilled liquid.

"Lawd, dat sho' is a messy white man!" she chatted to herself. "If Massah was dat messy, we'd sho have to 'spand de serving staff."

There! The ugly spill was now collected into her cloth. As she started to draw herself up, her hand caught on the edge of the dueling case and brought it crashing to the floor, scattering the beautiful ivory-handled pistols hither and yon. Her eyes widening, she hastily looked around, thankful that Mr. Aldrich had not chosen that moment to return. Scooting about on her knees, she collected the pistols, holding them carefully so as not to discharge them, then righted the overturned case. She returned the spilled accoutrements to the niche where she was sure they belonged, then picked up one of the pistols she had lain in the clean folds of her apron. Lawd! Which one goes where? she wondered, looking at the two indentations in the velvet where the pistols belonged. Then she shrugged her shoulders. What did it matter, as long as they were back where they belonged?

"Nobody'll ever know de dif'rence," she said to herself as she returned the case to its place on the desk, then scooted from the suite before she could be detected. Of course Aldrich would know she had been there, because the wine was cleaned up, but he would not know she had spilled the case and the pretty guns. She made sure it was exactly where she had seen it upon first entering the alcove.

She hummed a tune as she sauntered down the corridor, heading toward the kitchen to make a pot of coffee. If she was going to stay awake, she needed something to help her do just that.

Suddenly, Aldrich Emerson loomed above her. She released a startled gasp. "Mistah Emerson, didn't mean ta startle ya," she said.

"I think, girl, that I am the one who startled you."

"Yas, suh . . . Mistah Emerson needs Daisy to fetch somethin' fo' him?"

He lifted a bottle of whiskey and a goblet. "I think I've got everything I need." His voice suddenly hardened. "Now, be on your way, girl."

"Yas, suh," Daisy responded in a softly sarcastic tone, and one that Aldrich surely noticed.

With the footsteps of the uppity girl fading behind him, Aldrich entered the suite, closed the door, and moved toward the small, cozy alcove, noticing at once that the girl had cleaned up the wine he'd spilled. He sat down, opened the dueling case, and stared at the pistols.

He'd been doing a lot of thinking these past few hours. As children, Grant had always chosen the pistol to the right. As a grown man, he would, sensibly, remember that. Aldrich had mused over this until his brain was a stir of confusing thoughts. At first, Aldrich anticipated that Grant would choose the opposite weapon, but of course he would expect Aldrich to think along those lines. Thus, he would still choose the weapon to the right, because he would believe Aldrich would put the rigged gun to the left, expecting him to choose that one.

Caressing the weapons as a man might caress a beautiful woman, Aldrich reversed the guns in their plush velvet case. There! The rigged gun was now on the right.

He prided himself on his sensible thinking and his ingenuity. The way he had rigged the guns, the faulty weapon would be undetectable, even under expert scrutiny.

Now that he had taken care of that important matter, he dropped onto a comfortable settee and poured himself a goblet of whiskey. Quickly gulping it, he poured another, relishing its warmth for a few moments against his mouth. When he felt the numbness against his tongue, he gulped that glass, then poured another.

He had no qualms about not accompanying Ellie to the cottage. Neither the sick Miss Mandy nor her son had shown any toleration for him at all. She would want *her* people with her, and that did not include him.

Soon, Aldrich Emerson closed his eyes, thinking of the beautiful face of the woman he had married, wanting her and imagining how the future would be with her.

As sleep claimed him, his goblet shifted, spilling its contents and leaving still another mess for Daisy to clean up.

Twenty-six

Surrounded by those she loved, including her physician, Tylas Miller, Miss Mandy slipped quietly into eternity shortly before five o'clock that mid-October morning. She had made one final request, and that had been of Grant Emerson, with whom she had shared a private moment.

While a solemn Philbus took the word to Shadows-in-the-Mist and eastward along the bayou, Grant took his place among family and friends in the parlor of Ellie's cottage. If the recently married Ellie wanted her new husband with her, she made no mention of it.

Looking at his pocket watch, Grant wondered if Aldrich still expected him to meet him in the field at six o'clock. That was a rendezvous he did not plan to keep, at least not today. Miss Mandy was much more important to him than his cousin's unreasonable need to seek revenge.

Drawing a somber Delilah beneath the wing of his arm, Grant looked around the large, spacious parlor. Already, the hands of the grandfather clock in the foyer had been stopped, mirrors had been draped in black, candles lit on the mantel, and the bier brought in and positioned to hold the casket Lancie himself was making from the fine cypress boards Mr. Mayhew had sent over from the mill.

From outside came the dull, monotonous tap of still another hammer as Maden posted the customary death notice on the door.

By midmorning, a host of people traveling by carriages, surreys, and horses had converged upon the cottage from the surrounding plantations to pay their respects and offer condolences. Delilah hadn't seen so many of their neighbors gathered in one place since the morning her father had been buried on the quiet, shady hill up from The Boeuf.

Grant had suspended work in the cotton fields that day, and many of the slaves from The Shadows had taken up quiet vigilance around the cottage.

Grant patted Delilah's hand comfortingly, and, leaving her with Ellie, descended the steps to make the rounds among the slaves. Soon, he entered the carriage house and moved along its dark overhang to the tack room where Lancie was working. He tucked his hands into the waist of his trousers and watched the labors of the silent Lancie.

"What brings ya out here, Mistah Emerson?" Lancie asked without turning.

"Your mother," he responded.

For one brief moment, Lancie's gaze connected with Grant's. Then he turned, took up another of the square nails, and positioned it upon the coffin he was building. "My mamma? What ya mean, Mistah Emerson?"

"She made a request of me and I have every intention of honoring it."

"What request is that, Mistah Emerson?" he asked with a hardness that came from the unconscious hostility reflected toward white people.

"She told me that I was the only person in the world who could make you happy, and that was

407

more important to her than anything else in the world. So I plan to do something that will achieve that end."

Lancie's eyes narrowed piercingly. "What can ya do fo' me, Mistah Emerson? What can any white man do fo' me?"

Pushing himself from his slouched position, Grant approached the big, barrel-chested man. "I'm going to offer Daisy her manumission papers so that she will be free to marry you. You do love her, don't you?" Grant had already planned to release Daisy as a wedding gift to Delilah, but he could find no excuse to take the credit away from the dear woman who had died that morning. "You do love her, don't you?" Grant repeated the question.

"Rumor has it Massah Wickley paid mo'n fo' thousand fo' Daisy's mamma at de auction in N'Awleans," Lancie stated. "Top-o'-de-line high-yella breeder. Why would ya give away Daisy jes' cause one ol' dyin' niggah woman asks ya to?"

"Just call me crazy," Grant responded matter-of-factly, aware that Lancie's thoughtless slur against his mother was just his way of reaffirming his dislike for whites. "If you don't want Daisy, all you have to say is no, thank you."

Lancie shot him a suspicious glare. "Gotta be strings attached, Mistah Emerson. Ya ain't goin' ta give me a purty wench like Daisy an' not 'spect somethin' fo' it."

"I do have a request." Grant could read the 'I knew it' in Lancie's gaze. "My request is that you marry Miss Daisy proper and be a good husband to her. And—"

Silence. Lancie allowed a respectable amount of time to pass before he prompted, "And—"

"And," Grant began again, "whether you stay here on Lamourie with her or follow a dream to some far, distant place, you always let us know how you and Daisy are doing."

"I don't read, an' I don't write."

"But Daisy does."

Lancie's dark eyes widened in surprise. This was something Daisy had never told him. Not only was it against custom for the blacks to learn reading and writing, it was not encouraged by the white masters. Stubbornness moved through Lancie's body like an iron rod. He turned about, taking up his hammer to resume his unhappy chore. He felt, rather than saw, Grant's retreat. "I'll be takin' Daisy off yo' hands, Mistah Emerson," Lancie said softly, when the master of Shadows-in-the-Mist had reached the doorway.

"I kind of figured you would." With that, he left the big man alone, to complete the chore that was breaking his heart. Grant did not hear the emotional quiver in Lancie's voice as he whispered, "Thank you, Mamma."

"Daisy will be so happy, Grant," Delilah said when Grant told her of his conversation with Lancie. "I only hope that giving my dear friend her manumission papers will not cause dissent among your other slaves."

"They'll be freed soon enough."

"What do you mean?"

"If I don't free them first, I'm sure the United States will get around to it."

"Back to that again, Grant. The government is not going to involve itself in the question of slavery."

He said nothing. He was well aware that Delilah was as much opposed to slavery as he was.

* * *

When Philbus returned to The Shadows with word of Miss Mandy's death, Aldrich put his pistols away for the time being. When he made rounds of the plantation with Ellie in these past few weeks, not a single person had neglected to inquire about Miss Mandy. Her death would require a period of mourning proper to her popularity, and Aldrich knew there would be no duel until after the funeral.

That morning, Aldrich, feeling very much left out, bathed and dressed, then sat at the desk in the alcove, and wrote a letter to be delivered to his beloved Ellie. When he set down the pen, he read the letter over, aware that if he had misspelled a single word, his astute wife would notice it. *Dearest Wife,* he had written. *My sincerest condolences in the death of your dear Miss Mandy. I do not feel that my proper place during your period of mourning will be at your side, so I will gracefully bow out and free you to spend your time with those others who love you, and loved your dear servant. Be assured of my deepest fondness and love for you. Always, Your Devoted Husband, Aldrich.*

Sending the young boy Hank on to Lamourie with his note, Aldrich saddled a horse and began the short trip to Dentley, where he had seen a stallion in the stables of Mr. Thomas Jefferson Wells he was very interested in purchasing for Ellie's herd. He had been thinking a lot of Ellie's business and ways to improve it. Purchasing a champion stallion would save her the considerable stud fees she had been paying to other breeders.

When he reached Dentley, however, he found that Mr. Wells had already ridden to Ellie's cottage to pay his respects. Entering the Dentley stable for the

410

purpose of taking a better look at the stallion, he met one of Dentley's slaves, a man Ellie had referred to as Swainie.

Cautiously, Swainie approached the visitor, his fingers wrapped firmly around the collar of the growling cur dog constantly at his side. "Mistah Emerson, what be bringing ya to Dentley?"

"I understand from speaking to Mr. Wells a week or so ago that he is planning to sell the black stallion," Aldrich replied. "I'm interested in purchasing the animal for my wife's stables."

From the darkness beyond Swainie emerged a tall lanky white man Aldrich could not remember meeting. Following the direction of his gaze, Swainie turned toward the approaching man. "This here be Mistah Pierre Neville. Mistah Wells done give him a job workin' at de stables fo' a few days till de head groom, ol' Thaw, git up from de sickbed." When the dog again growled, Swainie popped it hard across the nose. "Shut up, ya mangy ol' hound!"

"Another man's misfortune is your fortune," observed Aldrich, cutting his gaze sharply from Neville. "Do you mind if I look over that horse?" he asked Swainie.

"Don't mind a bit, Mistah Emerson. Jes' be sho' when ya's in his stall that he don't back ya into a corner. He's real bad 'bout dat."

When Aldrich blended into the darkness behind the two men, Swainie, who had taken an instant liking to the amiable white man at his side, said, "Come on, Pierre, let's go over to da cabin an' see if my ol' woman got dem biscuits all hot 'n buttered."

"Is that the Emerson who owns Shadows-in-the-

411

Mist?" Pierre asked in the short walk to the slave quarters.

Swainie laughed, releasing the collar of the dog now that they were out of sight of Aldrich Emerson. "Dat be his cousin what come down from de Nawth an' married up wid Miz Ellie. It be Mistah *Grant* Emerson what owns de Shadows. He be at Miz El's, since po' Miz Mandy passed away dis mornin'."

"Miss Mandy?"

They had reached the porch of Swainie's cabin. "Miss Mandy, she be's an' ol' niggah woman what works fo' Miz El. Some says she wuz her pappy's bed wench when she'uz young an' purty as a pitcher an' when he died he give Miz Mandy an' her boy, Lancie, dey freedom papers. But dey stay on at Miz El's, I reckon 'cuz it be's de only way of life dey know."

Moments later, the two men sat on the porch, drinking fresh, cold milk and eating biscuits coated with butter and honey. Pierre seemed more than a little interested in the happenings at Shadows-in-the-Mist. The talkative Swainie did not hesitate to discuss the plantation he had formerly served, but when Pierre casually mentioned he had heard there was some excitement over there a few months ago when a dead man was found in the woods, Swainie's mood changed noticeably. He became moody and quiet as he concentrated on his humble meal, frequently throwing bits of the bread to the waiting dog. "They did find a fellow, didn't they?" Neville continued, attempting to prompt him into conversation.

"Sho', dey was a fella found," Swainie reluctantly offered his answer. "But dat's over an' done wid, an' nobody talks much about it no' mo'."

412

"You know, I think that fellow they found in the woods was my baby brother, Paulie," Pierre said, as casually as he might have mentioned the weather.

Swainie promptly choked on a morsel of bread, then dragged in a deep breath, unaware that his wife Sukie stood behind the screen door of their cabin looking out at the two men. "What makes ya think dat?" Swainie questioned after a moment.

Having filled his belly and washed his last bits of food down with the rest of the milk, Pierre settled against the rough porch support. "Saw a notice sent by the sheriff in Alexandria. Described that fellow right down to the shriveled right arm. My baby brother was born with a shriveled arm, and when we was young'uns, he accidentally shot hisself in the leg. That was described, too. Yep, that was my brother, Paulie."

"Is that why ya's on de Boeuf?" Swainie asked, trying to still the tremble that moved through his body. " 'Cuz ya think dat dead man was yo' brother?"

"Yep." Pierre took a splinter of wood from his pocket and began digging at his teeth. "Ain't leavin' The Boeuf until I find my brother. Somebody stole him away, because somebody has somethin' to hide, an' I'm goin' ta stick around till he shows up an' I can take him back home to bury him right proper. That's why I'm here . . . an' to find the gold that got him killed off. Ain't leavin' without that, either, no, sir."

Setting down the tin plate that had been stacked with biscuits just moments before, Swainie stood. "I'd best be gittin' back to de stables an' seein' if Mistah Emerson is still lookin' at dat hoss."

"Swainie, I'd like a word with ya" came the soft

413

voice of Sukie from beyond the screen door.

"Cain't it wait, woman?"

"Cain't wait, ol' man," she responded, her annoyance easily matching his own.

"Pierre, will ya go over an' check on Mistah Emerson? I'll be along shortly."

Pierre stood, arched his back, then sauntered down the narrow steps. "Sure . . . and I'll get busy on those stalls that need to be swept out."

When Pierre Neville was well out of sight, Swainie felt himself slump. "What do ya want, Sukie?" he asked, his voice quiet now.

"I seen how ya acted, Swainie. Now, I wanna know 'bout what happened dat night when ya's an' Massah Wickley run dat fella off'n de Shadows."

Swainie looked toward his wife, then he moved the few feet across the porch, and opened the screen door. He sat on a hard bench just inside the neat cabin, his eyes sweeping across the circular road and the direction of the stable. If anyone approached, he would be able to see them. "What do ya wan' ta know, Sukie?"

"I knowed what ya tell me befo', how ya's an' Massah left dat fella alive out der in de woods, an' I remember when Missy come over here dis pas' summer an' tells ya Massah Wickley's watch was in dat grave wid de fella, an' how she took it out o' that bag o' bones befo' Massah Emerson finds out who it belonged to. An' I remember dat night when ya's come back to de Shadows, an' when Massah Wickley retired to his bed, ya's ride back out in de woods. Ya be gone fo' nigh onto three hours, Swainie, an' I's wantin' ta know right now if it be you what kil't dat white man an' buried him out dere."

Swainie dropped his face into the palm of his hands and wept softly. Sukie dropped an understanding hand to his shoulder. "I sho' did kill dat fella, Sukie, but I din't mean ta," he said. "I was real mad 'cuz he jumped on de massah like'n he did, and I wuz jes goin' ta teach him a lesson. Massah had said he could sleep in dem woods an' be on his way in de mornin' an' I jes' wanted to put the fear in him so's he'd leave like de massah told him to. My ol' gun went off by accident, Sukie. Lawd God, I din't mean ta kill dat fella. Jes' meant ta skeer him real good. But when he fell down, plum' graveyard dead, I jes' got dat li'l ol spade I always carried around so's I could dig up de honeysuckle what Missy liked to plant round de Shadows an' I buried dat fella right where he fell."

Sukie was now weeping with her husband. "Did you tell the master what happened?" she asked.

"Massah Wickley, ya mean?" She nodded. "Yep, Sukie, my conscience really wuz botherin' me, so I tol' de massah long 'bout de time he wuz gittin' all dem notices from Mistah Penrod at de bank. Lawd God, Sukie, Massah never did tell me he los' his watch dat night. If I'd a' knowed, I'd a' took it off'n that fella I kil't befo' I buried him. I sho' wouldn'a wanted Missy to think her pappy kil't that fella."

Sitting beside Swainie, Sukie dropped her hand across his shoulder. "Ya hush dat cryin', Swainie. Ya made a mistake. Ain't no good in dredgin' it up now. Jes' tell me now, ol' man, did ya ride over to de Shadows back in de summer an' take dat bag o' bones what Massah Emerson was goin' ta turn over to de sheriff?"

"Sho' did. I sho' din't know de new massah over der told de sheriff what dem bones looked like."

"Ya done wrong," Sukie said quietly. "Did ya take Massah Wickley's watch, too?"

He shook his head. "Naw, Sukie, dat watch, it weren't in dere. Somebody already took it out. I 'spect it 'uz Missy, 'cuz she was actin' real funny dat day she rode over to talk to me 'bout dat night I wuz wid de massah."

"Ya know, Swainie, dey hangs a slave what kills a white man," she reminded him. "Ya better have hid dem bones so nobody'll ever find 'em ever ag'in!"

Fear pierced all the way to Swainie's heart. "De day I took de bones, I wuz ridin' cros't the field where Massah Emerson's silo got struck by lightnin' an' I saw Massah Wells aridin' dat big ol' stallion he's now wantin' ta sell. I hid behind dat silo, an' when Massah wuz outa sight, I got skeert he catch me wid 'em an I took de bones inside an' jes' throwed 'em on de ground. Dat ol' boy Pierre, he goin' ta find dem bones, fo' sho'! An' he ain't goin' ta stop snoopin' an' apryin' an' araisin' plumb hell till he finds out it 'uz me that kil't his brother. An' fo' sho, I's goin' ta hang higher'n a cloud!"

Sukie moved toward the screen door and looked out, her gaze falling to the lazy dog at the foot of the steps. She knew now why Master Wickley had sold her and Swainie and their children to Master Wells, when they'd lived at The Shadows for all those years. It was because of Swainie's confession that he'd killed a white man. Master Wickley could not bear to look at him, but rather than split up the family, he had sold them all to Master Wells, hoping to distance himself from the brutality of the murder.

This past year, she'd hated Master Wickley for selling them. Now, she understood why.

"What ya goin' ta do 'bout dem bones, Swainie?" she asked, turning back to her husband.

"Reckon I better go out yonder, Sukie, an' bury dat fella right proper. Maybe ol' Pierre'll get tired o' looking fo' his brother an' go on back where he come from."

"Ya better hope he does, Swainie. If'n he don't, an' he finds dem bones, ya better start talkin' to God 'bout yo' soul."

"Yas, Sukie, reckon I better."

He stood, a pathetic shell of a man who'd known all along that his past would catch up to him. He wasn't sure if he could save his own soul, but he had to do what he could to protect the memory of Angus Wickley.

He'd never held it against his former master for selling them off the way Sukie had. He had understood why and he'd been grateful to Master Wickley for not turning him over to the sheriff.

Miss Mandy was buried in a quiet ceremony the following morning. She would rest forever beneath the overhanging limbs of a massive oak with a clear view of the cottage where she'd been happy and the quiet bayou where she'd often watched Lancie and Maden fish in the late afternoons when work had been done. Lancie himself put her in the ground.

After the service, Thomas Jefferson Wells drew Grant aside. The two men walked slowly toward the bayou, pausing at water's edge. "What's on your mind, Tom?" Grant asked.

"One of my slaves took off yesterday. Before I hire a bounty hunter, I want to give him time to come back on his own. Since he was formerly owned by The Shadows. I'd be grateful if you'd keep an eye out for him. His name's Swainie."

"Why would he take off like that? I know you're not cruel to your slaves. Delilah mentioned that Swainie and his family had settled down at Dentley and were happy."

"I thought so, but the fact is, the man's gone. I talked to his wife. She told me she didn't know where Swainie was, but I could tell she was hiding something. I don't know if it was because her young'uns were hanging on her like moss, but she said very little, and what she did say left a lot of questions."

"I'll keep a look out for him," Grant offered.

"I suspect he might have taken off in a pirogue on The Boeuf. His horse came back to the stables yesterday afternoon, but his old dog is gone. I think Swainie liked that critter better than his family and probably took it with him." Wells extended his hand to Grant. "Thank you for keeping an eye out for my man and . . . I'd appreciate it if you wouldn't mention it to Delilah. She's real fond of Swainie and his family. Comes out to Dentley often to visit them."

"You know," Grant said, "Delilah and I are going to be married."

Wells grinned. "Kind of figured you would. You're getting a fine little lady."

"Talking about me?"

Both men turned at the interjection of the soft feminine voice into their conversation. Opening his arm, Grant invited Delilah to him. Her stark black mourning gown hugged her slender figure. "Think you're the only fine little lady in these parts, do you?" Grant said lightly.

"I would certainly hope I'm somewhere high on

418

the list," she teased. Immediately, her voice softened to suit the grim occasion that had brought them all to Ellie's cottage. "Mr. Wells, how are you today? And how are Swainie, Sukie, and the little ones?"

A frown pressed upon Wells's brow. "Everyone is fine, Miss Delilah. I understand we'll be having another wedding soon."

Delilah cut Grant a shy glance. "We really haven't worked out any of the details . . . or even set a date. But, yes, Grant and I will be married."

"My congratulations." He paused for a moment, then went on. "Well, Miss Delilah, I've concluded my business with your future husband and I—"

"Oh? What business is that?"

Again, his brows knit grimly. "I've got a fine stallion for sale and Sukie told me Grant had come over to see the animal yesterday—"

"She's mistaken," Grant immediately responded. "I wasn't over at Dentley yesterday. Perhaps it was my cousin, Aldrich."

The three of them began to ascend the hill toward Ellie's cottage. "She said Mister Emerson . . . I assumed she meant you. Now that I think about it, it must have been your cousin. He had expressed an interest in adding the stallion to Ellie's herd."

The two men spoke business as if Delilah was not between them. "Oh?" Grant said. "Ellie had mentioned that she preferred to send her mares out to other breeders to be covered by their stallions. She never indicated to me that she was interested in adding a proven stud to her inventory."

"You men!" Delilah forced a note of indignation into her voice. "Talking about mares being covered and proven studs as if I'm not even here. I should be offended."

Thomas Jefferson Wells laughed. "I can remember times, Delilah Wickley, that you were the one bringing up these subjects. Don't you recall last year when your father wanted to purchase one of my stallions and sent you over to do the negotiating? You weren't at all indignant then. As I remember, you beat me out of a real good horse for more than a fair price."

Delilah coyly dropped her gaze, then cupped her hand to the side of her mouth in the pretense of hiding her words from Grant. "I'm trying to convince this man walking beside me that I *really* am a lady. Here you go, Mr. Thomas Jefferson Wells, revealing my true self without a single qualm." Then she grew reverent. "Will you two excuse me? I would like to rejoin Ellie."

The two men watched her as she lifted her heavy black skirts and moved toward the cottage. "I'll wager there's not another one like her within a hundred miles." Thomas said when she was well out of sight.

"Make that a thousand and I'll fold my hand," Grant quietly responded.

"Still the gambler, eh, Grant?"

"Only when it comes to women."

Twenty-seven

By week's end, life along the bayou had returned to some semblance of normalcy. Though he could never replace Miss Mandy in Ellie's affections, Grant had given her one of his slaves to assist in domestic chores. The "frog girl" as everyone called her, but who was more aptly named Peculiar, was rumored to be one of the best cooks in the quarters. Grant smiled as he recalled a brisk conversation with Philbus, who had recommended her for Miss Ellie.

"If she's such a good cook, why wasn't she working in my kitchen?" The question seemed reasonable enough to Grant.

"Because, massah . . ." Philbus promptly responded, "she's peculiar. An' 'sides, Mozelle'd kick her britches if she came within a arm's length of her."

"Is she trustworthy?" Grant asked, wanting nothing to disrupt Ellie's life and cause her more problems.

"Sho', massah. Onliest thing wrong wid Peculiar is dat she's—"

"Yes, I know," Grant grumbled. "She's Peculiar. Surely she wasn't born that way."

"Naw, suh, massah," laughed Philbus. "Used to be named Mary, but Massah Wickley, he changed her name when she 'uz 'bout sixteen. He found her sittin' down on de bayou bank an' she tells Massah she be pickin' frogs out o' her pigtails 'cuz de Lawd tell her dey don't belong dere. Yas, suh, been Peculiar ever since! De darkies in de quarters, ever' so often they whittle a li'l frog out of a piece of wood an' give it ta Peculiar. An' Missy, she used ta bring her a li'l glass one from N'Awleans when she visited her auntie. Peculiar, she used ta circle 'em all around her, den one day dey started goin' missin'. Young'uns runnin' in an' out prob'ly carted 'em away, but ol' Peculiar, she din't make a fuss o' nothin'."

"Will you be so kind, Philbus, as to ready a surrey and drive our Miss Peculiar over to Ellie's place?" Grant asked after Philbus finished with his narrative. "And tell Ellie I'll be sending her papers over in a few days."

"Sho', massah, won't mind a bit gittin' rid o' dat crazy wench . . . an' dem frogs she carries 'round in dem pigtails, too!"

That Friday afternoon Grant sat in the study, preparing Daisy's manumission papers and going over the births and deaths among his own slaves in the past few months. Two had died, one of them being old Granny, and four had been born—a pair of twin boys and a girl each to two of the older women.

He was at odds over the issue of his slaves. Since Mozelle had been the one to boldly speak her mind, Grant had drawn her out into conversation on the issue of slavery. Their talk, when it had eventually led to the matter of freedom, had left him even more confused than before. "Yas, suh," Mozelle had said, "we's want freedom. But what we do's wid it, massah, onst we got it? Who gonna give a bunch o' freed niggahs a job makin' real wages. And where'll we live, if'n we don't live on de plantations where we always live. If'n we go on a long trip to find a place fo' ourselves, who 'mong de whites, even de po' trash, gonna want to live next do' to a freed niggah?"

"What are you saying, Mozelle?"

"Sounds purty clear to me, massah," she had responded without meaning to be impertinent. "If we be free, we don't wants ta, ya know, be free like ya might think about us bein' free. We's want ta be free to stay at de Shadows an' work fo' wages, jes' like a white man what works fo' wages. If'n de massahs here an' abouts be wantin' us ta be free an' leave, den we might as well be stayin' a slave an' stay where we be happy. An', 'sides, if'n we stay on de Shadows an' work like we always does, what be de diff'rence 'twist bein' free an' bein' a slave? We's still workin' de same ol' job an' livin' de same ol' way. Only diff'rence be dat we get paid fo' doin' it. But, massah, dat money we be making won't be buyin' us nothing we don't already have bein' yo' slaves, 'cuz ya be pervidin' us jes' 'bout ever'thing we need jes' like we be's yo' family. Now, ain't that so, massah?" Then she quietly left.

Though he knew his neighbors would frown upon it because it would cause dissension among their own slaves, Grant was considering freeing all the people at Shadows-in-the-Mist. Now, he wasn't sure what he should do. He realized there would be a few who would choose to leave and seek their own lives, but most would probably be willing to stay on at The Shadows and work for wages. He would discuss it with Delilah; as a wedding gift to her, he planned to file papers with the parish clerk that would recognize her as an equal owner of the plantation and its assets, and as such, the issue of freeing the slaves should be as much her decision.

Grant approached the sideboard where bottles of his favorite brandy were set in a neat row behind half a dozen goblets. Turning back with his half-full goblet, he immediately faced his cousin, standing quietly in the doorway.

"I thought you were moving over to the cottage today," Grant said, taking a sip of the amber liquid.

Aldrich's eyes narrowed spitefully. "We have unfinished business. Surely you didn't think I had forgotten?"

"I've forgotten nothing, Aldrich," Grant said, sitting at the desk to resume his work. "I thought by now you would have realized how ridiculous you are being."

"I'm afraid it's been slow to sink in, Grant," he replied, undaunted by his cousin's sarcasm. "In the morning, at six, in the field."

Grant picked up an old ledger he couldn't have had less interest in. "I'll be there, Cousin," he responded curtly, refusing to meet Aldrich's eyes; he wouldn't give him the satisfaction of seeing the concern in his own. "In the meantime, get the hell out of my house . . . and off my land."

"What has become of your tolerance?" asked a sarcastic Aldrich.

"You'll see it in a minute," Grant replied matter-of-factly. "It's about to fly out the window, along with your worthless carcass."

Aldrich turned, retreating down the corridor, his

boots echoing rhythmically upon the highly-polished floor. Just at that moment, Delilah entered. "What did you say to humor your cousin?" she asked.

"Threatened to throw him out the window," Grant replied, then changed the subject. "I thought you were napping."

"No, I was out at the stable. I've neglected Bella these past few days." She sighed then. "I understand from Philo that you've sent Peculiar over to Lamourie. Is she on loan, or do you plan to give her to Ellie?"

"She's a gift to Ellie. Do you have any objections?"

"Ellie won't keep her as a slave, you know. She abhors slavery even more than you do. She'll set her free."

"I figured she would, but I also figure Peculiar's too blasted odd to leave when she's got a bed to sleep in and food to eat." Taking her arm to guide her around the chair, Grant pulled Delilah down onto his lap. "Now that we're on the subject, what would you think about freeing *all* the slaves?"

"Well," Delilah said after a moment of silence. "I think if that decision is to be made, I'd rather you freed them than giving the government the satisfaction of doing it for you." When he gave her a puzzled look, she continued with haste. "Yes, Ellie mentioned to me your fears that the government would intervene in the issue of slavery." When he did not respond, she asked when he planned to free them.

"Before Christmas."

"How about tomorrow?"

"Tomorrow? That doesn't give me time to prepare the manumission papers."

"I'll help."

"Tell you what." His quiet tone still did not change. "Tomorrow's Saturday. Suppose you and I work over the weekend and make the announcement on Monday?"

"Suppose you're not alive on Monday?"

So surprised was he by her statement that his breath caught. "What do you mean? Why wouldn't I be alive on Monday?"

"I understand your cousin has called you to the field."

"Damn!" Grant frowned darkly. "Who told you?"

She would not drag the worried Philbus into this. "That doesn't matter. You're not going to meet him, are you?"

"I would be a coward not to. Besides . . ." He continued on a reassuring note, "my cousin will not kill me. And I certainly would not kill him. We're going to end this quarrel once and for all, and Aldrich is going to realize that I'm not the thoughtless bastard he thinks I am. I almost wish I hadn't returned to Massachusetts and found Madeleine pregnant with his child."

Delilah's face had grown ashen. Drawing in her bottom lip to cease its trembling, she quietly implored Grant to be a coward. "Don't meet him in the field. If you love me, you won't go. Oh, please . . . please, Grant —"

His fingertips pressed upon her mouth, stilling her words. "I told you, Delilah, my cousin will not kill me." His fingers moved to gently caress her pale cheek. "And don't try to assess my love for you by comparing it to my problems with Aldrich. Now . . . I need to see if Philbus has returned from Ellie's and enlist some of our men in the search for

426

Swainie. Wells seems to think he's still in the vicinity."

Mention of Swainie caused Delilah to drop her gaze. "Grant, there is something I should tell you—"

"And what is it that cannot await until tonight?"

"It really shouldn't wait. It has weighed heavily on my mind for many weeks now. Please, won't you let me get it off my mind without another moment's delay?" she softly beseeched him.

Sitting upon the corner of his desk, he motioned her to the chair he had just abandoned. "Now, what is this terrible burden on your soul?" he asked when she had neatly spread her skirts.

Last evening after dinner, while Grant had been at this same desk mulling over the business ledgers, Delilah had ridden over to Dentley to talk to Sukie about Swainie's disappearance. Sukie had told her everything, except where Swainie had hidden the bones of the man they now believed to be Paulie Neville. She had never seen Sukie so afraid, especially of Thomas Jefferson Wells learning of the secret Swainie had carried with him these past six years. She believed Swainie had run away because he feared being hanged. Sukie also feared being sold by the man who had owned both of them for less than a year. The luck of her family was bound to run out, and they would find their lives in the hands of a cruel master.

"So, what is this problem?" Grant prompted after a moment, stirring her from her deep thoughts.

She looked up, momentarily losing her train of thought. She had wanted to tell him about removing her father's watch from the evidence, but now perhaps it was best to wait until Swainie had been found and the whole story was out in the open. She did not want Grant to think for a single moment that her father might have been the murderer. "I've changed my mind. It's nothing that won't wait, Grant. I have more pressing problems now. Since I did not succeed with you, I am now going to try to talk some sense into Aldrich about this silly duel—"

He flew off the desk like a man struck. "You will do no such thing. Dammit, Delilah, don't beg for me! I simply will not have it!"

Had she not known him to be a gentle man, his tone would have frightened her. His eyes had narrowed and darkened to a rich royal hue. "I'm sorry, Grant. Of course I will not interfere in your problems with Aldrich."

Grant instantly regretted his outburst. Placing his hand softly upon her shoulder, he coaxed her to him. "No, I am sorry, Delilah." He buried his face into the rich depths of her hair. "Let's forget all this business for the day," he said. "I'll send Philbus over to Dentley with some of the men to help in the search for Swainie, and you and I can spend the day together."

"Doing what?" she asked, sniffing back the tears his angry words had caused.

"Would you like to journey into Alexandria and have dinner at the Exchange Hotel?"

"No."

"Would you like to visit friends?"

"No."

"Would you like to organize a singalong with the slaves?" he teased, brushing a kiss against her temple in the hopes of mending the hurt he had caused.

"No."

428

His warm breath assailed her cheek as his mouth sought the enjoyment of her own. "Would you like to make sweet, gentle love over dinner and the pale flicker of candlelight?"

"No."

His surprised gaze connected to her own. "No?" he repeated incredulously. "Then what would you like to do?"

"I'd like . . ." Only now did she manage a tremulous smile. "I would like to make wicked, wonderful love beneath the satin sheets I put upon our bed aboard the riverboat just this morning!"

"Satin sheets!" he chuckled. "And where did you get satin sheets?"

"I made them, and they're as red as a wanton hussy's lips."

"Good Lord, woman." He continued to laugh, glad that he had managed to take away her melancholy. "You didn't buy red satin to make a dress, then decide to make sheets instead, did you?"

"Of course not. I purchased it with the sole intention of making those red sheets!"

"I love you, Miss Delilah Wickley," he whispered.

"And will you still love me when I'm old and gray?"

"If those blasted red sheets don't kill me first! My heart beats madly just thinking about being with you upon them!"

Philbus charged his big gelding along the circular drive and dismounted at the gallery just as Grant and Delilah were exiting the house. He swiped his hat off his head as his gaze cut to Grant. "Massah, I needs a word with ya."

"Couldn't it wait?" Grant asked.

"Naw, suh, me an' some o' de men was out alookin' fo' Swainie, an' it be's about him—"

"You and the men have already joined in the search?" Grant asked, surprised that they wouldn't first consult him. He had, of course, intended to volunteer some of the men, but he didn't like the decision being taken out of his hands.

"I got men in the field pickin' de cotton an' I took a couple others to join in de search. Figured ya would want to help out Massah Wells since he sent men out when we thought Missy was lost in de woods. But, de men, dey's come in now. Ol' Swainie's been found . . . found on yo' land, massah."

"Was he hiding out?" Grant asked.

Philbus shook his head, his gaze cutting between Grant and Delilah. "Don't reckon Missy needs ta be hearin' dis, massah."

"Horse feathers!" retorted Delilah. "If it's about Swainie, I want to know what's going on."

Delilah gasped in horror when Philbus announced that Swainie was dead. Philbus gave her that moment before quietly continuing. "Dat ol' silo what burned in de summer collapsed on top of him. Wouldn'a found him, 'cept dat ol' cur dog that follows at his heels was lyin' right der awaitin' fer him to come out, an' de place was plum full o' flies."

"Hell!" Grant exclaimed. "What was he doing in there?"

"Don't know yet, massah. De men, dey is still tryin' to dig him out. But, Lawd, three days in dis hot weather done made it a real unpleasant chore." Delilah's expression turned ashen, and a shudder visibly shook her body. "Sorry, Missy," he said, "but

430

ya wanted to know."

"I'd better ride over to be with Sukie," she said to Grant.

"Of course," he replied, his mouth dipping to lightly touch her cheek. Then he whispered to her so that only she could hear. "Sorry about your friend. Those red sheets will have to wait."

That evening, a tearful Sukie sat in her cabin with Delilah, Grant, Thomas Jefferson Wells, and Pierre Neville, who had been quick to tell Wells that the bones found in the silo with his dead slave were those of his brother. Due to the condition of Swainie's body, he had been quickly buried, a small service spoken by one of the old black gentlemen who considered himself a self-ordained minister.

They were waiting for Sheriff Stafford from Alexandria so that Sukie could tell him her story. When he rode up with one of his deputies, Sukie immediately sent her children over to Ruby Mae's, one of Wells's other slaves who often took care of the children in the quarters.

With everyone sitting quietly around the room, Sukie gave all the details, just as Swainie had told them to her before he'd ridden out. She told them everything, including the part about Angus Wickley's watch being in the grave with the dead man. She did not, however, tell them that Delilah, thinking that her father had committed the murder, had taken the watch from the bag the morning Grant had reported the find to the sheriff. When she had completed her recitation, her eyes cut to the silent Delilah so that she could make her own confession.

Leaning across a small table, Delilah took Sukie's

hand and squeezed it comfortingly. Then she looked up at Grant, the shame in her eyes as readable as the love he usually saw there.

"We all know now that Swainie didn't mean to kill Paulie Neville." She refused to meet the eyes of Pierre Neville as he stood solemnly against the door. "In order to clear this matter up once and for all, I must admit my part in all this and take my just punishment."

"What do you mean, Miss Wickley?" inquired Sheriff Stafford. "Did you have something to do with Neville's death?"

Surprise touched her features. "Heavens, no . . . I was scarcely sixteen years old. What I did, Sheriff Stafford, was take my father's watch from the bag before Swainie stole it away." She did not implicate Daisy.

"I don't see much crime in that," the sheriff said.

"It would have been," she responded quietly, "if my father had been guilty of the murder and I had stolen away the only proof of that."

Looks were shared all around. Then Sukie stared hard at Thomas Jefferson Wells. "Massah, is ya goin' ta sell me an' my young'uns off?" she asked in a soft, trembling voice.

"Why on earth would I do that, Sukie?" he responded, his tone gentle, but still a little indignant that she'd think him so wretched and unsympathetic. "I do wish you'd have come to me when I thought Swainie had run off. Perhaps we'd have found him before—"

"Before the flesh started falling off his bones, just like my poor little brother out there in them woods with the dirt barely a finger deep over him."

All eyes turned to Pierre Neville. He had a right

432

to be bitter, but not to take it out on the gentle Sukie. "That's enough, Neville," the sheriff said. "You can take your brother and go home now."

"I'll be wantin' that gold he was hunting for."

"And you'll have to spend the rest of your life hunting for it." An irate Grant Emerson came to his feet. "Men have been searching for the last ten years."

"I'll find it," growled Pierre Neville. "Even if it does take the rest of my life."

"It won't take that long." All eyes turned to Delilah, who had placed a hand to her brow. Looking from one to the other of the men, she continued with haste. "I'll show Mr. Neville where the gold is. I think it's only fair that he have a good share of it since he lost his brother." Disbelief momentarily silenced the men, as each tried to find a proper response that would not make Delilah look as though she'd suddenly lost her mind. "Really, I know where the gold is buried," she repeated.

Grant was the first to find his voice. "And why have you not divulged this before now?"

"I only remembered where Papa had buried it a few months ago."

"And you did not retrieve it then? Why not?"

She shrugged gently, dropping her eyes from the face of the astounded sheriff. "Because something else became more important in my life than the gold that could have bought back The Shadows."

"What the hell could be more important than gold?" retorted Sheriff Stafford.

She looked him squarely in the eyes. "Love, Sheriff Stafford," she responded. "Now . . . please, don't press me to embarrass the man I will marry. Unless you plan to take custody of the gold on behalf of someone who has filed a claim to it, I will retrieve it and see that Mr. Neville gets a share of it." When he slowly shook his head, she looked toward Pierre Neville. "We'll ride out to where it's buried first thing in the morning."

That was fine with Grant. She would be out of the way when he met Aldrich on the field. But he would send Philbus along in the event the man got greedy. "Sheriff Stafford?" The man's gaze turned to Grant. "Has someone filed a claim?"

"Not that I've heard. Nobody can figure out where Angus Wickley got it in the first place . . . if it exists—"

"It exists," Thomas Jefferson Wells spoke up. "I saw it myself the night before Angus buried it."

Sheriff Stafford continued. "Nobody's laid a legal claim to it. I'd imagine that's because—pardon me for doubting you, Mr. Wells—everybody knew Angus was a little touched in the head and didn't believe the story about the gold . . ." He looked toward Delilah but did not apologize. "He never was the same after he run that rig into the bayou."

"I was in that rig," Delilah reminded him. "And I remember seeing that gold, just as clearly as I'm seeing you now. Daisy was with me, and she saw it, too. We may have been children, but we were old enough to know what gold looks like."

"You remember seeing that gold. Do you remember where your daddy got it? Or did that dip in the bayou cloud your memory, too?"

"I never did like you, Sheriff," Delilah snipped. "Now I know why." Putting his insult aside, she lightly shook her head, trying to remember more details of the week-long trip back from New Orleans when she was just a girl of twelve. She remembered

434

clearly that she and Daisy had fallen asleep in the back of the wagon and when they'd awakened the following morning, the chest had been beside them. Considering the gold to be her father's business, she had not questioned him about it. For a child to have done so would have been considered impertinent.

Finally, she looked up and said, "It was there . . . a chest containing thousands and thousands of gold coins. I only know that it wasn't in the wagon when we left New Orleans." Again, she squeezed Sukie's hand, which she'd continued to hold in her own. "For the time being, this matter is settled. We lost another good friend this week."

"Can't compare Swainie to Miz Mandy," Sukie mumbled, looking up at the sheriff. "Is I in trouble, Sheriff Stafford?"

"No." Rising, he turned toward the door and his deputy waiting outside, his glare a silent request to Pierre Neville to clear a way for him.

"How about me?" Delilah asked, with every intention of being impertinent.

"Wouldn't be doing any good to be filing charges against you. You'd just charm your way out of them before the judge."

"There is no need to insult Miss Wickley," Grant retorted. "I don't care if you *are* the law around here. I won't stand for it."

"I apologize to Miss Wickley, and to you, sir," Stafford mumbled, dropping his hat onto his head. "But this was a hell of a ride not to be taking anyone into custody." Then he ambled across the porch toward his waiting horse. Soon, he and his deputy were spurring their horses toward Alexandria.

"He is a most exasperating man," Wells said, rising, squeezing Sukie's shoulder before withdrawing toward the door. "If you let him get on your nerves, Grant, he'll think he's got the upper hand on you." When Wells reached the porch, he found Pierre Neville standing in the overhanging darkness. "You're welcome to sleep in the empty cabin at the end of the row," he said to the man. "Then I think it's best that you be on your way."

"After I get some of that gold," he mumbled.

"You need to be clearing out," he reiterated. Turning to Grant and Delilah, he lightly bowed his head. "Good evening to you. Be sure to send me over an invitation to your wedding."

"You're at the top of the guest list," Delilah responded.

With the adults departing, Sukie's three children moved cautiously onto the porch, then eased toward the protection of their mother's arms. "Mamma's got ta talk to ya 'bout yo' pappy," she said softly to her little ones.

Twenty-eight

The silence lay about the riverboat like a deep sleep. Delilah feared that even if she heaved a sigh, the dark night would collapse and crush her beneath its heavy weight. Not so much as a nightbird called across the bayou, and the haunting sense of lifelessness caused a shiver to travel through Delilah.

She had drained the last of her father's favorite peach brandy into the goblet and sipped it absently as she watched the big house for some sign of life. Since their return to Shadows-in-the-Mist, a quiet, thoughtful Grant had absented himself from her, and she wondered if her confession had disappointed him to a point that he would avoid her. She was worried; it seemed that from the beginning she had done things to prickle him, and she wondered if this latest touch of hers had been the last straw.

She could not know that he sat quietly in the study, making last-minute preparations in the event that he had underestimated the degree of Aldrich's hatred for him.

Grant settled back and studied the items on the desk in front of him. A small mahogany case lined with black velvet displayed the items of Delilah's jewelry that he had purchased from Mr. Garrett. In

437

the event of his death, he wanted them returned to their rightful owner. To the left of the case lay a single sheet of linen paper upon which he had hastily written his final will and testament. He had bequeathed most of his worldly possessions, including Shadows-in-the-Mist, to Delilah, with a special bequest of money to Madeleine's son, Dustin. The bequest to Delilah did not include the slaves. To them he gave freedom, the sum of two hundred dollars apiece, and the seven hundred acres of land he had recently purchased from Montford Wells, which was to be divided equally among the families.

His mood was glum. Losing Delilah seemed predestined, his future nonexistent. He wanted to believe his cousin would not shoot him down in the morning, but he wondered if that small spark of humanity truly existed beneath his surface. He had never been tolerant of his fellow man and he had never played the game of life with a show of conscience. He was a liar, a cheat, and a self-centered bastard who would go to any lengths to accomplish his goals.

"Massah, ya wanted to see me?"

Startled, Grant lurched forward in the chair. "Yes," he said to the burly Philbus. "I hope I didn't take you from anything important."

"Massah can call Philbus anytime. He be his property by law."

Grant cringed from the softness of sarcasm. "I want to make sure you're going to accompany Delilah in the morning. I don't want her to be alone with the Neville fellow."

" 'Course, massah. I wouldn't let nothin' happen ta Missy. I seen her grow up from a little sprite of a thing an' she's like kin. But . . ." The moment of silence compelled Grant's dropped gaze to again meet his own. "Ya don't need me out yonder in de field, massah, when ya meets wid yo' cousin?"

"I'll take care of my cousin. You take care of Delilah . . . and keep her away from the field. Will you do that, Philbus?"

"Sho', massah, if I can." Silence. "Is dat all, massah?"

"That's all." When Philbus began to leave the room, Grant spoke his name. "Have you been told that I am going to free Daisy?" Grant asked.

"Yas, suh."

"How do you feel about it?"

"De truth, massah?"

Grant quietly nodded.

"Well, we is all happy fo' Daisy, massah. Some of us are skiert by it, but me . . . well, I jes' hope one day ya might think about givin' me them manumission papers. But I'll tell ya, massah, if ya ever got round to it, I'll be gone from de Shadows 'most befo' de sun comes up de next mornin'."

Grant appreciated his forthrightness. "Where would you go, Philbus?"

The big man grinned widely. "Got a hankerin' ta go over ta Texas an' be a cowboy. Drive dem dumb ol' longhorns nawth'erd an' breathe in de dust o' de trail. Dat be some ambition, ain't it, massah?"

"Indeed," he remarked. "Every man has to have a dream."

Nodding politely, Philbus stepped backward into the corridor and quietly retreated.

Taking a few moments to return some semblance of order to the items atop the desk, Grant soon retreated from the large, dark-paneled room. Having skipped dinner, he should have been hungry, but he was not. He knew only that he had left Delilah so quickly upon their return to The Shadows that she must wonder what was bothering him. Actually, nothing bothered him now that he had put his affairs in order.

Soon, he stepped onto the gallery and felt the cool night breeze rustle through his hair. He had left his jacket behind and the top buttons of his shirt were undone. As he looked longingly toward the riverboat, he did not bother to refasten them. Despite the coolness, he suddenly felt the hot surge through his body that came from allowing Delilah to flood his memories. She was across that short spanse of lawn and clamshell driveway, awaiting him . . .

He soon crossed over the driveway toward the bank of the bayou, where the riverboat gently rocked. The water's surface was a shimmering of moonlight; he could see the reflection of an overcast sky and the flurry of dark clouds threatening to drop a veil of dark over The Boeuf. He looked up, thinking that the moon would disappear beyond the distant rumbling at any moment.

He did not at first see his Delilah resting upon the rail of *Bayou Belle,* her leg drawn up and her skirts exposing a slim ankle. When the liquid gold of her gaze turned to him, he offered his hand, feeling her own come to rest within it. Then he coaxed her up the main stairway and into the dining parlor, where he immediately began preparing a fire in the stove to alleviate the dampness within.

Momentarily the large compartment was bathed in warmth and light as a bright fire crackled in the stove. Grant's pale-blue eyes quietly studied the beautiful Delilah and drank in her soft curves. Her tie had loosened, betraying to his lustful gaze the smooth, creamy flesh of her breasts peaking against the material covering them.

"I thought you were angry with me," she whispered as he approached and drew her into the circle of his arms.

"Why would I be?" came his husky response. "You've done nothing to anger me."

"I thought that . . ." Her shrug bore witness to the shame within. "Confessing that I had taken my father's watch from the—"

Instantly, he cut her off. "Horse feathers!" he retorted, employing her favorite expression. "I couldn't care less about that. It is in the past." Even as he spoke, he saw a transition come over her as she realized he was not annoyed with her. As he withdrew just enough to pull his shirt off, he watched her passion-flamed eyes dance with light; the mass of chestnut-colored hair framing her heart-shaped face. Dropping the bundle of matches he had continued to hold after lighting the fire, he touched his fingertips to her flame-warmed cheeks, then combed them through the wildness of her hair. Burying his face into its softness, he felt his body physically harden against her soft, yielding one. He wanted her so badly that pain shot through him, and yet something within him held back. He felt like a giddy schoolboy exploring the beauty and sensuality of his first lady love, and he savored the loveliness of his Delilah, just as if it was their first intimate meeting.

Delilah's breathing raced frantically, and her sinuous movements against Grant spoke eloquently of her need for him. He aroused her like no man ever had before—or ever would again. When he buried his face between her heaving breasts, she threw back her head, her fingers clutching into his naked shoulders. She felt herself losing touch with reality, wanting to soar with him into an unknown universe that had suddenly been created exclusively for their enjoyment.

His hands moved around her waist, to squeeze her to him. When they roughly gripped the material at the back of her loose-fitting gown and began to pull it downward, her arms became limp, allowing for its easy removal. When at last she stood naked before him, he drew slightly back, his narrow gaze drinking in the beauty of her. She loved the way his eyes raked her body with tormenting delight and her heart pounded fiercely when his mouth dipped, then captured one of her breasts to gently caress it. She lifted her fingers to his thick blond hair, entwined them among the rich depths, then traced a path along his jawline.

She had never felt so dizzy with passion, but when he released her breast and briefly kissed the other to firm peakness, the true exhilaration began. Her flesh flamed beneath the miracle of his touch, of his tongue tracing a path down her heaving chest and lower, to the flat plane of her belly . . . and lower. When his explorations and gentle caresses coaxed her to her knees, then eased her back to a thick plush rug, she felt her flesh tingling, her thighs gently prodded apart and her knees drawn up and over his hard, muscular back. She dug her hands into the pile of the rug and clenched her fists, her passion-glazed eyes scarcely able to discern him kneeling between her thighs. Though the flames of the hearth glistening upon his hair almost blinded her, too, she was still able to make out the full, hard maleness of him spring free of his trousers as he unclothed himself, raking the material down his legs and discarding them into the pile where her gown lay.

She couldn't remember him being so patient before, so deliberate in his movements and his caresses, his hands gently stroking her inner thighs and merely brushing her womanhood. Her gaze connected to his own and it seemed that a thousand erotic hours passed in the few seconds that he studied, then dropped his palms to her ribs just below the roundness of her breasts.

They rested there, unmoving; she was unable to interpret the silent message in his eyes. "What are you waiting for, Grant? Do you not want me?" she finally asked softly.

He smiled, a strange melancholy smile that momentarily took her off her guard. The hardness of him rested against the juncture of her thighs, but he had made no move to enter her. Then his hands rose and roughly cupped her breasts. "I still cannot get enough of looking at you, wondering how one woman could be so beautiful. I find not a single flaw —"

"And that is what you are looking for?" she teased in a soft, sultry voice. "A flaw?"

"If I was," he responded with impassioned huskiness, "I would be very disappointed."

Easing atop her, his palms now resting upon the rug on either side of her, his mouth found the warm, willing depths of her own for a moment, then his caresses massaged a path along the smooth column of her throat, dipping into the pulsating hollow between her collarbones, then beneath her breasts. Lower and lower went his caresses, and when his tousled hair tickled along her abdomen on

443

a deliberate course, she gasped, relishing the wonderful wickedness of his movements against her. Then, as her mind soared far away and she lost herself in the wonderful naughtiness, his mouth and his tongue sought the sweet, moist depths of her and aroused her to unknown heights. She thought she would faint, but fought to retain her senses so that she could fully enjoy the magnificence of him.

The desires of her body commanded her every movement and she felt the walls of the riverboat, with its ordinary furnishings, metamorphosing into swirling depths of blinding fog and wicked delight that were both hot and cold in the same moment. Had only a few moments passed, or had it been hours, before her body burst into spasms of delicious fire that wracked her body from head to toe and brought Grant's body up to lightly cover her own.

She knew only that he was above her, on top of her, driving into the honeyed depths of her. She was only vaguely aware of his mouth nipping playfully, teasingly, at her own, his hands easing beneath her buttocks to draw her up firm against him. Nothing mattered but being with him. . . . Words were not necessary to relay her needs . . . her body spoke the language he longed to hear, as she oh so sensually rocked against him, matching his ever-increasing pace with the frenzied expertise of the most accomplished lover.

Waves of fire consumed them, molding their bodies together as one. She drank in the sweetness of his breath with every kiss, greedily accepted the probing of his tongue within her brandy-sweetened mouth. The muscles of his back were like tight knots beneath the caresses of her fingers, his slim hips so masterfully pounding against her thighs that she again felt the dizziness of passion. When, at last, he filled her with his seed, driving himself against her in the culmination of his passion, she felt his damp forehead drop heavily against her tangled hairline.

His body remained joined to hers. She liked the fullness of him that felt so natural, the spasms of fulfillment still echoing, like a beautiful memory, within their bodies.

Too soon Grant lifted his weight from her. Delilah attempted to hold him close, but he chuckled and touched his mouth to her own. "Do not worry, my love . . . I will not leave you alone for long."

She turned into his arms, tucking herself against him, her eyes damp and her mouth trembling. "You made love to me tonight as though we would never see each other again . . . like a soldier going off to a war that he knows cannot be won. I am afraid, Grant. I am afraid of what the morning will bring."

Grant gazed lovingly over her melancholy features. "I told you my cousin will not kill me. I promise—"

"But you said he always cheated."

He touched his mouth to her cheek and caressed it for a moment. "I promise, I will make sure he does not do so tomorrow."

"Let me be there with you, Grant—"

Instantly, his fingertip pressed to her mouth. "No . . . you have other things to do. Didn't you promise a certain Mr. Pierre Neville that you would make him a rich man?"

"I offered to take him to where the gold is buried because I thought it would please you. I thought you would think that I would interfere in your

445

problems with Aldrich, and I did not want to be an additional worry to you." Pouting prettily, she continued. "Oh, I should dig out the bottom and let the riverboat drift down the bayou with us both aboard. That is what I should do. Blast, the mud banks! I will this crusty old tub not to get stuck, but to carry us far away—"

"Hush!" He spoke the word sharply, and yet with an underlying softness. "Enjoy the night with me and do not worry about the morning."

She snuggled against him, easing her forehead into the curve of his shoulder. "You won't die tomorrow, will you, Grant?"

He frowned into the darkness. "Of course not. I've promised you the future, and I never break my promises."

"We'll always be together, won't we, Grant?" she softly implored.

He laughed, though his heart wasn't in it. "Unless you throw me over for a younger man, Miss Delilah Wickley."

She was well aware that he was attempting to drive the worry from her mind. "Do you know what I would like to do?" she quietly asked the man she loved.

"You've already told me. Send this blasted boat to a far place." He closed his eyes as he held her close.

"Well, besides that. I would like to ride over to Ellie's cottage, call out Aldrich, and shoot him myself."

"Don't fret, Delilah," Grant lightly ordered. "No one is going to get shot, including me. Now, let us get off this hard floor and find a comfortable spot in your bed."

"Blast!" A wide-eyed Delilah suddenly shot to a

446

sitting position.

To which a surprised Grant replied, "What's the matter, love?"

"We were going to make love—"

"We did make love," he reminded her.

"But upon my red satin sheets! Ooh! We missed all the excitement!"

"I didn't miss it, Delilah." Touching his fingers to the small of her back, he laughed. "And you didn't seem to be asleep, either!"

Facing him, a smile gracing her full, sensual mouth, she dropped her head to his chest. "I do love you, Grant Emerson. Don't you ever forget it!"

Gently stroking her hair, he closed his eyes and enjoyed the closeness of her.

Shortly after sunrise, Aldrich swung open the door and stepped out to the gallery of his wife's cottage. Sitting on the settee, he nursed a cup of strong chicory coffee, his gaze meeting the awakening morning with little interest. Off in a pen the stallion he had purchased from Dentley pranced and tossed its full black mane, then snorted possessively toward the grazing mares that did not seem nearly as interested in him.

So deep was Aldrich in his thoughts as he looked at his pocket watch to mark the time that he did not hear Ellie approach.

She wrapped her arms around him from behind the settee. She brushed her soft dark hair against his cheek. "Good morning, husband," she whispered.

"Good morning, wife," he replied.

"You are up early this morning."

He smiled, taking her arm to guide her around

447

the settee and onto the plush cushion beside him. "How is your new domestic working out?"

"She made a good cup of coffee, did she not?" Ellie answered, nodding toward the coffee cup Aldrich was now setting upon the table. "She has also prepared sweet rolls and bacon and eggs, if you're hungry."

Aldrich raised a dark eyebrow. "Then you don't mind that she talks to herself and constantly picks at her hair, looking for frogs?"

Ellie laughed. "She keeps her hair very clean. I don't think there's anything in it we need worry about. Now . . . what has brought you out so early?"

"I have business with my cousin."

"Oh?" She settled against him. "What kind of business?"

"Nothing that would interest you."

Peculiar stepped out to the gallery to approach the couple. "Miz El wants a cup uh coffee . . . huh, Miz El?"

"Not right now, Miss P.," Ellie replied, employing the name she had chosen upon the woman's arrival. She really didn't like the servant's name, feeling it insulted her, and she didn't imagine she'd use it in addressing her, no matter how long she stayed with her. "Do you want anything, Aldrich?"

"No!" His gaze toward Ellie softened, a form of apology for his sharp reply. "I'm not hungry." He took Ellie's hand, held it tenderly, then waited until the new servant had left before smiling into his wife's eyes. "You know, Ellie, I love you dearly."

A moment of worry pinched her brows together. "You seem troubled, Aldrich."

"Poppycock!" he retorted. "I've got nothing in the

448

world to worry about. I have a beautiful wife, plenty of money in the bank, and we—you and I—are going to start raising some of the best horses in the state of Louisiana." He nodded toward the stallion. "That beast will see to it. He's certainly anxious to get to your mares."

"If he has your appetite," laughed Ellie, "then we will, indeed, have a rich herd. Now, you'd better get to your rendezvous with Grant so that you can return to the arms of the woman who adores you."

Tenderly, his fingers traced a path beneath her chin. He was glad that news of the duel had not reached her ears. "I must retrieve a portfolio from inside, then I will be on my way."

Ellie sat quietly sipping the still-steaming coffee Aldrich had left there. It was not as sweet as she liked it, but it accomplished its goal in helping her to awaken to the day.

Drawing himself from the lover's embrace he had shared with Delilah in those few hours of early dawn, Grant quietly dressed, his gaze sweeping over her still-sleeping form. She had pulled the satin sheet over her and had tucked it around her like a cocoon when he left the bed. Grant doubted she was even aware he was not still with her.

When he reached the stable, Philbus was just drawing his gelding out of its stall. "Missy ready ta be meetin' up wid dat white man?" he asked, referring to Pierre Neville.

"She hasn't yet arisen," Grant replied. "Why don't you let her sleep until the man rides over here?"

"Do ya really think Missy knows where dat gold is, massah?" Philbus asked.

"Hell, no," laughed Grant. "If *I* knew where so much gold was, I sure wouldn't leave it buried in the ground where it could be of no use to anyone."

"I reckon we'll see, huh?" Philbus's expression suddenly grew serious. "Ya gonna meet yo' cousin in de field dis mo'nin'?"

Grant kept his response light. "Yes, we're going to get this ridiculous feud over with once and for all."

"Sho' hope ya don't git yo'self kil't, massah. Kinda gittin' used to havin' ya round."

Grant forced a grin. "Thanks, Philbus. Coming from you, that's a big compliment."

Philbus was first to admit that he could be difficult sometimes. It was only normal that his master would take every opportunity to point it out to him. "Well, I'll be round back atalkin' to my pappy," Philbus said, tipping his hat. "I'll git Missy's hoss saddled up fo' her."

"While you're inside, will you saddle mine?" Grant politely requested. "I need to take care of some things at the house before I ride out."

"Sho', massah," he replied, dragging the big horse around.

"Philbus!" The gelding immediately halted and Philbus turned back to face Grant. "Philbus," Grant spoke on a lighter note, "I've been here for a few months now and I've been indulgent of practices and traditions that have not set well with me—"

"What'cha sayin', massah?"

"Would it be so difficult for you and your people to call me Mister rather than Master? I'd prefer it."

Philbus grimaced, drawing his floppy hat farther down over his forehead. "It might take a while, but if dat's what ya want, I's sho' relay yo' request to de

450

others. Ya might want ta be patient wid de young'uns."

"I will . . . Thanks."

"Ya know, ya's nothin' like what we's expected when we heerd they's be a Yankee buyin' de Shadows," Philbus said quietly. "Naw, suh, ain't nothin' like we 'spected, at all."

"I hope that's another of those strange compliments of yours," Grant laughed.

Philbus snapped his index finger up against the brow of his hat. "Well, suh, it sho' ain't no insult." Once again, he pulled the horse around and entered the long hall of the stable.

Twenty-nine

Grant mulled over the idea that Aldrich might ride over to Shadows-in-the-Mist and call off the duel. Louisiana had incorporated an antidueling clause into its Constitution, but Grant knew that would not matter to Aldrich if he insisted on settling the issue of his marriage to Madeleine Vail. He was hoping that, for the first time in his life, a little common sense might sink into his cousin's thick skin.

Sitting at the desk, he wrote a short note and tucked it into the case of jewelry. Smiling to himself, he recalled the several times these past few months that he had wanted to return the jewels to Delilah but had feared embarrassing her. Her pride would certainly be stung if she found out that Mr. Garrett had been purchasing the jewelry, and at more than a fair price, because Grant had asked him to.

He pulled his jacket from the back of the chair and drew it on. He needed to keep the rendezvous with Aldrich, or risk losing face. Beyond the clean pane of glass at the window he saw his horse tied at the stable; he needed to ride out before Delilah arose. In those moments before dawn that they had made love, he had seen the plea in her golden eyes. He even imagined that she had not been asleep when he had left the riverboat.

452

Gathering his wits about him, he quietly left the house.

He was right about Delilah. The moment he had left the riverboat, she had drawn herself into a sitting position, a tremble of fear rocking her slender body. She wanted to be with Grant, but that was not what he wanted. All she could do was wait and pray and worry. She wasn't the least bit interested in her father's buried gold, or in lining the pockets of the embittered Pierre Neville, but she had to take her mind off the impending danger Grant faced on the field where he and his cousin would face each other with guns.

She wished she could have as much faith in Aldrich as Grant seemed to have. He trusted Aldrich not to kill him, or was he merely trying to reassure her with lies so that she would not worry? Delilah was at odds with herself; should she do something to stop the duel, tell Ellie what was happening and let her intervene, or simply sit back and wait?

The latter was the most painful of the three choices, but she knew it was the only one Grant would accept.

After she had dressed in a tan riding skirt with matching vest, then pulled on her favorite and most comfortable pair of boots, Delilah sat on the deck of the riverboat that faced the big house. At the stable to the right she saw Grant's horse tied and she knew he had not yet left the plantation. She ached for a last glimpse of him, and when, after several silent moments of waiting, he emerged from the house, she drew in a deep breath, rising from the chair to lean against the rail.

The morning sun gleamed like gold upon his bare head; he held his hat limply in his left hand as he approached his horse, which he quickly mounted and turned southward toward the bayou just as the man, Pierre Neville, was riding in. Delilah could not take her eyes off Grant. She watched him coax his horse into a trot, and she could tell that he deliberately did not look toward the riverboat. If he had, he would have seen her against the rail, tears torturing her golden eyes and her mouth softly trembling.

She felt a trifle foolish. They were probably being boys again, facing each other in a challenge of wills, two boys, mending their differences by playing silly games.

Still, an apprehension clutched her within. So fearful was she for Grant that she knew she could not obey his order to keep away from the field.

Ellie had dressed soon after Aldrich's departure and now sat quietly in the parlor, working on a quilt she was making for a friend who had recently given birth to a daughter. She stared at the squares of pink and rose in her basket awaiting the finishing touches, then stared absently out the window. She wondered how long Aldrich would be away on his business with Grant.

A knock sounded at the door. When Peculiar did not answer it, Ellie called for the person to enter.

Lancie stepped in, then grabbed his hat from his head. "Don't mean ta alarm ya, Miz El, but I's just talkin' to one o' de men from de Shadows what was passin' by on de bayou, an' he says de word be gittin' around dat Mistah Aldrich an' his cousin . . .

dey be—" Dropping his eyes, he twisted his hat between his nervous fingers.

"They're what?" Ellie coaxed.

"Dey's meetin' in de field on de other side o' de Shadows. They's gonna face each other in a duel, Miz El."

"Oh, dear Lord," responded Ellie, scarcely able to believe Lancie. "Are you sure?"

"Sho', Miz El. He say some o' de slaves over dere, dey's be hidin' in de woods so's dey can watch—"

"Saddle my horse quickly," she ordered.

"Yas'sum, Miz El. But I's ridin' wid ya."

"I expected you would," she responded, moving toward the back of the house to change. "I'll be out directly."

Scarcely fifteen minutes had passed before Ellie was pressing her horse on the trail with Lancie close behind. She did not feel the chill of the autumn morning or hear the sounds of the bayou . . . only the fear swelling within her like a tangible thing. She had just become a bride . . . would she become a widow again so soon?

She was furious that Delilah would allow something like this to happen. Couldn't she have calmed down the two childish men? Was she even aware of the duel? Dear Lord! Was Delilah even now taking her place among the spectators?

Ellie had underestimated Delilah. Even at that moment, she was telling Pierre Aldrich their mission would have to wait and she and Philbus were racing toward the field. She had decided that, no matter what Grant had said, she was not going to allow such foolishness, even if he had assured her it was nothing more than an empty threat on Aldrich's part. She loved Grant too much to take any chances, and if her only way to save him was to go against his wishes, then she would do just that. Grant had told her that he trusted his cousin to be fair and gentlemanly. Delilah did not have that much faith in him.

As they sped along the trail, Philbus yelled, "Dat Neville fella's hot on our heels, Missy."

To which Delilah replied, "He probably thinks we're going to beat him out of the gold. Let him follow." Whether he heard her, she really didn't care. First and foremost in her mind was reaching the field and stopping two men from being ridiculous.

She couldn't bear the thought of losing Grant.

She would rather die.

When Grant had dismounted his horse, he had been aware that some of the slaves were attempting to hide themselves along the dark fringes of the woodline. He shrugged as if it didn't matter. The prospect of witnessing death was a magnet to just about any man. He could not fault them for their curiosity.

Aldrich was waiting for him. Grant threw his jacket to the ground and he soon stood just outside of touching distance of his cousin. "I gathered you would provide the weapons," Grant said, looking down at the fancy case.

"I always have, Grant. Don't you remember?"

Grant looked up, his pale-blue eyes connecting to dark, viciously narrowed ones. "I remember a lot of things." He snatched his watch from his pocket and glanced at it. "It's almost six. Do you want to get this over with?"

Slowly, Aldrich opened the case. He watched Grant's eyes cut between the two weapons. When he chose the weapon on the right, as Aldrich had predicted he would, he had to suppress the tiny smile fighting against his mouth. It was not the moment to gloat in self-satisfaction. His cousin's death would give him that.

Aldrich took his own weapon, the only one that would fire this morning, and faced his cousin. "Back to back, ten paces, turn and fire."

Grant was frankly very surprised that Aldrich had reacted so calmly to his choice of the weapons. Had Aldrich second-guessed his adult nature? "Just tell me one thing, Aldrich. Do you love Ellie?"

The question surprised Aldrich. "With all my heart . . . and all my soul."

"Then why? Why are we here this morning?"

"Because . . ." Aldrich shot out viciously, "you have always gotten the upper hand on me. And I am sick of it! You made a fool of me, first when you married Madeleine and second when you . . ." He hesitated to complete the sentence. "Second, when Ellie was not your woman. I demand satisfaction!"

"No, Aldrich," Grant calmly replied. "You made a fool of yourself. But you're a damn lucky fool to have a good woman like Ellie. Let's put these pistols away, shake hands, and be friends. Would it be so difficult?"

"It would be impossible." Behind his wall of outrageous pride, Aldrich truly wanted to embrace his cousin and call him friend. He wanted to walk away from the field, without dishonor, sweep Ellie up in his arms and swear before all witnesses that he would be a good husband and she would have a happy life with him. God, he wanted to, even as he moved a few feet away and quietly waited for his cousin to turn against his back.

"Are you ready?" he asked when he felt Grant against him.

"I am," Grant said.

A moment of silence followed. Then Aldrich paced off, and counted off the steps. "One, two, three, four, five, six, seven, eight, nine, ten . . . Both men turned, their weapons raised, a hush suddenly falling over the field.

"Wait!" Without warning, Aldrich raised his pistol to the air and yelled hoarsely.

Grant did not drop his arm, but pointed the pistol menacingly in the direction of his cousin. "What is the problem, Aldrich? Suddenly lost your eyesight?"

"I cannot do this, Grant." He almost choked on the words. "Your gun is rigged not to fire."

"I do not believe that," Grant responded, the weapon still extended before him. "That is something a spoiled boy would do, not a man."

With an irate groan, Aldrich threw his own weapon in the dirt and approached Grant, ripping the gun from his cousin's hands. "Dammit, I said your weapon is rigged not to fire. You must know that I never play fair!"

"I still don't believe you," Grant challenged.

"Then I will show you," Aldrich countered, pointing his weapon to the right and pulling the trigger.

A single gunshot rent the air and a horrified Aldrich looked down at the gun Grant would have fired at him. He distinctly remembered placing the rigged gun on the right, which was the one Grant had chosen . . .

Confusion suddenly broke out as a woman screamed across the meadow and four horses, finding themselves free of riders, rushed past the two men in a blind panic.

Delilah had thrown herself off her horse when Ellie hit the ground. She pulled her up into her arms, scarcely able to make out Ellie's still features through the blur of her tears. "Ellie . . . Ellie," she screamed, her sleeve covered with her friend's blood.

Delilah and Philbus had arrived at the field at the same time as Ellie and Lancie. They were riding in together when the shot had been fired and Ellie had fallen, struck by the bullet Aldrich had fired.

Aldrich and Grant looked on in stunned horror, joined by a group of slaves. With a loud, desperate groan, Aldrich's hand flew out and jerked Delilah away from his wife. Kneeling, he pulled her into his arms and held her close, his tears rushing upon her pale cheeks. "God, Ellie . . . no . . . dear God, don't let this happen."

Delilah rushed into Grant's arms, her tears mixing with his own. Lancie had dropped to his knees and was sobbing against his linked fingers.

"I'll go back to your place and get a wagon," Pierre Neville, keeping his wits about him, said, and remounted his horse.

"Aldrich?" Ellie softly spoke her husband's name.

He brushed back her dark hair, damp with his own tears. "Yes, my darling. Yes, I am here."

"You do love me, don't you?" she asked weakly.

"More than life, Ellie. You are my heart. Dear God, forgive me."

Touching her fingertips to his tear-stained cheek,

459

gentle Ellie dropped her hand and quietly closed her eyes.

Pierre Neville rode away from The Shadows that afternoon in deference to the tragedy that had stunned everyone along the bayou. Speculation was made that he would return when a respectable length of time had passed, but for now, he was forgotten, the gold was forgotten, and the people at Shadows-in-the-Mist had to try to put the terrible day behind them.

Delilah made all the arrangements for Ellie; she was surprised that Aldrich had entrusted her with the details. The sheriff's initial report recorded the shooting as accidental, but Aldrich was ordered to ride into Alexandria within a week to give detailed testimony.

Grant had never seen Aldrich so distraught. He wanted to hate him for what he'd done to Ellie, but he could not. His cousin had learned his lesson in the most painful manner.

Grant slept alone aboard the riverboat that night while Delilah kept a silent vigil at Ellie's house, accompanied by a group of slaves. Shadows-in-the-Mist was a very lonely place to be.

Mozelle was fussing miserably over Delilah as she stood before the mirror, tucking in a wayward lock, straightening her gossamer veil, and tugging at the bodice of her tight-fitting gown. The gown of shimmering cream-colored fabric, with rhinestone accents on the billowing net oversleeves, had taken four seamstresses two weeks to make. Her elegant headpiece of delicate silver bugle beading sat atop her sternly pulled-back hair; from its center a half-dozen tight ringlets cascaded. Her glittering diamond-and-pearl necklace hugged the slender column of her neck.

"Do I look all right, Mozelle?" Delilah asked for the hundredth time.

"Ya's purty as a picture," an indulgent Mozelle repeated.

Daisy entered, carrying the bouquet of silk roses and the bridal wreath she had spent four days constructing for Delilah. "Here's yo' bouquet," she said, enthusiastically tucking it into Delilah's hand.

Delilah drew Daisy into her arms. "You are happy being married to Lancie, aren't you, Daisy?"

"Sho', Missy, been de bes' two weeks of my life. Massah's a good man fo' givin' me my freedom to marry Lancie, a good man fo' givin' all us slaves the freedom." Daisy grinned widely, straightening down the folds of her own simple gown. "Now he's goin' ta be Missy's husband! Ain't it somethin'?"

"Is everyone downstairs?" a nervous Delilah asked.

"Everyone . . . Mistah Wells, he's real skittery 'bout givin' ya away, 'cuz he's a wishin' yo' pappy was here to do it, but he's real proud to be doin' it, too. An' the bridegroom . . . he's jes' a bundle of nerves down there, waitin' fo' ya to come down the stairs. Lawd, Missy, here it be the winter, an he's a sweatin' up a storm in his new marryin' suit—"

Delilah laughed. "You don't think our Yankee-Doodle gambler is going to skeedaddle it back East, do you, Daisy?"

"Naw," Daisy giggled. "He's mighty proud to be agittin' ya fo' a wife. I overhears him tellin' Mr. Wells ya's goin' ta have a half dozen children by the time ya's thirty!"

461

"And he'll have half of them himself!" she chuckled, remembering the last time she and Grant had spoken about children. Oh, how happy she was! She felt giddy, like a schoolgirl. She could hear the mutterings of the many guests who had gathered for her wedding to Grant, and she could smell the commingled aromas of food that had been prepared for the feast afterward.

"Ya two better stop all dat chatterin'," Mozelle fussed. "Dey's a weddin' to be attendin'."

The door opened, and the gentle fragrance of lavender drifted into the room. "Your matron of honor has arrived."

Delilah turned and smiled brightly for her friend. "Oh, Ellie, how lovely you look!"

Ellie held up her arm, immediately cringing from the lingering soreness of her shoulder wound. "Look, I had a sling made from my dress material." Then she turned, showing off her own gown of rich blue charmeuse with golden lace and billowing chiffon trim.

From outside the window suddenly came the sounds of singing voices, Delilah, Ellie, Mozelle, and Daisy all rushed to the window and threw it open wide. There on the lawn stood a dozen or more of The Shadows' residents, singing a merry song:

"If ya want to marry, come an' marry me-e-e:
Silk an' satin ya shall wear, but trouble you
    shall see-e-e.
If ya want to marry, marry de sailor's
    daughter;
Put her in a coffeepot and sen' her cross
    de water.

I marry black gal; she was black, ya know,
Fo' when I went to see her, she look like
  a crow-ow,
She look like a crow-ow-ow."

Delilah laughed. "Thank you for the song, my friends, but would you mind terribly if I married the Yankee?"

"Naw'm" came the answer in unison, all of them waving their hands as they moved toward the parlor windows for a good view of the wedding. "Will you sing your songs at the feast after the ceremony?" she asked before they were out of sight.

"Yas'sum, Missy," one of the young girls replied. "We'll be dere fo' sho'!"

Turning from the window, Delilah hugged all her friends one last time before the ceremony. Looking to Ellie, she whispered, "Please . . . please before I am officially married, will you tell me? I simply must know."

Ellie turned to Daisy and Mozelle. "Would you await us in the corridor?" she asked politely. "We'll be but a minute."

When they were alone, Ellie took Delilah's hand and coaxed her to the edge of the bed, where they both sat. "You want to know how Charles died. Now, my dear young friend, is the time to tell you."

"It will not spoil your good mood, will it?" Delilah asked.

"Heavens no! Charles was not a very nice man." When Delilah's brows knit with bewilderment, she continued. "The night Charles died, we were aboard a riverboat journeying from St. Louis to New Orleans. That is the night I met Grant. Charles was playing cards at Grant's table, and Charles was

463

cheating . . . dealing cards from his sleeve. When Grant called him out on it, Charles shot him from beneath the table. That is how Grant got his leg wound. The shooting so angered the other men in the gaming room that several of them threw Charles into the river . . . He drowned."

"Then Grant had nothing to do with his death. He merely accused him of cheating. Oh, Ellie, why wasn't I told before?"

"No one here knew . . . only Grant and me. I took care of his wound until we reached New Orleans. When Grant found out I had a son, he made me promise not to tell anyone how Charles had died, because he did not want Maden to be disgraced. And that is exactly what I did. I kept the secret of the disgraceful manner in which Charles had died."

"Oh, thank you, Ellie," Delilah said, hugging her friend. "Thank you for relieving my mind. I swear, what you have told me will never go any further."

Just at that moment, the wedding march began to play. Ellie had sent Lancie into Alexandria to borrow the magnificent organ from one of the local churches as her gift to Delilah on her wedding day. "Come, let us join Mozelle and Daisy, and then get you married off."

"I am ready," she whispered with a shaky smile. "I think."

Mozelle opened the door and stood aside. "Ya man's awaitin' fo' ya, Missy."

Dragging in a long, deep breath, Delilah rolled her eyes upward. "I really am ready," she said, and moved cautiously into the corridor.

Grant Emerson was wondering how it had gotten

so blasted hot in the parlor in so short a time. He stood before the altar that had been erected and looked toward the staircase where his Delilah would soon descend. When Aldrich, his best man, leaned forward and said, "You look like a frightened rabbit trapped against a butte by a coyote," Grant managed a very nervous smile.

"I wonder if my horse is saddled," he teased in a whisper. "Do I have time to make my escape?"

"Be quiet and take your medicine, Cousin. This is what you get for falling in love."

These past four weeks, Grant had seen Aldrich in a different light. He had seen a man devastated by the fact that he had almost killed the woman he loved, a man who now stood beside him as the only member of his family to witness his marriage to Delilah Wickley. Aldrich had committed himself to staying at Lamourie Bayou with Ellie and raising horses; Grant was glad to have him as a neighbor . . . and a friend.

Soon he heard a scurry of activity on the stairway. Again tugging at the neck of his tight shirt, he watched Thomas Jefferson Wells move toward the stairs. Then came Ellie, dressed in her lovely gown, and just seconds behind her, his future wife.

When Delilah's hand stole upon Tom's for the short walk to the altar and the reverend who very quietly awaited her, Grant drank in the beauty of her. She was like an angel descending from the heavens. Her golden eyes gleamed through the rich gossamer of her veil.

He should have heard the mumblings of the wedding guests, and yet silence settled all about him. He imagined that he could hear Delilah's shoes touching upon the planked floor, the rustle of her

465

voluminous skirts, even the fall of a silk rose that had come loose from her bouquet. And all the while, his eyes held her gentle ones, so full of love and adoration that he felt a lump rise in his throat. He wanted to cough and send the offending evidence of his emotion far away, but he could not interrupt the exquisite moment that drew her closer. Nodding politely, he accepted her arm from a beaming Thomas Jefferson Wells.

The minister's gaze gave silent approval to the man and woman standing before him. He began. "Dear friends of us all: Your love is to be crowned with the Blessings of the Church, which is the bride of Christ, and your feet are soon to stand within the goodly Land of Promise. You are entering into that holy estate which is the deepest mystery of experience and the very sacrament of Divine Love."

Delilah stood quietly, as if in a dream, and listened as the voice of the minister slowly drifted away. She knew only that she was beside Grant Emerson, the man she loved and with whom she wished to spend her life, and they were binding their love in the most cherished way of all. Later, she would vaguely recall the minister saying something about "perennial beauty and gracious visions" in his lovely wedding sermon, after which she'd spoken the words, "I do" and had heard them spoken by Grant in return. She would vaguely remember a cool band of gold slipped onto her finger and Grant's mouth gently closing on her own. She would vaguely recall the well wishes of wedding guests, kisses upon her cheek, and arms about her shoulders. She would recall the aroma of food that she'd felt too giddy to sample, and the lulling songs of the slaves entertaining throughout the afternoon.

The only thing that wasn't vague about her wedding day was the depth of her love for her new husband.

That evening, when the excitement finally died down and everyone retired to their homes, Grant carried Delilah over the threshold of the bedchamber they would share.

"We are home, Mrs. Grant Emerson," he whispered, touching his mouth to her own warm one as he tenderly laid her on the bed.

"Mrs. Grant Emerson . . . I like the sound of that." She propped herself on her elbows and watched him finally loosen the collar that had been annoying him all day. "Do you feel better now, husband?"

He buried his head against her tightly bound breasts. "I will feel better when I can rest my head here . . . and there is no fabric to bar me from you."

"Oh, Grant, Grant . . ." She wrapped him in her embrace. "Can it be possible that we are man and wife? I am so happy."

His pale eyes narrowed in humor, he cupped her heart-shaped face between his palms. "Yes, man and wife. The Yankee-Doodle gambler and his southern bride . . . Now blast it, woman," he mumbled good-naturedly, "get yourself out of these blasted garments . . . or I'll do it for you."

She arched a dark eyebrow. "Then, blast it, do it, my love. I am . . ." She forced herself to yawn, covering her mouth as she did so, "much too tired to do it myself. I need a good night's sleep."

"Sleep!" he chuckled. "I was thinking of a proper wedding night!"

"Horse feathers," Delilah responded. "Now that I

467

have you for a husband, I don't have to worry about pleasing you with such mundane things as wifely duties."

"Oh?" For a moment he was not sure whether she was teasing . . . then he saw the hint of a smile she fought so hard to suppress. "You little vixen, I'll teach you . . ." He suddenly shot up, leaving her weightless, and she looked at him questioningly. "I almost forgot my wedding gift to you." Approaching a large bureau, he opened the top drawer, removed a mahogany box. "This is for you."

Her curiosity piqued, she sat up and slowly opened the box. Surprise and delight gleamed in her eyes. "I don't believe it . . . my mother's jewels," she whispered, picking up the pieces one at a time — the cameo brooch and oval locket, the pearl necklace . . . "But how did you . . ." she asked.

Sitting beside her; he took the box, closed it, and set it aside. *"How* doesn't matter. The only thing that matters, Mrs. Emerson, is *now,* our waiting bed, a beautiful woman, and the man who loves her." As his hands moved to span her tiny waist, to begin popping what he was sure were no less than a thousand tiny buttons running the length of her back, she held him close, waiting . . . oh so patiently waiting for the exquisite moments ahead when they would lie in each other's arms and love away the long Louisiana night.

Part Four

Thirty

Delilah sat quietly in the parlor, reading Daisy's letter for perhaps the hundredth time. It was the first letter she'd received in the three years Daisy had been gone, and she couldn't get enough of her friend's news. Who would ever have believed that sweet-natured, uncomplicated Daisy would become a lady about San Francisco, wearing fancy gowns and high-stepping shoes and boasting of friends who knew the President personally? Sitting back in her chair, Delilah's gaze reached beyond the gossamer curtains and the window looking out over Bayou Boeuf, and she remembered the emotional day in the spring of 1857 that Daisy had left with her husband Lancie. They had packed all their worldly belongings in a sturdy wagon Ellie had given them and had begun the long, arduous trip to California. There, Lancie had struck up a friendship with a fast-talking fellow from Australia and the two of them had prospected for gold, eventually sifting enough through their pans to buy a saloon in San Francisco. Daisy had been welcomed into the elite circles of society—"as a curiosity" she had written in her own words—but it had worked out just fine.

Now, Daisy wanted to know what had happened on

The Boeuf since she'd been gone. *Oh, where to begin!* thought Delilah.

Aldrich and Ellie had gone East last year and won custody of the precocious Dustin from his mentally unstable mother. He was now residing at the cottage on Lamourie and liked to "take care" of baby sister, Aimée Claire. The family was raising some of the finest Thoroughbred horses in the South and had begun shipping some by rail to the auction houses in the East where they quickly sold to enthusiastic buyers.

Shortly after Daisy had left The Boeuf, Philbus had taken off to Texas without Mozelle, who had stubbornly refused to leave The Shadows, and their last word from him was that he was driving cattle on the Shawnee Trail between Brownsville, Texas, and Sedalia, Missouri. Mozelle had promptly married one of the other men at The Shadows and within the year had given birth to a strapping son. Since she'd had no children in the twelve years she had been married to Philbus, it led one to believe that Philbus was probably equal to those steers he was driving on the Shawnee . . .

That was a speculation she did not need to relay to Daisy! But she would tell her about her successful efforts at matchmaking, for which Grant had another word: Busybody! In the summer of 1857 they'd had a surprising and unexpected visit from Lyle Bishop, who had wanted to clear his conscience and apologize for dumping the critically ill Delilah on the steps of the trading post. Since she had invited Hilda Roswell to spend that summer with her, the two young people had struck up a friendship that had quickly flourished into romance, and Lyle had returned to Spring Bayou with a wife. This summer they would visit The Shadows once more, and would bring their two daughters.

Would Daisy want to hear about the fate of Mr. Wells's famous horse, Lecomte? After being sold to Mr. Richard Ten Broeck, the racing promoter, he had been taken to England to be raced, where he had died in October of 1857 of colic. Grant was still fretting about it; he'd always wished he'd had the opportunity to purchase the horse and keep him on The Boeuf where he belonged, among the people who had cared enough about the handsome beast to name their town after him.

Oh, yes . . . the gold. Daisy would want to know about Papa's gold. Pierre Neville had returned to The Boeuf in January of 1857. They had ridden out to the grove of oaks and had begun digging . . . Pierre, Philbus—who had not yet left for Texas—Grant, and three of the other men from The Shadows. They had found the box, rotting and corroded as it was, and they had found just over four pounds of privately minted gold coins whose origin could not be determined in the three months Sheriff Stafford held them. The coins had borne the profile of a beautiful Oriental woman with upswept hair and an unnaturally long neck on one side, and on the other side a single yew tree. No other markings or lettering had even remotely hinted at their origin. When no claim had been made after the three months, Sheriff Stafford allowed the coins, less the half dozen Delilah kept, to be given to Pierre Neville. The rest of the gold had disappeared, replaced beneath the rotting iron lid by carefully laid wooden frogs. Yes, frogs! Peculiar's frogs, to be precise. Grant had tried for months to talk to Peculiar about what she'd done with the rest of the coins, but she had merely tugged at her pigtails and responded innocently, "What money, massah? Dey frogs, massah . . . ask dem frogs."

One day someone was going to find the gold that

Peculiar had spirited away. Perhaps, too, someone might even find out where Angus Wickley had gotten it to begin with.

A wail erupted nearby. Startled from her reminiscences, Delilah bent to pick up her three-month-old son Edouard from his cradle. "Now, what are you fussing about?" she asked in a quiet, loving voice. "You just want your mother's attention, don't you?"

Another voice echoed from the gallery and presently her dear husband entered the room, their daughter Isabel and Ellie's daughter Aimée Claire scampering ahead of him. "Whoa, lassies," a laughing Grant called. "My dear wife is in one of her thoughtful moods." Holding the two squirming girls in his gentle grip, Grant knelt and kissed his wife. "You promised we'd take a walk. Have you ever tried to rein in a pair of two-and-a-half-year-old hurricanes?" He looked down on his son. "You know, I was just thinking, my dear Delilah," he said, "we're a third of the way to those half-dozen children."

"Horse feathers" came her response, even as her free hand scooted across his shoulders to share an intimate moment. "These two little angels will be your legacy. There'll be no more!" Handing Grant his son, at which time he had to release the girls to their mischief, Delilah stood. Daisy's letter fell from her lap and she quickly retrieved it.

"Have you decided what you're going to tell Daisy?" Grant asked. "You've been working on your letter for half a week."

"Everything," she responded. Moving toward the desk, she deposited Daisy's letter there with the one she had started. As Grant, carrying his son, moved toward the kitchen with the chattering girls at his heels, Delilah picked up a poem she had found just that week. It had fallen behind the drawer in the desk

474

that had been her father's and she had immediately
recognized the familiar hand. Quietly, she again read
the words her mother had written:

"For all the years I spent with you,
Caring
And all the tears I've shed
Despairing
And clouds were black.
I thought, they have no silver lining.
Without a smile I faced each dreary morning.
Had God forsaken me, and if so why?
My heart was filled with love
For all creation.

And suddenly so many years
Had slipped away.
Where did they go, so fast they flew
Then in the shady yard one day
I found a lovely rose
Blooming in the frosty air
How hard it struggled to survive
But still 'twas there
And then I knew
To make us strong some pain
we must endure
And behind the darkest cloud
The skies are always blue"

Delilah had always wondered why her mother had
been stern and unaffectionate, and she had concluded
unhappily that her birth had been to blame for her
mother's melancholy. But the poem — and finding a
letter her father had received from his aunt Imogen —
had erased that worry for her. Her mother had been
extremely ill, and almost from the moment she and

Angus Wickley had married, she had known she was going to die young. Delilah liked to think that she was the rose in her mother's poem. It helped her to better understand her mother's detachment. *Oh, thank you, Mother, thank you, father, for the wonderful life you gave me. I will always love you.*

"Are you coming, wife?" Grant called above the squeals of Aimee and Isabel.

Moments later, they were moving, hand in hand, around the fringes of the pond and toward the gentle waters of Bayou Bouef. A young buck darted into the underbrush across the bayou, but not before catching the attention of the girls, who broke into runs toward the water. Holding his son across his shoulder, Grant caught them both by the tails of their skirts.

"Papa . . . Papa, horse, Papa, —" Isabel squealed.

"Silly Im'gen, it's a deer . . . huh, Unca?" Aimée Claire responded.

"Horse, Papa!" Isabel argued impishly, dragging her small hands to her waistline in an indignant stand.

"Sorry, it's a deer, little lady," a shrugging papa responded, and Isabel promptly began wailing. She hated it when her cousin was right.

"They're *your* daughter and niece," Delilah laughed gently, immediately noticing Grant's frown. "Oh, you're not worrying about politics again, are you, husband?" she chastised in her same quiet tone.

He shrugged. "Sorry, Delilah, I don't mean to spoil the mood of the morning, but . . . I'll be perfectly frank. I suspect that within two years . . ." He'd been about to say, "there will be war in this country," but that would be unfair. They had left the house to enjoy the morning as a family, and he would not spoil the mood. He forced a smile as he took Delilah's hand to drag her along beside him. "Come on . . . I believe I

476

get a whiff of bacon and eggs. I'll bet someone in the quarters wouldn't mind sharing breakfast with a man whose wife did not cook this morning!"

"I did so," she countered with indignation.

"Oatmeal," he groaned. "You cooked oatmeal . . . and you won't even eat it yourself! Even Mozelle refuses to cook the disgusting stuff!"

"The girls like it," she replied apologetically.

How happy Delilah was as her husband put aside his duties and spent the beautiful hours of the first day of spring with his family. In the afternoon, Aldrich and Ellie, who had journeyed to the doctor's office with an ailing Dustin, arrived at Shadows-in-the-Mist. "Is the boy all right?" Grant asked.

"Dr. Tylas could find nothing wrong," Ellie answered. "Chalks up his listlessness to spring fever. We're to keep an eye on him. But enough worry . . ." she continued, managing a smile. "How is that barbeque you've promised us for the evening coming along?"

"Mozelle has cooked enough for an army," Delilah interjected.

"I'm famished!" Aldrich rubbed his stomach as his other hand scooted across Ellie's shoulder. "I will simply follow the aroma of good food to the quarters."

Everyone had a grand time. Neighbors dropped by. Dustin, already feeling much better, took over the care of his fretting little sister, and as the children eventually collapsed in weary bundles, the cool of the evening wafted among the haunting ballads of the slaves that capped their perfect day.

Toward the hour of ten, their visitors departed and a sleeping Isabel and Edouard were tucked into their beds for the night. Grant and Delilah lay together in each other's arms.

"Isabel showed me the necklace you had made for

her. The gold coin made a beautiful pendant."

"Yes . . . I want each of our children to have one of them."

"Is that why you kept six of the coins?"

Delilah lightly struck his bare chest. "Of course not. It just seemed like a nice round number."

"Just think . . . six little Emersons scampering along the bayou with matching gold pendants—"

Delilah, suppressing a smile, closed her eyes. "I'm not listening, husband."

His mouth touched her forehead in the gentlest of kisses.

The night was long . . . their love exquisite.

And their future . . . who could forecast the future?

"You know," Grant said, drawing his wife against him beneath the softness of the sheets. "I'll bet that one day ol' Peculiar's going to remember where she hid the rest of that gold."

"Yes, perhaps one day when it is really needed," Delilah said. "Perhaps fate has intervened and one day The Shadows will really need that gold. Perhaps when our children are grown and running this place, the gold will show up just when they need it the most—"

"Delilah . . . the night is long . . . and we are together . . ."

"Forever?" Delilah asked, brushing her mouth against his cheek.

"Yes . . . forever."

FEEL THE FIRE IN CAROL FINCH'S ROMANCES!

BELOVED BETRAYAL (2346, $3.95)

Sabrina Spencer donned a gray wig and veiled hat before blackmailing rugged Ridge Tanner into guiding her to Fort Canby. But the costume soon became her prison — the beauty had fallen head over heels in love!

LOVE'S HIDDEN TREASURE (2980, $4.50)

Shandra d'Evereux felt her heart throb beneath the stolen map she'd hidden in her bodice when Nolan Elliot swept her out onto the veranda. It was hard to concentrate on her mission with that wily rogue around!

MONTANA MOONFIRE (3263, $4.95)

Just as debutante Victoria Flemming-Cassidy was about to marry an oh-so-suitable mate, the towering preacher, Dru Sullivan flung her over his shoulder and headed West! Suddenly, Tori realized she had been given the best present for a bride: a night of passion with a real man!

THUNDER'S TENDER TOUCH (2809, $4.50)

Refined Piper Malone needed bounty-hunter, Vince Logan to recover her swindled inheritance. She thought she could coolly dismiss him after he did the job, but she never counted on the hot flood of desire she felt whenever he was near!

Available wherever paperbacks are sold, or order direct from the Publisher. Send cover price plus 50¢ per copy for mailing and handling to Zebra Books, Dept. 3765, 475 Park Avenue South, New York, N.Y. 10016. Residents of New York and Tennessee must include sales tax. DO NOT SEND CASH. For a free Zebra/ Pinnacle catalog please write to the above address.